D1374980

We hope you enjoy this book. Please return or renew it by the due date.

You can renew it at www.norfolk.gov.uk/libraries or by using our free library app.

Otherwise you can phone 0344 800 8020 - please have your library card and PIN ready.

You can sign up for email reminders too.

*Also by Catherine Mangan*

One Italian Summer

# Catherine Mangan

# The Italian Escape

SPHERE

SPHERE

First published in Great Britain in 2021 by Sphere
This paperback edition published by Sphere in 2022

1 3 5 7 9 10 8 6 4 2

A CIP catalogue record for this book
is available from the British Library.

ISBN 978-0-7515-7986-4

Typeset in Baskerville by M Rules
Printed and bound in Great Britain by
Clays Ltd, Elcograf S.p.A.

Papers used by Sphere are from well-managed forests
and other responsible sources.

Sphere
An imprint of
Little, Brown Book Group
Carmelite House
50 Victoria Embankment
London EC4Y 0DZ

An Hachette UK Company
www.hachette.co.uk

www.littlebrown.co.uk

*To Tom,*
*For being by my side*

# Chapter One

There are ten thousand and eighty minutes in a week. That is exactly how long Niamh Kelly has been feeling depressed. Well, not in the true clinical definition of the word, obviously, but at the moment anything else felt like a massive understatement.

Her iPhone vibrated on the kitchen table in front of her – more concerned friends checking in, no doubt – but she couldn't muster the energy to respond. She was tired of talking about it. She slumped back into the chair, tied her long, dark hair up into a knot, flicked the phone to silent and opened her thesaurus app. Surely there was a more appropriate word to describe her current state beyond just sad. But not even the app could offer much in the way of useful alternatives, proffering options such as 'Bereaved' (no one had died so that was totally useless), 'Forlorn' (sounded like someone from medieval England) and 'Lugubrious' (that sounded promising but she had no idea what it actually meant).

'How are you feeling today, Niamh?' she asked herself.

'Lugubrious,' she replied with an exaggerated sigh.

'Are you talking to me, love?' her mother asked from across the room.

'No, just talking to myself, Mam.'

'Oh, right,' her mother replied over the sound of the television.

'Lugubrious,' she whispered to herself, tapping the screen on her phone. The definition read 'mournful or gloomy'. Definitely accurate, she decided, but none of her friends would know what it meant, either, so she wouldn't be able to use it without sounding pretentious, so rather disappointingly it was another useless option.

She had gone to the trouble of calculating the number of minutes: twenty-four hours, times sixty minutes, times seven days. She couldn't do that kind of calculation in her head. Mathematics had never really been a strong point, not that she'd ever really cared enough to try. She'd never understood how Pythagoras' theorem would benefit any aspect of real life, or why anyone was forced to learn long division when calculators had already been invented. It all seemed like a massive waste of time when there were so many more interesting things to be learned. So tonight Niamh felt entirely justified that in just a few seconds her calculator app could tell her the exact number of minutes that she had been in this sad mental state, without the need to rely on mental mathematical gymnastics.

'Ten thousand and eighty-one now,' she sighed under her breath as she spun the iPhone on the kitchen table and topped up her glass of wine.

'What's that, love?' asked her mother from across the room, her eyes glued to the television screen.

'Nothing. Just talking to myself,' she mumbled.

'Nina, why don't you come over here and sit by the fire?' her mother asked, patting the sofa alongside her.

'No, I think I'll go to bed,' she muttered, examining a cluster of split ends in her hair.

'Bed? It's only nine o'clock. It's still bright out. It's a beautiful summer's evening,' her mother argued, tearing her eyes from the television programme. 'Will you, for God's sake, stop picking at your hair? Do you have lice or something?' She stood up slowly, rubbing her knee, and crossed the living room towards her daughter.

'What?' Niamh asked through the bottom of her wine glass.

'Why are you picking at your hair? There's an epidemic going around you know – of lice. And they can hop from one head to another so it's easy to get them.'

'Jesus, Mam, no, I don't have lice. I'm not dirty. It's just split ends,' Niamh cried, pulling on some strands of hair that had come loose.

'They like clean hair, actually.'

'What? Who likes clean hair?' Niamh asked, now utterly frustrated with the conversation.

'The lice do. They like clean hair. That's why they hop from one head to another,' her mother declared confidently, as if she had just eked out this nugget of medical certainty from the gospel that is the *Reader's Digest*. All of her facts and strong opinions originated from the *Reader's Digest*. Someone had once told her that if she subscribed to *Reader's Digest* she would be able to have a conversation about anything because it taught you a little about everything. Mrs Kelly had been a regular subscriber for eight years now and quite fancied herself as a great conversationalist. 'Anyway, it looks like you have lice or something when you pick at it like that. You don't want people talking about you, do you?'

'They already are, Mam,' Niamh sighed. 'I've provided plenty of fodder for the neighbours lately. No shortage of gossip this week. Niamh Kelly, thirty-three years old, newly single, no, wait . . . dumped, in fact, and jobless. No man. No

3

job. What a disaster.' Her voice was rising now. Her father lowered his newspaper a couple of inches. His glasses peered over the top momentarily, gauging the situation as he glanced from wife to daughter, but he quickly retreated back behind the temporary invisibility that the newspaper afforded him.

'You do have a job. There's nothing at all wrong with that job, Nina, and as soon as you're feeling better you'll go back to it. There's no harm in taking a week off. You were due a break anyway.'

'I'm not going back to it. I *can't* go back! How can I go back there?' She knew she was starting to sound hysterical now but she couldn't stop it. 'How can I go back and face him every day? I'd be the laughing stock of the place.'

'I'm sure there is a way to avoid him, love. You shouldn't have to give up your job just because you broke up. That's not right.'

'A, there is no way to avoid him, Mam. PlatesPlease is a startup – actually, even worse, it's *his* startup, so there's no avoiding him. And B, we didn't break up. I was dumped. Remember? Dumped, dropped and discarded, like it all meant nothing. Like the past four years meant nothing. What a dope. How could I not have known? You know everyone will say that I must have guessed something, known something . . . How could I not have known?'

'But you didn't know and that's not your fault. Sometimes things just don't work out. People change. You don't know what was going through his head, but if he could treat you like that then you're better off without him,' Una Kelly said, emphasising her words by jabbing her index finger on the table.

'I'm nearly halfway through my thirties, newly single and no job. How did I end up here? Seriously, how is this my life?'

Niamh asked, shaking her head. She poured the remainder of the bottle into her glass and watched as it reluctantly released its last few drops.

The theme tune to the Friday-night chat show – a Friday-night ritual in every Irish household – hummed along on the television, signalling the end of any other possible conversation and the urgent need to make tea. Parents and 'young marrieds with children' around the country were gathering in front of the television and the fire, settling in for the next two hours, happy to be entertained. It would be the usual rollout of minor celebrities promoting their new movie, losers who had found God, turned their life around and had now written a book to help all the other losers out there do the same, and some twenty-something-year-old who had rejected meat and dairy and embraced veganism the previous year, had started making granola in their kitchen and had just sold the company to Kellogg's for several million. At the end of the two hours, one half of the country would be motivated to fix or change their life and the other half would be depressed because their lives were just ordinary by comparison.

'Is the kettle on?' Niamh's dad asked from behind the paper. He wouldn't put it down until the programme started and it was safe to come out from behind it.

'I'm putting it on now,' replied her mother, opening a packet of biscuits. 'Will you have a cup?'

'I will so.'

Niamh smiled despite herself at the nightly exchange about the cup of tea that they drank religiously, and the easy way that her parents had with each other. She wondered then if relationships got easier with time and if, after so many years, you could just anticipate the other person so that there was never any need for angst or arguments. Did you just know the other person so well that you knew instinctively what they would or wouldn't like, what they would or wouldn't do, and so navigate conversations and situations easily, armed in advance with that knowledge?

'Night,' she said quietly, getting up from the table.

'Night, love,' they both replied at the same time, heads already directed towards the television.

'Have a good sleep,' her dad offered as he folded down the newspaper and stood to throw a log on the fire.

She picked up her phone and it flashed 21.10. This time last week she had been having dinner with Rick at the new tapas restaurant. Rick preferred to eat early in the evening so they always made an early dinner reservation.

'It's better for the digestion to eat early,' he would say whenever she questioned the need to race to a restaurant by seven o'clock. 'Plus, some places have an early-bird special before seven, so it's an added bonus. See, Niamh, there is value for money everywhere if you look for it,' he would recite smugly.

She was probably having dessert right around now, this time last week, in her new navy dress. Now that she thought of it, this exact time last week she was less than twenty minutes from being unceremoniously dumped and she was happily tucking into her tiramisu.

She hadn't noticed anything unusual about his behaviour. He had been distracted over dinner, but not more than usual. He was in the middle of raising another round of funding for the business. He was always stressed when he was fundraising, so she had assumed it was purely work related.

'Why do you think they have tiramisu on the menu if this is a tapas place?' she had asked.

'What?' he had asked, scrolling through emails on his phone.

'Tiramisu is Italian. Why does a Spanish tapas restaurant have tiramisu on the menu?'

'Niamh, I have no idea. Maybe the Spanish don't have that many desserts. Do you have any idea how many calories are in that thing?' he retorted. 'There are over six hundred calories in one slice of tiramisu, Niamh. That means you'd have to run for an hour and fifteen minutes just to burn that off,' he snapped as he stuck his phone back in his pocket.

'So I'll walk to work every morning next week.' She shrugged, and scraped the bowl.

'Niamh, I don't have time for this now. I have to work tomorrow.'

'But tomorrow is Saturday!' she whined.

'Entrepreneurs are always on, Niamh, you should know that by now. It's intense. We can't all saunter into the office five days a week at nine o'clock like you do.'

Niamh leaned heavily on the edge of the sink now, shaking her head. She sighed to herself, thinking back on the series of events last Friday night. She should have seen it coming, but she hadn't. Or maybe she had just refused to accept that there had been more arguments than smiles over the past few months.

She rinsed her glass in the sink and snuck two of her dad's night-time cold and flu tablets from the medicine basket over the sink, swallowing them with lukewarm water from the tap. Apparently they weren't addictive and they definitely helped knock you out at night.

She shuffled towards the kitchen door, thinking that she would have to burn that navy dress, but she couldn't burn it right now, even though the fire was perfect. It was roaring up the chimney, resembling a miniature towering inferno in the grate. But if she came back downstairs with the navy dress and tossed it into the fire, it might be too much for her dad. He would either abandon his current position on the armchair and flee from the room, not wanting any part of the madness (missing his show in the process – and she'd hear about that until next Friday's episode), or he'd think she had lost her mind and would start to worry about her.

She didn't need anyone else to worry about her. She certainly didn't need to have her dad offer any critical life advice. It was enough to deal with her mother and her *Reader's Digest* nuggets of wisdom. One thing was sure, however – she would never wear that navy dress again. It would always be the dress she got dumped in. Shame, really, because she thought she looked kind of skinny in it. Well, not *skinny* exactly, but slim, or at least slimmer than she looked in real life. Kind of like a sartorial magic wand.

'Waste of sixty euros,' she sighed, heading towards the stairs.

# Chapter Two

She could hear the high-pitched whine of the vacuum cleaner downstairs. The postman dropped some envelopes through the door and the dog went nuts.

'Mother of God, it's eight o'clock on a Saturday morning,' she groaned from under her duvet. She wasn't hungover, exactly, but her head ached behind her eyes and her tongue felt like chalk.

What was it about small dogs that they always had to start a fight? It was like they were always on the defensive because of their size. Niamh had refused to walk Marty any more because he was completely out of control. He was a small, hairy little thing, a cross between a wheaten terrier and something else – no one knew exactly what. Her dad had taken him in when the neighbour's dog got knocked up for the second time in a year and had another three puppies. They were all headed for the local shelter but everyone knew that the shelter had a seven-day kill policy, so the Kelly family had come to the rescue. Her mother had refused at first to have anything to do with it.

'If you bring him in here, Paddy, you'll have to take care of him.'

'Ah, would you look at him. Sure he's a lovely little thing,' her father replied, scratching his chin. 'He'll be no bother at all.'

After a few disastrous attempts to walk him, Niamh refused point blank to take him out again. 'He'll just have to get his exercise in the back garden,' she announced, coming in through the front door and opening the back one. 'It's mortifying to try to walk him. Honest to God, if there is a German shepherd in sight he's heaving and straining at the leash, frothing at the mouth, trying to attack him, and he wouldn't even reach the German shepherd's knees. I think he has a Napoleonic complex or something. He definitely has issues of some sort.' From then on Marty was sent out into the back garden to run around and get a bit of exercise.

'Get *out*, Marty,' she heard her mother roar over the sound of the vacuum cleaner. 'Niamh, are you up?' she shouted up the stairs. Her mother only ever called her by her proper first name when she was admonishing her.

'No! Can you turn off the hoover, Mam? It's only eight o'clock in the morning! That noise is torture at this hour!' Niamh roared, despite her headache. She heard footsteps coming up the stairs. Clearly she wasn't about to win this one.

'The day is half over at eight o'clock in the morning,' her mother said, throwing open the bedroom door. 'Look at the state of this place, and it smells like a brewery. The window cleaners will be here in an hour so you better get up and get dressed.'

'My curtains are closed, Mam! And they'll only be washing the outside of the windows,' Niamh argued, rubbing her temples.

'It's not right having those men outside your window and you inside in bed. Sure they'll know full well that you're inside in it if you have the curtains closed.'

'Jesus,' Niamh mumbled into the duvet. 'All right, I'm getting up.'

'Stop swearing, Niamh. And your sister Grace will be here any minute to drop off the boys for a few hours while she gets her hair done.'

Niamh didn't know why her mother always referred to her as 'your sister Grace', but she did. It was never just 'Grace'. It's not like she had another one and might get them confused.

'All right, I'm up, I'm up.'

She'd need something to dim the headache before the boys arrived. The sound level went up tenfold when Blake and Ben landed. Blake was a year older than his brother, but Ben was the mad one. No shortage of personality there. Niamh always felt that Grace should have swapped their names once she discovered their personalities, as Blake was way too weird a name to give any Irish boy. He'd definitely get beaten up over that in the future. Ben could have handled it as he was a bully already at only two years of age, but Blake was a quieter, more sensitive little thing. He was still terribly loud, but sweet and gentle. She'd have switched the names before anyone got too used to them.

'Do we have any more of those dissolvable things in the red box?' she asked as she padded slowly down the stairs in her pyjamas.

'Did you drink too much wine again last night?' her mother asked with a disapproving tut.

'No, I think I'm getting a sore throat,' Niamh lied. That was the only way to extract any sympathy, as hangovers were not tolerated. In fact, between herself and Grace, she was pretty sure that they had each only once ever made the rookie mistake of admitting to a hangover. Every other occasion for painkillers was the certain onslaught of strep throat, migraine or the flu. That way you stood a chance of getting tea and a blanket.

'You should go to the doctor and get yourself checked out.

11

You're getting a lot of sore throats lately. Now go up and fix yourself, will you? Look at the state of you. They'll be here soon. Oh, and dress the bed so the window washers don't think we're a bunch of tinkers.'

Now that Niamh thought of it, she probably hadn't washed her hair since last Friday. The Friday that she wore the new navy dress and went to the new tapas restaurant. The Friday she was dumped. She hadn't seen a mirror yet today, but she knew that her hair would be standing up in clumps from its unwashed roots. She might have hidden it under a baseball cap for the day to avoid the chore of washing and drying it, but she knew her sister would waft in wearing something expensive and looking like she'd just stepped out of a salon, even before she'd had her hair done. She always smelled expensive, too. Niamh had tried her perfume once to see if she could smell expensive as well, but it just smelled like bottled, overripe fruit on her skin.

Her sister was the successful one. She had a shining career as an architect, two perfect, if loud and berserk, toddlers and a doting husband. He was starting to lose his hair early, which Niamh was certain freaked her sister out. She wouldn't be surprised if Robert showed up with hair implants one day to maintain the outward veneer of perfection, because who wants to show off their balding husband? Otherwise he was fine, though, and they seemed happy together.

She was tall, too, in the way that successful people are. Niamh had read once (in one of her mother's *Reader's Digests*, of course) that successful people are, for the most part, tall. Someone did a study of the most successful men and women in the USA and something like less than 1 per cent of them were short. That particular week had been especially tough at work, so the article had made her feel better about herself.

Good to know that she could now righteously blame her five foot, four inch height for her professional shortcomings. In fact, she felt sure that the term 'professional shortcomings' was most likely coined by a successful, clever, tall person for short people everywhere.

She heard them before she saw them. The front gate was flung open with a clatter and both sets of little feet thundered down the gravel path. It always amazed her how much noise such small people could make. They were babbling in through the letterbox before anyone could even get to the front door. It was nine o'clock exactly. That was another difference between Niamh and her sister – Grace was always on time for everything. Niamh pulled open the kitchen door and scooped them up, one in each arm.

'You two monsters are getting heavy!'

Blake called her 'Nee' but Ben hadn't quite worked out his words yet so he just roared random sounds at people. Apart from 'Mama' and 'Dada', the only name he'd got a handle on was 'Granda', which came out like 'Gah'. It drove her mother mad, of course, that he could say 'Granda' but not 'Nana', so every visit was like a warped speech therapy session, with Nana repeating her name slowly in Ben's face any time he would stand still.

When he wasn't eating, he preferred to stomp on things and kill anything smaller than him, like random spiders or any sort of bug that had the misfortune to move in the back garden. He was the sort of silent but deadly type. Not even Marty was safe, and he knew it, retreating with a kind of terrorised screech whenever he saw Ben coming.

Grace was putting the kettle on in the kitchen. 'I brought croissants from the French place you like, Niamh,' she said giving her a hug.

'Sympathy croissants?' Niamh asked with a grimace. She was pretty sure that Grace hadn't allowed a croissant to pass her lips in over ten years. 'So is this tea and sympathy with a pity croissant thrown in for good measure?'

'It can be if you like, but they're bloody good croissants.' To Niamh's surprise, Grace pulled off a corner and stuffed it in her mouth. 'So, what kind of mental state are we in, here? What stage in the grieving process – depressed and dejected, mad as hell, or sad and mopey?'

'Definitely sad and mopey.'

'So, what happened exactly? Did you do something to piss him off or is he just having an early mid-life crisis?' Grace asked, pouring three mugs of tea.

'I didn't do anything!' Niamh insisted. 'We went out to dinner like I told you and when we got home he just said something like he didn't "want to do this any more".'

'What *exactly* did he say, Niamh?'

'He said, "Niamh, I don't want to do this anymore. It's not working. We're going nowhere. There's no point."'

'Sounds like a mid-life crisis to me. He's a knob, Niamh. You're better off without him.'

'That's easy for you to say. You're not the one who's turning thirty-four next birthday and newly single.'

Grace leaned against the kitchen table. 'Are you telling me that you'd rather be in an average relationship than be single? Will you listen to yourself for a minute? That's an absolute travesty! Women burned their bras for freedom in the sixties and there you are wishing you could hitch your wagon to some aspiring entrepreneurial loser.'

Mrs Kelly paused her attempt to scrub last night's casserole dish. 'No one burned any bras in the sixties. That's a myth.'

'Mam, everyone knows that feminists burned their bras in

the sixties. That's known all over the world,' Grace countered confidently.

'Well, anyone who thinks that is wrong. It's a myth. The demonstration that created that myth was the 1968 protest of the *Miss America* contest when loads of women threw bras, stockings, girdles – all sorts of underwear – into a rubbish bin, but it was never set alight. Psychologists call it the Rashomon effect, where different people have contradictory accounts of the same incident.' She rattled this off with gusto and resumed her scrubbing.

'*Reader's Digest*, Grace,' sighed Niamh. 'I'd just take that one at face value and leave it at that if I were you, or we'll be here all day.'

Grace rolled her eyes. 'So when are you going back to work? You can't loll around here for ever or you'll go out of your mind.'

'I'm not going back to that place. I can't!' Niamh whined.

'What? That's ridiculous! That's a fine job and you were good at it. Of course you're going back.'

'I can't. I'll be such a pity party. I'm mortified. Thirty-three years old and rejected by the man I thought I was going to spend the rest of my life with. God, what a mess.' Niamh put her hands over her eyes. 'Anyway, it's his company, Grace, so it's not like he's going anywhere. I should never have gotten involved in it. I can't believe I let him talk me into it. "Help me get started, Niamh ... Let's build this together, Niamh ..." I gave up that great job at that restaurant PR firm for the chance to work at a startup. I thought I'd be at the forefront of everything, pitching to the media and arranging press evenings. Then off Rick goes, raising money and doing media interviews, while I'm left running payroll. Wanker.'

'Language, Niamh!' Mrs Kelly said into the sink.

'Well, he is, Mam, to be fair,' offered Grace in support. 'Look, you're not actually losing your job; you are choosing not to go back to work. That's different. That's quitting. Or you could just pull yourself together and go back to work – how about that? You don't have to lose your job over this. It's not like you see much of him these days at work, or he's directly in charge of you or anything. Don't let him win. Fuck him. Just go back to work with your head held high.'

'Language, Grace!'

Grace rolled her perfectly made-up eyes. 'Or get another job.'

Marty let out a howl from under the table.

'Ben! Get off of him!' Grace shouted under the table. '*Off!*' Ben was sitting on Marty who was, at this stage, flattened to the floor.

'Ugh. Get another job?' Niamh dropped her head into her hands. 'What do I tell them at the interview? Oh yeah, my boyfriend dumped me, and I worked for him for the past four years, helping him build his startup, so I've gained no real experience apart from buying birthday cards, processing invoices, trying not to die of boredom overseeing payroll, and making sure the company cactus doesn't shrivel up and die. Did you know it's almost impossible to kill a cactus? It's that sort of killer knowledge which makes me employee of the year material. They'll be lining up around the block to hire me.'

'Yeah, you sound like a bit of a sad, co-dependent loser when you put it that way.'

'Thanks. Oh God. I'm mortified,' Niamh said, cringing. 'How did this happen? What am I going to do? I can't stay out on sick leave for much longer. I already sent in one fake doctor's note.'

16

'How did you manage that?' Grace asked, breaking off a second piece of croissant.

Niamh threw a look in her mother's direction and lowered her voice. 'I just wailed and bawled and talked about not loving myself under these circumstances, until he gave me a note to say I was incapable of work right now.'

'But you've been out for a week. You made one claim of having lunatic tendencies and you got a sick certificate for a whole week?'

'Yes, all I had to do was think of everyone talking about me at the office and I worked myself up into a right state. I can't claim that I wasn't actually a bit of a nutcase in the doctor's office.'

'Well, the longer you leave it the worse it will be. You're still on sympathy leave right now 'cause people feel sorry for you, but if you stay out much longer then they'll think you've actually become a bona fide nut job over this. Is that what you want?'

'Of course it's not what I want. I didn't want any of this. I wanted to get married and live happily ever after.'

'Well, that's shot to shit.'

The dog gave another screech.

Mrs Kelly sighed. 'For the love of God! I'm up to my elbows in suds here. Will one of you please rescue that creature and put him out in the back garden?'

Grace grabbed Marty and shoved him out of the back door. Ben gave a roar, which was intended to mean, 'I want to go out, too.'

'Use your words, Ben. I can't understand you if you don't use your words! O-U-T. Say *out*.' Ben gave another roar and she shoved him out through the back door too.

'What was it he said, again? That he can't do it?' she asked Niamh as she closed the back door.

'"I don't want to do this any more."'

'That's so pathetic. Who says that? I mean, what actually was wrong with him? Do you think there's someone else?'

'I don't know. I mean, no I don't think so. I think I freaked him out.'

'How so?'

'Well, I had been dropping hints about moving in together and stuff like that and the last time I was over at his place I left some *Homes & Gardens* magazines lying around. Plus I had been hinting about the new batch of apartments being released next month, you know, the fancy ones on the canal? Then I asked him if he wanted to take a spin to IKEA on Saturday, just to have a look around. I think it all freaked him out. Are you going to eat the rest of that or what?' Niamh nodded towards the mostly uneaten croissant.

'No, you can have it.'

''Tis no wonder you have such a good figure, Grace,' Mrs Kelly said as she folded up her rubber gloves. 'I wish I had your discipline.'

'Marvellous,' Niamh said, rolling her eyes. 'Oh well, I might as well add chunky and undisciplined to my list of offensive character traits.' She stuffed the remainder of the croissant into her mouth.

'You're not chunky, Niamh. Stop being so hard on yourself. You've just been comfort-eating for the past week and you feel like shit. It's a thing, you know. People comfort-eat when they are sad, then you put on a little weight and feel even worse about yourself. Look, shitty things happen, relationships end. It's just really, really bad luck that you worked with him, too, so you've got a double dose of crap to deal with, but honestly, Niamh, you are better off without him. He's self-obsessed, vain and hell-bent on world domination with that little food app of his selling subscriptions to people who can't cook. You just need a bit of distance, that's all,' Grace said emphatically as she sipped on her tea.

'It's not a *little* food app, Grace. It's doing really well, actually,' Niamh said with an indignant huff. 'Our early customers were people who couldn't cook so those subscriptions that deliver a box of ingredients to your home were useless because you still have to actually cook the meal, but in the last few months we've started getting real traction with people who are entertaining at home. They order the PlatesPlease meal that they want, it shows up fully cooked, and they serve it as if they had cooked it themselves. That's what is so unique about the product and that's where the real growth opportunity is, so that's where our focus . . . '

Niamh's voice trailed off. She leaned forward in despair, resting her head on her folded arms. 'Our focus . . . I just said "our focus", but it's not, is it? It's all his. I'm out,' she groaned, banging her forehead on the table for emphasis.

'You need to get out of here,' Grace declared as she stood up from the table, brushing crumbs from her cream-coloured pants.

'She can't go anywhere. The window washers will be here any minute and she'll have to deal with them because I have to run to the shops.'

'Not *now*, Mam. Not right this minute. I mean you need to get out of here – your routine, this house. Get out of town.'

'Right. I'll just grab my overnight bag and head to the airport. Catch the next flight somewhere exotic with . . . oh wait . . . with no one. You mean a "sad and alone" trip for singles?' She knew she was being mopey and dramatic again, but her sister always thought there was an easy solution for everything. Her life was always nice and breezy. She just coasted through life with salon hair and perfectly groomed eyebrows.

'No, come with me next week to Italy!' she exclaimed with a wide smile, as if she had just solved one of the world's more pressing concerns.

'What are you doing in Italy?'

'I'm going to a conference. You know the one I go to every year? It's just three days but I'm staying on for the weekend too. Come on, it'll do you good. It will be fun!'

'Grace, I haven't left the house in a week!'

'That's precisely why this is a great idea. You need to get out. You need a distraction.'

'No, I can't. I'm just not up for it.'

'Oh, come on. It'll be fun. You won't have to do a thing – it's all organised. All you need is a flight. Everything else is sorted.'

Una Kelly turned from the sink to face her daughters. 'Sounds like a lovely invitation to me, Nina. It might do you good.'

'I dunno . . . I haven't been to Italy for years,' Niamh mused.

'I'll send you my flight details. Just book yourself a flight. Do you think you can get another nutcase certificate? Buy yourself another week off work?'

Niamh giggled for the first time in a week. 'Trust me, it doesn't take much to go from my current resting nutcase state to extreme lunatic. All I have to do is think about my life right now and I'll lose my mind all over again. What day are you going? And where?'

She realised that she was considering this trip without knowing the first thing about it. Maybe she did need to get out of town.

'I'm on the morning flight to Milan on Monday. The

conference is Tuesday to Thursday and I fly home Sunday. Robert is looking after the boys for the weekend and the nanny is going to do full-time during the week. We're not staying in Milan, though. I have a driver picking me up and taking me to the hotel in Liguria. We're staying at the Grand Hotel Miramare. It's part of the Leading Hotels of the World group. It'll be fabulous!'

Niamh could feel herself perk up already. She couldn't remember the last time she had made a decision so quickly. 'Shit, today is Saturday. I need to go buy some new outfits.'

'You can go after the window washers leave,' Mrs Kelly protested. 'But I think that's a great idea. A week away will do you the world of good. You can get your head straightened out and you'll be well able to deal with all of this nonsense when you come back.' She nodded approvingly.

'And for the love of God will you get something done with your hair today?' sighed Grace. 'You don't want to frighten the Italians.'

Niamh ignored the snarky comment, mostly as she had to agree that something needed to be done to tame her hair. 'I'll get an appointment for this afternoon.'

'OK, I'll text you all the details. Mam, I'll be back by lunch to pick up the boys.'

'All right, love. See you later.'

'And Grace?' Niamh said as she stuck her head into the hallway after her sister. 'Thanks!'

'It will be an adventure,' Grace replied with a wink.

# Chapter Three

The air was different. It didn't just smell different; it felt different, different to the air back home in Dublin. It felt lighter. Maybe it was just drier and not as damp, but it felt good. It was warmer than it was back home, too. Not yet hot, as it was still only May, but warm enough that Niamh didn't need her jacket. She felt like a creature shedding a layer of skin that it no longer needed as she slipped it off. She had seen snakes do that on *National Geographic* documentaries on television and always thought it looked cool.

Grace had told her more or less what she should pack. Niamh had asked her some very specific questions about the kind of clothes she should bring, as she suspected that she and Grace took very different types of holidays and she didn't want to look like the hired help accompanying her more glamorous sister. Grace was a bit of a pro by now, as she travelled to Italy twice a year – once for the annual conference and once a year on holiday with Robert – whereas Niamh hadn't been in years.

'I know you think that my clothes are fancy and that I overdress for certain things, but you have to take my advice on this, and don't think I'm exaggerating.'

'OK,' Niamh responded slowly.

'Pack for your most glamorous self because you'll still feel like you look like a homeless person next to these Italian women. Honestly, I don't know how they do it. It's like they have an innate sense of style, or some internal gene that allows them to look effortlessly elegant all of the time. *All* of the time, I swear. And they are all skinny as rakes!'

'What about all the pasta and wine?'

'I don't know. Maybe they just eat it at lunch or something, 'cause honestly they all look fabulous.'

'But Italian grannies all look tubby and round.'

'Well that's just it – they are all skinny and fabulous until they hit fifty or so, then they all get the midlife spread. I think they just actually stop caring at that point, because they're married and can now eat pasta for dinner every night. I don't know, but every Italian woman under fifty looks amazing.'

'You've just convinced me that nothing I own is suitable, so basically I'm going shopping for a new wardrobe for the week. I just hope they've got summer stuff in the shops already,' Niamh sighed.

'A few cute dresses and some wedge sandals and you'll be fine,' Grace said with a shrug.

As they waited for their luggage, Niamh texted their mother to tell her they had landed safely in Milan. The orange beacon atop the luggage carousel started to flash along with a siren sound that was so unnecessarily loud it could warn of a threatening invasion. Niamh wrestled with her case and tried to heave it off the carousel without maiming anyone. She had definitely overpacked, she thought, as she hurled it to the floor. She probably should have used the smaller one, but she hadn't been able to decide on what to pack. This one had been labelled 'heavy', with a frown at the check-in desk in Dublin, and it was certainly not easy to manoeuvre as it only had three good wheels.

Grace always checked in a suitcase when she travelled as she always packed so many cosmetics and sprays that she couldn't possibly qualify for the carry-on luggage requirements, but she had one of those sleek, hard-shelled RIMOWA cases that seemed to roll all by itself. She spoke pretty good Italian and she certainly seemed to know her way around the airport. She had called the driver as they were walking from the luggage claim area. She was speaking Italian on the phone to him and laughing. It wasn't easy to laugh in another language. Niamh had studied French and Spanish for five years in school and couldn't remember a single conversation that had made her laugh. They say you've really mastered it if you can make someone laugh in another language.

The driver stood holding a sign reading GRACE QUINN, and greeted them with a wide smile.

'*Ben arrivata, Signora Quinn. Sono Vincenzo,*' he said, shaking her hand warmly before reaching for her suitcase.

'*Ciao, Vincenzo. Grazie,*' Grace replied, as she twirled her sleek RIMOWA suitcase around to face him.

Niamh hesitated for a moment, rooted to the spot, as she'd never been met anywhere by a driver. Was she supposed to hand him her suitcase, too, or was that only for the person who actually made the booking? She wondered if he could even drag both suitcases? He looked pretty old.

'*Buongiorno, signora,*' he said, leaning towards her and grasping the handle.

She watched as he strode away, her old black suitcase with the rickety wheel bouncing behind him.

Grace turned to face her, shaking her head. 'Seriously, Niamh, the charity shop wouldn't accept that thing if you tried to donate it.'

Niamh rolled her eyes. 'I didn't realise that my luggage was going to be judged too. "Niamh get your hair done, Niamh buy some new clothes, Niamh make sure to use your Louis Vuitton suitcase,"' she said in a mock whiney voice as she skipped to keep up with Grace.

Grace seemed to navigate the clusters of people easily, but then Grace, older by two years, always seemed to manage things with ease.

'I still can't believe you took Robert's name and changed your last name to Quinn,' Niamh said, jogging alongside her sister.

'That's a random statement, even by your standards.'

'No, the driver had a sign saying "Quinn" back there when we arrived. I almost forgot that you're no longer a Kelly. I couldn't imagine having another name – that would be weird.'

'Are you kidding me?' said Grace defensively. 'I couldn't get down the aisle fast enough to drop Kelly and take Quinn as my surname. You didn't have to deal with being mocked and called "princess" at school! I wasn't sorry to see the back of Grace Kelly!'

The two of them followed the driver through the terminal towards the waiting car. Niamh felt bad for the man. He must have been her father's age and he was dragging the two cases in his black blazer and black hat. Her father wouldn't be seen dead in that hat. It didn't seem to cost Grace a thought, though, as she pulled her sunglasses from her handbag as they stepped out into the sun.

'Of course, they were just sitting there conveniently at the top of your handbag,' Niamh muttered to herself as she rooted through her oversized bag. She bumped into an impossibly tall, elegant Italian woman.

'*Attento!*' the woman exclaimed. '*Porca miseria!*'

She didn't know what the second part meant, but it sounded mean.

'Wow, what a cow!' Niamh said incredulously. 'It was an accident!' she growled over her shoulder at the woman.

The woman made a hand gesture at her that she'd seen Italians do in movies. Even that looked effortless and elegant. She'd have to find out what they each meant.

Grace breezed ahead of her in layers of pale grey and cream. She seemed to have this great wardrobe of monochrome pieces that all worked together effortlessly. By comparison, everything Niamh owned was either black or brightly coloured. She decided that she'd have to try the monochrome look and see if it would make her feel any more elegant. She might talk to Grace about it and maybe they could go shopping together while in Italy.

Grace slunk into the back seat of the car, whipped out her phone and started dialling.

'*Allora, signora, siamo pronti?*' the driver asked, looking in his rear-view mirror at them both, wondering if they were ready to go.

Niamh nudged Grace.

'*Scusi, sì, grazie, Vincenzo.*' Grace nodded in his direction.

'Off we go,' he said in a strong accent, making it sound like 'Off-ah we-ah go'. He caught Niamh's eye in the mirror and winked.

Niamh leaned back into the cream leather seat. There was plenty of room for her legs, she noticed, much more so than the regular taxis back home. She placed her handbag on the ground next to her feet. She should have polished her shoes before she left, she thought to herself, peering down at them. They looked scruffier than normal against the cream interior of the car. There was a box of tissues on the ledge behind the passenger seats, little bottles of water in the compartment between them and a magazine tucked into the pocket on the back of the two front seats. She plucked out the one on her side but it was in Italian. Still, though, she could flick through the photos, as it looked like an Italian edition of *Vogue*.

'This is unreal.' She grinned at Grace. 'Do you always travel like this when you go for work?'

'Every time. The company pays for it,' Grace replied casually.

'Wow, I'd be on a bus by now, or trying to find a bus if I was doing this myself. This is the way to travel! It's no wonder you don't mind travelling as much as you do.'

'Don't mind it? Are you mad? This is what keeps me sane. I look forward to these trips away. I love the boys, but they are full on and demanding, and these trips give me a couple of days to be myself, or actually allow me to be the person I used to be before I became a mother.'

Grace's phone rang and she launched into a work conversation. Niamh rested her head back against the headrest and stared out of the window. She realised that the two of them had never been away together before and she had just had a previously impermissible glance into her sister's life. Her mother did always say that travel broadens the mind. She smiled, thinking that for someone who had lived her entire life in Dublin and had only ever travelled outside the island of Ireland twice, her mother knew a lot about a lot.

The car had tinted windows, which was just as well as she hadn't managed to find her sunglasses. She must have packed them in her suitcase.

'That was pretty stupid,' she sighed as she rummaged one more time through her handbag. It was a two-and-a-half-hour journey from Linate airport to their hotel in the town of Santa Margherita. Niamh had looked up the hotel online and didn't think she had ever stayed anywhere that looked more glamorous – and that was just from the photos, which everyone knows never truly do a place justice, except for in those package resorts where she normally went on holiday. They always had great photos of sprawling swimming pools and when you got there you wondered if you were even looking at the same thing. They looked massive in the photos, but the photographer was obviously using some lens trickery. It shouldn't be allowed, really, as it gave a different impression of what you actually got in reality. The truth was that she had never yet met a swimming pool in real life that exceeded the opinion she had had in advance, based on the photographs.

Niamh had never been to this part of Italy. She had been to Rome years ago for a weekend in August and, between the heat and the crowds, she swore she'd never go back. It wasn't as hot this time. The first half hour of the drive was the usual nondescript, grey scenery you encountered in most countries as you left the airport and navigated a series of ugly highways. The more developed the country the worse the initial drive seemed to be upon leaving the airport. Everything seemed dull and industrial – the roads, the fields, just a series of flat shapes alternating grey and green as they flashed by, interrupted by the odd, ugly factory.

She thought about Rick as she watched the signposts for Genoa whizz by. He'd like it here, she thought to herself. She wondered why they had never travelled like this together, on an adventurous sort of trip. They had always booked package holidays and usually returned to the same few places in Spain or the Canary Islands every year. They had gone to Turkey one year, to a city on the coast called Bodrum. She had thought it sounded exotic and adventurous, but when they got to the place they were staying, it was just a small resort with a couple of swimming pools and two restaurants. It was just like all the other places they had been, except for the food. The food was definitely more exotic. She remembered telling her mother about it when she got home.

'They grill their lamb there, Mam, and it's served pink in the middle!'

'What do you mean pink in the middle? It can't be pink in the middle, Nina, sure that's not even properly cooked!' her mother had exclaimed, horrified.

'I swear, Mam! It's pure pink in the middle. It was good, too.'

'You won't find me there, so then,' her dad offered from the armchair. 'Sure that's half raw.'

Niamh had felt quite sophisticated, regaling the two of them with tales of all this foreign food. Her dad was the classic meat and potatoes kind of man. If the dinner didn't have potatoes, then it just wasn't dinner.

'And we had whole grilled fish. It was delicious. First I thought it was a bit weird, 'cause it was the whole fish, but I covered his head with a bit of lettuce so I couldn't see his eyes and then it was grand.'

'What do you mean you could see his eyes?' her father asked.

'Yeah, they serve it whole. It's supposed to have more flavour, Dad, if it's cooked on the bone and served whole. Rick didn't mind it, but I had to cover his eyes so he wouldn't be looking at me while I ate him.'

'We definitely won't be going there, so! I couldn't eat him if he was looking up at me. Did they throw him on the grill too when he was still alive?' Her dad chuckled. He was a pretty good cook and he liked to cook fish (her mother didn't like the smell of fish cooking, so that was her dad's job), but it was all neatly filleted by the time he brought it home from the fish shop.

The drive was starting to get prettier now. The countryside was spectacular. Every so many kilometres there were little clusters of villages, each chock full of autumnal-coloured roofs and tall church steeples. The fields were littered with farming outhouses and only a scant number of cows or sheep from what she could see. Grace spent most of the journey talking or typing on her phone.

'You're missing the views, Grace!' Niamh admonished as she craned her neck to see out both sides of the car.

'Seen it all before.' Grace smiled, continuing to type with fury. 'The more I get done now, the less I have to do when we get there and it's almost time for cocktails, so we've no time to waste!'

'Ooh, cocktails! Fun!'

'Even better – cocktails Italian style! *Aperitivi*, right, Vincenzo?'

'*Sì, Signora Quinn! Sempre una buona idea,*' he laughed. 'Always … how you say … the good idea,' he said over his shoulder to Niamh.

She could feel herself getting excited. Her tummy had that little knot of butterflies as the car turned off the main road and onto a smaller one. They passed a sign for the Grand Hotel Miramare on the side of the road.

'Even the sign for it is posh looking,' she gushed.

'Honestly, you'd swear you'd never been out of the country before, Niamh!' Grace laughed, although secretly she was pleased to see her sister smile. She'd never admit it to Niamh, of course, as God forbid she'd remind her that she was supposed to be in some sort of relationship-mourning state. She'd just retreat back into a cloud of moping. This trip was the perfect opportunity to shake her out of her miserable, self-indulgent, sad reverie and point her in the direction of 'get a grip'. She was mad as hell at Rick, but she refused to indulge in the usual 'what if' type conversation with her sister. All that did was encourage more obsessing over the 'what might have been' scenarios and prolong the inevitable. Rick knew exactly what he wanted out of life and he always had done. He had simply decided that, for whatever reason, that no longer included Niamh. It was time for Niamh to get over him and move on.

# Chapter Four

The car followed a winding road lined with a series of tall, exotic palm trees on both sides. The footpaths were gloriously wide and paved with a series of perfectly even grey flagstones. Niamh couldn't help but compare them to the footpaths at home, which were small and uneven. She had read about the Italian tradition of *passeggiata* – when the locals took a stroll before dinner each evening. It all looked so pleasant from her vantage point in the car that she could even imagine herself taking a leisurely stroll in the evenings. She turned to suggest the notion to Grace but she was still engrossed in her phone.

Everyone seemed to walk more slowly here, too, as if they were really going for a stroll and enjoying it. She had been to New York once and remembered being amazed at how everyone there walked insanely fast, but this was the opposite. Everyone looked so elegant, too. She hoped she had packed enough nice things. She'd have to ask Grace what she should wear before she changed for dinner tonight.

Every now and then she got a glimpse of the water, sparkling an iridescent turquoise. Little sail boats bobbed up and down and larger yachts sat imposing and immobile but for the fluttering of a flag declaring ownership or place of origin.

'*Allora signore – Santa Margherita Ligure,*' Vincenzo announced with a little flourish of his right hand as they approached the town.

'Wow,' Niamh gasped as they rounded the bend and the sea presented itself fully, lapping up just underneath the wide footpath on the right.

The road narrowed into a two-lane street with a smattering of shops along the left side. All of the façades were a similar shade of white, the only differences being the colours of their shutters or the signs that hung outside each shop.

The car slowed and turned left into the driveway of the hotel.

'*Signore, siamo arrivati,*' Vincenzo said, proudly announcing their arrival.

Even with no Italian, Niamh was able to work that one out.

'*Arrivati . . . arrivati . . .*' she repeated to herself quietly, as she rolled down the window and took a deep breath of air. She liked the way the words felt on her tongue.

The hotel stood imposingly at the foot of the driveway, with the sea curving to one side and behind it. Lofty trees, tilted to one side from years of strong sea breezes, lined the driveway. Teal-green shutters flanked the tall, narrow windows, with some offering their residents pretty wrought-iron balconies beneath them.

After pulling up beside the entrance, Vincenzo got out and opened the door for each of them. Niamh was fairly certain that she'd never had anyone open a door for her like that before. She'd have simply got out by herself but her door was locked, so she had no choice but to wait for him to round the side of the car and open it for her.

'*Grazie,*' she said, feeling a little self-conscious. She could smell the sea on the breeze and turned her face up to the sun, closing her eyes and soaking in the warmth.

'*Prego, signora,*' Vincenzo replied, with a smile and a nod.

A bellman had already rolled a shiny brass cart in their direction and he quickly whisked their luggage from the car.

'*Benvenuti al Grand Hotel Miramare, Signore Quinn,*' the bellman said, welcoming them as he loaded both cases onto the cart.

'I thought you said you hadn't been here before,' Niamh whispered, leaning in towards Grace.

'I haven't, why?' she responded giving her an odd look.

'Well, how does he know your name then?'

'The driver radios in advance to let them know when we're almost there. Didn't you hear that in the car? That way they can greet each guest by name. It's kind of a nice, personal touch.'

'No, I didn't hear that, but then again I don't speak Italian so how would I know what the driver was saying?' Niamh retorted.

'Oh right, that's right,' Grace said distractedly. She was back on her phone again. 'I'll have to get the Wi-Fi code and check in with the office before we get changed.'

'Why, where are we going?' Niamh asked. She was trying to keep up with Grace, but was trailing behind, her eyes darting in every direction.

'Nowhere. We're not going anywhere, we're staying here, but there's a cocktail thing starting at five o'clock. I just told you that in the car, Niamh!'

With a mounting sense of panic, Niamh got the sense that she was included in this cocktail thing by default. Grace had mentioned cocktails in the car, but Niamh had assumed that it referred to the drinking of them, not an actual official event. She had expected that they would go to some nice restaurants, have some nice meals and do a little exploring. She had packed for that, but she hadn't reckoned on anything that involved actual cocktail attire. In fact, she wasn't sure that anything she owned would qualify for cocktail attire, at least not in her sister's eyes.

'You didn't tell me that we were going to a cocktail party, Grace,' Niamh hissed as they followed the bellman.

'Oh relax, Niamh, for God's sake. It's not a cocktail party, it's a reception.'

'Oh right, that's fine then, it's just a reception,' Niamh responded sarcastically. 'What the hell is the difference? Not that it matters, 'cause no matter what the difference is I don't have a cocktail dress conveniently stuffed into my suitcase.'

Grace rolled her eyes. 'Look, it's just a welcome reception for the people who are going to the conference. It's basically just a drinks thing. You don't have to go if you don't want to but you're not allowed to sit in your room and be mopey. You're here to have fun, so stop brooding over Rick and cop on to yourself. You're in Italy. Just throw on a cute dress if you want some free drinks. It'll be over by about seven o'clock and we can go for dinner then.'

'I'm not being mopey! I haven't thought about Rick in at least an hour! And a "drinks thing" I can definitely get behind. It'd be rude not to go and leave you all alone, especially when there are free drinks,' she said, grinning.

The interior of the hotel was opulent but not fussy. The foyer rose up into a lofty, cavernous, cathedral-style roof. The walls were a soft white that was almost a light grey, and the mottled glass in the tall, narrow windows diffused the light so it had an almost velvety quality to it. The floor tiles were massive slabs of old stone and had the same lambent grey-white hue as the walls.

Their footsteps echoed softly on the stone floor as they entered through the double doors, following the bellman across the hallway, which was flanked by six-foot-tall floral displays on each side. It was easily the most beautiful hotel she had ever seen.

Their room was equally impressive, with original parquet flooring and two queen-sized beds covered in crisp white linens and a stack of pillows so lush that they could probably induce fatigue in the most die-hard insomniac. Double doors led to a panoramic balcony overlooking the *Golfo del Tigullio* and a light sea breeze came through the open windows, bordered by white linen curtains that felt as light as gauze.

Grace changed into a simple, fitted red dress that fell just to her knee, and wore a single strand of dark grey pearls.

'Wow, you look fab!' Niamh said admiringly, as she tugged on the material of her shirt. 'There isn't an ounce of fat on you!'

'You won't be saying that by the end of the week.' Grace laughed as she leant towards the mirror to put on her earrings. 'I'll be properly chunky after a week of pasta, pizza and wine!'

'There's no hope for me, so. They'll be rolling me onto the plane on Sunday.'

She winced at the thought of home and all the awkwardness and messiness that awaited her there. She'd much rather forget about it entirely for the week so she decided there and then that's what she should try to do.

'OK, I'm heading downstairs,' Grace said, picking up her purse. 'This meeting will only last about an hour and then the drinks thing starts at five o'clock on the balcony. See you in a bit!'

'OK, bye.'

Niamh showered and wrapped up in a large, fluffy white

robe that was about four sizes too big for her, but enveloped her in a delicious softness. She sat on the balcony transfixed by the view. The sun wasn't yet ready to set but the light was beginning to soften. The Gulf was flat calm and a few stray, thin clouds diffused the light onto the surface of the sea below. She watched a parade of tiny sailing boats, like minuscule versions of themselves, moving slowly on the horizon. She'd never been on a sailing boat, just a ferry from Dublin to Wales once. She imagined the silence all the way out there, with only the sound of the breeze and the water slapping against the boat. There were mountains to the left, a series of grey and black shadowy mounds that both fell into and sheltered the Gulf below. Church bells chimed and seemed to echo across the water, only adding to the perfection of the scene.

'Oh shit!' she cried, realising that the bells were signalling five o'clock. 'Dammit! I'm not even dressed!'

She stared, horrified, at her hair in the mirror. She must have been outside for more than half an hour and her hair had dried slowly in the sea breeze. It stood in different directions on top of her head.

'Fuck! I'm like a goddamn scarecrow.'

She teased her hair as best she could and sprayed it with enough hairspray to freeze a bird in motion. She slipped on a pale blue dress that she had bought just two days before. She had decided that Italy wasn't ready to see her pasty, white legs so this dress was perfect as it fell below her knees. Grabbing her wallet, she gave a cursory glance in the mirror.

'You'll have to do now. You're late enough as it is.'

The elevator opened onto the first floor. She followed the corridor towards the restaurant, off which was a large terrace overlooking the extensive gardens and the Gulf beyond.

There must have already been a hundred people in little clusters, chatting easily and laughing softly. A table was laid out at the entrance with dozens of name cards. Running her finger down the line with H–L she found hers, and pinned it to her dress.

She felt awkward walking in alone, and scanned the crowd for Grace. Waiters stood with trays of champagne on either side of the doors and there was a bar to the left and another to the right. She made her way to the bar on the far right, hoping that the barman spoke English.

'*Buongiorno*,' she offered slowly.

'*Ah no, signora, buona sera*,' he corrected her with a warm smile. 'After five o'clock is *buona sera*.'

'Oh sorry, yes ... I mean, *sì, buona sera*.' She could feel her face start to flush.

'No problem, *signora*. My English is so bad it will make you cry,' he replied with a grin. 'Now, what would you like?'

She hesitated, looking at a group of women to her left. Each one of them was holding the same orange-coloured drink.

'What's that drink?' she asked nodding in their direction.

'Ah, is an Aperol spritz, *signora*. Is perfect for *aperitivo*!'

'OK then, *sì*,' she smiled.

She scanned the crowd as he mixed her drink. She knew they were largely an international crowd as Grace had talked a bit about the conference on the plane. They were architects from all over the world who converged in a different part of Italy each year to network and discuss advancements, challenges and opportunities in the industry. They were a well-dressed, elegant-looking bunch. The women were without exception stylish and slender.

'Must be a money thing,' she mused under her breath, ''cause they're all successful and loaded – and every one of them is skinny.' She tugged self-consciously at the waist of her dress, willing it to sit lower.

'*Ecco, signora*,' the waiter said as he handed her the Aperol spritz.

She retreated behind several clusters of people and made her way towards the balcony. There was still no sign of Grace. She had no interest in making small talk with a bunch of strangers with whom she had nothing in common. Grace would show up eventually and force her to meet some people, but for now she was content to be alone in the crowd. The view was transfixing and she stood, motionless, staring at the horizon.

Her straw started to make noise at the bottom of her glass. She turned to make her way back to the bar and accidentally reversed into a waiter directly behind her, carrying a tray of Aperol spritz drinks. He in turn was propelled into the man walking past him, toppling one of the drinks over the side of the tray in the process.

'*Dio, io*,' the waiter exclaimed, and was suddenly surrounded by two other waiters brandishing clean white cloths and attending to the man in the suit.

'Oh God! Oh my God, I'm *so* sorry!' Niamh exclaimed in horror.

The man's pristine white shirt had a large orange stain spreading across the front. It was like a scene in a movie when someone gets shot and the blood starts to expand in a fast-growing puddle, except this one was bright orange alcohol.

'I'm *so, so* sorry,' she offered again, mortified as she watched his shirt change colour.

Her sister would kill her. Please God let him be a stranger that she doesn't know. The waiter mopped it off as best he could, apologised again in Italian, glared at Niamh and slunk away.

'It is fine. After this I go home,' the man said in a strong Italian accent as he stared down at his shirt.

'Jesus, your shirt is ruined. I'm so sorry!' she said again, her face flushed.

'It is fine. No problem. Perhaps now I should have a drink.' He smiled, signalling a passing waiter. 'You will have another, no?'

'Well, you're wearing one, thanks to me, so you might as well. I'm really sorry . . . and yes, I'll have another. I promise I'll stand back here,' Niamh said, backing up to the balcony.

'I am Giorgio,' he said, smiling as he extended his hand to her.

'I'm Niamh.' She was utterly mortified at the massive orange stain on what was clearly an expensive white shirt. He attempted to say her name but paused and made a sound not unlike the one Blake made when he called her.

'Nee . . . No, you must say that again for me. My English is not so good,' he said, shaking his head.

'Oh, sorry. It's Niamh, like "nee-uv",' she said, trying to pronounce it phonetically.

'But your name tag, they have written it in the wrong way?' he asked, frowning at the name tag.

'No, it's spelled correctly,' she responded, staring at it upside down on her dress.

'But where is the M? I did not hear an M. It sounds like you said a V sound.'

'Yeah, sorry, I know. It's Irish. Some Irish names completely freak people out 'cause they can't pronounce them. Like Saoirse, you know, the Irish film star?'

'No, no, I don't,' he said with a classic Italian hand gesture. He nodded towards her name tag. 'What is Kelly? This is also a girl's name, no?'

'That's my last name.'

'So, this would be similar if my name was Giorgio Francesco or Giorgio Alberto? Two men's names,' he said with a laugh, his dark brown eyes never leaving hers.

'I never thought of that before,' she said, mirroring his laugh. She couldn't help it. His laugh was contagious. 'I wasn't able to pronounce Niamh when I was small so I called myself Nina until I was about four. Bit of a late bloomer, apparently.'

'What is a bloomer?' he asked, a confused look on his face.

'A what? Oh sorry, umm, it's someone who starts late or grows late, you know like a flower that takes a long time to bloom.'

'No, I don't know what you mean still,' he replied, shaking his head. But ... Nina! *Perfetto!* This is much easier for me.' He extended his hand and switched to Italian. '*Piacere*, Nina. I am pleased to meet you.'

Niamh smiled shyly. '*Piacere*, Giorgio,' she said, hoping she hadn't totally butchered the pronunciation.

She noticed that he wasn't wearing a name tag. Hopefully he wasn't part of the conference group and her sister wouldn't know him.

A waiter came over with a tray of Aperol spritz. Giorgio took her empty glass from her hand and picked up two more drinks.

'*Ecco. Salute!*'

'*Ecco. Salute!*' she replied.

'No.' He laughed. '*Ecco* means "here", or "here you go". *Salute* means "cheers!"'

She could feel herself flush again.

'Oh, right, sorry. I don't really speak Italian.'

'Nina, do you always apologise this way for everything that you say?' His English was fairly good but his accent was ridiculously strong. He sounded like an Italian trying to speak English in an American gangster movie. Or like someone from *The Sopranos*.

She had never thought about it, but now that he mentioned it, she did say sorry a lot. Maybe it was an Irish thing? Or maybe it was just her. She couldn't be certain, but she didn't want to feel any more foolish than she already did tonight.

'No, it's an Irish thing. We say it a lot,' she lied.

He nodded, seeming satisfied with her answer.

'Are you an architect too?' she asked, in part because she wanted to change the subject and in part in the hopes of confirming that he had nothing to do with the conference attendees and her sister would never have to know of the unfortunate drink incident. If he was the CEO of some big fancy architect firm, she was dead.

'No, no, but I know many of these people here. I do some work with them.'

Christ, I hope my sister isn't one of them, she thought to herself.

'Oh? What kind of work do you do?' she asked, trying to sound casual.

'That depends if you mean for my work or my real life,' he replied with a smile and a shrug of his shoulders. 'For my work, I am a lawyer. I work with architects and engineers, so many of these people here are my clients. I like my work, but it is just my job, not my real life. My real life begins every evening when I leave the office and all weekend until the sun comes up again on Monday. Here in Italy, we work to live, unlike many other places where they live to work.'

She plucked another Aperol spritz from a passing tray. This was her new favourite drink, she decided. She had downed the last one in seconds. It must have been the shock of ruining this gorgeous creature's shirt. She watched him as he turned to wave at someone across the room. She liked how his eyes crinkled at the corners when he smiled.

'So do you work to live or live to work, Nina?' he asked with a grin. She noticed that he tilted his head slightly to one side every time he asked a question.

She hesitated and looked down into her drink. She wasn't sure what she was doing at present – faking a mental breakdown, taking time off from her job, running away from her life to Italy for a week. She definitely didn't live to work. Work was grand and she never minded going to work, but she didn't *live* for it. But she also didn't work to live in the way he meant. She liked her life in Dublin, but it was kind of small in a way. They never did anything much besides go on a sun holiday abroad every year for two weeks and take a few weekends away around the country. 'They' ... she caught herself automatically referring to a 'they' that she no longer had a right to, or a claim on. She felt her face flush and took a sip of her drink, hoping to hide momentarily in the glass.

'Well, I ... ' she started.

'Giorgio! *Andiamo!*'

Niamh's head turned to follow the Italian voice. A tall, slender, dark-haired woman in a figure-hugging, cream satin dress waved her arm in the air from the door of the terrace.

'*Sì, cara. Arrivo subito,*' he called back with a wave of his hand.

'I am sorry, Nina,' he said turning back to Niamh. 'But if I don't go now I will be in trouble.'

'Oh, sorry, of course. No problem. My sister will be here soon anyway, and we have dinner plans.' She frowned, realising she was rambling on to this stranger. Why did she feel the need to babble on like that?

The brunette weaved her way through the small crowd

and came to a stop alongside them. She hooked her right arm through Giorgio's in a gesture that looked overtly possessive to Niamh.

'*Amore, andiamo,*' she implored in a low, honeyed voice, without making eye contact with Niamh.

'*Certamente,*' Giorgio responded with a smile.

Niamh thought that he was just about to introduce her to the sultry Italian woman, when she leaned in the direction of the door, tugging on his arm. Giorgio shrugged his shoulders as if in resignation.

'Now, I must go,' he said to Niamh with a smile. 'Nice to meet you, Nina.' He placed his glass on the table next to them.

The brunette gave her a small smile that didn't quite reach her eyes.

'You too, and sorry again about your shirt,' she replied sheepishly.

'Ah! Now you are apologising again!' He laughed. '*Arrivederci!*' He smiled and headed for the door.

She looked over the balcony and watched as they exited from the door downstairs, noting that they were still arm in arm.

'Figures,' Niamh mumbled into her glass.

'Who was *that*?' Grace asked as she came up behind her and leaned over the balcony. 'He was divine!'

'I spilled a drink on him. Well, not "spilled", actually, but sent one flying in his general direction. That gorgeous creature is his wife or whatever,' Niamh replied as both sisters leaned over the balcony and watched them walk away together. 'She's like something out of a Pantene shampoo commercial with that hair.'

'Yeah, and that dress. The Italians are so stylish, aren't they?' Grace replied.

'She came to rescue him, obviously, before I caused him any more harm.' Niamh sighed. 'Cold as ice she was, too. And he was so friendly. I don't know what he's doing with her, apart from the obvious.'

Grace gave her a nudge. 'Maybe she thought you were a threat!'

'*Ha!* My little blue Zara dress can't compete with that! Where the hell have you been, anyway? I'm starving!'

'Sorry, I got stuck with that group over there just inside the door. I did some work with them in the past and they are trying to hire us again. Anyway, I could see you chatting to that guy so I figured you were fine!' Grace laughed. 'I'm starving, too. I'm done here. I'll be seeing enough of this lot for the next few days. Let's go find a bowl of pasta the size of our heads.'

'Grace, do you think we say sorry too much?' Niamh asked as they made their way through the crowd in search of dinner.

# Chapter Five

The next morning Niamh got up early with Grace and pored over her guidebook at breakfast, trying to plan her day. Grace had been surprised to see her get out of bed so early.

'Niamh, it's only seven a.m.'

'I know. I couldn't sleep – bad dreams,' Niamh replied with a sigh. 'Anyway, I bet the breakfast here is divine and I'm determined not to be sad and gloomy in Italy. I'm not going to waste another minute moping over that moron back home.' She sounded more determined than she felt.

'Good girl!' Grace said with a smile.

'I don't know what I'm going to do, though. I'll have to get a map so I don't get lost.'

'You won't get lost, Niamh. Just pick a spot on the map and ask the concierge to map out the directions for you. It doesn't matter where you go, everywhere is fabulous,' Grace said, as she tucked her long, brown hair up into a neat bun.

'I think I'll go to Portofino, that's not too far away. It's where all the fancy yachts are. Sounds lovely.'

'Lucky duck!' Grace responded, getting dressed into her conference-appropriate outfit. 'Don't do too much 'cause I'll want to go exploring too once this conference is over on

Thursday. You can be the advance team and bring me back anywhere absolutely fabulous that you discover!'

'I will. I'll take notes.'

'I definitely want to go to Portofino, it looks beautiful from what I've seen online and I've heard there are some amazing restaurants.'

'OK, I'll go there today and see what it's like. Then if it's fabulous we can go back together,' Niamh replied, rummaging through her selection of dresses. 'Will this be OK for daytime?'

'Yeah, that's cute. You don't want to be the same as all the other tourists in their ugly shorts and T-shirt combos, do you? It's Italy, for God's sake.'

'Yeah, that's what I was thinking,' Niamh said, pulling on a short, khaki sundress.

Horrified at the cost of taking a taxi from one town to another, Niamh quickly discovered that the easiest and most cost-effective way to get around was by ferry. It was also the most picturesque way to travel as it afforded views of the mainland and the various towns along the way, from the perspective of the water. From March to September the ferry ran all the way from Santa Margherita to Portofino and continued up the coast to Genoa. She was dying to get to Genoa as it was rumoured to be a crumbling, authentic maritime city, but she had limited time and that trip required the commitment of an entire day. There were numerous other little towns along the coast begging to be explored and the hotel was so beautiful that she planned to hang out and read in the sun, poolside, for a few afternoons.

This morning she opted to explore Portofino, as it was an easy fifteen-minute ferry ride. She would have lunch, wander around and take the ferry back in time to meet Grace for drinks at six o'clock. She had asked the concierge for some recommendations for the area and he had mapped out a series of day trips along with recommended spots for lunch, coffee and gelato along the way. He had given her a list of restaurants for Portofino and had recommended one in particular that he proclaimed was the best in town. She took a peek at the menu on her Foodie app and recoiled in horror at the prices.

'I could buy a week's groceries for the price of that fish!' she exclaimed as she adjusted the app's filters to highlight other travellers' recommendations. 'Ah, that's more like it. This fish is priced like it was just pulled from the sea, not from some special intergalactic space mission. What is wrong with people? Who pays that kind of money for fish?' She shook her head and, with a few taps on her phone, made a reservation at the highly recommended and totally affordable local option.

A crowd had already gathered on the pier waiting for the ferry, and judging by the outfits they were almost exclusively tourists. Most of them wore trainers, ill-fitting T-shirts and oversized cameras. She wondered if they all knew how to work the cameras properly or just fancied themselves as professionals while taking mediocre point-and-shoot photos.

There was an excited buzz of chatter on the pier, with everyone eager to head off for the day and explore the various towns along the route. She heard three or four different languages, one of which she couldn't even identify. The ferry pulled in and a man stood on deck announcing 'Portofino' at the top of his voice. The crowd crushed forward, everyone eager to get what they thought was the best seat. She moved along with the swell of the crowd and handed her ticket to a man balancing with one leg on the ferry and the other on the pier.

'*Grazie*,' he said taking the ticket and extended his hand to help her on board.

'*Grazie*,' she replied with a smile. How gallant! she thought to herself.

She couldn't imagine why anyone would choose to sit in the enclosed bottom deck unless it was the depths of winter, so she skipped lightly up the steps to the top deck. The sun was full in the sky and she could feel the air warming up already.

She leaned over the side and watched the crowd board the ferry. She noticed that the man didn't extend a hand to other men, only the women, but she supposed that the men would be too proud to take his hand, even if they thought they might slip between the wobbling boat and the pier. It was most likely a testosterone-driven decision.

The engine revved and the ferry turned and headed straight out into the bay. Portofino was directly south of Santa Margherita on the map, but the ferry headed out in a westward direction before making a loop and heading south. It was an easy, fifteen-minute boat ride, with stunning views along the coast. The sea was calm and the wind was light. She sat back and closed her eyes, her face up to the sun. She always thought it was amazing that a two-hour plane ride could transport you to such a different climate. Despite being so close to home, southern Europe had proper summers and not much rain from May to the end of September.

Niamh thought that if you grew up in these climates in Italy, Spain and France, it must be very hard to get used to miserable weather in places like Ireland and the UK. Back home you could never be guaranteed a good day and any-thing planned outdoors always had to have a backup plan. Hardly anyone she knew had a barbecue as there was just little point, given the usual state of the weather. Grace had

had one once. They had bought it when they bought the new house and had invited the family over for a barbecue one Sunday. It had rained solidly all day and Robert had spent two hours standing under an umbrella trying to keep the coals alive while he grilled a bucket of sausages and chicken. They had had to concede to the rain and eat indoors. It had all seemed a bit pointless, really, not that Niamh ventured that thought out loud, after Robert had spent the afternoon in a damp shirt. Still, though, sitting at the kitchen table eating sausages and chicken skewers was hardly exciting.

Her thoughts were hijacked by someone speaking English with a loud, foreign accent. She opened her eyes and squinted in the direction of a young man in a short-sleeved, crisp white shirt. He carried a clipboard and was surrounded by a cluster of American tourists. Niamh wondered why he carried the clipboard. In this day and age surely all of his information could have been accessed digitally. Unless maybe it was provided by the tour guide company to make him look official. She decided that he definitely looked the part, and even though he had a strong accent – which she presumed to be Italian – he spoke pretty good English.

As the ferry started to turn to the right and make its way south, the tour guide pointed out some impressive-looking properties dotted among the trees along the cliff top. As they rounded the headland and made the turn in towards the town of Portofino, Niamh was provided with a free guide to the various celebrity houses visible from the water. He talked of celebrities who had holidayed there in the past, including Rita Hayworth, Liz Taylor and Clark Gable and some more recent, less dead stars, like Robert de Niro.

She gazed at the expansive homes and wondered if she'd bump into anyone famous today. She'd never met a celebrity.

The closest she had come was seeing the girl from the SuperValu ad on television cross the street in St Stephen's Green, but she didn't think that that really counted as she wasn't a celebrity in the true sense of the word. She hadn't looked as skinny in real life, either, and Niamh had decided there and then that professional hair and makeup made all the difference to a person. The SuperValu girl was living proof of that.

She heard her free tour guide say something excitedly about 'the Curse of Tutankhamun'. She remembered something about Tutankhamun from school. He had been an Egyptian pharaoh of some sort, but that was about all she remembered and she certainly didn't remember that he had a curse named after him. But apparently he did, as did all the other dead pharaohs, according to her adopted tour guide, who was gesticulating wildly with both hands. She squinted in his direction, wondering why on earth he was talking about an Egyptian pharaoh on the coast of Italy.

'According to the legend, the curse of the pharaoh is cast on anyone who disturbs the mummy of an ancient Egyptian person, especially if it is a pharaoh,' the tour guide said to the rapt attention of his little audience of American tourists. 'They don't care whether you are an archaeologist or just a thief,' he continued, 'but if you disturb the body you will be cursed.'

'Oh my God, I'm totally never going to Egypt,' one older American woman drawled loudly, as she blessed herself with the sign of the cross.

'Well, you can go to Egypt, but you must not disturb any mummies, that is all.'

He had a bit of an alarmed look on his face as if worried that he had terrified the woman and would get a bad review for his tour guide skills.

'So who died from Tutankhamun's curse?' asked an American boy, clearly fascinated with the idea.

'According to the legend,' the tour guide continued, 'a man called George Herbert, who was the Fifth Earl of Carnarvon, was present at the excavation of the tomb. He was the financier of the project, and when they opened the tomb in 1923 he was bitten by a mosquito and he died four months later. This was the villa that he lived in.' He gestured to a sprawling property overlooking the bay.

The American woman blessed herself for the second time. Niamh rolled her eyes, got up and made her way down the steps.

'Someone was obviously desperate for a good story back in 1923,' she muttered to herself. 'Imagine getting a mosquito bite and blaming a dead pharaoh because you died four months later.'

Still, though, she decided that she'd refrain from telling her parents that story as her mother already had strong feelings about mosquitos. In fact, ever since they were blamed for carrying and transferring the Zika virus, Una Kelly had sworn she'd never again leave Ireland.

'Thank God 'tis too cold and damp for them things here,' she had said in horror one night, having watched the nine o'clock news divulge the latest Zika virus epidemic stories. 'That thing is from Africa, you know.'

'What thing, Una?' her father asked from behind his newspaper, beating Niamh to the question.

'The Zika virus. They say it originated in the Zika Forest in Uganda and they can trace it all the way back to 1947.'

'Is this another nugget of wisdom from *Reader's Digest*, Mam?' Niamh asked, adjusting the strings on her pyjama bottoms.

'Be careful and don't spill that wine down my good sofa,' her mother admonished, glaring at Niamh on the sofa in her pyjamas with a glass of wine in hand.

'You'd think they'd have come up with a cure for it if it's been around that long,' her father offered.

'You'd think so, wouldn't you, but no, there's no cure.'

'God, that's terrible. But you can't get it here, can you?' he asked, dropping the newspaper a few inches and looking over it at the images of mosquitos on the news.

'No, you can only get it in hot places where they have mosquitos. Out foreign, you know? It's too cold for them here.'

'Out foreign' was a term reserved for faraway countries that 'normal' tourists didn't visit on holiday, and included anywhere on the continents of Asia, Africa or South America. The United States, Australia and New Zealand were considered foreign, certainly, but civilised enough not to be in the same classification as other places 'out foreign', most likely something to do with the fact that those countries all spoke English.

'Thank God for that. We'll be staying here, so,' her father said in closing, retreating back behind his newspaper, happy in the knowledge that Zika wasn't something he had to worry about any time soon.

# Chapter Six

Portofino grew larger in front of Niamh as the ferry inched its way towards the pier. The bay narrowed into a channel with mega-yachts and sailing boats moored on the left and just in front of the little town that curved around the water's edge in a large semicircle. Wide pedestrian streets led from the water to an expansive piazza, at the back of which stood four- or five-storey buildings, each of them variations of muted, warm pastel colours. The buildings were tall and narrow and huddled together as if they had gathered conspiratorially for a clandestine meeting. The shops were a collection of luxury brands, offering everything the discerning, wealthy client never knew they needed. She strolled past shop after shop with wide, glittering window displays.

Even the mannequins are glamorous here, she mused, and insanely skinny.

It quickly became apparent that this was tourist central, but for a very specific type of tourist – wealthy. The Italians appeared to be outnumbered by tall, leggy blondes speaking Russian and toting multiple shopping bags. They were the fancy, cardboard kind of shopping bags that only posh shops used to send you on your way with your newly acquired luxury goods. She heard Eastern European languages that she couldn't identify. In fact, the only Italians, as far as she could see, were those working in the various cafés or restaurants.

She followed the path as it curved along the water's edge to the right. The street narrowed and it appeared to have less tourist traffic, as it was quieter and sat in the shade cast by the buildings that flanked it. She liked the fact that the crowd had dispersed a little and she chose a quiet café with a blue and white striped awning.

'*Buongiorno, signora.*' The waiter smiled and handed her a menu.

'Oh. Umm . . . *buongiorno. Caffè?*'

'*Un caffè o un cappuccino, signora?*' he asked.

'Oh, *sì, un cappuccino,*' she corrected herself, following his lead.

'*Subito.*'

She didn't know what *subito* meant. Couldn't even guess. 'Sure?' she wondered out loud. It kind of sounded like it, but she'd have to check with Grace.

He took the menu from her hand, smiled at her again and disappeared as quickly as he had appeared. Minutes later he was back with a small hand-painted cup and saucer and the most perfect cappuccino she had ever seen. He shooed away a pigeon pecking near her feet and placed the cup and saucer in front of her.

'*Ecco, signora.*'

'*Grazie.*'

She sat back in her seat, savouring the warm creaminess of the froth and the tease of the strong coffee underneath. This was nothing like the kind of cappuccino you'd get back home, she thought. She'd even tried the Starbucks version in the new place near the office, but the cups were the size of her head and the foam took up half the cup and felt like she was drinking air.

'The office,' she sighed, slumping down in her seat. She immediately thought of Rick. It was Tuesday morning. She was an hour ahead in Italy but he would already be at his desk back in Dublin. He always got there before everyone else and would already have put in forty-five minutes at the gym.

'Bloody overachiever,' she muttered into her cappuccino foam. It made her angry that she had allowed him to crawl unannounced into her thoughts. One thought of the office back home and he had slithered right back in there. 'Fuck you, anyway.'

A lady at a table nearby turned her head slightly in her direction but didn't make eye contact.

Shit. Inside thoughts, Niamh, inside thoughts. She wondered if Italians swore like the Irish did. 'Probably not, but even if they did I wouldn't be able to understand them, so maybe they are swearing all day long but I just don't know it,' she muttered angrily. She sat quietly, engrossed in her thoughts for a few minutes and then waved at the waiter, giving the universal hand-signature-in-the-air gesture for the bill.

'Holy shit! Seven euros for a cappuccino? That's mad,' she blurted out loud. The lady nearby turned her head again. OK, Niamh, time to move on, she said to herself as she poked out coins from her purse. You clearly can't afford to drink leisurely cappuccinos in this town or at this rate you won't be able to afford lunch!

The shock of the overpriced cappuccino had banished all thoughts of Rick from her mind. She strolled along the narrow streets, admiring the clothes in the windows, but she had no interest in even entering one of the shops. The price of the cappuccino was evidence enough that she could barely afford to have breakfast in this town, let alone look at clothes. All the top couture brands had shops here, along with some Italian brands that she was unfamiliar with. The most glamorous of all was a shop called Brunello Cucinelli. She had never even heard of it. The window display had waif-like mannequins draped in soft, muted shades of beige, cream and grey. She could tell that it was expensive as it was obvious from her side of the glass that the materials were exquisite. All the pieces seemed to flow without any obvious structure.

'If I was rich, I'd shop here. Brunello ... Brunello.' She repeated the first word as if lodging it in her memory. She would have to tell Grace about this store but she knew she wouldn't be able to pronounce the second part of the name so she took a photo surreptitiously on her iPhone.

The sun got warmer as the morning slipped by. It was easy to pass the time here, wandering the narrow streets and ducking into the non-couture shops. She bought a fridge magnet for her mother and two cute Portofino T-shirts for the boys. She wandered aimlessly, enjoying the fact that the only thing she had to do was show up for her lunch reservation at half past twelve.

She sat on the low wall surrounding the marina, staring in amazement at the massive yachts moored in the bay. She had seen many marinas before, at home in Ireland and on various holidays, but they had always run the gamut from small fishing vessels to bigger yachts with sails. She had never seen anything like these boats. Some of them were the kind of glamour yacht that you'd see in the movies, but some of these boats were so large that she wondered if they ever left the marina. There were two in particular that were enormous, almost the size of a supermarket back home. Both were black.

One appeared to be deserted, but the other had a number of bikini-clad girls on the deck. They were, without exception, blonde and skinny.

She wondered what women like that did when they were in a place like Italy. She and Grace had talked about that very topic the previous evening at dinner.

'I mean, how do you not eat the pasta here when it's so good?' Niamh had asked her sister as she dipped a slice of crusty bread into olive oil. 'What are all the models and skinny people supposed to do – just ignore all the pasta and eat vegetables and fish? That's so sad! Imagine not being able to eat what you want?'

'I don't know, I suppose if they are models or whatever and they make their money from being skinny and looking a certain way, then they have to be disciplined.' Grace shrugged as a plate of steaming *spaghetti alle vongole* was placed before her. 'Mother of God, this looks divine.'

'Thank God we're not models.' Niamh sighed as the same dish was placed in front of her. 'You can't possibly eat a load of pasta and stay skinny, so I don't know what all these skinny people do, but I feel bad for them right now. God, this smells amazing. I don't think you can get clams at home, can you? I don't think I've ever seen clams for sale back home.'

'I don't think I have, either. Maybe they just don't grow in Ireland. Maybe only mussels grow in Ireland for some reason, I don't know.' Grace shrugged and twirled her fork in her bowl of spaghetti, spearing a clam at the same time.

'Do mussels grow?' The question was out of her mouth before she had a chance to stop it and pull it back.

Grace stopped twirling her fork to look up at her sister. 'What? Are you seriously asking me that question, Niamh?'

'No, I mean, I know they grow, but like … when they

are born, or whatever, are they like seeds and they just grow, or what?'

'I swear, Niamh, sometimes you have the weirdest mind.'

'No, but really . . . I mean I know they don't grow on a bush or anything. They grow in the sea.' She giggled. 'But, like, are they actually born like the tiny fish are born in *Finding Nemo*, or what?'

'*Finding Nemo*?'

'No, wait. This is starting to sound weird, but all I asked was how do they, you know, become mussels like we know them? Like, for instance, are there male mussels and female mussels?' She tried to rescue the conversation and make it sound like it was a completely rational question to ask. 'Do they start off as little seeds or eggs and if so then how do they all attach themselves to rocks where we find them in the wild? Do they each cling to a rock for dear life and grow there until one day a human comes along and tears them off it and eats them? Kind of a sad existence, isn't it?'

'Honest to God, Niamh, sometimes I worry about you,' Grace said, shaking her head. 'I've never spent much time wondering about mussels so I'm afraid I can't answer your questions. Google it when we go home. Now, shall we get another bottle?'

'Honest to God, Grace, sometimes I worry about *you*,' Niamh said mockingly. '*Yes* would be the answer to that question. If I ever say no to that question that's when you should start to worry!'

She was smiling to herself now, thinking back on the conversation about mussels. She still didn't know the answers. She leaned back on the wall, her arms supporting her from behind, and wondered if the skinny girls on the boat in front of her were happy. They looked amazing, but they obviously weren't having spaghetti for every meal. She couldn't imagine not being able to order whatever she wanted off the menu – especially here.

'This is why you are chunky, Niamh, and why you are not exposing yourself to the world in a bikini,' she said quietly to herself. 'A burka would be more appropriate based on the amount of food you eat – and it is usually not salads.'

'I'm sorry, are you talking to me?'

She turned to see a young blond man sitting directly behind her on the wall. She had been so intent upon the boats that she hadn't noticed him sit down.

'Oh, no, sorry! I was just talking to myself,' she replied, hoping he hadn't heard what she had said.

'No problem,' he said with a smile. 'I do it all the time.'

His accent sounded American, but not like the strong American accents she had heard earlier that morning.

'You here on vacation?' he asked.

'Um, yeah. We're staying in Santa Margherita. I just took the ferry here this morning.'

Hopefully the change in conversation meant that he hadn't heard her berating herself about the lack of salads in her life.

'Ah, smart move. Traffic around here is nuts. The ferry is the way to go. That's a nice town.'

'It seems nice. We only got here yesterday so I haven't really seen much of it. I was dying to see Portofino so I thought I'd come here for lunch.'

'Good idea. There are some amazing restaurants here. Some of the best around, actually.'

'Have you been here long?' It sounded like he knew quite a bit about the area.

'A few months.' He shrugged. 'I'll probably just stay until the fall.'

Definitely American, Niamh thought, noting the use of

'fall' instead of autumn. She also noticed that he said 'probably', which meant that he wasn't here to do something practical and finite like build a bridge or open a new hotel or something – probably another American just off around the world to find themselves and do something utterly useless in the process until they were summoned back home by the call of a real job. She couldn't tell what age he was but he was most likely in his mid to late thirties.

'That must be nice,' she said. 'I'm only here for a week.'

She wondered what it would be like to be able to gallivant around like that and decide when you might want to leave. He must definitely come from money, she decided.

'It sure is. I'm making the most of it while it lasts,' he said with a grin as he stood up. 'I'm going up to the little square there for a coffee. Would you like to join me?'

'Oh, that's kind but I actually have a lunch reservation in a few minutes so I have to get going.'

It was a bit of a lie as she still had half an hour before her reservation, but she wasn't about to get into a conversation about her disaster of a life over an overpriced coffee with a privileged American stranger who was just killing time in Liguria until he buggered off again to do something else, somewhere else. She figured a white lie was a safer bet.

'Where are you eating?'

'Um, Da Puny?' she said it in a hesitant voice, as if it were a question. She frowned, wondering why she always did that when she was shy or nervous.

'Excellent choice! It's a great local spot,' he exclaimed, turning to face the piazza. 'Well then … Da Puny: one; Jeffrey: zero. My loss is their gain.' He smiled.

She returned his smile shyly, thinking that he was obviously a complete charmer and wondering if women really fell for

61

those kinds of lines. She faked a laugh, as she didn't know how to respond to that. '*Ha!* Thanks, bye,' she said as he turned to walk away. She pretended to look busy on her phone.

'Bye, Niamh. Nice to meet you. Enjoy your lunch!' He grinned and walked away.

I didn't tell him my name, she thought, frowning again as she watched him go. *Fuck!* He *did* hear me rabbit on about bikinis and salads. She felt her face flush. Jesus, Niamh, the one cute, friendly foreigner you meet ever in your life thinks you're a nutcase talking to yourself in the middle of town. Excellent way to improve upon your disaster of a life.

She stood up from the wall, brushed off her dress and made her way in the direction of the restaurant. She couldn't tell if he had been flirting with her or if he was just genuinely nice and well mannered. Her flirting radar had become obsolete from lack of use. He was definitely cute though, she thought to herself with a smug little smile as she crossed the cobbled streets in search of her restaurant and her lunch.

# Chapter Seven

The restaurant was at the very back of the piazza, facing out in the direction of the marina. It had a large covered terrace out front and was surrounded by pretty, dark green trellises, with a creeping plant of some description making its way up and around the latticework. It was the second of six restaurants in a row and was by far the busiest. A few doors down she could see the restaurant that the concierge had recommended and decided that she had definitely made the right choice. It was the kind of place that you could judge based on the clientele and how they were dressed.

Definitely dodged a bullet there. I probably couldn't even afford the bread basket in a place like that, she laughed to herself as she made her way towards the restaurant that she had booked.

The young woman who stood at the check-in podium out front couldn't have been more than her mid-twenties. She was statuesque and strikingly beautiful, Niamh thought as she walked towards her. She must be a model when she's not working here, she mused.

'Eh . . . *buongiorno*,' she said hesitantly.

The young woman greeted her with a wide smile. '*Buongiorno, signora.*'

Perfect teeth too, Niamh thought. 'Eh ... I have a reservation for half past twelve. Under the name Niamh Kelly.'

'*Scusi*. For when, madam?'

'Umm ... for twelve-thirty?' She heard herself saying it as if it was a question again. She stood up taller and pushed her shoulders back and her chin up. The woman still towered above her.

'Ah, OK. And what is the name again please, *signora*?'

'Niamh Kelly. I've reserved a table outside.'

'OK,' the woman said, in a lilting Italian accent. 'Is your entire party here now?'

'Umm, no. It's just me.'

'But the reservation is for a party of two, *signora*.'

Niamh knew she was probably imagining it, but she could almost feel the entire piazza go quiet and tune in to the conversation. She felt her face begin to flush. 'Well, no, it should only be for one.'

'Hmmm.' The young woman frowned and shook her head. 'No, *signora*, I'm sorry but the only reservation we have for Niamh Kelly is for a party of two.'

'OK, well, there is only one of me so what do you suggest I do?' Niamh asked shortly, feeling a rush of colour make its way up her neck.

The hostess raised one eyebrow and stared down at her. '*Signora*, I can see that we have a table for Niamh Kelly reserved for the outside, but it is for a party of two. We don't seat singles on the terrace.'

'Excuse me?' Niamh asked, incredulous. This bitch was actually going to argue with her because she was a single?

'We might have a table inside available in an hour or so, but we are very busy, *signora*.'

'But I have a reservation, *signora*,' she replied emphasising the last word.

'Madam, you have a reservation for two, not one.'

'Are you telling me that I can't sit here because I'm on my own?'

'Yes, madam, exactly.'

She could tell that the hostess was beginning to enjoy this now.

'That's ridiculous. What kind of a discriminating policy is that? You mean single people can't eat here?' She knew she was getting angry now and she should just walk away, but she was humiliated and she didn't want to give in.

'No, madam, single people cannot eat on the terrace as we only seat parties of two or more outside. And you made a reservation for two, but you are only one, so I cannot seat you outdoors.'

'This is ridiculous. I made the reservation online and the system probably just automatically booked it for two people. It's not my fault if the operating system defaults in favour of happy couples as the norm.'

Niamh was fuming and was just about to make one final smart comment and storm off when she heard someone speak behind her.

'Excuse me,' the woman said in a deep voice. She stood alongside Niamh at the podium and placed a hand lightly on her right arm.

'Monica, darling, apologies for being a little late,' she said to the hostess in a posh British accent. She turned towards the back of the terrace and waved towards the grey-haired, impeccably dressed man who was rushing towards her. 'Giacomo,' she said kissing him on both cheeks.

'Emilia, *piacere*,' he replied, bending to kiss her free hand.

'Giacomo, I'm late. Please forgive me.' She spoke slowly and enunciated her words beautifully.

'Emilia, is never a problem,' he insisted in a strong Italian accent. 'Please do not worry. We have your table ready for you just here, just as you like,' he said, indicating to a corner table alongside the trellis.

Niamh could do nothing but stare at her. She was meticulously put together. She wore a three-quarter-length, off-white jacket with matching Capri pants. Beneath, she wore a high-necked black top that looked like it might be cashmere, and black sling-back heels. Her blonde hair was knotted in an elegant chignon and pinned at the base of her neck. She finished the look with massive, oversized dark sunglasses, perched on top of her head.

'Marvellous. *Grazie*. Oh, and one more thing. Could you please help my friend here ...?' She turned and looked directly at Niamh.

'Niamh?' Niamh replied with a question, as she wasn't sure what was happening or what she was supposed to say.

'My friend Niamh,' the woman continued. 'There seems to be some confusion with her reservation and she would like to sit outside.'

'Certainly, *signora*,' Giacomo replied with a deep nod of his head. He threw a warning glance in Monica's direction. 'Any friend of yours, *signora*, is a friend of ours.'

He reached out and shook Niamh's hand. '*Piacere, signora*.' He glanced down at the reservation book and saw that she did indeed have a reservation. He glared one more time at Monica. 'My apologies for the confusion, *signora*,' he said to Niamh with a smile. 'We have a lovely table for you outside, just as you requested. *Un momento*.'

The blonde lady winked at Niamh and smiled, patted her

arm twice, then turned and drifted in the direction of her designated table. Giacomo fired off a rapid stream of Italian and a bow-tied waiter appeared by Niamh's side and escorted her to her table. The second place setting was whisked away as the waiter held her chair for her. Niamh's heart was pounding. She had no idea what had just happened or who that lady was, but she certainly had some serious influence in this restaurant.

She gazed around at the diners, each of whom was elegantly dressed. They all chatted quietly together over the chinking sounds of cutlery and crockery. She was glad that she had worn a cute dress, as she didn't think she would even have approached the bitch-in-heels at the podium if she were in her usual shorts and T-shirt holiday attire.

Her heart rate had returned to normal and she was relieved that none of the other diners seemed to be paying her any attention. She could see the profile of the lady who had rescued her in the opposite back corner, engaged in animated conversation with three other diners. 'Emilia,' she said to herself. 'What a pretty name.'

'*Allora, signora*. May I offer you a menu in Italian or you would prefer English?' The waiter who had seated her had returned with menus in hand.

'Oh, English would be great, thank you.'

'*Certo, signora*.' He smiled and placed it in front of her with a flourish.

He no sooner had left, than Giacomo reappeared at her side. '*Signora*, may I offer you a glass of prosecco?'

She hesitated, not knowing if he meant offer in the sense of 'offer on the house', or in the sense of 'Would you like it?' If the price of the cappuccino was anything to go by she should probably decline.

'As my gift, *signora*,' he continued, sensing her hesitation, 'for the earlier confusion.'

'Oh no, that's fine, honestly,' she said waving her hand.

'*Signora*, it will be my pleasure,' he said with a smile as he poured her a glass. 'Enjoy. *Salute!*' And he was gone again.

She spied the other tables to see what everyone was ordering. It looked like people were having either pasta or fish. The menu was dazzling and she suddenly realised how hungry she was. She had read that their *pasta pescatore* was one of their most famous dishes. It was a seafood spaghetti dish in a light tomato sauce. She spotted at least two other people with a dish that looked like it could be just that, which is always a good sign. It was thirty-two euros, so she figured that it had to be a life-alteringly good bowl of pasta. She reached out for a sip of prosecco but realised it was gone. She had obviously drained it in the flush of embarrassment of what had happened.

'Well, that's just classy, Niamh,' she muttered to herself. 'Eh, *scusi*,' she called to a passing waiter. 'May I have the wine list, please?'

'*Certo, signora, subito.*'

'*Subito, subito*,' she repeated quietly, exaggerating the pronunciation and enjoying the sound the word made. Italian words with their big vowels seemed to roll about in her mouth. She had no idea how to spell it but it sounded wonderful. '*Subito ... subito*,' she continued. She stopped abruptly when she realised that the lady at the table next to her was staring at her. She caught her eye, mortified. The lady gave a kind of small, sympathetic smile. The kind of apologetic, fake, half smile you'd give to a person with no legs who was sitting, begging on the street and had turned to catch you staring at them. Her face flushed. 'Great, you look nuts again, Niamh,' she muttered under her breath.

'*Ecco, signora,*' the waiter said with a big smile. 'Here are the wines by the glass.' He pointed to the first and second pages of the menu.

It's probably frowned upon to order an entire bottle for yourself, especially as a woman, she guessed, as she ran a finger down the list. 'Singles don't eat outside and they certainly don't drink a whole bottle of wine with lunch,' she muttered quietly as she munched on a breadstick. She ordered a glass of Pinot Grigio, even though she could easily have polished off an entire bottle. 'Best not to push one's luck!'

The waiter took her order and suggested that she have the minestrone soup as an appetiser. 'Is very good, *signora,* and is light.'

'OK, sure.'

Her glass of wine was poured at the table. She thought that was a nice touch, rather than just plonking an already-poured glass of whatever it might be in front of you. This way you got to see the bottle and you actually knew what you were drinking. She was given a taste first. It was nicely chilled. '*Grazie,*' she said, and she nodded her approval.

No sooner had the wine waiter left then a plate of tiny bruschetta was placed in front of her.

'From the chef, *signora.*'

There were three pieces of bruschetta, each piece no more than two inches long. The tomatoes glistened with oil. She bit into the first piece and decided that she had never tasted anything quite as good. The toasted bread was warm and crusty on the outside but gave way to a softness in the centre, not like the hard crusty things you got at home that resembled croutons more than this softly yielding, melting creation.

That feeling of intense satisfaction continued through the other courses as she sat surrounded by a happy hum of sounds. She hadn't felt this content in a long time, she realised. The food, the wine, the warm air, the foreign sounds all worked together in a happy little harmony. It was a perfect blending of sensations, tastes, sounds and emotions. She ordered a second glass of wine. The bruschetta had indeed been a precursor of great things to come, as she had never in her life had anything like the seafood spaghetti dish. It had mussels, clams, shrimp and squid all melded together in a light tomato garlic sauce.

'Insane. Insanely good,' she murmured to herself contentedly. She would have to tell Grace about this place, although she wasn't sure she would have the courage to come back and face the bitch-in-heels again. She scraped her fork quietly along the bottom of the bowl, trying to scoop up the last of the sauce.

'How was your lunch?'

She looked up to see Emilia towering over her, with her oversized handbag slung over one arm.

'Oh my God, divine.'

'Yes, it's good, isn't it?' She smiled.

'And thank you for . . . you know . . . earlier.'

'Oh, don't mention it, darling. It was good to take that wretch down a notch or two. She has the most God-awful superiority complex. Good to bring her back to earth every now and then.' She laughed. 'Now, I don't want to disturb your lunch . . .'

'No, I'm finished. Um, would you like to join me for a drink or a coffee? It's the least I could do. I think this food might have changed my life and I would have been having a slice of pizza elsewhere if you hadn't rescued me.'

'Well, when you put it like that, how can I refuse?' Emilia laughed a big laugh again and pulled out a chair.

There was a rush of waiters to the table. One helped fix her seat, while another dusted off the table with a napkin. Giacomo appeared at her side almost immediately.

'*Signora*, what can we get for you?'

'What are you drinking, darling?' Emilia asked, nodding towards Niamh's glass.

'Um, the Pinot Grigio.'

'Well, that won't do, will it, Giacomo?'

Giacomo smiled. 'An Arneis, perhaps, *signora*?'

'Two please, darling.' She turned back to Niamh. 'The Pinot Grigio is fine, but the Arneis is divine.'

'Excuse my ignorance, but what is the ... what was the name of the wine?'

'It's pronounced *ar-neys*. It's from Piemonte, in the north of Italy. Have you heard of Barolo wine?' she asked without any hint of judgement.

'Yes, of course.'

'Well, Barolo is from Piemonte, as is Barbaresco, another famous red wine. And it so happens that the region produces the most divine white wine called Arneis.'

Niamh didn't recall even seeing it on the list of wines by the glass. She'd certainly have wondered what it was as it was such an unusual name. 'It doesn't sound very Italian. Would I have seen it on the list?'

'No, they don't serve it by the glass, only by the bottle, which is normally not a problem, but given the amount of wine I've already had it would be a little precarious to dive into another entire bottle.' She laughed her big laugh again.

Niamh didn't think she could imagine the lady diving into anything, especially not wine, as she seemed so elegant and refined. She also guessed that pouring Arneis by the glass was another concession made without hesitation in her favour. Who on earth is she? she wondered.

'I'm Niamh, by the way, as you already know from earlier,' she said, extending a hand.

'Oh my, how rude of me. That's right, we haven't been properly introduced. Forgive me. Emily,' she said shaking her hand firmly.

'I thought they called you Emilia earlier?'

'They did. The Italians will find an Italian version of anything if they can get away with it. Though Lord knows what they'll do with Niamh. Irish?'

'Yes. Are you British?'

'Yes, I'm from London. Or at least I was. I live here now.'

The waiter reappeared and poured two large glasses of white wine. Niamh couldn't help but study the man as he stood over them.

'So how come all the waiters are in black tie if this is a casual, local place?'

'It's a cultural thing here. The black ties don't necessarily mean that the restaurant is fancy,' Emily explained. 'It's just the traditional uniform. They are mostly always men too, the waiters that is. It's actually viewed as a real career here. They call them career waiters – absolute professionals who spend their whole lives in restaurant service, and more often than not at the same restaurant.'

'Really? At home it's something that people do temporarily while they're trying to figure out what to do next, or life in general.'

'Yes. Not the case here. They take great pride in their work and they tend to stay with the same company or restaurant for years.'

'Hmm, that makes sense. I was in Paris once and I noticed

the same thing – all the waiters were men. I bet it's the same career waiter sort of thing. This is divine,' Niamh said appreciatively, as she tasted the wine.

'It is rather, isn't it?' Emily agreed.

'Do you live here in Portofino?'

'Good Lord, no. I couldn't handle all these tourists.'

'Yeah, I did think it was a bit touristy when I got here this morning. It's beautiful though. So pretty.'

'Yes, awfully pretty, but far too many people. Most days I find that people are overrated.' She laughed. 'Are you here on holiday then?'

'Yes, we're staying in Santa Margherita.'

'And who is the other part of your "we"?'

Niamh laughed. 'I'm here with my sister. She's here for a conference and we're staying at the Grand Hotel Miramare.'

'Wonderful property, and Santa Margherita is a nice town – very grand.'

'Where do you live?'

'Not far from here in a small fishing village called Camogli.'

'Called what?' Niamh asked.

She spelled it out. 'C-A-M-O-G-L-I, but the g is silent. It's pronounced *Cam-ohl-yee*.'

Niamh found it hard to imagine this lady in a fishing village. She seemed so elegant and worldly and almost larger than life.

'You absolutely have to visit it. It's the most divine little village, very Italian. Small and quiet but with an abundance of wonderful restaurants.'

'I've never heard of it.'

'That doesn't surprise me. Most people who live there, and even those who visit religiously every year, tend not to talk much about it. It's almost like an unspoken pact. We want to keep it just as it is and not have it overrun with tourists like some other towns nearby.'

Niamh hesitated. Portofino was quite stunning and this restaurant had been amazing, so she found it hard to see how another place could be even more perfect.

'You'll understand when you get there. It's as if no one wants anyone else to know about it. It's that wonderful.'

'I'm intrigued. I'll go with my sister at the weekend when she's done with her conference.'

'Marvellous idea,' Emily said, as she finished her wine.

Niamh was relieved to finally meet someone else who drank as fast as she did. All she got back home was criticism for it.

'Now, I must be off. My driver has been waiting for half an hour for me, poor man.'

'Oh, I thought that Camogli was one of the little villages on the coast.'

'It is, yes, why?'

'You don't take the ferry?'

Emily laughed. 'Darling, I haven't been on a ferry in twenty years! Now, must run. Here's my card. Call me when you get to Camogli if you would like to. I'll tell you where to eat and such.'

The card just had her name and phone number. It was made of heavy paper stock and her name was embossed: EMILY DRAKE. Who *was* this woman?

Giacomo and a waiter appeared at her side as she stood up from the table. She shook Niamh's hand and waved goodbye before she disappeared in the direction of the restaurant entrance, with Giacomo escorting her by the arm. Niamh motioned to a waiter for the bill. Giacomo reappeared minutes later with a tiny glass of limoncello. 'For you, *signora*, as a *digestivo*.'

'Oh thank you. I mean, *grazie*.'

'And the bill, it has been paid, *signora*.'

'Sorry?' she asked, looking up at him.

'Signora Drake has taken care of this. She said that you are a friend, no?'

'I . . . oh . . . what? Wow. Thank you.'

'Don't thank me, *signora*. Signora Drake is a kind and generous woman. You are lucky to have a friend such as this.' He smiled and disappeared, leaving Niamh to her thoughts.

She could feel tears sting the backs of her eyes and blinked furiously to ward them off. A random act of kindness, she thought, incredulously. Who does that? I want to be like her when I grow up. I want to be that woman who walks into a restaurant and spots someone who clearly needed to be rescued at some level and just say, 'I've got this.' How cool is that?

She leaned against the back of her chair. This was definitely the nicest thing anyone had done for her in a long time and she marvelled at how subtle it had all been. She slid her credit card back into her wallet and drummed her fingers on the table. It was hard to put an age on Emily. She was one of those women who had clearly aged well and life appeared to have been kind to her. She barely had a wrinkle on her face but she must have been in her early fifties.

Kind of like Nicole Kidman, she mused. She always looks amazing, not to mention skinny. I know she's loaded and wealthy women always look good – except the ones who've had too much Botox – but still, she looks amazing for fifty-something. Julia Roberts too – she still looks amazing. Oh and Sandra Bullock! She's fabulous. *And* she dumped that loser American actor after he cheated on her. Imagine being stupid enough to cheat on someone like Sandra Bullock? Isn't she still single? And then she adopted a black kid? These women have it all together. I really need to make more of an effort and get my life back together – and this time on my own terms.

She decided then that Emily must be in the same age range as those actresses. 'She's about twenty years older than me and is in better shape than I am,' she sighed. 'You really need to get your shit together, Niamh. A diet wouldn't be a bad idea, for starters. Maybe tomorrow you can make it through one meal without devouring an entire basket of bread?' she berated herself as she wove her way through the clusters of tables and out into the streets of Portofino.

# Chapter Eight

I feel like a fraud, Niamh thought as she studied her reflection in the full-length mirror. She had read about something called imposter syndrome in one of her mother's *Psychology Today* magazines – essentially self-sabotage over irrational feelings of inadequacy. I wonder if that also applies to wearing someone else's clothes to fit in at a fancy restaurant, she thought.

'Hmm, maybe maxi dresses are the way to go, though. That actually doesn't look too terrible on you, Niamh, and it hides any evidence of years of doughnuts having been a preferred breakfast choice,' she said smugly, turning to look over her shoulder. She had borrowed a dress from Grace for tonight's dinner. They had a reservation at an elegant restaurant up in the hills behind Santa Margherita. 'Thank God Grace packed a few loose, floaty numbers,' Niamh mumbled to herself as she rummaged around in her bag for earrings.

The past couple of days had flown by. Niamh had surprised even herself at the extent of her wanderings around the peninsula. She had walked the length and breadth of Santa Margherita, happily ordering pasta at every meal. She had even explored the nearby beach cove of Paraggi and made a point of telling Grace that she'd tried spaghetti and sea urchin for the first time in a tiny seaside trattoria. Although, if she was being totally honest, that was really only because she had ordered the wrong thing and was in fact expecting spaghetti with shrimp.

Grace had an important presentation this afternoon and, as a result, she had been stressed and preoccupied for the past couple of days. Niamh was hoping that tonight her sister would finally be able to relax and get into holiday mode – and stop picking at her in the process. As a result of Grace's stress, nothing Niamh had packed had been deemed suitable enough for their dinners every evening.

'Honestly, Niamh, I told you this would be a fancy trip. Did you really only pack those three dresses?'

'Well, I didn't think I'd need to dress for royalty every night.'

'Don't be such a smart arse. We're here for a week so you should have packed an outfit for every evening. All the restaurants are fancy around here, especially at night.'

Niamh rolled her eyes. She didn't mind the idea of getting dressed up a couple of times, but having to wear a dress and heels every night was not exactly her usual style.

'Can I not wear flat sandals with this dress?' she had asked Grace earlier that evening.

'No. You'll look like a hippy. Do you want to look like a hippy? Put on a pair of wedge sandals at least, for God's sake. And don't be late. I'll meet you at the bar at seven o'clock.'

'I won't be late,' Niamh retorted, rolling her eyes. 'Good luck with the presentation!' she shouted from the bathroom, as Grace left for the afternoon.

Now, standing at the bar in Grace's maxi lemon chiffon dress, she felt like an entirely different version of herself, but it was easier to wear the damn thing than to listen to her sister moaning about her inappropriate choice of outfit again.

She ordered an Aperol spritz as she waited for Grace to arrive and was hoping that she would be easier to live with now that the conference was over. She had tried hard to put on a front and be cheerful all week, but her mind had wandered often to Rick and the situation back home. She must have worn her thoughts on her face one evening earlier in the week, as Grace had jumped all over it. She grimaced now, as she thought back on the conversation and the realisation that her relationship with Rick was definitely over.

'What's the matter with you? What's with the face?' Grace had enquired.

'Nothing. I was just thinking, that's all.'

'Don't tell me you are moping over that loser back home, are you? You're better off without him, Niamh. Honestly I wish you'd just get over him and move on.'

'Way to go there, Grace, with that large bucket of patience and understanding,' Niamh replied snarkily, as she chugged the remainder of her glass of wine. 'It's only been two weeks, you know. Give a girl a break, will you?' She reached for the bottle and poured two more glasses. 'I thought you were taking me away so I could feel sorry for myself and wallow in self-pity and self-loathing?'

'No, I brought you away so you could see that there is more to life than "Rick the Dick" and pull yourself together. You don't think he's sitting at home moping over you, do you?'

Niamh had been quietly checking her phone twenty times a day. She had secretly hoped that he might have regretted his decision and had been waiting for him to call to say that it had all been a giant mistake, but she refused to give in and contact him in any way.

'No, of course not.'

'Well, he's not. So the sooner you move on the better.'

'What do you mean by that?'

'Nothing, nothing,' Grace replied, looking down at the menu.

'Do you know something?'

Grace hesitated and sipped her wine. 'Well, it's just that I saw something on Facebook, that's all. But it's probably nothing.'

'What did you see on Facebook?' Niamh could feel the colour drain from her face. She had deleted him in a rage but had forgotten that her sister might still be friends with him on social media. Shit, she thought, this was a missed opportunity – I could have been stalking him on Facebook on Grace's phone this entire time, damn it.

'Nothing, just a photo, just forget it. There's no point.'

'Hand me your phone, please.'

'I didn't bring it with me to dinner.'

'That's a flat-out lie. That device is *never* not on your person. It's like an extension of your arm. Hand it over, please. Unlock it first.'

Grace sighed and reached into her bag. She tapped out her four-digit code and opened the Facebook app. She scrolled for a few moments and then stopped. She hesitated for a second before handing the phone across the table. 'Just don't freak out, OK? Don't make a scene. I had to beg to get this table.'

Niamh took the phone and stared at the photo in front of her. It was Rick, looking handsome in a dark suit, with a young blonde woman sitting on his lap. She looked vaguely familiar. She was sitting on one knee, with her hand on his other thigh.

'They look cosy,' she said slowly. 'Wow, didn't take him long, did it?'

'Give it back to me,' Grace said, waggling her hand across the table.

'Who is she?' Niamh zoomed in to get a better look at her. 'I don't believe it . . .' her voice trailed off as she frowned at the screen.

'What? Do you know her? Don't tell me you know her,' Grace replied.

'I don't believe it . . .'

'Not helping, Niamh! What?'

'That's Boobra.'

'Who?'

'Boobra from Sales.'

'Who's Boobra? What does that even mean?' Grace asked, her hands spanning out at her sides.

'Barbara,' Niamh offered, still not looking up from the screen. 'Her name is Barbara something-or-other. She's kind of new. I don't remember her last name, her dad's Vietnamese or something and I've no idea how to pronounce it. I don't really know her, I just know she works in Sales.'

'At PlatesPlease?'

'Yes. She went to Slovenia or Slovakia or somewhere like that in Eastern Europe last year for a cheap boob job. They had some promotional thing going on – some two-for-one special – two people, not two boobs, obviously – so she went with a friend.'

'What? What kind of dope goes for a discounted boob job?' Grace asked, aghast.

'This clown did. But in fairness, she did have boobs like fried eggs. I saw a before and after photo. Anyway, she wanted to go up two cup sizes but when she woke up the surgeon was standing over her saying that he had a surprise for her. He said that as he was doing it he decided that she would look fantastic with even bigger boobs, as she was so lovely and tall. So he went up three cup sizes while she was unconscious.'

'What? Are you serious?'

'Deadly. Now they just look ridiculous, as is clearly evident here.' Niamh, with the beginnings of a grin, turned the zoomed-in photo around for Grace to see.

'Ah come on, you're making that up!'

'I'm not, I swear. So now she has these obviously fake, massive boobs, hence Barbara became Boobra.'

'Did she sue him?'

'How could she sue him?' she exclaimed. 'She couldn't afford a full-priced boob job in the first place, let alone the cost of a lawyer to sue a plastic surgeon on the other side of Europe.'

'But that's absolute malpractice surely,' Grace said incredulously.

'I swear, Grace, you're the only person in my life to not see the funny side of this. Come on, it's hilarious – going for a discount boob job and waking up with more than you even wanted? It's like God poking at you for messing with plastic surgery in the first place!'

'That poor girl. Give me back the phone,' Grace said, waggling her hand in front of Niamh.

'I don't know her that well but she's not the brightest of sparks, to be honest, and what the hell is Rick doing with her, anyway? She didn't wait long for me to be out of the picture, did she?' Niamh pushed the phone back across the table towards her sister. 'They deserve each other!'

'Don't go all mopey and make me sorry I told you now. I thought seeing this might actually help you get all self-righteous and be all strong feminist-type and realise that you're better off without him. Please don't go wallowing, for the love of God.'

'I *am* better off without him, but allow a girl a moment to react to something as shocking as the visual of Boobra implanting herself on his lap – no pun intended,' said Niamh with a giggle.

'What?'

'Implanting herself ... nothing, forget it. Is there more wine in that?' she asked, tipping her head towards the bottle in the ice bucket.

Grace drained the bottle into their glasses and motioned for another. 'I'm sorry that you had to see that. I hope you're not all upset and just putting on a brave face for my sake, but you really are better off without him. I know that's a cliché and all, but it's true.'

'No, maybe I'm actually really in shock or something, but now I feel like a complete gobshite for wasting a minute feeling sad over him. I've been hanging out mentally in Loserville for the past two weeks and he's been getting his rocks off with Boobra. And she's not even pretty!' Niamh fumed. 'She's just skinny! Oh, but she has enormous boobs.'

'No, she's a bit of a dog, actually. Flat nose. Looks like she got whacked in the face with a frying pan,' Grace said, pouring two large glasses from the new bottle.

Niamh giggled at the idea of being whacked in the face with a frying pan. 'Yep, he's really dredging the bottom with that wench. Well, she can have him. She'll find out soon enough. The man has no stamina in bed. He leaves it all on the gym floor and whoever he's taking to bed gets seconds.' She held up her glass in a fake toast. 'Your competition isn't other women, Boobra – it's the bench press. Good luck with that!'

The two of them laughed uproariously. It might have been just the kind of release that Niamh needed because, for the first time in weeks, she slept like the dead that night and woke up without feeling anxious. Whopping headache, of course, but that could be easily cured and it had been worth it. An anxious heart isn't as easy to fix and she was grateful to wake up feeling some level of peace, at last.

She shook her head, dispersing the memory of the Boobra conversation that night at dinner with Grace and sat now quietly at the bar. She twirled her glass of Aperol spritz, keeping one eye on the door as she waited for Grace to finish her presentation, so the holiday could really begin. She regretted having lost her cool and gotten so emotional about the whole situation, but in hindsight it had been coming for a while. She couldn't believe that had only been a couple of days ago. It seemed like weeks ago, now, looking back on it, and she felt mentally exhausted from all of the emotional energy of the past couple of weeks. It was almost as if seeing the photo of him with that wench cemented everything in her mind. It was clear that he was moving on, and it was as if that photo had given her permission to do the same. She had decided that there was no point in mourning someone who doesn't want you any longer. So instead she had focused the next few days on exploring, pasta and plenty of wine.

'Well? How'd it go?' she asked Grace as she finally saw her approaching. She was relieved to see her with a smile on her face.

'It went great! But I'm so glad it's over. Now we can plan some stuff for the next few days. Where should we go first? Two whole days of no work, just play. Fabulous,' Grace said, plucking Niamh's glass from her hand and taking a sip. 'Cheers!'

'Well, you had said that you wanted to go to Portofino, and I'd like to go to that place the lady who rescued me is from – Camogli.'

'Do we take a boat there?'

'Yes, to both of them, they're both on the same route from

here. Portofino is the first stop, then the ferry continues on to Camogli.'

'Well, you've already been to Portofino, so why don't we go to Camogli first and wander around, have lunch and all that and then we can stop off in Portofino for a drink on the way back?'

'Good plan. Let's go in the morning, then.'

'Did she give you the names of some good restaurants for lunch?'

'No, she gave me her card and just said to call her if we were going and she could recommend some places.'

'Oh God, that doesn't mean we have to meet her, does it? I know she rescued you and all that, but we only have two days. I don't really want to have to have lunch with a stranger and make polite small talk. Is that mean? Sorry if that's mean, but I've spent the past three days talking to people so I'm kind of over it.' Grace grinned.

'No, that's fine. I don't have to call her. I'll look up some recommendations online later.'

The next morning started later than planned. Three bottles of wine might have seemed like a good idea at the time, but they rarely do so the next morning. The girls struggled down to breakfast before it finished at eleven o'clock.

'Do I look as bad as I feel?' asked Grace at the breakfast table.

'Yes. Woof. No offence.'

'God,' she groaned. 'Did we finish the third bottle?'

'Yes, and ordered two limoncellos, 'cause we still hadn't had enough.'

'I don't even remember getting home.'

Niamh plucked bits off her croissant. The large bottle of sparkling water in front of them was a telltale sign of chronic overindulgence the night before. 'My head is pounding,' she moaned, her chin resting in one hand. 'I don't think I can have a cappuccino yet. I'll have to have black tea. Here, take these.' She handed two painkillers across the table. 'They're the ones you dissolve in water. They work the fastest.'

'Thanks,' Grace replied, looking up at her. 'You still have makeup on from last night.'

'Oh God, I didn't even look in a mirror before coming down.'

'That's probably a good thing. You would never have left the room.'

'Are you serious? Am I a state?'

'You look like a racoon. You have eyeliner or mascara or both smudged a solid inch below your eyes.'

'Oh, Jesus. No wonder the waiter looked at me funny. Why didn't you tell me, Grace?' Niamh shrieked, sitting up and wiping her fingers beneath her eyes.

'Stop shouting,' Grace moaned, her head face down in her hands. 'I feel like roadkill. Will you pour more water please? I'm so stupid, I swear. I wish I could remember the night before just how bad I feel the next morning so I could trigger some kind of stopping action, but no ... I just keep on going. Ugh. I need to eat something.'

Copious amounts of sparkling water and carbohydrates later, they made their way back to their room and lay on their beds.

'There's a ferry in an hour. We should try to make that one. It gets us to Camogli by about one o'clock,' Niamh said, hoping that the room would stop spinning soon.

'I just hope the sea is calm, that's all.'

'We can go up on top, that way we'll have a breeze. That will wake us up a bit, then we can have a nice late lunch.'

'How can you talk about lunch? I've just inhaled enough carbs to feed a small family. How long did you say it takes those tablets to work?'

'Usually twenty minutes or so. Come on, get up and take a cold shower. That will help.'

'OK. If I'm not out in fifteen minutes I may have just slipped down the plughole, so come rescue me,' Grace moaned as she stumbled towards the bathroom.

'I'll look up some restaurant recommendations while you're in there. A glass of wine will do you good. That will fix you – hair of the dog and all that!'

'Shoot me,' was all she heard in reply as the bathroom door closed.

# Chapter Nine

It was the most perfect palette of colours, Niamh thought, as the ferry rounded the edge of the promontory and made a right turn in the direction of Camogli. They were still a few miles out from the town as they turned and faced into the bay, but even all the way back out here the town looked like a warm orange glow at the foot of a lush, dense green hill. The buildings were taller than in Portofino and they stretched far left and right beyond what looked like the beach and the pier.

The strong sea breeze had helped shake off some of the overindulgent cobwebs, and Niamh was starting to feel a bit more human. Grace was still unusually quiet and sat back against the railing with her eyes closed and face tilted up to the sun. The ferry continued steadily towards the village of Camogli, the burnt orange buildings getting larger as they drew closer.

The bay was protected by massive, overgrown cliffs on the right side, dotted here and there with pretty villas. To the left was Genoa, resembling little other than a white Lego town in the distance, and straight ahead of them sat Camogli. As the ferry slowed and made its approach, it veered right and followed the still waters around the pier, into the marina. The difference in the boats at this marina was notable. These were fishing vessels and small pleasure boats, nothing like the hyperbolic statements of wealth and affluence she had seen in Portofino.

The coloured collection of buildings stood five or six storeys tall in front of them. Many of the windows had been flung open, as if to invite in the warm, early summer air. Lines of laundry flapped in the breeze. Not uniformly starched, white linens but rather a more domestic, honest kind of laundry of underwear and towels. The ferry chugged to a stop, pulling up at one of two piers, and began to disgorge its passengers along a narrow wooden plank.

'Are we there?' asked Grace as she stood and followed Niamh down the stairs.

'Yep. Let's go find a coffee.'

'Definitely.'

They followed the long line of passengers along the pier and up towards the town. Everyone ambled along, with no one appearing to be in any particular hurry. Niamh noticed that they hadn't heard any English spoken since they had left their hotel earlier that morning.

'Oh look!' Niamh gushed as she pointed at one building after another.

'Can we please just get a coffee first? I promise I'll be more human then. Just a large injection of caffeine and I'll function much more normally,' Grace said quietly, as she hid behind a wide-brimmed hat and oversized sunglasses.

'There's an Illy coffee sign right ahead.'

'Best news I've heard all day,' Grace mumbled, following Niamh through the meandering clusters of people.

The crowd splintered once they had left the marina and they made their way easily up into the town. Cafés, restaurants and gelaterias were clearly in abundance. A narrow street sloped up into a piazza with commanding views of the marina and the bay. From there the street climbed higher to a wide pedestrian promenade. It was late Friday morning now, and the promenade was getting busy, but everyone looked and sounded Italian.

'They can't all be Italian, can they?' Niamh asked, as they pulled up two white chairs outside the café.

'Why not? We are in Italy, after all. What were you expecting? Arabs?' Grace asked sarcastically.

'God, I had forgotten how pissy you get when you're hungover. I'm going to stop speaking to you now until you have mainlined some caffeine and normal levels of human decency back into your system.'

Niamh ordered two cappuccinos and a couple of biscotti in the little café. The girl behind the counter clearly didn't speak English and so the short exchange was conducted solely in Italian, with strong support from hand gestures. The girl motioned for Niamh to take a seat, indicating that she would bring the coffees out once they were ready.

'The coffee is so good here, isn't it?' Grace said, sipping her cappuccino. 'Why does everything taste better here?'

'Dunno, it does though. Are you up for a walk around before lunch?'

'Yes, I'm starting to feel human again. Sorry for being such a witch all morning. My headache is starting to ease now, too. Good biscotti!' Grace wiped crumbs from her mouth.

'Ooh look, Grace! An estate agent's. Let's take a look. I'd love to know what a place here would cost. You know the way people stick things on their fridge for motivation? Mine could be an apartment here in Italy. Ooh! Maybe we could get a place together and I could just live here and you could come on holidays with the boys.'

'Are you sure you're sober?' Grace asked, draining the end of her cappuccino.

'Yes, why?'

'Umm, because last time I checked I already had a mortgage and you were recently out of a job. Reality check, perhaps?'

Niamh slumped back into her chair. 'Since when are you so negative on everything I say? You're the one who dragged me here, remember?'

'For a week, Niamh! We've got this glorious week to enjoy and then come Sunday we get back on the plane and go home. That's how it goes.'

'OK, OK. I just wanted to take a look. You're the one always telling me I should invest in a place of my own.'

'I meant in Dublin, Niamh, where you'd have a hope of working to actually pay for it! Now, what's next on the agenda? Where's lunch?'

'I got some recommendations from the concierge this morning for some local places here in Camogli. He said we wouldn't need reservations here at this time of year. Apparently it doesn't get really busy until the height of summer.'

'OK, what are the options?'

'Well, two of them require another boat ride, and one is right here in town.'

'I don't think I'm up for another boat ride just yet. What did he say about the one in town?'

'Just that it's one of the best seafood restaurants in town. It's a bit pricey, though, for the fish dishes, at least.'

'Ah, who cares?' Grace shrugged. 'We've only got two days left. Two lunches and two dinners ... how badly crippled financially can we get in two days? Plus this place feels more casual than Santa Margherita, so it's bound to be less expensive.'

'It definitely feels more casual than Portofino, and this cappuccino was only three euros. That's less than half what I paid in Portofino, so that's a good sign.'

'What's the restaurant called?'

'Da Paolo. It's a local seafood restaurant. It's down a tiny alley somewhere.'

'OK, we'll keep an eye out for that. Let's go wander,' Grace said.

They gathered their things and left the café.

The village of Camogli was built on two levels and locals referred to them as the upper and lower streets. The lower street was mostly pedestrianised and bordered the bay, with a long, wide promenade overlooking the beach below. In typical Italian fashion, the beach was dotted with a series of private beach clubs providing loungers, changing and bathroom facilities. They were all closed for the season, poised to reopen the following month, and so the beach was deserted, save for a few locals walking their dogs along the water's edge.

They walked the length of the lower level, and climbed the steep steps to the upper level, pausing halfway up to catch their breath, pretending to be taking in the view of the bay.

'I swear, I think that little granny up ahead with her bag of groceries is going faster than we are,' Niamh huffed.

'How many bloody steps are there?' Grace asked as she doubled over and placed her hands on her thighs. 'This is not a recommended activity for people in a delicate condition like us.'

'At least it's not raging hot. Look at the view, though!' said Niamh, pointing behind them at the glistening bay. She watched a solitary sailing boat bob along on the horizon. 'It's beautiful!'

They continued to the top of the steps and stood to catch

their breath again. The upper level had a hip-height wall that ran the length of the village. It was larger than they had first imagined. Upon arrival to the pier, it looked as if the entire village was contained on the level along the beach and promenade, as the upper level was neatly tucked away out of sight. They could see now that this was the true local heart of the village, with little fruit and vegetable markets, a small grocery store, a post office and everyday kinds of services on offer. They wandered the length of the street slowly, looking in shop windows along the way. Smaller, narrower streets ran off this main thoroughfare, deeper into the village.

Local women wore housecoats and headscarves as they swept the footpaths outside their shops or houses. Old men wore flat caps and dark suits as they went about their daily business. Mothers fussed over children as yet too small to be in school, and a couple of skinny stray cats darted from one side of the street to the other in search of their next meal. Without exception everyone nodded or smiled a greeting as Niamh and Grace passed by.

The sun beat down on them warmly as they wandered the narrow, cobbled streets happily.

'I haven't seen that restaurant yet. Have you?' Grace asked, tilting her head upwards to admire the small church in front of them.

'No, but I kind of forgot to look for it, to be honest, I was so busy just looking around. Should we ask someone?'

'We better, it's almost two o'clock and we're lost. Will you do it? I don't have the energy to speak Italian.'

Niamh stopped to ask the next housecoated lady where they might find the restaurant, but clearly failed to pronounce it correctly. She pulled out the note that the concierge had written and showed it to the lady.

'*Ah, sì*. Da Paolo,' said the woman, correcting Niamh's poor attempt at pronouncing the name. '*Giù.*'

'*Giù?*' Niamh asked not understanding.

'*Sì, sì, giù,*' the woman repeated, indicating furiously with her arm to the level below.

'OK. Down. *Grazie.*'

'Oh well, at least it's down and not up again,' Grace laughed. 'We'll have worked up an appetite for lunch anyway, that's for certain.' She started to walk in the direction the lady had pointed, but Niamh remained leaning against the wall, gazing out at the bay. 'Come on, who knows how long it will take us to find this place.' Grace grabbed Niamh's elbow. 'What are you doing? Come on!'

'It's just so beautiful, isn't it? So peaceful.'

'Yes, it is. I'm starving. Come on.'

They turned back in the direction they had come and made a right turn onto a narrow side street. They passed another minuscule vegetable store with its crates of vegetables stacked carefully outside on the footpath, a fabric store of some sort, with linens, aprons and tea towels on display in the window, and a pharmacy.

'Is that the third pharmacy we've passed or do we keep passing the same one?' Grace asked, confused.

'No, we haven't been here before. I think the steps down will be at the end of this street, though. What a pretty street.' Niamh sighed as she admired the flaking, colourful buildings flanking them on either side. They could see the bay sparkling in the sun at the end of the street, which meant that they were at least going in the right direction. 'It's like something out of a movie back in time.'

With that the church bells began to chime out their hourly announcement. They reverberated somewhere overhead, echoing against the buildings and seemingly surrounding them. Niamh tilted her head up to the sky, breathing in the clear air and the melodic chiming sounds. 'Magical.'

She rushed to catch up with Grace. 'Grace, look!' she exclaimed, stopping suddenly and peering through the window of a shopfront.

'What?' Grace asked, turning back to face her.

'Look, isn't this just adorable?'

'It's closed. As in, shut down, closed down.'

'I know, but look at it. Isn't it sweet?'

'I suppose it used to be at one time. It's a bit of a mess now.'

'No!' Niamh urged again. 'Look at the tiles and the little counter. It's so cute. It must have been a restaurant or a café or something. Look at the tables back there in the corner.'

'Dunno, come on. I don't want to be late.'

Niamh put her hands up to create shade around her eyes and pressed her nose to the window. She didn't know if it was the bells, or the warm air, or the feeling of contentment that she felt here, but this little town had captivated her imagination. She peered through the window of the dilapidated, abandoned building, imagining what it used to be in its past life. And then she saw the sign.

AFFITTASI, followed by a phone number.

It was handwritten in thick black ink on a piece of card, tucked on the inside bottom corner of the window. Niamh's breath caught in her chest and she glanced from the sign into the interior of the room and back to the sign. She didn't know exactly what it meant as she didn't speak the language, but she knew it wasn't a for-sale sign, as she had seen those around town – VENDESI, which looked similar to the French version that she knew. 'It must mean that it's for rent,' she whispered against the glass.

Grace had reached the end of the street by now, either oblivious to, or choosing to ignore Niamh's stalling.

'The steps are right here. Come on, hurry up, will you?'

Niamh drew her breath to tell Grace what she had seen, but hesitated when she turned and saw her, hands on her hips, impatient to get to lunch. Deciding against it, she whipped out her phone and took a photo of the handwritten sign, dropped her phone back into her bag and jogged the length of the narrow street. She glanced up at the corner, noting the street name because, without it, given her appalling sense of direction, she may never make her way back again.

'Via dei Limoni,' she whispered under her breath.

After a couple of wrong turns, the girls found the restaurant, housed in an old stone building. You couldn't access it from the main road as it was tucked away down a three-foot-wide alleyway. The only indication that there was anything at the end of the little alleyway was a small wooden sign, hanging overhead with the name of the restaurant etched on it. They followed the alley one behind the other as it wound around in a wide curve, ending in a tiny courtyard with eight outdoor tables.

From the courtyard, they could see in through the back door of the restaurant. Two female cooks were busily stirring and chopping inside. To get to the front of the building, and the main entrance of the restaurant, the girls continued along the alley and circled around to the other side of the building. They were greeted with warm smiles and shown to a small table inside. It was dark and cosy with tall, lofty ceilings, and the place was already packed with diners. Ceiling fans whirred overhead, attempting to regulate the heat being generated within the thick old walls of the building.

Relieved that their waiter spoke a little English, they asked if they could order a bottle of wine.

'White or red?' was all the waiter had asked. There was no wine menu.

They asked for a bottle of white wine, and a few moments later he presented them with a bottle of crisp Vermentino. 'Is from the hills nearby,' he explained in a strong Italian accent.

There was no lengthy ceremony and no tasting, instead he simply opened the bottle and placed it on the table. '*Salute!*' he said with a smile. He returned and handed them a menu. 'English is OK?'

'Yes,' Grace giggled. 'English is fine.'

The translations left a lot to be desired – 'head of shrimp' and 'white fish, cooked' – so they scanned the room to see what other diners had before them. Almost every plate that they could see had a version of the same thing. They couldn't make out what it was, but it was some tiny, silvery fish that had been flattened and was served with either lemon or tomato.

'Ah, *alici*,' the waiter replied loudly when they asked him what everyone was eating. 'Is a local speciality!'

The girls exchanged glances, neither one of them wanting to admit that they didn't know what kind of fish it was.

'Ah-lee-chee' Niamh repeated slowly.

'*Sì, signora*, Camogli is the best place in Italy to eat *alici*!' he exclaimed, with no small amount of pride.

'OK then, we will have that … them, please,' Grace decided. 'And the fish in salt, is that a good—'

'*Certo, signora!*' he responded excitedly. 'Is the best dish. I bring you the fish.'

He returned moments later with a large platter of

just-caught, shiny, fresh whole fish. He advised on one in particular to share, and when they nodded their agreement he was gone again.

'Well, I'm not sure what we're actually going to be eating, but that was easy enough,' Grace laughed. 'Cheers!'

'Cheers! It all looks amazing,' Niamh replied, watching the various dishes come out from the kitchen.

A basket of warm bread was brought to the table and local olive oil was swirled onto a small plate. The sisters chatted happily as they awaited their first course. The overindulgences of the previous night were quickly forgotten as they enjoyed the local wine in earnest.

'I could just die happily here with this bread and oil. It's so good,' Niamh sighed.

'I know. Why is it so hard to get good bread like this at home? Although, to be honest, everything tastes better here. All the food is just so much better, not just the pasta, which is totally amazing. Everyone seems to be happier or more easy-going, too, don't they? I don't know, they don't look as stressed out as people back home. I wonder if it has anything to do with the weather or the *dolce vita* that Italians talk about all the time?'

'Well, in fairness, Grace, you'd be a lot happier too if you could eat like this every day, not just for one or two weeks a year on holiday. I could live here ... I think I could actually live here, you know?'

'Of course you could, until you ran out of money and had to go to work!'

'No, seriously, people do it, Grace. People move to new countries all the time and start over.'

Grace smiled across the table at her sister. 'I think everyone engages in the fantasy of running away from life and starting over in some exotic new place at some point in time, but then reality crashes in around you and you realise that you have to actually work to make a living, and you get back on the plane and go home.'

'Yeah, I suppose . . . ' Niamh responded quietly.

The waiter interrupted the conversation on their Italian life commentary by placing a plate in front of each of them. They had thought they had ordered the same thing, but he brought out two different variations of the seafood appetiser; one was prepared in olive oil and lemon and the other in olive oil with thin slivers of tomato. They ate in silence for a few moments, savouring the light flavours on their tongues. The fish was so delicate it seemed to melt in their mouths.

'I have to ask him what this is,' Niamh said, halfway through the plate. 'Do you want to swap and try this one? It's divine.'

'Sure, so is this,' Grace replied, passing her plate across the table. One dish was as delicate and delectable as the other.

'*Alici, signora,*' the waiter replied when he heard Niamh's question.

'But what is that in English? What kind of fish?'

'Anchovy, *signora.*'

'Anchovies?' they both repeated in unison.

Grace stared down at the remaining few fish; they were about three inches long and flattened out in the middle so they lay like butterflies. They were silver grey and glistening under the oil. 'These are anchovies?'

'He must have the wrong name in English. They can't be the same thing. I'll have to look it up,' Niamh said. She pulled out her phone and found Google Translate. 'He's right,' she continued, looking up at Grace.

'I wouldn't touch an anchovy at home with a barge pole.

Those ugly, salty, crumpled-looking, hairy things,' Grace said shaking her head and enjoying the last morsel. 'How can this be the same fish? See? Even anchovies taste better here.'

'Have you really never thought about living anywhere else?' Niamh asked, topping up their glasses of wine.

'Of course I have. I have thoughts of running away from my life on a regular basis. Particularly on a Sunday night and Monday morning.'

'But you love your job,' Niamh frowned.

'I do, but it's just hard sometimes with the two boys and all the rushing around, and Robert is away a lot for work, which is a pain. I always thought I'd like to live in America, actually, and work for a great big architecture firm, but it's so hard to get a visa.'

'What about in Europe?'

'Nah, Robert and I both make good money at home, so we have a decent quality of life. The only way we'd move at this point is if one of us landed a big corporate gig in the States and they were throwing gobs of money at us. God bless the Americans and their big corporate salaries!'

'Yeah, I suppose you're right,' Niamh replied distractedly, twirling her fork between her fingers.

'Look,' Grace said quietly, as she leaned across the table and put a hand on Niamh's arm. 'You're going through a lot and you've got a whole load of things to figure out. Change is hard, so don't try to solve everything at once. I'm not worried about you, Niamh. You'll figure out what's next, you'll find another job – a better job. Lord knows you were underappreciated at Rick's company. You'll find something better, you'll get a lovely new apartment and you'll start over. Everything will work out – it always does.'

Niamh was saved from any further conversation about her future as the waiter delivered their main course to the table. The fish was encased in a massive, hard mound of salt, which he hacked at carefully. The salt came away in large chunks, revealing the whole fish inside.

'It kind of looks like the lumps of ice you hack off when you're defrosting the freezer at home,' Niamh giggled.

The waiter freed the fish from its salt casing and divided it into two halves, placing two fillets on to each plate. Another waiter brought a plate of potatoes sautéed with garlic and lemon and another of green vegetables.

'I think this might be the most divine piece of fish I've ever had in my life,' Grace mumbled, not taking her eyes off her lunch.

'I don't understand what is happening in my mouth! Unreal,' Niamh agreed.

When they had finished, they ordered two espressos. The waiter brought them, along with a plate of almond biscotti.

'You stay here in Camogli?'

'No, we're staying in Santa Margherita,' Grace answered. 'We're taking the ferry back later this afternoon.'

'Ah, but you must stay for the sunset. Here in Camogli is the best sunset in all of Liguria. The sun – she looks you in the eye as she says goodnight,' he said, drawing circles in the air with his hand. 'It will be a little after seven o'clock tonight.'

They looked at each other across the table and Grace shrugged. 'Why not? We're not in any hurry, as long as we're back in time for dinner. We have a reservation at that place near the hotel tonight.'

'OK. Is there somewhere we can go and get a drink to watch it?' Niamh asked the waiter.

'Yes, you must go to La Terrazza. Is in the hotel at the other end of the pier. You have seen the hotel, no?'

'Oh, yes, I saw it as we came in on the ferry earlier,' Niamh said, nodding.

'*Va bene* – OK. You will go there before seven o'clock, no? It will be the most beautiful thing you will see in Italy, *signore*!' he said enthusiastically.

'How do we say no to that?' Grace said. 'How about a limoncello?'

'Well, now that we've got a few hours to kill that's not a bad idea at all!'

# Chapter Ten

They left the restaurant sated and happy and spent the next few hours exploring Camogli, popping into bookshops, small boutiques, churches and markets. A little after six o'clock they made their way towards La Terrazza. The streets were quieter now, with only small clusters of children playing in alleyways. Boats approached the pier, ready to tie up after a day of fishing. A couple of scraggy cats sniffed around in corners near restaurant bins, and new batches of laundry were hung out to dry from apartment windows.

As they walked along, Niamh wondered why he had sent them to that particular place to watch the sunset. They passed dozens of places right on the promenade, overlooking the bay on the way to the hotel. The air was getting cooler now and she pulled a wrap from her bag. They strolled in silence, each of them lost in their own thoughts. She saw the ferry leave the pier, heading back in the direction they had come from this morning. She wondered if there was a second one servicing this stretch of the coast, as she watched it make the turn from the marina out into the bay. If not then this one would deposit its passengers in their towns of choice and then turn around in Santa Margherita and come back to pick them up. The thought of it made her smile, as if it would be coming back especially for them.

They entered the hotel and were greeted by front-desk staff with friendly smiles. They asked for directions to La Terrazza and were escorted by a smartly dressed, slender young woman down a long corridor and through a series of double doors. Her chestnut-brown hair was neatly tied up in a huge bun and she was immaculately made up. Niamh instinctively pulled her wrap around her and vowed to lose a few pounds, watching the woman's waistline as she walked ahead of her. The hotel corridors were quiet but they could hear strains of music playing as they approached the entrance to the terrace.

The brunette stood to the side and opened the right-hand door for them. '*Ecco, signore,*' she said with a smile.

No sooner had they stepped onto the terrace than they were greeted by a smiling man in a black waistcoat and bow tie. '*Buona sera, signore.*'

'*Buona sera.*' Grace smiled in return, taking in the scene in front of them.

The double doors had spilled out into the centre of a protected terrace, shaded from the breeze by tall, white walls on either side, with only the front remaining open and unobstructed. From their vantage point they could see that the terrace swept wide left and right and directly ahead, and the Golfo Paradiso seemed to arc around them. They were high enough not to have the beach or the beach clubs obstruct the view of the bay and the horizon, flanked on one side by the massive, lush green hills and on the other the colourful town of Camogli petering out and continuing in a series of villages all along the bay as far as Genoa. It was truly the most spectacular view that either of them had ever seen.

The waiter escorted them to the last free table on the far right and he and another waiter held their chairs as they sat down. Neither of them had said a word since they stepped onto the terrace. The waiter just smiled, as if he recognised this look of awe, and gave them a moment to take it in. The terrace was full of well-dressed couples and small groups of people chatting quietly, everyone facing towards the bay and the horizon. The sun was still high in the sky, but it was as if everyone had gathered for the screening of something special, and the show was about to commence.

'Do you think anyone would mind if I went out to the front to take a photo?' Niamh asked, standing up.

'I'm sure not, but you know you'll look like a total tourist if you do. Can't we just pretend to fit in here for a minute?' Grace said, rolling her eyes. 'I want to feel like I belong with all these beautiful Italian creatures, and not like some moron who just dropped in for an hour and would soon scurry off to her lowly hotel.'

'Fair enough.' Niamh smiled and turned to sit down.

'Ah, so you came after all!' Niamh heard the voice ahead of her but the sun was in her eyes. 'I wondered if you would flee the normal tourist-trodden route and venture further afield.'

Niamh shaded the sun from her eyes. It was Emily.

She flushed momentarily, embarrassed to have been spotted in Camogli and not having called her, especially as she had been so kind to her at lunch in Portofino. Emily crossed the terrace to their table, oblivious of the stares of people around her. She wore a long, off-white, buttoned dress that fell to her ankles and high wedge sandals in a similar shade. She looked like she had just stepped out of a Dolce and Gabbana advertisement.

'Hello, I'm Emily,' she said graciously to Grace as she shook her hand. 'Welcome to Camogli.'

'Grace, this is the lady who rescued me at lunch the other day, the one I told you about.'

'Oh wow, hello! It's nice to meet you.'

'I'm sorry I didn't call, but we just decided to come here last minute. It wasn't really a proper plan,' Niamh said sheepishly, glaring at Grace.

'Plans are usually overrated and lead to unrealistic levels of expectation, darling. You are far better off travelling on instinct rather than sticking to a rigid plan. Good Lord, you really can't see anything back here behind this wall. Come and join me at my table, won't you?' She motioned to a table all the way at the front, alongside the little terraced wall. 'Unless you like being tucked away back here with the masses, that is.' She laughed.

Niamh threw a quick glance at Grace and could tell that she was intrigued. 'We'd love to, thank you.'

Emily turned and motioned to the waiter who had seated them. 'Gianni, they are going to join me at my table.'

'Certainly, Emilia. *Prego.*'

Niamh recalled the quiet fuss that was made of her in Portofino and wondered if Emilia was treated this way at every restaurant and terrace bar she ever visited. She had an easy elegance about her, such that the expectation of excellence that she so naturally assumed seemed fitting. It suited her demeanour but it was all done effortlessly, warmly and graciously. It was very impressive. With a flurry of waiters, the three women were escorted to the front and seated at Emily's table.

'Oh, there's a lovely breeze here,' Grace said, smiling. 'This view is really incredible.'

'Yes, I don't know how anyone can bear to sit back there. It's stifling,' Emily said in her strong British accent. 'Now, drinks.'

Gianni reappeared at the table with a platter of various

little *aperitivi* for them to nibble on. 'Orange happiness, *signora*?'

'Yes, Gianni, *grazie*. Ladies, what would you like to drink?'

'What did you order?' Niamh asked, leaning into the table.

'I'm having an Aperol spritz, just like most people out here, as you can see. It's the drink of choice for *aperitivo*.'

Niamh had to agree that almost every table on the terrace had Aperol spritz, the only exception being a couple sipping on two tall beers.

'Germans,' Emily said with disdain, rolling her eyes in her head. 'No class whatsoever.'

'But what did you say to Gianni when you ordered the drink? He called it something else but I couldn't catch it. Is there another name for it?'

'Oh, no!' Emily sat back and laughed. 'It's orange happiness. Orange happiness in a glass, darling! I called it that the very first time I ordered it on this very terrace and I've been calling it that ever since.'

'That's cute,' Niamh said with a smile.

'It's true, darling. You sit here with this incredible view, on this lovely terrace, in this quaint little village and life slows all around you, and then as you watch the sun set you drink the most perfect drink of the same bursting orange colour. I mean, it's perfect. What else is there?'

'How long have you lived here?' Grace asked, taking the first sip of her orange happiness.

'Not long enough,' Emily replied ruefully. It was the first time they had seen her without a smile since they'd sat down. 'When you live somewhere like this, or move to a place like this, at least, then you almost resent any time you wasted elsewhere. It's that powerful. This place can put a spell on you quite easily, if you let it. I moved here ten years ago and now my life in London feels like eons ago, and terribly superficial and small. I know that sounds like a contradiction in terms, but it's not. It was superficial as it was mostly about exterior pleasures, not pleasures of the soul, and small because everyone has a permitted circle of people and places, and people are mostly creatures of habit. If we let it, our lives can become small without us even knowing it, and we become smaller people as a result.'

'Don't you miss anything about it?' Niamh was intrigued.

'No, I get back often enough to satisfy whatever needs I might have for big city life, but honestly, darling, you can get that in Milan, too – and much more elegantly.'

Niamh thought about her life in Dublin. It wasn't superficial, but it was definitely small. What did she have back there apart from her family? It was always the same people, same places, same restaurants, same boring routine – yes, definitely small. She wasn't sure when it had become so rote. She had always had plans to travel and see the world, get an exciting job, earn good money, go on exotic holidays, wear great clothes, but along the way she had settled for less. She had met Rick and they were happy – or at least she had thought that they were. She had tried at first to keep things interesting, given that they worked together. He was a workaholic and a bit of a gym addict. Now that she thought about it, he did have a bit of a compulsive personality.

They had each had their own routine. Thursday night was Chinese takeout at home with a bottle of wine (he wasn't a big drinker but one bottle was never enough for two, so she always made sure they had a second stashed away on standby). On Friday night they would go to a restaurant in town and go for drinks afterwards. They'd usually have sex when they got home, and when she wasn't completely wiped out after the week, she'd make a big effort to be sexy and wear her fancy, matching underwear. On Saturdays Rick went to the gym – he went religiously six days a week – and she shopped for the week's groceries. Then they might go to a movie or get takeout pizza and watch something new on television. On Sundays he played rugby with the lads and she'd clean the house and then go visit her parents.

Niamh had always cooked a traditional Sunday dinner of roast chicken, beef or lamb because Rick loved that kind of food. She had been passionate about food and cooking since she was three years old, helping her mother bake pies and cakes, and dropping chopped vegetables into a large soup pot that would simmer for hours. The traditional Sunday dinner was something she could whip up in her sleep, and it was always the same, but Rick didn't like it when she tried to do something inventive and, frankly, it just wasn't worth the ensuing argument. After several disastrous dinners she had given up and resigned herself to Sunday nights of Irish recipes created in the 1960s.

Instead, she'd entertain herself by lighting candles to make the place look pretty and open a bottle of wine. The only night Rick would let loose at any level was on a Friday night and he wouldn't have more than two glasses of wine on a Sunday night. Two glasses felt to her like she was just getting warmed up, so she'd open a bottle and have a couple of glasses while she was cooking dinner, to get a head start.

'Niamh! Hello?' Grace said in a sharp hiss, conscious of being on a posh terrace where the only other sounds were of clinking glasses.

'Sorry, what?' She hadn't realised that she had drifted miles away.

Grace shook her head. 'Emily was asking if you wanted another drink.'

'Do we have time? What about the ferry?'

'Oh, the ferry runs until late, don't worry about that,' Emily said with a wave of her hand that both dismissed the thought of bolting for the ferry and summoned another round of drinks at the same time.

The sun sank lower and moved quickly, casting orange and pink shadows across the clouds above it. The terrace grew quiet as the bottom round of the sun dipped into the sea at the horizon and continued to sink below it. The hues of orange, red and pink grew stronger and wider, and then suddenly as it disappeared below the surface of the bay, they softened and dissipated. It was like a theatrical production. Niamh felt as if she should applaud.

Chatter resumed on the terrace and at their table and Gianni reappeared with a bottle of bubbles and three glasses.

'I have an unspoken rule, you see,' Emily explained. 'One cannot drink Aperol spritz once the sun has set. Luckily, the Italians have a wonderful alternative to champagne called Franciacorta.'

They chatted easily for the next hour. Emily talked about her life in Camogli, Grace talked about her boys and her work and, to her surprise, Niamh heard herself talking about her recent disasters back home. She suspected that the various drinks might have something to do with it.

'I should call and cancel our dinner reservation. We'd have to leave here in the next twenty minutes to make the ferry in time for dinner. You're not ready to leave, are you, Niamh?'

Niamh turned and looked at her distractedly. 'No,' she said quietly. 'No, let's stay here for ever.'

Grace stepped away from the table to call the concierge back at their hotel. Emily raised her glass to her lips and looked across the table towards Niamh. 'It's easy to decide to stay, isn't it?'

'Hmm?'

'Here in Camogli … I can understand why you would decide to stay. I mean, why bother going anywhere else? Right now, where else is there?' she asked, raising a glass in a silent salute.

'I don't know, actually. I don't think I've ever felt further away from everything and everyone in my life, and that's not a bad thing right now.'

'Separation creates distance and distance can bring either peace of mind or heartache, it just depends on your perspective. If you know where you are going, then there are no wrong decisions because you are following your true north.'

'We're not talking about me deciding to stay here for dinner any more, are we?' Niamh smiled.

'We never really were, darling,' Emily replied with a wink.

# Chapter Eleven

'I'm not leaving.'

'Agreed,' mumbled Grace. 'How on earth are we supposed to make it to lunch today? I'm not even sure I can make it to the bathroom safely, my head's spinning that bad.'

'No, I mean I'm not going back.'

'Back where?' Grace asked, swearing under her breath as she tripped over the dress that she had hastily discarded on the floor the night before.

Niamh took in her sister's dishevelled appearance in the bathroom mirror. It was comforting to know Grace still had the capacity to look terrible.

'Back home. Back to Dublin. I'm staying here.'

'What? Don't be ridiculous, Niamh. You have to go back. You have a job.'

'I quit.'

'What? When?'

Niamh turned to face her sister. 'Last night.'

'Last night after a bucket of orange drinks and three or four bottles of wine?'

'Yes,' Niamh replied, dropping two soluble paracetamol into a glass.

'Niamh, you know I don't function well when I'm hungover,

so I really don't have the energy to deal with this *Eat Pray Love* shit right now. It's like all my patience and tolerance seeps out through my pores and is replaced with clouds of alcohol fumes,' Grace sighed, sitting down heavily on the edge of the bath.

'I'm serious, Grace.'

'Why did I mix my drinks last night?' Grace sighed. 'I'm such an idiot.'

'Grace, I'm not joking.'

'Sure you're not. Well then, you know what? I'm not going home either!' Grace retorted, now losing her cool. 'I have a few slivers of freedom when I get to travel for work. My normal life is an intense, full-time job, two toddlers who think I'm a mess-mopping, toy-fixing, walking snack machine and a husband who moans that I work too much but has no problem blowing through the second wage on rugby weekends. So, here's an idea. Why don't we both just run away and move to another country?'

'God, you get so ratty when you're hungover,' Niamh replied, rolling her eyes. 'I'm not being all *Eat Pray Love*—'

'In fact,' Grace cut across Niamh, 'I'm going home to tell my husband that I'm leaving him and moving to France because last year I went to Cannes for a conference and thought it was the most fabulous place I'd ever been. I'm going to drink rosé every day, live on baguettes and Niçoise salads and live happily ever after.' She fixed Niamh with a superior and satisfied stare that said 'point proved'. 'Now, come on, let's go to breakfast. I need coffee.'

'GRACE!' Niamh roared, exasperated. 'I'm deadly serious! I sent an email last night officially handing in my notice.'

'What the fuck, Niamh? You can't just quit. You were drunk.'

'Actually, I can. And, yes, I was a bit, but I still feel the same today, just with a wicked headache.'

'This is madness. Even if you do want to quit your job, you have to do it the right way. You have to go home, hand in your notice . . .'

'Since this is all sort of Rick's fault he can deal with the details. It's not as though we have an HR team. His problem, not mine!'

'Oh, for Christ's sake, Niamh, this is insane even by your standards. I know it sucks right now, but shit happens, people break up. You have to face reality, move your stuff out of Rick's apartment, move *on*. Get closure! You can't just decide you're not going home.'

'I've already taken all my stuff from Rick's apartment. Everything is back in Mam and Dad's place again.'

'Fine,' said Grace, exasperated, and changing tack. 'Say you do stay here, what's the plan?'

'Well, I don't have all the details figured out exactly but I did have one idea about . . . ' Niamh hesitated, reluctant to share her thinking with Grace and have it dismissed as utter nonsense. 'I mean, I don't have it all figured out exactly, but I know I want to live here. Well, not here in this hotel, obviously,' she said, gesturing around the hotel bathroom. 'But I want to live in Italy. I know that much. I want to do something crazy, Grace, something different.'

'You want to do something crazy? Well, this qualifies. And you'll live where, exactly?'

'In Camogli. I—'

'But you've only been here for a week!' Grace was pleading now. 'You don't know the area, you don't know anyone, you don't know the *language*. What will you do about money?

'I have savings that I can live off.' Niamh was very grateful

114

she'd been working this plan out over the past couple of days, and that she wasn't having to field this inquisition on the hoof. There was a strong chance her head might have exploded. She walked back into the bedroom hoping distance would deter Grace, but she followed without drawing a breath.

'What do you mean you have savings? Like what? What are we talking about here?'

'I have about twenty thousand euros in the bank.'

'You have *what*? How the hell do you manage to have twenty thousand euros in the bank?'

'I'm good at saving.'

'Holy shit, I'll say. I have about two thousand euros in savings and my credit card has a constant revolving negative balance that I treat as a second source of income.'

'Well, I didn't have much of a life with Rick in Dublin. I didn't do that much, so it was kind of easy to save.' Niamh shrugged.

Grace stared at her in disbelief. 'So, what am I supposed to tell Mam?'

'Tell her that I'm grabbing life by the arse, like she always told me to do.'

'I don't think that quitting your job and extending your vacation indefinitely in an Italian fishing village was what she meant, Niamh. I mean, spoiler alert, but Mam never was a massive fan of Rick so I think that her advice more likely related to dumping that mopey cretin in the first place, getting out from under his feet at work and getting out there on your own. That's the type of life she was talking about grabbing by the arse – one that was *yours*. Not one cooked up over a bowl of pasta.'

'You know what? I always do the right thing.' By now Niamh was pacing the bedroom and her voice was rising. 'I always do what I'm supposed to do, what everyone thinks I should do, or what I think they expect of me. And where has it gotten me? Nowhere. For the first time in my life, I'm going to do something that makes no sense to anyone else, but it does to me. I'm going to do what I *want* to do for a change – even if it's a mad idea.'

'It *is* a mad idea, Niamh. It's a totally mad idea that you will regret. Why not just stay for another couple of weeks? You don't have to quit your job. Call them and tell them you've made a mistake, get your job back and just take a couple of weeks out. Rick owes you that. I'm sure he'll figure out a way to get you some more paid time off.'

'No, I'm not changing my mind. I can't face going back there. Anyone can get another job, Grace. What I actually want is another life. One that I build for myself, one that I actually like, the one you say Mam wants for me. Even if you think it is a mistake.'

'You're being ridiculous, Niamh, completely and utterly ridiculous. This isn't some movie, you know, where you get to drop your real life and create a new one in a foreign country where you don't speak the language. This is your life and you are being totally juvenile about it.' Grace was furious now and flung some things into a bag. 'I'm going to breakfast and then for a walk. We have a lunch reservation at one o'clock. Text me if you come back to your senses and want to join me.'

The door slammed behind her. Niamh winced from the noise and grabbed her bag. She checked the ferry schedule for Saturday morning. The next ferry was in thirty minutes. She had four hours before lunch. She grabbed a croissant from the breakfast buffet and headed out to the pier. She dialled the number from the photograph on her phone as she walked.

'*Pronto?*' a deep male voice answered.

'Oh, hello. Umm, *buongiorno*. I'm calling about the café.'

'Sorry, you have the wrong number.'

The phone cut off.

Niamh frowned as she pulled up the photograph on her phone again and compared it to the number she had just dialled. It was the same number. 'Idiot.'

She dialled again.

'*Pronto?*'

'*Buongiorno*. Hello? I'm calling about the café for rent in Camogli. On Via dei Limoni? I saw the advert in the window,' she said in one quick rush.

'The café?'

'Yes. I got this number from the notice in the window.'

'You are calling about the café?'

She rolled her eyes. Who was this idiot and why was this so hard to understand? 'Yes, can I speak to someone about the café, please?'

'You can speak to me, *signora*.'

Marvellous, she thought sarcastically. 'Is the café still for rent?'

'Yes. Yes, it is.'

'OK, can I see it?'

'*Certo*,' he said slowly. 'When do you want to see it?'

'Is this morning possible? I can be there in an hour.'

'Today? *Signora*, it's Saturday.'

'Yes, I'm aware of that but I'm supposed to get on a plane tomorrow to go home to Ireland and I want to know if this crazy idea I have of renting a café is even a remote possibility.' She spoke hurriedly, afraid he might hang up again.

There was silence.

'So you are here on holiday and you want to rent the café?'

'Well I don't know, I mean, I think so, but I would like to see it before I throw everything else away. Would that be possible?'

He hesitated again and sighed. 'OK, I can meet you in one hour. You know where it is?'

'Yes. OK, thank you. I'll see you in an hour.'

'*Va bene*,' he said, sighing again as he hung up. He hadn't even asked her name.

She arrived a few minutes before 10.30, feeling quite proud for having only got lost once along the way. She had tried to retrace her steps once she got off the ferry but was confused when she reached the upper level of the town. The fact that she had zero sense of direction was no help. She checked Google Maps on her phone and stuck it back into her bag, leaving the bustle of the main promenade and followed one narrow little cobbled street after another, until she'd made her way back to Via dei Limoni.

She hadn't paid much attention to what was around her last time she was here, as Grace had been in such a hurry to get to the restaurant to inhale carbs. Checking the time to make sure she wasn't late, she wandered the length of the street, stopping to peek in through the windows of the shops along the way. There were all kinds of artisan shops, one selling leather gloves, another showcasing embroidered tablecloths and linens. There was a tiny place with wooden crates of limoncello displayed outside the door, and dried red chillies pinned, in bunches, to the doorframe. She put her hands to the glass and peered through the window of a shop with a sign that read PROFUMERIA. The shelves were laden with miniature glass bottles, each with their own tiny handwritten sign.

'A perfume shop,' she sighed quietly to herself, her breath fogging up the window pane before her.

Finally she reached the old café. It looked so forlorn in its dejected state, compared to the other pretty little shops further down the street. She stared through the window, admiring the original tile along the window sill. It was in worse shape than she had remembered, and this time she noticed more splintered wooden shelves and chipped counter tiles than she had done previously. She paced up and down outside the café. There was no sign of anyone.

Maybe it's for the best, she thought, still pacing. Maybe Grace was right and this is just a mad idea. What was I thinking? I don't even speak the language!

She sat on the window ledge outside the café and put her head in her hands.

She could feel her heart beat louder in her chest and a nervous swell in her belly. Have I made the right decision? Is this really nothing more than an unrealistic fantasy? she wondered. Maybe I could call the guy and tell him I had made a mistake and I'm sorry and now you don't have to waste your time showing me the café on a Saturday. She massaged her temples as she stared down at her feet with a classic case of buyer's remorse, even in advance of making any significant financial commitment.

But it was my idea. I know it's not for everyone, and Mam and Grace wouldn't understand, but I'm doing it for me. It makes sense to me, even if the details are marginally terrifying. So just don't think about the details. then, Niamh . . .

She closed her eyes, took a deep breath and placed both her hands on her knees. 'Stick to the plan. Be brave!' she whispered to herself.

'*Signora*, you are speaking to me?'

Startled, she whipped her head up and stared into the sun.

'No, sorry. I was just talking to myself.' She was mortified as she stood up.

'It is you again.'

She stopped in her tracks and looked up at him again, her jaw dropping slowly. This can't be happening, she thought as she stared up him. He's divine! He looks like he stepped off the pages of Men's *Vogue* and I'm not even wearing mascara.

He took off his sunglasses and smiled at her. 'Yes, I am right. It is you. You are ... umm ... Nina, no? Why are you here?'

'I came to see the café,' she replied slowly. She had forgotten how handsome he was.

'Yes, but I thought you stay in Santa Margherita, at the hotel.'

'I do. At least until tomorrow. After that I'm not sure.'

'But you are thinking of renting this café?'

'Well, yes, I had been. I saw it yesterday and wanted to come back and see inside. How is your shirt? Did you get the stain out?'

'The shirt, it will never recover. It died that evening, but there are many more shirts. Don't worry,' he said graciously, as he put the key in the door. 'Be careful, *signora*, is very dusty. Everything is dusty. It has been closed for a long time.'

'Oh, why? What happened? Why did the owner close it?'

'The owner is my brother. His wife was the one who ran the café but she died.'

She put a hand to her mouth, horrified. Can you not just for once in your life keep your mouth shut and your stupid, nosy questions to yourself, Niamh? she admonished herself silently. She took her hand down from her face. 'Oh my God, I'm so sorry. I shouldn't have asked. I'm really sorry.'

'Is OK, it was a few years ago. She died in a car accident.

They were married only one year. So he closed the café and he left Camogli.'

'Oh my God. That's awful. How sad.'

'Yes, this is why I was surprised to get your call this morning. I had not thought about the café for many years.'

'But is it actually for rent?'

'I think, yes. I will have to check with my brother if you decide that you are interested, but I think yes. It was a great place. She was a great ... how do you call it ... hostess? And she was a very beautiful woman. Everyone in the village came here. It always had a heart if you understand what I mean. When she died he moved to America. He wanted to be far from Camogli. He is a doctor so he ... how do you say ... he made a transfer to a hospital in Chicago. He wanted to start over with a new life.'

'I know that feeling.'

He looked at her curiously. 'You have this sadness in your life, too?'

'Well ... no, not like that. Nothing like that, thankfully, but something else that is making me want to run from my life.'

'Perhaps you run *towards* something, not *from* it? You never know in this life until you try it. Perhaps you don't run from something, but this something, whatever or whoever it was, is no longer for you and something else is for you, but in another place that you must find.'

His English was broken and it wasn't expressed in the most perfect way, but the sentiment was powerful and sent chills down her spine.

'*Allora*,' he said changing the subject. He turned the key in the door and leaned against it. It was wedged stuck in the door-frame and wouldn't budge. It took two shoves with his shoulder to release it. '*Ecco il caffè.*' He gestured with his right arm around the room as a small cloud of dust settled around his shoulders.

Niamh stepped in behind him. The place was a mess. It wasn't just dust, but also damage from years of neglect. There was mould on the tiles, sagging timbers, a broken countertop, chipped floor tiles. It was in a terrible state, but it was still beautiful. The woodwork was a deep mahogany and the tiles were a pretty blue and yellow pattern. She could imagine just how charming it once might have been.

'How much is it?'

'I do not know,' he said, shaking his head. 'We never had to think about this.'

'No one ever enquired about renting it?'

'No, *signora*, the people from the village would not do this out of respect for my brother and his wife, and we do not get so many crazy tourists here in Camogli,' he said as he shrugged his shoulders.

'There isn't, like . . . a bad omen or anything in the place, is there?'

'What is an "omen"?' He frowned.

'I mean, if no one from the village would ask about renting it, it's not like there is a curse or anything on it, is there? Is that a bad question to ask?' she asked, grimacing.

'Ah, OK. Yes.'

'Yes?' she replied, horrified.

'No, I mean, yes I understand now your question. I am sorry for my English.'

'Oh, no it's fine. Sorry, it was a weird question to ask.'

'No, *signora*, there is no curse. It was just a sad ending and the building has been in my family for many, many years so my brother did not have to worry about needing to rent it, so it stays like this. As for the price, I can ask my brother.'

'Oh right, yes, of course. How long will that take?'

'I don't know. I will call him but it is now very early on Saturday morning or late on Friday night in Chicago. If he is working at the hospital then he will not have his phone, of course.'

'Yes, of course. It's just that my flight back to Dublin is tomorrow.'

'I see, and when you will return to Italy?'

'Well, that's just the thing, you see – I saw this place and thought I could stay, and, you know, fix it up and maybe open a café here.' She heard the words come out of her mouth and realised just how insane she must sound to him.

'*Un momento*. I don't understand. You are here for a holiday and are thinking to not go back tomorrow, yes?' He was staring intently at her and she couldn't read his face.

'Yes. That is what I am thinking.' She realised that she was beginning to speak in broken English now, too. 'But now, if I don't know how much the rent will be then I don't know if I can afford it. So it's more complicated.' She sighed.

'Ah, I see.' He rubbed his hand across his chin. He wore dark stubble, whereas last time she met him he'd been clean-shaven. She wondered if she had dragged him from bed with her phone call, or if he always sported a casual look at the weekend. 'I will call my brother now and leave a message. Then we wait. If he does not reply soon then we think of something else, yes?'

'OK.'

Niamh nodded as she watched him pull out his phone. She wondered what his idea of 'something else' might be, but hoped irrationally that this would be straightforward and his brother would just answer the phone in the middle of the night and give him a figure for the rent. She listened to him rattle off a stream of Italian.

'He was not there,' he shrugged. 'Now I must go. I must meet a friend at eleven o'clock. We can meet back here at noon, no?'

'Sure. I can come back. Do you think he will call back?'

'I don't know for sure, *signora*, he is in America and sometimes he calls back at crazy times because he works crazy hours, but you are out of time, no? We must think of something so that you can make your decision.' He locked the door and gave her a wave. 'See you in one hour. *Arrivederci*, Nina!'

He made it sound straightforward, as if a Plan B was something that could be conjured up, giving her some momentary relief. What were the chances that his brother would be awake, get the message and call back within an hour? She decided then that she would leave it to fate. If it was meant to be then she would have her answer in an hour and, if not, she'd forget about the whole thing, catch the ferry back in time to meet Grace for their last lunch and say nothing of the morning's misadventure. Satisfied with her decision, she made her way down the steps to the lower level of the village and walked to the little café on the pier that she had visited with Grace to pass the next hour.

# Chapter Twelve

Niamh was so busy stirring and staring into her cappuccino that she didn't notice the blonde woman walk in.

'Back so soon?'

She looked up from her reverie to see Emily grinning down at her from behind yet another pair of massively oversized sunglasses.

'Exactly how many pairs of sunglasses do you own?' Niamh asked as she looked up at her.

'I can't say I know,' Emily replied, pausing to think. 'Quite likely a dozen, I'd say, if I were to venture a guess. What on earth are you doing here this morning?' She pulled up a seat and joined Niamh at her table. 'An espresso please, Massimo,' she said in the direction of the owner behind the counter.

'It's a long story,' said Niamh.

'Well then, get started.' Emily nudged her and smiled.

'I don't want to go back.'

'I know.'

'You know? How do you know?'

'I could tell last night. It's easy to recognise something in someone else when one has already experienced it, my dear. I'm not talking about the usual end-of-holiday blues, but something close to absolute distraction at the thoughts

125

of having to extract yourself from your current existence here and reinsert yourself back into what used to be your life before. I'm afraid, once you reach this point, darling, nothing will ever be the same again.'

'So you don't think it's a mad idea?'

'On the contrary! I think it's a solid idea. It's mad, certainly by normal people's standards, but solid. All that awaits you at home is depression or embarrassment, if not both, based upon what you have told me, and how could any sane person with a shred of self-respect ever go back and try to continue a professional career in the company of a maggot like that? It's just unthinkable.' Emily stirred two sachets of sugar into her espresso before she continued. 'By all means, go home, but be realistic about it if you do. Everything will have to change. Everything will be different. You will have to find a new job, as you won't be able to stand working in such close proximity to him and, let's face it, most of your friends are probably shared friends at this point. Am I right?'

'Yes.'

'Awkward! And you are back at your parents' house full time? Darling, that's enough to force anyone out into the back garden to dig a very large hole in the ground and want to sit in it in perpetuity.' She knocked back the espresso in one shot. 'If you stay here then all you've got to figure out is what to do with yourself. One problem, not three.'

'What do you mean?'

'Look, if you go home now then you'll have to figure out a new place to live and that will likely be determined by your next job, so you're stuck at your parents' house until you figure out the job part. Plus you're going to have to make new friends because it will become immediately apparent to you that you're going to lose some in the "divorce", as it were.'

'What do you mean?' Niamh asked in a confused tone.

'Well, it's my experience that when a couple splits, friends take sides. Right or wrong, friendships are just another casualty of a breakup. Your true friends will be staunch defenders and fiercely loyal. They'll stand by you, but some will skitter off, as they won't want to be stuck in the middle of any awkwardness. You just have to accept it for what it is. By comparison, if you stay here then you have no friends to start with, apart from me, of course, so any new addition will be a plus, not a minus. And this place is so small that it really doesn't matter where you live in terms of your work location.' She sat back, clearly pleased with her detailed diagnosis.

'I've figured out the work part. I think.'

'Well, don't keep me in suspense, for heaven's sake.'

'I'm thinking of renting the old café up on Via dei Limoni. I have to meet the owner's brother in about twenty minutes to see if he knows what it will cost. I can't make the decision until I know that much and he called his brother when we met earlier.'

'Lena's old place? Good Lord, that place must be a shambles. It was closed up in a hurry and hasn't been touched since. How on earth did you stumble upon that?'

'We were just wandering around yesterday before lunch and I saw it. Was Lena the brother's wife?'

'Yes, her actual name was Elena, or Helena, or something like that, but everyone called her Lena. She was from Milan originally. What a beautiful woman.' Emily sighed. 'I think she used to be a model at one point. Anyway, she fell in love with Marco and when she moved here she opened the little café. It was the heart of the town at one point, not least because of her charm. It must be in a terrible state now, though. I'm pretty sure it has been abandoned since she died.'

'Yeah, it's pretty rough, but it's still charming. It kind of seemed like it was waiting for me or something – I don't really know how to describe it. I know that sounds really wishy-washy, but I thought it looked beautiful, even in its current state. To be honest this whole place kind of . . . I don't know how to say it without sounding like I'm on *Oprah* or something, but it kind of spoke to me.' Niamh stared down into her coffee cup. 'What made you decide to move here in the first place?'

'What's not to love? Life is more pleasant here, more relaxed, darling. There is truth in that well-worn Italian expression, *la dolce vita*. Life is simply sweeter here: the antiquity of it all, the countryside, the seaside, the views, the food, the wine, even the language. I came here not really speaking any Italian but it just sounded so melodic to me. English is just so . . . I don't know . . . mainstream or pedestrian by comparison.'

'I know,' Niamh said. 'It's honestly just so beautiful here.'

'Don't get me wrong, London is marvellous, but you'll find that most people who live there do so out of necessity. It's where they work, or where their children are schooled. Then, they get into a routine and it becomes familiar, it's what they know, so it's easy and it just becomes the place they live. For most people it would be difficult to up and move, even if they wanted to.'

'I suppose I was kind of forced into the decision, given that everything was pulled from under me at home,' Niamh mumbled into her cup.

'Don't underestimate yourself. Not everyone is cut out for moving abroad, Niamh. It's not for everybody. It takes a lot of work to make it work. The language is an obvious challenge, as is the bureaucracy and the logistics of it all. The act of

128

moving abroad is not unlike the notion of wanting to write a book, actually.'

Niamh squinted in her direction, wondering where this was going.

Emily tilted her head in feigned exasperation and continued. 'People read a book and say, "I could do that, I could have written that," just as they look at someone who has uprooted their life and moved to another country. But they don't, do they? They don't write the book. They don't relocate elsewhere, they just talk about it and are quietly content in the knowledge that they could if they wanted to. Niamh, darling, these honestly are the most frustrating conversations ever, as one is forced to listen to these self-imposed excuses for not doing ... well, anything. frankly.' Emily shook her head and rolled her eyes in mock frustration.

'What did you do there, in London, I mean?'

'Same as I do here, just more of it.'

'You work here? I didn't know that.'

'Very few people can afford to just sail off into the sunset and not work, darling. Plus I think one would soon get bored of the idea of infinite free time. If all we had was free time then where's the joy in it? One relishes it all the more when it's limited, rather like most of the good things in life.'

'I suppose,' Niamh responded, reluctantly. 'Although I think it would take a long time for me to get bored of infinite free time. I can think of a long list of things I could do! So what do you do, exactly?'

'I'm an interior designer. I just charge more for it now because I'm more discerning about which clients I choose to work with. I ran a very successful business in London for years while I was married. Then I changed my life and moved here.'

'You were married?' Niamh asked, unable to mask her surprise.

'I don't like to talk about it. I'd prefer to scratch it from memory entirely if I had the opportunity. It's so long ago now that it seems like someone else's life.' Emily turned her head in the direction of the horizon, her eyes narrowing almost to a squint. Her face seemed to take on a hardened expression, clearly practised from years of actively trying to eliminate any memory of this man or her life with him.

Niamh's jaw was actively disengaged from the rest of her face in absolute shock.

'What? How come? What happened? Am I allowed to ask that?'

'Oh, it's terribly predictable, I'm afraid,' Emily replied, with a small wave of her hand. She turned back to meet Niamh's wide-eyed gaze. 'He was the kind of man for whom one woman was not enough, but sadly I was blissfully unaware of the fact for years.'

'He was having an affair for years and you didn't know it?' Niamh asked, her mouth falling open.

'Precisely.' Emily lifted her cup to her lips. 'She was an artist, apparently. Very creative and wildly inspiring – his words, not mine.'

'He told you that?'

'In so many words, yes. We even had two of her paintings hanging in our home in South Kensington. I never liked them. He just showed up with them one day. I thought it might be some client ... you know, that he felt obliged to support. They always struck me as being rather angry looking, but apparently I just didn't appreciate her talent and it was a reflection of her wildly expressive nature coming out on canvas.'

'What did you do? I hope you kicked his cheating ass out immediately?'

'I called my lawyer an hour later and had divorce papers drafted in a matter of days.'

Niamh stared across the table at her new friend, shaking her head. 'I can't believe someone treated you like that and you had to go through a divorce because of it.'

'I didn't.'

'You didn't what?' Niamh asked with a confused frown.

'I didn't have to go through a divorce.'

'You didn't end up divorcing him? OK, now I'm confused.'

'I didn't have to, as it turned out. I had his whole sordid affair publicly announced at his club. He was a member of the British Bankers Club – a very exclusive members-only, mahogany-and-dark-leather furniture sort of place, where successful, wealthy, executive types engage in verbose, self-congratulatory, hubristic conversations. He had been a member for years and had a standing Thursday evening drinks appointment with some of his cronies. Anyway, I lost all rationale and drove a very large Wüsthof chef's knife right through the centre of both of her angry paintings and had them delivered to him at the club, so it was clear to everyone in the room that I knew and that I was not about to take it lying down.' She smiled a small smile.

'How totally badass of you!' Niamh said with a laugh.

'Well, that was about the only satisfaction I got and, in the face of the humiliation and the deceit, it was fleeting.'

Niamh stared at her in disbelief, trying to reconcile the image of this angry, revenge-seeking woman-scorned with the kind, gentle, generous woman she had come to know in the past few days.

'I hadn't counted on the shock factor. You see, most of

them – his cronies that is – are, or at least, were, still married. Divorce is not something that the super-wealthy like to engage in. It's messy, undignified and far too public. The wives too buy into it, because they don't want their lives to change. They have large homes, expensive cars, high-profile social lives and social circles. Divorce means downsizing and airing one's dirty linen in public, so many couples choose to remain together, despite irreconcilable differences in the marriage. Many of them cheat, of course, or have mistresses, and still others have a whole other relationship that their partner is aware of, but chooses not to oppose or challenge. The women are often guilty of the same behaviour, of course, and are not without blame.' Emily paused for a second and her gaze shifted slightly, as if moving elsewhere momentarily. 'I think I knew of two couples who seemed genuinely happy together. But, then again, I thought we were doing OK, so what do I know?'

'I can't believe someone could just turn a blind eye to the fact that their husband has a whole other relationship!' said Niamh. 'I've never heard the likes of that!'

'Oh, trust me, there's a lot more of it goes on than you'd rather think,' Emily said with a slow shake of her head. 'Anyway, I was never certain if it was the shock of the threat of divorce itself, or the mortification of having his affair so spotlighted in such a public manner at his club, but, as it turned out, I never got the chance to ask him. He stormed out apparently and went back to his office, presumably to make some calls to get his legal team on standby. He never came home that night. He went to the artist's house in a rage. Of course I heard all of this after the fact – even the wealthy love to gossip. The following day he suffered a massive stroke and collapsed. He died in the hospital two days later.'

Niamh sat and stared at her in shock. 'I actually don't know what to say. It sounds like a scene from a soap opera!'

'Indeed,' Emily said, raising one eyebrow. 'Another coffee?' she asked Niamh as she motioned for the waiter.

'*Si, signora?*'

'*Altre due, per favore,*' she said, pointing at the two cups in front of them.

'*Subito, signora,*' he replied, with an almost imperceptible nod.

'The real tragedy was that I never even got to mourn him. If the bastard had dropped dead a week earlier I'd have been none the wiser,' Emily continued. 'As it was, I had to act the part of the grieving widow in public, all the while fuming at the thought of the deception and the lies.'

'Did you ever meet her?'

'The artist? God, no! What good could ever come of that? Once I heard that he had died, I shredded the divorce papers and instructed my lawyer to stand down, as it were. So, it turns out that dying was the only decent thing he had done for me in years.'

'Wow – so you ended up getting everything,' Niamh said in quiet admiration.

'Yes, I did.' Emily gave a defiant tilt of her jaw. It was evident that she had had to justify or defend that reaction previously. 'Word got out, of course. His balding, simpering cronies couldn't help but spread word of what had happened at the club that night. Don't for one minute think that gossip is the pursuit solely of bored housewives. Once their respective wives got hold of the story it quickly became fodder for the finest salons across London. I stuck it out for four months as I got our . . . *my* affairs in order, and then came here.'

'But did you know about this place before that?'

'Yes, we had spent many summer holidays in Portofino, so

I knew it well. He had always loved the glitz and the ostentatious glamour of Portofino, whilst I had preferred the quieter comfort of Camogli. He would play golf or whatever and I would come here, alone, for hours at a time, drinking in the sounds of local Italian village life and wandering happily amongst contented people, so much so that when the time came to leave London, this was an easy and obvious choice.'

'Crikey. I'm actually stunned,' Niamh said. 'What an unreal saga! It's honestly like something you'd read or see in a movie.'

'Quite. My life as a Hollywood blockbuster – except that no one would believe it. They'd say it was too far-fetched a notion!'

'Yeah, probably,' Niamh agreed, sipping her second cappuccino. 'So you ended up being married to a nasty piece of work and you're the one who had to give up the life that you knew and start over?'

'Well, everyone has their own struggles. Life may look simple or perfect from the outside, but everyone is dealing with something. My "somethings" just all came barrelling down on me at the same time. Some things in life you can fix, change, improve, but sometimes you just have to accept them and move on.'

Niamh thought for a moment about her own situation and her current longing to stay in Italy and start over. The circumstances were different, of course. Rick had ended the relationship, after all, but the hurt was the same. She had been rejected and had taken herself and her wounds off to another country. Now she found herself not wanting to return. She frowned as she thought how different it might have been had she stayed in Ireland, hoping for a second chance but instead being brutally shut out of Rick's life. She still thought he might reach out, that she might have heard something from him, but she hadn't heard a word. She felt a sudden sadness at just how cold and decisive people could be when it came to deciding that they no longer wanted you in their life.

'I'd never thought of it like that,' she said quietly, picking the errant, sticky-up piece of skin on her left thumb. There was surely a more clinical name for it, but she was damned if she could think of it now.

'Anyway,' Emily said abruptly, brushing nothing in particular off her white pants. 'I don't like to talk about it or dwell on it, for obvious reasons, so let's please change the subject. And please do me the favour of not bringing it up again.'

Niamh watched her adjust her posture and her expression simultaneously as she prepared to once again bury the memories and the unresolved pain. 'Wow, so the "stiff upper lip" British thing is actually a thing!' she exclaimed. 'Sorry, that was supposed to be in my head, but I just watched your expression change as you changed the subject. I didn't mean to cause offence.'

'None taken,' Emily said with a small smile. 'And yes, it is in fact a thing! I'd rather wear an exterior, glossy appearance of inner contentment any day, than wallow for ever in a large vat of gloom and self-pity, exuding strains of misery such that no one would come anywhere near me. Wouldn't you?'

Niamh shrugged. 'Yes, I suppose so,' she replied, wondering if she herself would have the grace and resolve to compartmentalise and banish her grief and anger in similar circumstances.

Emily stood, picking up her purse and adjusting both her sunglasses and her composure, looking nothing like a woman who had just poured years of pain and sadness onto the little round table that sat between them.

'I have to go and meet Giorgio again to see if he has any answer about the rent. Do you want to come with me?' Niamh asked.

'Why not? I quite like the idea of escorting you to what might potentially be your next life adventure. Onwards, Niamh,' she said linking Niamh's arm with hers.

# Chapter Thirteen

'So you've already met Giorgio, then?' Emily asked, raising an eyebrow as they strolled towards the abandoned building.

'Yes, I met him this morning when I went to see the café, but I had met him last Monday night at the hotel in Santa Margherita. He was there for the cocktail thing, at my sister's conference. I think we talked about that last night – the architects' conference.'

'Sounds vaguely familiar, darling. I think you'll need to repeat much of what was said late last night – at least the important bits.'

'It was a bit embarrassing this morning, actually. I accidently toppled an Aperol spritz all over him that night, then I called the number to see the café this morning and he showed up. I was mortified all over again,' Niamh replied, shaking her head at the memory of it.

'Ah, yes, it makes sense that he would have been at that conference. Some of those architects would be his clients. He's quite a fine individual of a man, wouldn't you agree?' Emily asked, looking sideways at Niamh as they walked towards the steps.

'He's gorgeous, yes. He seems nice, too – friendly – but I'd say he's kind of quiet . . . is he?'

'He wasn't always quiet. Poor man has had a rather rough time of it. After Lena died, his brother was devastated, naturally. He tried to carry on with his life but he never got over her. So, he put in for a transfer and a year later it came through so he moved to Chicago. They had always been close, so Giorgio missed having his brother around. Then their father died suddenly – while Marco was in Chicago. He couldn't come home because of some visa restriction, so he missed the funeral. Giorgio had to be the rock for their mother and try to carry on with his own life, changed as it was. After all that, his fiancée – Giorgio's, that is – left him for another man about a year ago. She said that he had changed drastically after everything that had happened and was too sorrowful and he wasn't fun to be around any more. She claimed he had lost interest in her, but that just wasn't so, she was a terribly selfish individual. She got bored and didn't want to play the role of supportive partner. She wanted some diversity, so she found someone else and just left. He was devastated, and I'm not sure that he has got over it yet. To be honest, he shouldn't have bothered being so overwrought over her – the fiancée, that is – because she was really not a good person,' Emily continued. 'She was incredibly beautiful and I think she felt that her beauty was enough to endear her to anyone, including Giorgio. He fell for it. Then, once things got tough she took off. So now, with his brother in America, it's just him and his mother here in Camogli, and you know how close Italian men are to their mamas.' She rolled her eyes.

'He doesn't live with his mother, does he?'

'Heavens, no. He's more sophisticated than that, darling. In fact, he has the most gorgeous house up in the hills behind Camogli, but he takes care of her and they're very close. He's all that she has now that her other son, Marco, lives abroad.'

'But what about the woman I saw him with at that party?' Niamh asked, with a small frown.

'Ah, yes. They've been good friends for many years and I think it was perhaps a case of turning to a close friend for comfort in a time of need. I never thought they were the right fit, but then they surprised me and ended up as a couple. Then again, given my track record with men, I'm hardly qualified to pass comment on anyone's relationship.' Emily laughed.

'That's not the impression I got,' Niamh said, as they rounded the corner onto Via dei Limoni. 'She was kind of glued to him.'

'Wouldn't you be, darling, if you had been invited in to live life by his side?' Emily replied with raised eyebrows. 'One would hardly need a second invitation!'

'No, I suppose not,' Niamh agreed.

They arrived outside the café and Emily peered in through the window. 'It's in a worse condition than I thought it would be. Good grief. Are you sure about this?'

'Well, it depends on the price. I have no idea what he's going to say, to be honest. It's entirely possible that I won't be able to make it work.'

'One thing I've learned in life, darling, is that no matter what it is, if you want it to happen badly enough, you can make it happen.' Emily frowned as she scanned the room through the dirty glass. 'You just have to make sure it's what you really want. Are you sure this is really what you want, Niamh? It's going to take an awful amount of work.' She shook her head.

'I don't mind about the hard work. The only thing I'm uncertain about is whether I can afford it or not. Where the hell is he, anyway?'

'Giorgio?' Emily asked standing, up straight. 'Oh he's

always late for everything. I don't think he has ever been on time for anything in his life!' She laughed. 'It's a bit of an Italian trait, but he's particularly talented in that aspect. If you live here you will have to get used to that.'

If you live here . . . Niamh repeated in her head. The words sent chills down her spine with excitement and anticipation.

Giorgio rounded the corner suddenly, talking on his phone and carrying a bundle of files. The blazer of his dark grey suit was unbuttoned. He wore another pristine white shirt, she noted, and his body was lean and taut beneath it. He stopped a few feet from them and wrapped up the call with multiple frustrated repetitions of *sì* and *va bene*.

Niamh's breath caught just a little. His hair looked dishevelled, as if he had just run his hand through it.

Christ, you're gorgeous, she thought, instinctively wanting to reach out and flatten out his hair.

He greeted Emily with a smile and kissed her on both cheeks. '*Ciao, Emilia.*'

'*Ciao, Giorgio, come va?*'

'*Bene, bene, grazie,*' he said. He pulled the keys from his pocket and dropped them to the ground. '*Ciao,* Nina,' he said, looking up at her with a grin as he stooped to retrieve them.

'Working on a Saturday, Giorgio? That's most unlike you,' Emily said, playfully.

'No, no. I just help a friend with a problem. On Saturday I don't work. *Sicuramente, no!* OK, we go in,' he said, jiggling the key in the lock.

The door was sticking in the doorframe again so it took a couple of shoves to get it fully open. As he gave it a final shove there was a loud crack. He peered around the other side of the door to see that one of the panels had cracked. He shrugged his shoulders and looked at Niamh. 'You want to rent this?'

He dropped the keys on the dusty countertop and went to lean against it. He hesitated, wiped it with a hand and shook his head, deciding to remain standing upright. '*Allora . . .*' He placed the bundle of files on a small table near the counter. The leg buckled under the weight and the whole thing collapsed to the ground. 'You want to rent this?' he asked again, shaking his head.

'See – even Giorgio thinks you are mad,' Emily said, waving a hand in an effort to dispel the small cloud of dust that had risen from the collapsed table.

'What did he say? What did your brother say about the rent?' Niamh asked. She tried desperately not to sound overly concerned, but she wasn't sure she could take much more generic conversation without knowing what the actual outcome was going to be.

'My brother, he did not call me back. I think he must be working.' Giorgio shrugged.

'Shit,' Niamh said. 'Well, I can't just stay here indefinitely.'

'No. I understand. So this is what I have done. I cannot speak with my brother right now, so I called my friend who has a . . . *come si dice* . . . a shop that sells and rents the houses?'

'An estate agent?' Emily offered helpfully. She was clearly used to interpreting meaning and intent from poor attempts at English and converting them into proper English.

'Ah, *sì*. Yes . . . this. I called my friend who has this kind of shop in the next village and asked him what would be a fair price for a small building such as this one in his village. Don't worry, his is a normal village like Camogli, just slightly bigger. It is not a very large expensive place like Santa Margherita or not a very fancy place like Portofino. There you cannot afford to rent anything! So I asked him what he thinks. He told me that there is one café similar in his village, maybe a bit smaller, I don't know. So, he tells me that this café, in his village, he rents for three thousand euros each month, but it is new, no?'

Niamh looked around in dismay. She had no idea what it might cost to get this place in working order, but it surely wouldn't be cheap.

'So, I think this is what we can do. You pay half of that rent and we sign an agreement for six months. If my brother does not like the agreement, you can make a new one with him in six months, but this way, you can know what you must do and you know that this building will be yours for six months, so you have chance to see if you can make a good start, no?'

She nodded slowly, thinking that half the rent was a pretty fair deal. 'But what if your brother freaks out? Can we have an agreement that he can't cancel the contract for the six months?'

'*Signora*, I am a lawyer. Yes, I can create the right agreement,' he said with a smile. 'So, do you want to rent it?'

She looked around at the dust, the broken furniture, the neglected counters and shelves and the chipped tiles. 'Yes, I want to rent it.'

It made no sense, that much she knew, but whatever uncertainty she had about this impulsive project, she knew that she couldn't go back home tomorrow. At least this way, with a six-month guarantee, she could defer the ultimate decision and give this a real shot.

'OK, when would you like to start the rent?'

'Right away, please. I mean, it's available immediately, isn't it?'

'Yes.' He shrugged again. 'Obviously it is available. We have done nothing with the building since my brother left. He didn't think that anyone would want to rent it, but he cannot do any work to improve it, so you must rent it in the condition that you find it. This is OK with you?'

'Yes,' she nodded. 'This is OK with me.'

'I will do one thing more,' he added. 'I think there is a lot of work to be done here, no? So, we can sign the agreement in my office on Monday, but you will start to pay the rent only in one month. You must pay the money to . . . how you say . . . *come si dice* . . . '

'Renovate it?' asked Emily.

'*Sì, grazie!* Yes, to renovate it. So, for this I will offer you first month free of rent. This is OK with you?'

'Yes, that is very fair.' Niamh beamed.

'Oh my God, you are out of your mind, darling,' Emily said with a laugh, peeling a dangling cobweb from her hair. 'Giorgio, she's not signing anything today. Between now and Monday I'm going to try my best to talk her out of it.'

'*Va bene*,' he said, smiling. He turned to Niamh. 'If Emilia has some success then I don't see you on Monday. If Emilia has no success then I see you on Monday morning at ten o'clock at my office. *Ecco*. Here is my card.'

She took his card and smiled at him. '*Grazie*. See you Monday.'

'Don't count on it,' Emily shouted over her shoulder as she dragged Niamh from the dusty interior into the sunlight.

'*Arrivederci*,' Giorgio said with a nod. As a lawyer he dealt with people in challenging situations all the time and he knew determination when he saw it. He was pretty certain that he would be seeing this Irish woman again in his office at ten o'clock on Monday morning.

143

# Chapter Fourteen

She was late getting back to the hotel. She had texted Grace to say that she was coming back for lunch but probably wouldn't get there until about 1.30. It was now a quarter to two. Grace had already been seated at their table and was tapping away furiously at her phone. Thank God she has a glass of wine in front of her, Niamh thought, as she was ushered through the restaurant to the window table. That's about the only thing that has any chance of keeping her calm and patient.

'Sorry, sorry, sorry!' she gushed as she sat down.

'It's fine, as long as I have wine for company I'm never alone,' said Grace with a shrug. 'So, where were you?' She pulled the bottle of white wine from the ice bucket and poured Niamh a glass.

'I went back to Camogli.'

Grace rolled her eyes. 'To the café?'

'Yes, I met the owner's brother to see how much it would cost to rent it.'

'Jesus, I was hoping that this was just a mad notion that you had yesterday and that it was powered by alcohol. So you're actually serious about this?'

'Yes, I am. Very.'

'I don't know what to say. I've never heard anything so

naive or ridiculous in my life – running away from your life and your problems like that.'

'Well, Grace, I'm staying, for better or for worse, so you can decide how this goes. Do we spend lunch arguing over it because you don't approve of my decision or do we talk about it like normal people? It's up to you.'

She surprised herself with her assertiveness and, judging by the expression on Grace's face, she had surprised Grace, too.

'Well, first of all, "normal people" don't make rash decisions like this and toss the return portion of their ticket and just not go home. They deal with their problems instead of fleeing from them, but fine, yes, we can talk about it. I'm not going to argue with you. I just think you are insane, that's all.'

'Think what you want, but for the first time in my life I'm terrified and excited about something. I've never been terrified of anything, ever.'

'And that's a bad thing?'

'Well, don't you think it says a lot about my life back in Dublin? It was boring and safe. I never made any of the decisions; Rick did. He was in charge of our lives and he was the one who made plans and forged ahead with his career. He was doing well, I was just happy to follow along like some kind of sheep on a leash.'

Grace remained quiet and let Niamh speak, which in itself was unusual.

Niamh looked down into her wine glass as if looking for inspiration of some kind. 'It was a small life, Grace. He was in charge and I just limped along like some sad individual, grateful to be included in his plans. He didn't mean any harm – it wasn't intentional, or anything. I mean, I was happy to go along with it all, but that's what I was doing. I was just going along with everything. He made all the plans and big decisions. I just

145

decided what to make for dinner every time I stood in front of the butcher counter in Tesco. He had the great apartment that I kind of half lived in, but didn't own. He made more money and paid most of the bills, so he always had the final say in where we went on holiday, or which hotel we picked. He never compromised on his football or rugby, no matter what else was going on. It was always a priority, even over me, sometimes.'

'But you never had a problem with it before, did you? Why didn't you say anything?'

'I didn't even realise it, Grace,' said Niamh in a loud whisper across the table. 'I know this is going to sound soft, and like something you'd hear on a *Dr Phil* show, but it's like I was living it ... in it ... and so I couldn't see it. I had no perspective. I didn't know that there was anything else. I didn't want to know or need to know, because that was my life and it was safe – or so I thought. God, how wrong can a girl be?' She shook her head and continued. 'I never went anywhere on my own before. I never travelled without him, so it's as if any time we went anywhere, he was kind of in charge and I was happy to follow along. Grace, this is the first time in my life that I've been out of the country and not with a boyfriend. This is the first time in my life that I've gone and done stuff on my own in another country, like when you were at the conference those few days. I only ever went on package holidays, or a weekend to London. I never got off a plane in another country with no plan, only to have to figure it out myself. This is the first time in my life that I've felt like I've been on an adventure and it's not as if this is Nairobi or Madagascar or somewhere mad and exotic. It's Italy, for God's sake.' She gestured with her right hand, her glass of wine in her left. 'And I feel like I'm in charge of me for the first time in my life!' She leaned forward and hauled the bottle from the ice bucket, draining it into their two glasses.

'Oh, sweet Jesus,' Grace said quietly. 'This is my fault. Mam is going to kill me. It's all my fault. I brought you here. I plucked you from your safe, quiet little life that you were happy with. I insisted you come here with me and now you don't want to go back.' She motioned to the waiter to bring another bottle of wine. 'This is going to be a two-bottle lunch, I can already tell. We should order some food.'

'It's not your fault, Grace. It was my decision. Now, granted, if you had brought me to some other place like Romania or something I mightn't have been as fast to decide to change my life, but I love it here, and why the hell not?'

'Doesn't matter,' Grace replied, her two hands covering her face. 'Mam's going to think you've lost your mind and will blame me for dragging you here in the first place! Where is that waiter?' She gave a small laugh. 'I need a drink.'

They continued chatting for another hour over lunch. By the time they had finished, Grace was resigned to the fact that Niamh had made up her mind.

'All right. I still can't believe you are doing this, but I will accept the fact that you are not coming home with me on one condition.'

'What's that?'

'You have to call Mam and tell her before I get home. There is no way in hell that I am getting off that plane having to explain this to her. She'll lose her mind as it is, so it has to come from you.'

'OK, fine.'

'But you can't call her now. You can't be drunk talking to her or she'll think it was a mad idea based on too much wine, not just a mad idea all on its own merits.'

'Fair enough.' Niamh giggled. 'Do you really think it's a mad idea?'

'Yes, completely and absolutely insane. But kind of badass

too, in a way.' Grace smiled from behind her wine glass. 'Not, to be clear, that I condone it in any way. But if you had to pick some place to drop out of life then I suppose Italy would have to be top of the list. Just don't go falling for some randy Italian. If you are going to do this then make it your own adventure. You've been somebody else's project for too long. Be your own for a while.'

How is it that other people always seemed to have good advice for your own life and how to improve it, but from the inside it was hard to see what was even wrong, let alone put together a cohesive plan to fix it, Niamh wondered as they left the table.

They spent the rest of the afternoon wandering around the elegant town of Santa Margherita. The weather was a perfect mix of bright sunshine and light sea breeze. They strolled, stopping for a gelato, neither of them mentioning the fact that only one of them was returning home tomorrow. They were both in denial for different reasons.

On returning to the hotel, the concierge handed them a message. It was from Emily.

*Hello darlings,*

*I know that tonight is Grace's last night and I wondered if you two had plans for the evening? If not, a friend of mine owns one of the best restaurants in town – Sara's – and tonight they reopen for the season. It's always a marvellous affair! If you don't have plans then I would love you two to be my guests.*

*No need to call if you are coming. Just meet me at La Terrazza at six and wear something absolutely fabulous!*

*(Oh, and bring a wrap. We're going on the water!)*

*Ciao darlings,*

*Emily*

Niamh read the note over Grace's shoulder.

'Jesus,' said Grace, turning to her sister. 'How do you refuse an invitation like that?'

'Umm, you don't?'

'Absolutely. OK, I've got to go see what outfits I have left to wear. If Emily says to wear something absolutely fabulous, then that's about as glam as I've got.'

'Well, I'm trotting behind you in the fashion stakes, so I may need to go back into town to those boutiques.'

'Let's just do that then. Come on,' Grace said, grabbing Niamh by the elbow.

Three boutiques and six shopping bags later, the girls returned to their hotel for the third time that day. They had an hour to get ready before the 17.30 ferry departure. By the time they were ready to leave an hour later, the room was filled with a cloud of steam, perfume and hairspray.

They opted to sit inside on the short ferry journey to Camogli so as not to demolish the hair creations so carefully sculpted just minutes earlier. The ferry ride was easy, and less than thirty minutes later they pulled up to the pier in Camogli. The two sisters made their way to La Terrazza to find the place completely packed. Apparently opening night at Sara's – wherever it was – was clearly cause for celebration, and half the town had turned out to kick off the evening at La Terrazza.

They made their way through the throng of people. The terrace was standing-room only tonight and the air crackled with excitement and laughter. Niamh stayed close to Grace as they weaved through the crowd, feeling more than just a little bit intimidated.

'What are we doing here? Who are all these people?' she asked Grace nervously, as she scanned the elegant crowd. 'I feel like I'm in some kind of movie or something.'

'I don't know. This is nuts. Just smile. That's what I do when I'm in a large group of people I don't know. It helps make you look more confident.'

Niamh planted a small smile on her face, hoping it looked more authentic than it felt. Emily was holding court alongside the pop-up champagne bar and waved at them to come join her. The crowd was very well dressed and everyone was drinking champagne served in old-fashioned coupe glasses instead of the usual Aperol spritz cocktail routine.

'Wow, what *is* this?' Niamh asked Emily above the cacophony of laughter and chatter.

'It's opening night, darling! Tonight marks the first night of the season and Sara's is one of the best restaurants in town. It's not something one can get on the list for – rather, it's strictly invitation only, and the way Sara thanks her local and loyal customers for their patronage and support during the season. But she's a dear friend of mine, so I throw an annual opening-night party here at La Terrazza before we go to her restaurant.'

'Crikey, this is your party?' Grace asked as she looked around and took in the crowd.

'Yes! Isn't it fun?'

'I'll say,' Grace said in agreement, as a waiter in a white waistcoat offered her a glass of champagne.

'I'm glad we shopped, Grace,' Niamh said, hissing into her sister's ear. 'I'd have looked homeless if I'd shown up tonight wearing anything in my suitcase!'

'Me too. Can't let the side down, you know? Especially as you're going to be living here now. You've got to represent!'

Just hearing the words sent shivers down Niamh's spine. She looked around at the glamorous crowd and her stomach flipped with both anxiety and excitement. She felt giddy as she realised that she might actually live here from tomorrow on. It wasn't just about tonight, with its glamorous setting, elegant outfits and champagne party. If she were to be honest, that was a little more intimidating than it was enticing right now. But rather it was more about this place here, these people, the snippets of Italian conversation that she couldn't possibly understand. This might actually be her real life from tomorrow.

'What did you mean in your note about going on the water?' Grace asked.

'Ah, yes. Well, the restaurant is not here. This is just the gathering point. From here we take a boat to Punta Chiappa.'

'We just passed that on the way here, didn't we?'

'Oh yes, that's right, you would have done coming from Santa Margherita. Punta Chiappa is the stop before Camogli. Look.' Emily pointed with one slender arm towards a cluster of tiny lights in the distance.

Both sisters looked in the direction she was pointing. The cluster of lights was at the base of the lush mountain range that ran along the left side of the bay. Niamh had seen Punta Chiappa on the ferry timetable but hadn't taken much notice of it on any of her journeys to Camogli. Emily explained that it was so small that it didn't even qualify for village status and was really just a little hamlet. There were two restaurants, a church and a cluster of houses, and it could only be reached by water or by a vertiginous hike through the lush mountain range. There was no road access, which only added to its sense of remoteness.

The restaurant clientele arrived either by ferry or at the end of a one-hour hike (not possible at night), and the wealthier clientele arrived by private water taxi or, better still, private boat or yacht.

'In the summertime there is the most spectacular collection

151

of antique *gozzo* boats and gorgeous yachts moored out in the bay. The owners swim and sunbathe and then have lunch at one of the two restaurants in Punta Chiappa. They are both great restaurants, but tonight is the opening of Sara's. So grab another glass of champagne and we'll get moving in about twenty minutes or so.'

'Are we taking the ferry to the restaurant?' Niamh asked, as she plucked two glasses of champagne from a passing waiter.

'Darling, I don't do ferries,' said Emily, laughing loudly. 'Giorgio is taking his boat over and I've hired a few of the local water taxis for people. They're much faster than the ferry and far more fun.'

'Oh, Giorgio is going?' Niamh asked, sipping her champagne.

'Anyone who is anyone is going and, yes, he said he was. He should be here somewhere, but I haven't seen him yet.' Emily craned her neck to see around the terrace. 'Then again, he's always late for everything.'

'I feel like I'm missing something here. Who is Giorgio?' Grace asked with a raised eyebrow.

'Oh, he's the guy who I'm renting the café from. It's his brother's place.'

Grace narrowed her eyes and stared at her sister. 'What are you being all coy about? You're not the coy type, Niamh.'

Niamh rolled her eyes. 'I'm not being coy, Grace. I don't think I'd know how to be coy if I tried.'

'So, what then?'

Emily grinned and gave Niamh a nudge. 'Go on, tell her . . .'

'Nothing. It's just that when I showed up to meet him at the café it turned out that he was the guy I'd met at your cocktail thing that first night.'

'Ah! The guy you threw a drink at, on the terrace?' Grace said, with a shriek of laughter.

'I didn't throw a drink at him, Grace. It was an accident,' Niamh said defensively.

'I bet he stands well back from you tonight,' Grace replied, giggling, prompting another eye roll from Niamh.

'As you two are my guests this evening, you should come on the boat with us. The mayor is a friend of Giorgio's, so he and his wife will be on it, and a couple of other friends from town. I'll introduce you to everyone later on.'

'Oh, lovely, that sounds fabulous,' Grace said appreciatively. She turned and leaned in towards Niamh. 'Where on earth have we landed? Who are these people and what is happening?'

'I know, it's weird, isn't it? I mean, in a good way obviously. It really feels like a small village and everyone is so friendly.'

'If this is anything to go by then getting integrated here isn't going to prove too difficult,' Grace said, looking around and taking in the crowd and the setting on the terrace. 'You might be on to something, Niamh. I might be dropping out of my life and turning around to follow you back here! Is that him? The guy with the café?' She was pointing at a tall, well-dressed man who was making his way through the crowd on the terrace.

Niamh followed her gaze and saw Giorgio greet Emily with a wide smile and a kiss on each cheek. 'Yep, that's him,' she said, looking him up and down.

'He's divine looking. Is he single?'

'Umm ... no. Emily said he's involved with someone. I didn't get all the details. I don't really know him. I've only met him briefly a couple of times. He's pretty hot though, isn't he?'

'That's an understatement, Niamh.'

'Actually, he has a kind of sad story.'

'Jayzus, why is it that they are either gay or have some kind of sad sob story? Are there no non-screwed-up hot straight guys any more?' Grace asked, plucking another glass of champagne from a passing tray. 'Thank God I don't have an early flight tomorrow. This is way too much fun to pass up!'

'No, I don't believe there are, but you are probably asking the wrong person, given my train-wreck history with men.'

'Fair enough. He's handsome, though. I'm pretty sure I could help him get over his tragedy, whatever it was. It could be my personal pet project,' she said, gazing in Giorgio's direction. 'He doesn't seem too distraught or sad right now,' she added.

Niamh looked in his direction. He was laughing along with Emily and another couple.

'By the way, did you call Mam today?'

'No, I'll do it in the morning.'

'Niamh, you better call her! I swear to God I'm not dealing with this when I get home. She's going to lose her mind completely over this, so I need to make sure that she has enough time to stress about it in advance before I get there and have to listen to it.'

'I know, I know. I'll call tomorrow, I promise. Drink up, it looks like this party is moving out.'

Both girls downed their glasses of champagne as Emily ably corralled the crowd towards the exit. The sisters strolled to the marina arm in arm as part of a larger contingent slowly snaking their way through the town.

'I feel like I'm in a Christmas nativity play, you know, that scene from *The Little Drummer Boy*,' Niamh giggled, as she glanced over her shoulder at the crowd behind them.

'I can't believe I have to go home tomorrow and you get to stay. So unfair!' Grace cried.

'I know, it's a bit weird just thinking of it. Oh, and if you don't want to pack all your stuff you can leave any cute pieces you want here with me.'

'Nice try. I'll need them for when I come back to visit you.'

'I'm starving.'

'Me too,' Grace agreed, as the two of them reached the top of the marina. 'Let's wait here for Emily. We don't want to miss that boat, wherever it is.'

Emily and Giorgio were the first to reach them.

'*Buona sera*, Nina.' He smiled as he stood alongside them. 'Emily tells me that you ladies need a . . . *come si dice* . . . a lift to the restaurant?'

'Yes, please!' Niamh grinned, and introduced her sister.

Giorgio led the way down the steps to the pier and stepped lightly onto a classic mahogany-panelled motorboat, extending a hand first to Emily and then the two sisters. 'Take a seat. We wait for a few more people,' he said as he readied the engine.

'Wow, this is a beautiful boat, Giorgio,' Niamh gushed.

'*Grazie*. Yes it is old, but very elegant. It is a traditional wooden boat that you find in Italian bays and around the islands. Perfect for sailing.'

'Everything about this evening is elegant,' Grace whispered to Niamh. 'Look at us, sitting on this gorgeous boat, waiting for the mayor and his wife and then zipping off to a restaurant opening! I have a feeling that this is going to be epic!'

'Me too. I'm beside myself right now. I think I've pinched myself twice already!' Niamh agreed excitedly, as the last guests stepped aboard and Giorgio revved the engine.

# Chapter Fifteen

There was already a crowd at the restaurant as their boat pulled up and docked at the little pier in Punta Chiappa. Before they were able to see anyone, there was no mistaking the sounds of a party in play. Giorgio's boat had sped across the bay in less than twelve minutes, the sky backlit orange with the setting sun. Emily was first off the boat, followed by the mayor and his wife, and the two sisters, with Giorgio staying behind to tie up the boat safely. It was only a short walk from the pier up the winding path, through a grove of trees to the restaurant.

The entire place was lit by strands of tiny fairy lights, strung from the eaves of the restaurant roof to the palm trees and olive trees lining the bay side of the terrace. White linen tablecloths and simple silver candelabras decorated the two long tables, each of them seating twenty-four people. Bowls of cream and white wild roses were placed at every four seats down the length of each table. A string quartet decked out in black tie played classical pieces in the corner, and a pop-up Franciacorta bar stood ready to serve the evening's invited guests.

Everyone appeared to know each other and the two sisters stood quietly, taking in the view back across the bay towards

Camogli. Emily was nowhere to be seen; presumably she had dashed inside to greet their host and her friend.

'I can't believe I passed this place on the ferry from Portofino,' Niamh commented as she leaned on the wall and stared down into the crystal-clear water in the bay below.

'It's like something out of a movie. I've never been to a more stunning restaurant setting,' Grace gushed.

'Ladies, you do not have a drink. You will have champagne, no?'

The two sisters turned around to find Giorgio coming up from the pier behind them. 'It is not a party without champagne, and tonight it must be a party, no?'

'Yes, please,' they replied almost in unison and walked with him to the pop-up bar. The bottles of Franciacorta were displayed in oversized vintage wine coolers and had been perfectly chilled.

'Ooh, isn't this what we had the night we met Emily on the terrace?' Niamh asked, with an excited clap of her hands as she turned to face Grace.

'Probably, yes,' Giorgio interjected with a smile. 'If you were with Emilia then I am sure you were drinking Franciacorta. Tonight will be a feast.' As he talked, he poured them each a glass. 'Sara is a wonderful chef. I am sure that you would have . . . how do you say . . . found your way to her restaurant during the summer, but to be here tonight is special.' He held up his glass. '*Salute!* To the start of summer.'

They clinked glasses and drank to the start of summer.

'*Allora.* You must excuse me as I must go now to find our host.'

And with that he was gone again.

'There's something kind of elusive about him, isn't there?' said Grace, as they watched him walk away. 'I mean, he's divine, obviously, and friendly and all that, but he's kind of distant too.'

'Yeah, maybe he's just quiet or shy,' Niamh commented, as she too watched him go.

They could see a tall brunette in a flowing red silk dress make her way slowly through the crowd in the distance.

'Don't tell me that's the owner,' Niamh muttered to Grace. 'For the love of God, she's stunning. She's like a model.'

They watched as Giorgio greeted her warmly with a kiss on each cheek, followed by a hug.

'He's not quiet and shy now,' Grace commented from behind her champagne glass.

'She looks familiar,' Niamh said, squinting in her direction. 'Wait a second! She's the woman who was at your cocktail thing the other night. The woman who came to pull Giorgio away.'

'The night you destroyed his shirt?'

'Yes, that's her. Emily said they've been friends for years and they're an item now.'

'They look good together. Imagine what their kids will be like.'

'Yeah, like "the Clooneys: the sequel",' Niamh muttered in reluctant agreement.

They heard Emily introduce their host to some people nearby as the 'illustrious and accomplished Sara Rovella'. She looked like a film star or a model and must have been at least five foot eight.

'That's definitely her,' Niamh sighed. 'How does one person get to be so stunning and obviously talented and successful as well? Talk about winning the life lottery.'

'Yeah, but didn't you say she was kind of mean to you that night?'

'No, not mean exactly, just didn't really acknowledge my existence . . . whatever.' Niamh shrugged as she looked around in awe at their surroundings.

Emily waved in their direction and approached the two sisters.

'Niamh, Grace, please meet my friend Sara, our host for the evening. Sara, these are the Irish girls I was telling you about.'

'It's a pleasure to meet you,' Sara said, shaking both of their hands.

'Likewise, and thank you so much for inviting us this evening,' Grace said.

'It is my pleasure,' Sara said, in almost pitch-perfect English. 'Which one of you is Nina?'

'Oh, that's me.' Niamh smiled. Grace looked sideways at her but she continued uninterrupted. 'It's a real pleasure to be here. We've heard such wonderful things about your restaurant.'

'That is kind of you to say. I understand you are about to embark on your own adventure, and you will open a café? Camogli has captured your heart and your imagination, no?'

'Yes, it has.' Niamh nodded in agreement. 'I've never been anywhere like this.'

'I understand how you feel. The same happened for me when I came to visit from Rome. I never went back. That was many, many years ago.'

'Yes, I have to call my mam tomorrow and explain that I'm not coming home.'

Sara and Emily both laughed.

'Sara had a similar dilemma,' Emily said, smiling.

'Yes, except it was my husband at the time who I had to call,' Sara said with a strained expression. 'He wasn't very understanding. It was quite a difficult phone call, as you can imagine. But I hope that your phone call to your mother will not be as dramatic.' She frowned slightly and put a hand to her mouth. 'You look familiar to me. Have we met before?'

'Oh, yes, at the drinks thing, em ... cocktail event at the hotel in Santa Margherita,' Niamh said hesitantly.

There was no doubting the change of expression on Sara's face as she registered having met Niamh a few days earlier.

'Ah yes, that is right. Well, you must excuse me as I need to put on my apron and continue my work, or no one will eat tonight.'

She nodded her goodbye and turned in the direction of the kitchen.

'She is the most delightful person,' Emily said as Sara turned and left. 'Now, just wait until you taste her food and you will wonder if there is nothing that she cannot do.'

Niamh wasn't sure she'd describe Sara as 'delightful', based on the two brief encounters she had had with her, but thought it wise to say nothing for now.

'What happened with the husband?' Grace asked.

'She left him that time and never went back. He raised his hand to her once and one belt in the face almost fractured her jaw. That was what it took for her to come to her senses and leave. She wasn't exaggerating when she said that she never went back. This is home to her now, and we are her family.'

'God, that's terrible. Imagine having something like that happen to you. I'd run a mile and never look back if any man did that to me. That's inexcusable,' Grace said in horror.

'Indeed,' was all that Emily said in response. 'Come, let me introduce you to some people. Remember, Niamh, these people could be your customers in a few weeks,' she said with a wink.

'No pressure, Niamh, just don't cock up any of these

introductions tonight,' Grace said wickedly. 'Your whole future career could depend on it.'

'I'm glad to see that my notion to open a café is such a source of entertainment to you,' Niamh replied, as they followed Emily up the slanted walkway to the main terrace.

'Oh, wait,' Grace said, once Emily had left their side. She turned to face her sister. 'Why did Sara call you Nina? What was that about?'

'Oh yeah, Giorgio thinks my name is Nina, or actually, he'd prefer if it was as he thought Niamh was too difficult to pronounce.'

'That's interesting.'

'Why? It's just because of the spelling of Niamh and the V sound and I told him that as a child I used to call myself Nina so he just started calling me Nina, that's all.'

'Well, she said she had heard about the Irish girls and then asked which of us was Nina. I presumed Emily had told her about us.'

'Well, of course she did, she's the one who brought us here so she'd have had to.'

'But Emily calls you Niamh.'

Niamh hesitated and frowned.

'Yes, Emily calls you Niamh,' Grace continued, 'so Sara must have heard about the Irish girls, and in particular the one called Nina, from someone else.'

'Did you notice her expression change back there?' Niamh asked her sister quietly.

'I did. What was that all about?'

'I don't know, but that was definitely weird.'

'It's opening night. Maybe she's just stressed.' Grace shrugged. 'Don't give it another thought.'

The next hour passed in a blur. Waiters proffered platters of tiny hors d'oeuvres as dozens of bottles of Franciacorta were popped. The sun had set entirely now and Camogli was a cluster of glittering lights in the distance. The last of the guests had trailed in by eight o'clock, just as the waiters got ready to seat everyone at the long tables. Emily pointed them in the direction of two seats next to each other towards one end of the long table. Niamh and Grace turned to make their way through a group of eight or nine people, with Grace saying '*Scusi*' as they did so.

'Hello again,' came a voice from behind in a soft American accent.

They both turned to face the blond man who was grinning in their direction. Grace's face remained blank as she glanced at Niamh. Niamh frowned. He looked vaguely familiar in the way that a bit-part actor in a film you had seen once a long time ago might look familiar.

'You don't remember me, do you?' he asked Niamh directly.

Grace glanced at her again inquisitively.

'Umm, well ...' she stuttered, racing through facts and places in her mind to place this man who stood before her, certain that she knew him somehow.

'It was a pretty wild night, so I'm not surprised you don't remember,' he offered. 'It is Niamh, right?'

Niamh stared at him blankly. 'Shit, he does actually know me,' she said quietly to Grace as he made his way towards them.

Grace had stopped fully in her tracks by now and was staring in amusement at the situation developing in front of her. 'Niamh, aren't you going to introduce me?' she asked, grinning. She couldn't remember when she had last been so entertained by her sister's infamously poor recollection of faces and names.

Niamh was racing through her internal mental filing

cabinet and coming up with nothing. What the hell kind of night was this man talking about, and when? 'Well, I ... umm, this is my sister, Grace.'

'Pleasure to meet you Grace. I'm Jeffrey.'

'Jeffrey,' Niamh said aloud in the hope that it might trigger some sort of memory. 'Jeffrey.' Suddenly recognition lit up her face and she slapped him on the arm. 'You're Jeffrey the American, from Portofino,' she shrieked. 'You had me quietly freaking out there trying to remember what wild night I met you.' She laughed with relief and felt her face flush.

'I'm sorry. I couldn't resist it. It was clear that you had absolutely no idea who I was and, as crushing as that was, it was even more fun to tease you.'

'Jesus, don't frighten a girl like that, will you? I was wondering what kind of wild night you meant.' She turned to Grace, who was still watching with amusement. 'I met Jeffrey the day I went to Portofino for lunch. He caught me talking to myself at the pier and was gentleman enough not to comment on it. Gentleman until now, that is. You just lost that status!'

'Yes, I'm sorry. That is all entirely true,' he said, shaking Grace's hand. 'It was the middle of the day and I tried to buy her a coffee but she was not to be persuaded. She was intent upon her lunch date and she stuck to her guns. You are wrong about the American part though,' he said turning back to face Niamh. 'I'm Canadian.'

'Oh, sorry. I just assumed you were American. I can't tell the accents apart. What are you doing here?' Niamh asked, hoping for a change in conversation.

'Here in Liguria or here in this restaurant?'

'Well, both I suppose.'

'I've been studying at the university in Genoa for the past two semesters as an international student and, apart from a few inconvenient exams in a couple of weeks, I'm just about done. And as for this restaurant, well, my friend is on the guest list and I'm tagging along for the free food.'

'Oh, right. You did say you were here for the summer or something like that.'

'Aha, so you do remember,' he said, smiling.

'The conversation is coming back to me now. What are you studying?'

'Law and international business. I've been working my tail off for the past few years and when I go home I have to take up a placement with one of the big law firms in Canada or the US, so I'm planning to take the summer off. I figure it might be the last chance I have to do something utterly irresponsible and selfish.'

'What better place to do that?' Grace offered. 'I'm beginning to feel like I'm the only person here who is not changing her life in some way and choosing Italy. It's really all a bit depressing. I may need another drink.'

'Allow me,' he offered without hesitation. 'Franciacorta? Two?'

'Yes, please,' they said, again in unison.

Jeffrey made his way to the champagne bar as people were starting to take their seats at the tables. Grace turned to her sister and raised both hands in the air. 'What are you out here? Who are you? Some kind of man magnet? What the hell is going on?'

'What? What do you mean?' Niamh asked in a high-pitched voice.

'First Giorgio with the café and the boat and now this Canadian taking the summer off and just hanging out here. I mean, who are these people and how do you know them all? This is not the quiet Niamh from Finlay Place in Dublin that I know, the one who orders Chinese food every Thursday night of her life without fail. Who the hell are you and what have they done with my predictable sister?'

Niamh giggled. 'Grace, I just met this guy sitting on a wall at the marina in Portofino. He asked me if I wanted coffee, just like he asked you if you wanted champagne just now. That's it. That can happen to anyone. It's nothing more than that. Before he walked up to us here I had spent an entire three minutes in his company in a piazza in Portofino. I have no idea what he's doing here at this opening night thing or who he knows to score an invitation from. And, as for Giorgio, his brother owns the café and his fiancée ran off and left him for another man, so he was sad and depressed and apparently hooked up with that goddess in the red dress. It's not like either of them are here hanging off my arm or dancing with me under the stars. You're exaggerating this like you always do everything! It's like you have this vision of me slotting into life here, finding the perfect man and living happily ever after.'

'Well, of course I do. Then I can come visit and stay in your fabulous villa! I think it's a perfect life plan for you.'

Jeffrey returned with three glasses of champagne. 'Where are you ladies sitting?'

'Over there in those two seats,' Grace said, pointing to the chairs Emily had indicated.

'My friend's not here yet. Mind if I join you?'

'Sure!' Grace answered before Niamh had a chance to draw her breath. 'As long as there is a free seat.'

'I'll make sure that there is. This is a much better idea than trying to follow a conversation with someone else in Italian. I've been here six months and my Italian is still pretty awful.' With that, he took off in the direction of the tables and their allocated seats.

# Chapter Sixteen

Jeffrey had somehow managed to shuffle the place cards so that he was able to sit next to Grace and across from Niamh. Sara had changed from her red silk dress into her chef's whites as course after course came out from the kitchen. She came and introduced each of the courses as they were served, describing the ingredients and the preparation of the food. The sommelier did the same as the wines changed with each course. It was a study in Italian fine dining, an exquisite meal from beginning to end.

Jeffrey and the two girls chatted and laughed easily across the table. He was very good company – charming, witty, self-deprecating and utterly easy to be around. Emily sat a few seats from them and checked in after the first course was served to make sure the girls were having a good time. She needn't have worried. Niamh couldn't remember the last time she'd had such a wonderful evening and she was pretty sure that Grace felt the same way, judging by the constant grin painted on her face.

The sky had grown black and the stars sat like splatters on a canvas far above their heads. Cicadas creaked and croaked in the bushes and a light sea breeze slapped miniature waves against the cliff face beneath them. It was heady and intoxicating.

After dinner the string quartet resumed as a display of desserts was set up on one side of the terrace. Coffee and after-dinner drinks were served along with more champagne, and the festivities carried on for hours.

'So you two are here with Emily tonight?' Jeffrey had asked in a break between courses.

'Yes, we're her guests. What about you? You said you were here with a friend?'

'Yeah. My buddy from law school in Genoa is Sara's younger brother. He asked if he could bring a friend, so here I am.'

'So where is this friend?' Niamh asked looking around. She hadn't seen him with anyone else all evening.

'Well, I took the ferry here from Genoa earlier today. I wanted to wander around and have lunch before going on to the restaurant, but my buddy decided he'd take his own boat. His own, very old boat, that is now sitting somewhere out in the Golfo Paradiso waiting to be tugged in to shore.' He sat back against his chair laughing. 'In hindsight, the ferry wasn't such a bad idea after all.'

'Oh no, his boat broke down?'

'Yep. He's fine. I mean, the coast guard people, whoever they are, have already been in contact with him and they are arranging for a tug, but he just has to sit there and wait until the tug reaches him.'

'But do you know anyone else here?' Grace asked.

'Nope. He just told me where to go and said he'd meet me here if he got towed in to the port in time.'

'Oh God, the eejit! Imagine missing a party like this because his boat broke down.' Niamh giggled.

'Excuse me? What's an "eejit"?'

'Oh, it's an Irish word for idiot or gobshite.'

'Gobshite?' Jeffrey looked even more confused.

Niamh giggled again. 'Sorry, another Irish word for idiot.'

'"Gobshite." I like that. It's very emotive. I'll have to use that one. Oh, speak of the devil!' he continued. 'Hey, Franco! Over here!' he said, waving furiously at his friend. 'You're just in time. Dinner is over!' All four of them laughed.

Sara came out and hugged her brother, rattling off a rapid stream of Italian and gesturing towards the kitchen.

'If you will excuse me, my dinner has been saved for me in the kitchen,' Franco said with a faint American accent.

Once he had been fed he rejoined the group at the table and regaled them with the story of being stuck in the middle of the bay with only darkness and the odd jumping fish for company until the coast guard came and berated him for being so stupid in the first place.

'I thought they had come to rescue me, not to yell at me,' he said in perfect English. 'I was happier in the bay in the darkness before these men showed up to tell me how reckless I had been.' He laughed, and sipped his wine.

'Your English is excellent,' Grace said appreciatively.

'Oh, thank you, that's kind of you to say. It's the result of years of international schools. My father was in the military and wherever we lived, we were educated in international schools, with English being the common language.'

'Where do you live now?' Niamh asked.

'Well, my family are all in Rome, except for my sister Sara. I've been studying in Genoa for the past few years and that is coming to an end this summer, so I guess I have some decisions to make.'

'Did you study law, too?'

'For my sins, yes, and now I embark on a legal career, but not until the end of summer. Right, Jeffrey?'

His accent might have almost been American, but he looked very much Italian.

'Amen to that. One perfect, lazy summer coming up,' Jeffrey replied, raising his glass in salute.

'God, I'm so envious of you all! I can't imagine an entire lazy summer anywhere, let alone in Italy,' Grace said, draining a bottle of red wine into her glass.

'I think I know where she stocks that,' Franco said with a smile, nodding to the bottle of wine. He got up and moved out past them towards the kitchen.

'I'll give you a hand,' Jeffrey said, and he stood up to help his friend scout out more wine.

'I can't believe I have to go home tomorrow,' Grace said, twirling her wine glass and watching the legs roll down the inside. 'I'm depressed at the thought of it.'

'Well, if it's any help, I won't be having a lazy summer. I'm about to get up to my ears in God knows what crap to fix up a ramshackle café and try to make a living from it.'

'Fair enough.' Grace grinned. 'Hardly the glamorous life, but still, it is Italy.'

'Yep, that's true. I'll have to learn some Italian in a hurry, though, or I'll be lost before I even start.'

'Well, how many weeks do you think it will take you to get the place ready to open?'

'I don't know – a few weeks, certainly. It needs a bit of work, and not just cleaning.'

'Well then, just apply yourself to learning Italian at the same time. You'd be surprised at how quickly you'll pick up the basics.'

'Yeah, good idea. Maybe I could get a tutor or something?'

'Is that code for lover?' Grace asked mischievously.

'Grace. The last thing I want is a man. I'm just getting over the last one.'

'Well, you know what they say about the best way to get over a man . . . '

'No, I don't, and I don't think I want to know,' Niamh said firmly. 'I'm here to fix my life, remember? Not complicate it further by adding another man into the mix. Give me a break!'

'Fair enough. Suit yourself, but celibacy is overrated. Just look at the number of nuns leaving the church. They're running screaming from convents looking for a penis.'

'Grace! That's disgusting! You can't talk about nuns like that!' Niamh was horrified.

'What's this about nuns?' Emily asked from behind them. 'I haven't spoken to you two all evening, but by the looks of things you were having a fine time.' She smiled.

'Oh, so much fun! Thank you so much for inviting us, Emily. What a fabulous evening,' Niamh gushed.

'Now, tell me, where are you going to stay until you get yourself settled? Have you thought about it?' she asked Niamh.

'Well, I took a look online and there are all kinds of Airbnb options in Camogli, so I rented one for the next month. It's a little one-bedroom apartment on the third floor of one of those old buildings on the upper level of town. It's small but really cute. Plus, I get a discount for renting it for a month, so I'm checking out of the hotel tomorrow.'

'Good idea. I think that's a smart move. It reduces your overheads significantly and in the meantime you can decide what you want to do on a more long-term basis.' Emily nodded in approval. 'And that will give you enough time to get the café up and running, and you can fix up the place upstairs at the same time.'

'What do you mean the place upstairs?' Niamh asked with a frown.

'Do not tell me that she's going to be able to live over the café?' Grace asked, turning to face Emily. 'If it all works out this perfectly I swear I'm just going to shoot myself.'

'Well, of course, darling. What did you think was upstairs?'

'I didn't know, I mean ... I didn't think that the upstairs went with the café!'

Emily sighed. 'Niamh, darling, you are renting the entire building. That means the bottom half and the top half.'

'Sweet Jesus, she doesn't even know what she's renting.' Grace shook her head. 'Emily, will you please keep an eye on her when I'm gone?'

'Of course, darling. But Niamh, you had to know that you were renting the entire building, surely?'

'I didn't think about it. I only saw the downstairs, and I haven't seen the contract yet, so I've seen nothing in writing. I just looked around the café and thought I could make it work, I never thought about the upstairs,' she replied, feeling entirely foolish.

The two boys returned with a bottle of champagne and two more bottles of red wine.

'Oh, marvellous! I'll have another glass of red wine please, Franco,' Emily said, handing him her glass, 'and then cut me off or I shall die tomorrow. And welcome back, darling! We haven't seen you in Camogli in ages.'

The group continued chatting for the next hour, with Franco entertaining them with story after story. Niamh was relieved to have someone change the subject, until Giorgio suddenly appeared by their table with Sara by his side.

'I'm sorry to interrupt, but I must take the boat back soon,' he said, more to Emily than to anyone else. 'The mayor and his wife have already left, so we have room for two more if you boys want to return to Camogli on the boat.'

'Well, given Captain Franco's adventures earlier today, I'd be delighted to take a ride back with you, that's very kind,' Jeffrey said, grinning at Franco.

'Yes, as I am without a boat, a lift back to Camogli would be great, thank you, Giorgio,' Franco said graciously.

'Oh, boo, must we break up the party so early, Giorgio? It's only half past midnight,' Emily said feigning a sulk.

He laughed. '*Sì cara*. I'm afraid so. Tomorrow I will sail with some friends in the morning and must be up early to get the boat ready. You will thank me for this tomorrow, no?' He nodded in the direction of the collection of empty wine bottles.

'Yes, I suppose I will,' Emily sighed. 'Sara, are you coming back with us?'

'No, my dear, I must stay here. Tomorrow is my last day off for the season and we reopen to the public on Monday, so it will be a busy day.'

'Spoilsports, all of you! Now, Giorgio, I have a question for you—'

'Don't!' Niamh insisted, but Emily continued, unfazed. 'The building that Niamh will rent from you . . . '

'Who?' asked Franco, confused. 'Who is Niamh?'

'Oh, for goodness' sake, these names get very confusing after a few glasses of wine, Niamh . . . Nina . . . I'm referring to the building that she will rent from you. Is she renting only the ground floor, or the entire building?'

'I don't understand the question, Emilia,' Giorgio replied, sounding confused.

'You quoted her a price to rent the building, to open the café again. Is that for just the ground floor or does it also include the upstairs?'

'It is the whole building, of course.' He turned to Niamh. 'You did not know this?'

'Umm, actually, no, I didn't realise … I mean, I hadn't thought about the upstairs …' She faded off quietly, realising that everyone at the table was now staring at her. She felt herself begin to blush.

'So, you think it was a good price for the lower half, no?'

'Yes,' she agreed.

Giorgio threw his head back and laughed. 'So now, is an even better price, no? Because you get the upstairs half for free, no?'

To Niamh's mortification, he found this hilariously funny and roared with laughter, causing her to blush a crimson red.

'So glad that I could provide the entertainment tonight,' she grimaced.

'Don't worry, I can show you tomorrow, when I return from the sailing. I will be back by lunchtime and can show you in the afternoon.'

'OK. Grace has a car picking her up at noon, so I could make my way to Camogli then.'

'Don't remind me,' Grace groaned. 'The holiday is over and back to the grind I go.'

'Very well. I have your number. I will text you in the afternoon to show you the other half of your building,' Giorgio said. '*Va bene?*'

'OK, yes. *Va bene.* That sounds good,' Niamh said quietly, mortified at her mistake.

'See you all at the pier in twenty minutes,' he said as he walked off with Sara. Niamh watched as she accompanied him down the slope to the pier.

Niamh found herself feeling irrationally envious of Sara. She had hardly spoken to her during the evening, but it was clear that she was a very talented chef, had her own successful business, as well as being tall, slender and beautiful – the kind of woman who could pull off a long red silk dress. Sara seemed to be a woman for whom life had come together, but there was definitely something cold and aloof about her that wasn't in keeping with the kind and generous descriptions Emily had shared of her. And then there was the fact that she was accompanying Giorgio down to the pier to say goodbye, alone . . .

Niamh sighed and turned her gaze towards the glittering lights up in the trees.

'What's the matter?' Jeffrey asked her quietly.

'Oh, sorry, was my sigh that loud?'

'Yep. Was that one meant to be in your head?' he asked, turning his head sideways to look at her.

'I suppose so. Sorry, there's nothing wrong. I was just thinking, that's all.'

'That's a dangerous pursuit and not one that I'd recommend. You'll never find contentment if you are constantly thinking and weighing up your life.'

She looked at him, wondering if he had read into her sigh and guessed correctly what was going on in her head, or if he had just said the right thing by chance.

'You're right,' she smiled. 'Sometimes I get stuck in my own head so much I don't even know if I'm thinking or speaking out loud. Gets me into all sorts of trouble!'

Jeffrey threw his head back and laughed. 'I bet.'

'All right, you lot,' Emily said, corralling the five of them towards the pier. 'Giorgio is always late for everything but he hates it when others keep him waiting. One of life's ironies, I'm afraid, but it's either him or call a water taxi, and I, for one, don't plan on missing this ride.'

They made their way to Giorgio's boat. He kissed Sara and hugged her before stepping aboard. The rest of the little group thanked Sara again and said goodnight, stepping onto the boat one by one. As Niamh, last in line, stepped on board, Giorgio turned and offered her a hand, but Jeffrey had been standing, waiting to do so. Giorgio directed his attention back to the controls and turned some dials. Emily looked from one to the other of them, then patted the wooden deck alongside her and indicated for Niamh to sit.

'Hold on tight. He likes to go fast in the dark!' Emily said, as Giorgio reversed out from the little pier towards the open bay.

The boat took off and the blast of cool air was intense. No one said a word. It would have been hard to shout above the engine and instead each was lost in their own thoughts as they powered towards the marina. An exhilarating ten or so minutes later they slowed down to round the bend and enter the still waters of the marina, backlit by streetlights glowing orange along the pier.

Emily said goodnight to the group and goodbye to Grace and headed home.

'Come back and visit us soon!' she threw over her shoulder to Grace.

Jeffrey called a taxi for Niamh and Grace as they had missed the last ferry going in the direction of Santa Margherita. Minutes later a car pulled up and Jeffrey opened the back door for them, telling the driver in Italian where to take them.

'Meet me for lunch tomorrow,' he said quietly to Niamh, as she went to step into the car.

She hesitated and looked up at him. 'I don't know. I . . . '

'I heard you say that you're coming here anyway tomorrow to see the upstairs that you didn't realise you had.' He grinned. 'Look, no pressure. It's up to you. But it's just lunch and you have to have lunch anyway, you know?' He shrugged and waited for her answer.

'Yes, OK. You're right, it's just lunch. I can probably be here by about one o'clock, after Grace leaves.'

'OK, I know exactly where I'll take you. Meet me right back here at one o'clock then.'

'Right here?'

'Yes, it's as easy a place as any, right?'

'OK.' She smiled as she got into the car.

'*A domani*,' he said closing the door and tapping on the roof.

# Chapter Seventeen

The next morning the two sisters awoke reluctantly to the sound of church bells ringing out throughout the town.

Niamh stumbled out of bed first, rummaging through her bag for headache tablets. 'Ugh,' she groaned. 'How can they possibly be gone? I brought two boxes.'

'They're in the bathroom,' Grace mumbled through sheets in the next bed. 'I took some last night.'

'Smart. I should have done that. Ugh, I've a red-wine headache,' Niamh moaned, padding into the bathroom.

'Well, we were also drinking champagne like there was an alcoholic drought forecast and we might not see a drink for six months. Mixing is the worst—'

'Can we not talk about it please, Grace? It's not helping.'

'What time is it?'

'Ten. I counted the bells just now. I can't find my phone.'

'Oh God, I need to get moving, my car comes at noon.'

'Do you want to get breakfast first or pack first?' Niamh asked, before chugging back a glass of misty-coloured dissolved medicine.

'Breakfast. I can't pack now. My head hurts. I need carbs. Bread, toast, butter ... everything that is bad for me. Do you think they'd make spaghetti carbonara for breakfast?'

'Probably not. Let's get some bread and tea and things. You'll feel better once you've eaten.'

The two of them moved slowly, rooting through bags for suitable clothes – nothing too tight, too short or too bright. If they could have gone to breakfast in sweatpants they would have, but it just wasn't that kind of place.

'You know, if Jennifer Lopez was staying here, or one of the Kardashians, they'd rock down to breakfast in a pair of sweatpants and still look hot,' Niamh grumbled, as she threw on a loose, lightweight shirt.

'Well, first, they'd be wearing some four-thousand-dollar version of sweatpants, and, second, they are all skinny as razors and would have some amazing crop top showing off a perfectly toned midriff, so no one would be focused on the sweatpants, even if they had cost four thousand dollars,' Grace mumbled matter-of-factly.

'Fair point. Are you ready yet? If you're not ready then I'm going to have to lie down again. Standing up is hard work this morning.'

'No, I'm ready. Let's go.'

They stumbled their way quietly through breakfast, downing black tea and sparkling water. As they got back to the room, Grace turned to her sister, squinting back the headache that sat behind her eyes and said, 'OK, I'm going to pack and you are going to call Mam. I'm not getting on that plane if you haven't dealt with this, and you've just run out of time. Got it?'

'Oh God, I was hoping I wouldn't have to do this with a hangover.'

'Niamh, I—'

'All right, all right, I'll call her now,' Niamh groaned. She retrieved her phone from under the bed and stepped out into the corridor to call home.

'Hello?'

'Hi, Mam, it's Niamh.'

'Oh, hello, love. Well? Have you two had a great week?'

'Yeah, great. It was fabulous.'

'You sound tired. Are you all right?'

'Oh yeah, I'm fine. Just a bit of a sore throat, I think.'

'Was the hotel lovely?'

'Gorgeous. Very fancy, actually, but not pretentious, if you know what I mean.'

'Oh, that's lovely. Are you all set for your flight tonight?'

'Actually, that's why I'm calling.'

'Oh, before I forget to tell you, the internet is gone out here so you won't have any when you get home. The man is coming out to look at it tomorrow but he said he mightn't get to us until the afternoon, but I said that would be fine. I don't know what happened to it, but it went out two days ago, and sure, I hardly use it so I kept forgetting to call about it.'

'That's fine, it doesn't matter, actually.'

'Now what time do you two land tonight?'

'Not until about midnight.'

'Oh Lord, that's very late. Are you coming straight home or will you stay at your sister's place?'

'Well, actually, that's why I'm calling. I won't be going home.'

'No problem. I thought you might stay at Grace's anyway tonight because I knew the flight was landing at some late hour. Sure, there is no hurry anyway. You're not going back to work tomorrow, are you?'

'No, Mam, I'm not going back to work tomorrow.'

'Good, you can have a bit of a rest so when you get home. Oh and your dad said to tell you that your magazine arrived during the week.'

'What magazine?'

'The new one your dad got for you. The cooking one.'

'Oh. Right.' Niamh rolled her eyes, hoping this wouldn't be an extended segment of the conversation. She had completely forgotten that she had signed up for a new *Food & Wine* subscription weeks earlier. Her dad had read out an advertisement from his fishing magazine about a special offer.

'You should get that, Niamh,' he had said, explaining that he thought it would be good for her. 'You could try new recipes and they teach you about wine, too. That sounds like something you'd like, doesn't it? And it's only twelve euros for the whole year. Sure that's great value.'

She had agreed that it was and he had filled in the coupon and pulled it out of the fishing magazine. 'Una, will you post that tomorrow for her? If I ask her to do it herself it'll end up at the bottom of her bag, or will be stuck on the fridge for the next month and the special offer will be gone. It says that it expires at the end of the month, so get it in the post.'

'I will,' her mother had replied, rooting in the drawer for an envelope. 'And she can be cooking all kinds of weird things for you to try. Won't you, Nina?'

Niamh shook her head, jolting back to the present conversation.

'Mam, it doesn't matter about the magazine,' she said, interrupting her mother's banter. 'I'm not getting the flight home tonight.'

'What? Is something wrong? Did something happen?'

'No, nothing happened.'

'What about your sister Grace? Is she coming home tonight? Was your flight cancelled? Is there a problem?'

'No, there is no problem, and yes, she is still on the flight tonight.'

'Grace is coming home, but you're not? Why on earth aren't you coming home? Have the two of you had a fight or something?'

'No, Mam, it's nothing like that. It's just ... I don't know how to explain this so it won't sound ridiculous, but I've just decided to stay.'

'For how long? Another week, or what? What are you talking about, Nina? What about work? When are you going back to work?'

'I'm not going back, Mam. I quit.'

'Quit?' her mother gasped. 'What do you mean, you quit?'

'Mam, I can't go back there. I just can't. I can't face going into work every day and seeing him there. It's just not going to work.'

'Jesus, Mary and Joseph, she's after quitting her job, Paddy. Your father is coming to the phone now.'

'Mam, will you stop? Look, it's this simple. I'm not going back there to work. I don't want anything to do with him or that bloody place. I have savings so I'm fine. I got here and it's just fabulous, really fabulous, and I know it sounds crazy but I just feel right at home here. The people are lovely, the place is stunning, the food is amazing, I just love everything about it.'

'But, love, you're on holidays. Everything is supposed to be lovely, but then at the end of it you're supposed to come home. I know that the breakup was hard, but you can't just abandon everything you've worked for. You're just not thinking straight.'

'What I've abandoned or given up is nothing, Mam. The job was an average job, I never loved it, and to be honest it was just a job that paid the bills. I won't miss it and I won't miss going in there every day. I'm thirty-three years old and I've never done anything that I've actually loved. You're always telling us to grab life by the arse and get out there and do something with our lives, so that's what I'm going to do.'

'Jesus, Mary and Joseph,' her mother recited again. 'So now you're going to take my advice when you're off out in a foreign country? You never took it at home when I meant that you should get another job or go back to school.'

'See, well, I'm doing it now instead … and no, I never listened to you before and nothing ever changed. All I ever did was the same thing, day in and day out, boring, reliable, uninteresting Niamh with a boyfriend who clearly didn't give a toss about her in the end. Well, that stops now. I'm going to stay here and give it a shot.'

'What on earth are you going to do? And where are you going to stay? You can't afford to stay in that fancy hotel, surely?'

'No. I found an Airbnb for a few weeks until I get settled.'

'A what?'

'Airbnb. It's like an apartment that you rent for a few days or weeks at a time. You know, short term rentals. I rented it for a few weeks until I figure out where I'm going to live.'

'Good Lord, no, I've never heard of it. And what about work? Money?'

'I'm going to rent a little café. It's a place in the village that needs some work. I'm going to fix it up and open with a simple menu – you know, sandwiches, salads, stuff like that. It's nothing fancy, not a restaurant or anything, it's just a small place, but it's cute and I got it for a great deal.'

'Good God, but you don't know anything about running a café. I don't know what to say. Your father wants a word.'

She could hear mumbled chatter as her mother handed the phone to her father.

'Niamh?'

'Hi, Dad,' she replied, grimacing and bracing herself for his response.

'Are you all right?'

'Yes, I'm fine, Dad. I'm grand, honestly.'

'And what's going on? You want to stay there, is that it?'

'Yes, I'm going to stay here and open a little café. I've already found one, Dad, a small place in town.'

'When did you decide all this?'

'Earlier in the week. Grace has seen it too, and the village that I'll be staying . . . I mean, living in. And I'm moving into an apartment later today, after Grace leaves.'

'I see. And is everything else all right?'

'Yes, everything's grand, Dad. Why, what do you mean?'

'Do you need money?'

'No, I have savings. I have enough to do this and live for about six months.'

'Good girl. I'm glad that you saved while you had that job. No woman should ever be dependent on anyone else, or any man, for that matter. Your independence is everything, Niamh, that's your freedom. If you have that, then you can stand on your own two feet and you don't need anyone. I'm glad you have that, that's good. Good girl.'

She felt her eyes sting with tears. She hadn't expected him to get mad, but she had thought that he might not understand her rash decision and instead think she was crazy to throw away 'a good job', as he put it. She could hear her mother gasp in the background and could imagine her trying to pull the phone out of her father's hand.

'Sure you couldn't go back to that job and face that little fecker every day, not after the way he treated you. So, if this is what you want to do then just go for it, but do it right. It's a big decision to walk away from your job, so make sure you do something properly, not half-arsed. Do you hear me?'

'Yes, I do,' she said quietly. She bit her bottom lip and

blinked back tears, trying not to let her emotions register in her voice.

'Well then, that's that so. Sure, you're only in Italy. It's not as if you're moving to Australia. Isn't that right, Una?' Niamh could hear him chuckle. 'Right, I'll put you back on to your mother. She's huffing and puffing here next to me, but don't worry, she'll calm down eventually. At the end of the day you have to try new things, otherwise what's it all for? Isn't that so? You'll be grand. Here's your mother, bye now,' he said as he handed the phone back to his wife.

'Yep. Thanks, Dad. Bye.'

'Well, I don't know what's gotten into him,' her mother huffed. 'He must have been reading one of my psychology magazines, because normally he'd be a raging lunatic at the thoughts of you giving up a fine job.'

'It's no longer a fine job, Una,' Niamh heard him retort in the background. 'That prick ruined it for her and she's better off without him, if you ask me. If I got my hands on him I'd give him what's what, the little runt. Now, will you let the girl alone and let her get on with her life?'

'Lord God Almighty, it's like I'm living with Gandhi suddenly,' her mother said sarcastically. 'I'm just worried about you, Nina, that's all. I'm not trying to ruin your fun, I just want to make sure that you're not making a mistake, that's all.'

'I know, Mam, and I'm not. Or, if I am, then I'll just come home. I just want to try it, that's all. I've never done anything like this in my life and it just feels right. I just want to get settled in here and then I'll come home in a few weeks and get more of my clothes and stuff.'

'Well, this is quite a surprise. Tell your sister that I'll want to see her when she gets home to get the whole story. And you're sure that everything else is all right?'

'Yes, Mam, I promise. Everything is good. I'm fine, honestly.'

'All right so then, well, mind yourself and call again in a few days to let us know how you're getting on, will you?'

'I will. Thanks, Mam.'

'All right, love. Chat to you soon.'

'OK, Mam. Bye.' Niamh heard her mother begin her chant of 'Jesus, Mary and Joseph' as she took the phone from her ear to end the call. No doubt this conversation would go on for a while yet in the Kelly household this evening. Niamh was relieved that conversation was over and grateful that they had tried to be somewhat understanding. She was most surprised by her dad's reaction. Who knew that he'd be the supportive one in all this? she thought as she waited for Grace to zip up her bag.

The car was waiting for them downstairs.

'Being hungover actually helps with goodbyes, I think. It's hard to focus on anything 'cause my brain is fuzzy on the inside, so I won't get all sad and weepy,' Niamh joked.

'Just be grateful that you're not travelling in this condition for the next seven hours. What was I thinking?' Grace moaned out loud. 'Good luck with everything and don't sit and dwell on stuff too much. You've made your decision so just get stuck in. Everything else will fall into place as it's supposed to.'

'OK, thanks. And sorry in advance for the Spanish inquisition that you'll get at home.'

'That's all right. I'll just avoid them for the next few days. Call me during the week, OK?'

'I will. Bye!' Niamh waved madly as the car turned and made its way down the long driveway.

# Chapter Eighteen

Niamh sat on the top deck of the ferry, her head hanging out over the side. She figured she probably looked like a dog with its tongue hanging out and its head stuck out of the window of a car, but she didn't care. The air felt good. She had raced to get her luggage packed up and stored with the bellman before checking out at noon and she was already regretting agreeing to meet Jeffrey for lunch. That had definitely been the wine talking. She barely knew him, she generally didn't like meeting new people, she was sleep deprived and the last thing she wanted right now was to get involved with a man at any level. Those were four solid reasons not to show up as planned on the pier, but she felt bad about standing him up. She wouldn't like it. 'Do unto others, Nina . . . ' She could hear her mother's words ringing in her head.

She got to the pier at two minutes past one and made her way to the spot where they had disembarked the night previously. She frowned and looked around. There was no sign of Jeffrey. She sat on the low wall at the pier's edge and dangled her legs over the side, staring down into the water. She pulled out her phone and texted Grace to see how she was doing. She checked the time. She strolled to the end of the pier and back, snapping some shots of the boats in the harbour. She checked the time again. It was quarter past one.

'Am I in the right place?' she muttered, before she noticed Giorgio's boat moored just a few feet away. 'Yep, you're in the right place, Niamh, but he's not here. He stood me up!' She fumed. While she was busy working herself up into a small, quiet rage, she also acknowledged that, while she was pissed off, she was actually a little relieved to not have to sit through lunch with a practical stranger. 'Who does that!' she huffed, and headed back in the direction she had just come, making her way up the steps and walking briskly to the far end of the promenade.

The restaurants were already busy with families and groups of friends out for Sunday lunch. She walked to the last restaurant at the opposite end of the pier and did a quick scan of the crowd. Perfect, no familiar faces, she thought as she stood in the entrance.

'*Allora, signora, buongiorno,*' the host said, as he came to greet her.

'*Umm . . . Buongiorno, solo uno per favore,*' she said, raising one finger as if it weren't clear enough that she was alone. Jilted, party of one! she thought to herself.

'*Ah, brava. Un momento, signora.*'

'Did he just say "brava"?' He did. He just congratulated me for dining alone, and on a Sunday too,' she muttered, shaking her head. 'How very Rosa Parks of me it was to venture out alone to have lunch. Niamh Kelly, single, radical and fearless – not afraid to eat alone in Italy in public on a Sunday. Her actions might just change the world for singles everywhere,' she mocked. 'Clearly not the done thing in Italy.'

The waiter sat her at a corner table and she scanned the other tables to see what people were eating. The menu made her mouth water just by reading it. A basket of warm bread was placed to her left and another waiter appeared and poured her a glass of something bubbly. She looked around again and realised that all the tables had glasses of bubbles. Must be a Sunday thing, she thought appreciatively.

She ordered a glass of local white wine, caprese salad and a bowl of *spaghetti pomodoro*. She moved her chair so she wasn't facing directly into the sun, and adjusted her sunglasses to sit up high on her nose. She spent the next two hours luxuriating over bread, wine and food, and all with the most perfect views of the bay. She sent a photo of her lunch to Grace by text.

*Jealous! I'm still in the car, ravenous and queasy at the same time.*

She ordered an espresso and replayed the conversation with Jeffrey in her head. She tried to convince herself that she wasn't too bothered, but it actually had stung a little to have been stood up. Even though she was glad that she hadn't had to feign interest in any kind of conversation or make small talk, she couldn't help feeling rejected for the second time in a matter of weeks. Maybe he had changed his mind in the cold light of day? Maybe he'd forgotten? It didn't matter, she decided. The chances were she might not even see him again as he lived in Genoa. Anyway it was best not to complicate things right now.

She got to the café early and waited for Giorgio. He was late, as usual. Her phone buzzed and a message flashed up from an Italian number. It was Giorgio. He apologised, explaining that he was delayed and directing her to where a key was stashed outside, telling her to let herself in if she was there already. She fished the key from the hanging flower basket that held the remains of some dead weeds and dried, crumbling earth and unlocked the door. It felt different being here alone. There wasn't a sound to be heard, except for her footsteps on the old tiles.

She stood behind the little bar and ran her hand along the counter, leaving a trail in the dust. There was all manner of boxes stashed behind the counter, some unopened and others in disarray. The coffee machine was thick with dust and grime and what she suspected might be a coffee grinder had spider's webs running from its lid to the coffee machine, making a footbridge for the tiny spiders that called the place home.

She wandered down the narrow corridor behind the counter. The last time she was here she had assumed that it led to a bathroom and nothing more. This time she noticed a second door, which revealed a staircase behind it.

'OK, that's why I didn't see any stairs. Well, at least you're not entirely thick, Niamh,' she muttered to herself. 'It's not like there was a staircase staring you in the face that you just completely missed. Anyone could have missed this!' She felt marginally vindicated from not having realised that there was an upstairs to her building.

She made her way upstairs, the steps creaking as she went. The small landing at the top gave way to three rooms. The first door at the top of the stairs revealed a bathroom. Like the rest of the place it was dusty, but she couldn't help but admire the original pedestal sink, the old mirror on the wall and the antique glass doorknobs. The floor was tiled with vintage dusky pink and black tiles and a similar colour scheme complemented the walls. The other two rooms had clearly been used as storage rooms as they contained dozens of boxes – again, some unopened, and some with all kinds of paraphernalia spewing out like entrails from the inside and onto the floor.

One of the two rooms faced onto the narrow street below, while the other faced west and looked out over rooftops towards the bay. 'Not only did I not know I had an upstairs, but I have an upstairs with a sea view!' she exclaimed, as she threw open the two windows and leaned out. She took a picture of the rooftops and the glistening bay in the distance and sent it to Grace.

*Where's that?* came the immediate text response.

*That's my upstairs! Can you believe it?*

*Holy shit, that's fabulous! Can you live there?*

*I don't know, I suppose so. I'll have to ask Giorgio. There might be rules about the use of the building.*

*OK, keep me posted. I'm getting ready to board here soon. Will text you when I land and I'll call tomorrow!*

*OK, safe flight!*

'It is quite a view, no?' Niamh jumped and dropped her phone, whipping around to see Giorgio standing in the doorway. 'Damn it, Giorgio, you can't just walk up on someone like that. You frightened the life out of me.'

'Oh, I am sorry. I thought you heard me come up the stairs.'

'No, I didn't,' she said, bending to retrieve her phone from the floor. 'Jesus, my heart is pounding.'

'I am sorry. I did not mean to frighten you. I see you have found the upstairs.' He grinned, still enjoying the fact that she hadn't known she was renting the top half of the building. 'I have not been up here for a very long time. It is ... how you say ... a big mess?'

'Yeah, but it just needs a good cleaning, to be fair. What was this place used for?'

'It was never really used for anything. My father bought the building a long time ago and the café was downstairs, but this was always just used for storage.'

'Did anyone ever live here?'

'No, I don't think so. At least not since my father

bought the building.' He crossed the room and sat on the window ledge alongside her. 'What are you thinking to do up in here?'

'Well, given that I didn't even know that it existed all along, I haven't really thought about it,' she said, shrugging. 'Are there any usage restrictions?'

'No, this building is old. It was built before any usage rules were created, so there are no restrictions for what you can do inside. Outside you have to maintain the building as it is – no changes are allowed.'

'OK, that's cool,' she said, looking around. 'And what should I do about all this stuff? Does someone want it? Or should I put it somewhere?'

'I think if it has been here for so many years, then no one even remembers that it is here, so you can just get rid of anything that is in your way. Some of these things might be helpful,' he said, standing up and turning some boxes so the labels faced him. 'Some were for the café, so you can use them if you like. Some are just rubbish.' He gestured to the open boxes with their contents spilling onto the floor.

'OK, what do I do with rubbish? I mean the big stuff like these boxes?'

'There is a place to take it to but you need a car or . . . *come si dice, un camion . . .*'

'A truck?'

'*Sì*, yes, a truck. You need a truck to get there. If you move the things that you do not want and put them inside the door downstairs, I will have someone come to take it for you.'

'Oh, that would be great, thank you.'

'Just let me know when you are ready and I will send someone. Now, I must go. *Ecco* . . . these are for you.' He reached into his pocket and handed her a set of keys.

'I'm getting the keys already? But I haven't signed anything yet.'

Giorgio smiled. 'Nina, what are you afraid that you will do? I am not afraid, so I give you the keys. Don't worry so much . . . is bad for you. Tomorrow I will come back with the agreement for you to sign. You will be here tomorrow, no?'

'Yes, I'll be here first thing in the morning. So you don't want me to go to your office?'

'No, no, I come here to you. Is easy for me. This time I will make more noise so I do not frighten . . . what did you say . . . your life out of you?'

'Something like that, yes.' She grinned.

'*Arrivederci*,' he said, with a small nod of his head. '*A domani.*'

She hadn't intended to get stuck into any real work, but as she poked through some boxes it became clear that most of them would need to be dumped. She spent the next few hours opening boxes, labelling those that she might use in the future and stacking them in a corner. Any open boxes containing stuff that was of no use to her were shoved to the landing at the top of the stairs. She found a roll of black bin liners and filled six of them with pieces of old paper and cardboard, old paper cups, receipts, magazines and newspapers, lugging them down the stairs one at a time.

Several boxes contained foil packages of coffee beans. She would have to ask someone if they were even any good any more or if coffee beans had a shelf life. She couldn't even guess how long they had been stored there, and they had no expiration date on them.

'You don't want to go poisoning your first customers with dodgy coffee beans,' she grunted, as she shoved the boxes into another corner of the room. She had all the windows open upstairs to let in some fresh air and every now and then she would pause to listen to the church bells ring out over the village.

The only indication that it was getting late was that the light had begun to change. 'I've been here for four hours!' she gasped, as she checked the time on her phone. 'I really must get a watch some day.' She calculated the time it would take to get to the ferry and decided that, if she hurried, she could make the 19.30 departure. That would get her back to the hotel by eight o'clock, to collect her luggage and take a taxi back to her new apartment. 'Yeah, after you've scraped the layers of grime off of you,' she muttered as she turned to lock the front door. She stopped and looked around the room downstairs. 'Congratulations, Niamh, it looks like you've made the place worse than it was, not better.' She rolled her eyes and locked the door, walking lightly down the deserted, cobbled street towards the steps to the lower level and the marina. Still, not a bad day's work, she thought, pleased that she had at least gotten started. More tomorrow, she reminded herself, resolving to get an early start and begin her new life as she meant it to continue.

# Chapter Nineteen

Niamh was spending every waking hour at the café. She was completely absorbed in the renovations and had lost all track of time. She had bought cleaning supplies, gallons of paint, paintbrushes and rollers, and a stepladder at the local hardware store. To her relief, she realised that the walls didn't need to be painted – a good cleaning would suffice – but the skirting boards, doors and cupboards were scuffed and chipped and would definitely benefit from a refresh. Niamh was on her hands and knees behind the counter when he came into the café.

'*Ciao*, Nina? Hello? You are here?' Giorgio asked, his head poking through the door.

'Yes, I'm here,' she shouted from underneath the counter. She stood up and brushed her hands on her jeans. 'Hi.'

'Ah, *buongiorno*. You are busy.'

'No, it's fine, I'm just cleaning,' she said, aware that she looked like she had just crawled out of a dumpster. She tried in vain to beat the layers of dust from her sleeves and her jeans.

'I just bring you a copy of the agreement,' Giorgio said, placing the document on the countertop. He was wearing a navy blue suit and another stunningly crisp white shirt. She wondered exactly how many white shirts he owned.

'Oh, great, thanks. Your brother was OK with everything?'

'Yes, he is just surprised that you wanted to rent it, I think.' Giorgio looked around at the chaos. By the look on his face she guessed that he too was surprised.

'I just made some coffee. Would you like some?'

She watched as his gaze went to the large espresso machine behind the counter.

'Nina, is not possible to make coffee with this machine in this condition.' A look of horror flashed across his face as he wondered for a moment if she had used the machine in its current disgusting state. 'How can you make coffee like this?'

'No, this coffee,' she laughed, putting a steaming French press on the counter. 'Will you have some? It's freshly made.'

'What is this?'

'It's coffee, Giorgio, what do you think it is?' Niamh asked, confused at why he was being so difficult. 'I bought them in the hardware store yesterday. You can get them for single cups or multiple cups. Look – you just put the ground coffee in here like this,' she said, picking up another French press to demonstrate. 'Then you add boiling water and press it down – like this. See?' She looked up at him with a wide smile.

'But why you are giving this to me? I cannot drink this.'

'Why not?'

'Nina, why are you not using the machine?' he asked, gesturing to the enormous Simonelli espresso machine behind the counter. 'Why have you not cleaned the machine to use it and make real coffee?'

'I can't work that thing.'

'What do you mean you cannot work this machine? You have never worked a machine like this?'

'No.'

'Then why are you opening a café?' he asked, confused.

195

'Well, it's mostly about the food. I'm going to focus on healthy salads and light sandwiches and things like that. You can get a coffee anywhere in this town but there is no healthy lunch place,' she said indignantly. 'I'm going to do different stuff. I love to cook and I'm pretty good at it *and* I worked in restaurants for years every summer at college. I just have to figure out some of the stuff that I don't know about yet, and that coffee machine is one of them. But in the meantime I can make French press coffee. They use them in French cafés, you know.' She placed her hands on her hips, feeling fully justified in her explanation of her coffee workaround solution.

He stared at her for several seconds, rooted to the spot. 'Nina, how much experience you have working in cafés?' He crossed the tiled floor and stared at the French press steaming on the counter. He touched the lid and shook his head.

She hesitated, wondering how honest she should be right now. 'Why? What do you mean?'

'Nina, is a simple question.' His hands were gesturing now in that typical Italian way, but she still hadn't learned how to decipher them. 'How long you have spent working in cafés in other places?'

'Well, if you want to be that scientific about it, then none,' she huffed. 'But, as I just told you, I worked in restaurants for three summers. All I have to figure out is the financial bits and the coffee. But it can't be that hard. I mean, these machines practically make the coffee themselves, don't they? It's like having a motorbike behind the counter. Look at the size of this thing!'

'*Mamma mia*, Nina. You do not understand how important coffee is to Italians! You cannot serve coffee like this, in a plastic thing like this, to an Italian. They will never come back.' He placed the French press back on the counter and ran his hand though his hair. 'I will help you before you are doomed to die for ever with no customers and lose all of your money.' He was gesturing furiously now. 'You need to learn. Come.' He sighed, shaking his head. He started dialling a number on his phone as he strode across the tiles and was gone out of the front door. She darted after him, stopping only to turn the key in the door. She heard him chattering in short, rapid sentences and ended with '*Si, adesso*'. Yes, now.

'Yes, now . . . where?' she asked, but he was already too far ahead of her to hear.

She caught up with him at the end of the street. 'Where are we going?'

'To teach you to make coffee,' he said, without losing stride.

She followed obediently, trying to keep pace with him. 'Man, you walk fast!'

At the bottom of the steps he turned right and shortly afterwards he stopped in front of the Illy café.

'Oh, we're going here?'

'Yes, this is where they make real coffee. You will learn how before you make yourself crazy with this idea to open a café without real coffee and you are crying to me in two weeks because you have no customers and you are . . . how do you say . . . bankrupt?'

'I've been in here a few times. It's nice.'

He stopped and stared down at her in disbelief. 'Yes, it is real coffee. Here, they make real Italian coffee . . . this is why it is nice.'

He walked through the door, up to the counter and shook hands with the man she recognised as the owner. They chatted in rapid Italian for a minute or two, with the owner throwing several glances in her direction. She stood sheepishly, wondering what exactly was being said, with no way of knowing what would happen next. She caught two well-dressed ladies looking her up and down and realised with no small degree of horror that she was standing at the entrance of the coffee shop covered in dust and filth.

'Ah, you are the Irish girl who will open the café on Via dei Limoni, no?' the owner asked her as he approached and extended a hand to her. 'I am Massimo. Don't worry, *signora*, Giorgio has explained everything to me. I will help you,' he said with a wide grin and a strong handshake.

'Yes, that's me. I'm Niamh,' she answered quietly, returning his handshake and just now realising that she would be in competition with this man's business.

He hesitated, looked at Giorgio and said something in Italian.

'Ah *sì*.' Giorgio nodded. 'When I tell him about you and the problem you have on Via dei Limoni, I tell him your name is Nina. Then you say your name is Nee . . . I still cannot say it. How do you say it?'

'Oh, right. No, Nina is fine,' she said to Massimo.

'Nina is OK?'

'Yes, Nina.' She smiled.

'Ah, OK, good . . . is better for me.' He grinned. He seemed a happy sort of individual.

'*Allora*,' he continued. 'And you cannot make coffee?'

'No. Well, not on one of those machines.' Niamh pointed to a similar-looking machine.

'No, she cannot make coffee,' Giorgio said firmly, glancing at her sideways.

'No problem, Signora Nina! You will do free labour for me and I will teach you to make the best coffee. At the end you will buy me free lunch in your new café! You are going to do new food, no? Is good agreement, no?'

'Yes.' Niamh smiled. 'Is good.'

'But you cannot learn to make coffee in one day. It takes time.' He hesitated and looked down at her jeans and shirt as he raised his shoulders to his ears in classic Italian style. 'And perhaps today is not the best day for you. You were busy with the cleaning, no?'

She felt her face start to flush. 'Yes, I'm sorry. I was cleaning. I didn't know I was coming here.' She glared pointedly at Giorgio. She thought she saw him attempt to hide a smile.

'*Allora*, Nina, you will come here every day for two hours. Then, in a week or two you will be able to make coffee. Anything less will be a disaster and you will have no customers and your business, it will die. *Capice?*'

'*Sì, capisco.*' Niamh nodded, indicating that she understood.

'Now I must go back to work,' Giorgio interrupted. 'Massimo, I will not come back here for coffee for two weeks, until it is safe to have coffee again. But, before I go, I will have one espresso now – that you make, please.'

'*Subito,*' Massimo replied, as he turned to face the coffee machine.

'You are with the best teacher now, Nina. Massimo has been making coffee since . . . *come si dice* . . . how do you say . . . since you are a baby.'

'*Sì, è vero.* It is true. I am more than forty,' Massimo said with an exaggerated shrug of his shoulders. He placed an espresso in front of Giorgio. '*Ecco.*'

Giorgio smiled and tipped back the espresso, turning to Nina. He nodded at her with a smile and said '*arrivederci*' as he left the café.

She watched him leave and realised that so too did every other woman in the café. He cut a fine figure as he dashed out of the door and turned to make his way back to the office. He was being so sweet to her that she couldn't help feeling drawn to him. It was the most kindness she had felt from a man in a long time. She was clearly attracted to him, but didn't want to give in to that notion. After all, she couldn't imagine any woman *not* being attracted to Giorgio. But she knew that any feelings she might have would lead nowhere, involved as he was with the 'illustrious and accomplished' Sara, and she sensed that Sara would act like a ferocious lioness in defence of her man.

You're the new girl in town, Niamh, she thought to herself. Best not go knocking off someone else's man as you try to ingratiate yourself with the locals.

She washed her hands and face in the bathroom and did her best to beat off some layers of dust from her clothes. Massimo showed her around the little café. She stood outside the counter as he made a *macchiato* for a customer and then he invited her to join him for a coffee.

They sat at a table in the back of the café and he told her about Italians and their coffee. He talked about their preferred brands and the different types of coffee. She was shocked to hear the price of the commercial coffee machines that were standard in every restaurant, café and railway station café in the country. Some of them cost several tens of thousands to buy.

'So how can a small café afford to have one?'

'Well, they don't buy it, they lease it from the coffee manufacturer,' he explained. His English was a lot better than Giorgio's, most likely because he dealt with foreigners every day of the summer season. 'The coffee makers want you to use their coffee beans, so they will offer you the machine and you can keep it for as long as you order their beans. So, they make the investment up front for the machine, but they know that you will be a customer for many years.' He leaned back against the chair. 'As long as the coffee beans are good, you will continue to order from them, so they are building many, many customers for many, many years.'

'So how come there is a machine sitting in the café on Via dei Limoni all this time if no one is buying coffee beans any more?'

'I don't know, but probably Giorgio or his brother made a deal with them when they closed the café, or probably they bought it at the beginning. The café was opened many, many years ago, Nina.'

'Yes, I heard a little about it. It's very sad.'

Massimo shook his head. 'Lena was such a beautiful woman. Marco has never been the same since that time. They were so happy together. Everybody loved her. She was a kind and beautiful woman. Everyone was so sad when she died.'

'Did Marco leave right away?'

'No, he stayed for a while and tried to . . . how do you say . . . put his life together once again, but I think that everywhere there were too many reminders of her. He and Giorgio were always the best friends, no? So it was hard for Giorgio, too, to see his brother in this much pain, you understand?'

'Yes.' Niamh nodded. 'I understand.'

'I'm sorry, my English is not so good.'

'No, it's great,' she said encouragingly.

He smiled and continued. 'So Marco applied for a transfer to a hospital in America. He could continue his medical practice there and hope to start a new life at the same time. He got a visa, and one evening he told the family at dinner that he was leaving. He left the next day. It was as if he could not wait to leave the sadness behind.'

She watched Massimo as he told the story and she could see the sadness in his face, recalling the details. 'Then, he was gone, and Giorgio was sad for this reason, too. His fiancée left him two months later.'

'That's awful. Had they been engaged long?'

'I don't know, maybe a few months. I know that he loved her, but I do not know how much she loved him. Giorgio is a kind man. He has a good career and he is a hard worker. His family has some other businesses – different real estate – that he also is involved with, as well as his own job, so he is always busy. But, I don't know how much this woman really loved him, and how much she loved the idea of him. To leave so soon after so much has happened, it says to me that she ... how do you say in English? ... She was not willing to live the hard parts of life, to have problems and stress, only easy. She wanted only the good life. That is not right.' He stood abruptly. 'I am sorry. I am keeping you from your work. I talk too much!'

'No, not at all. I enjoyed chatting with you,' Niamh said, standing too.

'Chatting? What is chatting?'

'Oh, speaking ... it's speaking, you know, casually, just like we were doing.'

'Ah, OK! So I teach you to make coffee and you teach me to speak better English!' he said with a wide grin. 'Now, I must get back to my customers. Tomorrow I will see you at ... at what time is good for you?'

'Oh, any time is fine, Massimo, honestly. You tell me what suits you and what is best for your business.'

'OK, so we see you tomorrow at nine o'clock. That way the Italians will have gone already to work and so will have had their coffee and we will not upset anyone, and the less serious people, like tourists, will not be here until after ten o'clock, so we will have some time to prepare.'

'Sounds good. Thank you again, Massimo.'

'Signora Nina, you forget – you will work for free for me,' he said, grinning. 'So don't thank me yet! *Arrivederci! A domani!*'

'*A domani*.' She waved as she stepped back out into the sun.

# Chapter Twenty

She quickly began to look forward to her mornings at Massimo's café. She had completely underestimated the amount of work involved in operating a small café, and she had wildly misjudged her lack of experience. Without Massimo's help, her attempts at running a little café would have been, as Giorgio had predicted, a disaster of massive proportions. The coffee machine itself and the skill required to properly make good coffee were only part of the challenge. There was so much more involved that she hadn't even begun to plan for or consider.

She was also gaining a sense of the importance of relationships within the community. Massimo knew everyone in the village, it seemed, but then he had lived here his entire life, so this was understandable. Most of them – the locals, that was – came to his café for coffee or pastries in the morning. She didn't intend to compete on the basis of coffee alone, and she explained that to Massimo, but rather she wanted to create a unique place for light, healthy lunches as opposed to the usual Italian fare of pasta and pizza. Her customers would most likely be tourists more than locals, at least initially. Tourists would be more accustomed to having salads, soups and sandwiches for lunch, as opposed to the traditional bigger

Italian midday meal, and she did have relevant restaurant experience that she could put to work.

She also learned some useful cultural information, such as the fact that Italians didn't really go in for breakfast like other cultures, but kept it simple and light, with a coffee and croissant, or *un cornetto*, as the Italians called it. Massimo explained that breakfast is such a non-issue for Italians that most of them choose to stand at the counter in the morning to have their cappuccino or espresso, rather than sit down at a table.

Massimo was a sweet man who was devoted to his family. His adorable two-year-old twins burst through the door each morning screaming, 'Papà! Papà!' and he would scoop them up into his arms. It made her smile every time she saw it. He introduced her as Nina and they each clung to one of her legs and stared up at her wide-eyed, chanting her name loudly on repeat.

Massimo's mother would take up residence at a table at the back of the café each morning a little before nine o'clock. It was a ritual that gave purpose to her day. She was a small, sweet old lady who always had a smile for anyone who came in. She would sit at the table drinking coffee, doing crossword puzzles and reading until some of the local women showed up, at which point she would hold court for very lengthy, important conversations. She was known in the café as *Nonna*, the Italian for grandmother, and it was a badge that she wore with pride.

Nonna had also started to call Niamh Nina, as she had heard the twins loudly and enthusiastically rattle off her name each morning. The old lady shook her head, and made a dramatic hand gesture that involved both shoulders, when Massimo tried to explain that Nina wasn't her actual name. It was becoming clear to Niamh that at this rate she would soon be known exclusively as Nina among the Italian community, and she took pleasure from the fact as she began to feel more and more as if she were being accepted by this new tribe.

Nonna spoke no English so their conversations were limited to the little Italian that Nina had acquired, supported by a lot of hand gestures.

'Why does Nonna always dress in black?' she asked Massimo one morning.

'Ah, she is in mourning for her husband, my father,' he replied over the screech of the coffee-grinding machine.

'Oh, I'm sorry to hear that. I didn't realise that your father had passed away.'

'Nina, it was twenty years ago, but my mother has refused to wear anything but black ever since.'

'Aw, that's kind of sweet, you know, like a great romance that she doesn't want to let go of.'

'Yes, it is sad. They were best friends and had been married for almost forty years. Now she is in her early eighties, but she looks so much older because of all that black she wears,' he sighed. He shrugged his shoulders and continued. 'But, she will not listen to anyone, so what can I do?'

'Sounds like something out of an old black and white movie, you know? The widow wearing only black and mourning her husband for the rest of her life?'

'She was a very beautiful woman, but now she wears her sadness on her face in lines. I think if she did not wear all this black, it would be better. How would you say ... it would make her feel lighter? Do you understand?'

'I do. There's a thing now called colour therapy. It's all about how different colours make you feel and when you should wear them. You know, like red is a power colour so you should wear it when you have a big meeting, or presentation, or when you want to feel in charge.'

'*Ha!* This is good information! I will wear red the next time that I go to visit my bank manager,' Massimo said, and he threw his head back and roared with laughter. 'This must be an American theory, no?'

'Probably,' Niamh agreed, giggling. 'I doubt the Irish invented it, anyway, and it does sound like something that the Americans would come up with.'

The conversation continued in easy banter for two hours each morning. Massimo would interrupt her every time she used a word that he didn't understand and he would repeat it over and over until he got used to saying it. In return he taught her some common, everyday Italian expressions, phrases that she could use right away in her new life. He taught her that it was important not to worry about grammar and structure and pronunciation, but just to start with simple words and phrases and build on them.

Giorgio had been true to his word for the first few days, but reappeared just after she arrived one morning at nine o'clock.

'*Buongiorno a tutti,*' he said, with a smile to the little crowd in the café.

'Ah, Giorgio, I was afraid that you would not come back until Nina had finished learning,' Massimo joked as he shook his friend's hand.

'I thought you were avoiding this place for the next two weeks?' Niamh asked, with her hands on her hips.

'I tried, but it is the best coffee in town. I had no choice but to return,' he sighed with mock exaggeration.

'You are late this morning, no?' Massimo asked in English with one eyebrow raised.

'Oh, ah, yes, today I start later,' he responded, sticking his hand in his pocket and plucking out his wallet. '*Un cappuccino, per favore.*'

'I think you had better make it, Massimo,' said Niamh. 'Now that he's returned you don't want to scare him off by having me make his coffee. I don't think he is ready for that just yet.'

'*Va bene*, OK, I will make,' Massimo responded, turning to face the coffee machine.

Niamh had busied herself filling the grinder with fresh coffee beans when she heard a gasp behind her.

'*Ah, Giorgio, caro,*' Nonna exclaimed as she shuffled towards him. He bent to kiss her on both cheeks. She placed her hands on the sides of his face and spoke in rapid, gentle Italian. Niamh could only guess by the expressions and the gestures that she was saying she hadn't seen him in a long time. Massimo came and stood alongside her behind the counter, placing Giorgio's cappuccino cup on a saucer.

'Yes, we don't usually see you here at this hour of the morning, Giorgio. It is unusual, no?' He turned and winked at Niamh. She saw Giorgio flash a look at Massimo that she didn't understand.

Nonna turned to him and demanded to know what he had just said to make Giorgio look flustered. When he explained in Italian, she clearly agreed with Massimo's statement. She turned back to Giorgio, putting an arm around his waist and patting his chest with her other hand.

'*Sì caro, sì,*' she said, and continued in Italian.

'She says that he always comes in too early for her so she never gets to see him. She says that it has been too long since she has last seen him and she is angry with him for this. Angry in her own kind of way, that is,' Massimo translated. 'She is telling him that she wants him to come to dinner on

208

Saturday night. Nonna is such a wonderful cook.' He gestured wildly with his hands. 'How do you say in English . . . she is a magician with the food! She used to have some wonderful dinner parties in the past, but now she just cooks for family. *Mamma mia*, she can make the pasta that will make you want to cry it is so good.'

Nonna turned and pointed towards Niamh without even slowing her rapid stream of Italian. Niamh had no idea what was being said, but based on the series of hand gestures in her direction, it clearly had something to do with her and she could feel her face start to flush immediately. Why does my face do this every time, she wondered, frustrated, putting both hands to her cheeks.

'Ah, Nina, Nonna wants you to join us all on Saturday night. You will come, no?' Massimo translated again.

'Oh, really? Well, yes, of course, I would love to but . . . ' she said, surprised to have been invited. 'What did she say?' she asked Massimo quietly.

'Yes. She said that Giorgio must come for dinner as he has been . . . how do you say in English . . . not seeing her as much recently?'

'You mean avoiding her?'

'Ah, yes!' he exclaimed loudly. 'This is the word I was looking for. Yes, she says that Giorgio has been avoiding her so he must come to dinner on Saturday now that she has seen him again.' He wore a wide smile, pleased with his use of his newly acquired English word.

'Yes, but what does that have to do with me?' she asked Massimo. 'Are you sure that she invited me?'

'*Sì, sì, certo.* She said that you must come to dinner also because you are the reason she has seen Giorgio again.'

'How so?' Niamh asked, now utterly confused. She wasn't

sure if it was his English or if the old lady just wasn't making any sense, but she couldn't see what she had to do with the reunion of Giorgio and Nonna.

'Yes, you see, Nina, Giorgio comes here every day for coffee at seven-thirty in the morning,' he said, leaning in and speaking quietly to her. 'Nonna is never here that early in the morning. He has come here at that time every morning on his way to work for many, many years, but today he is here at nine o'clock, because, I think, you are here, no?'

'That's daft, Massimo,' she said, feeling her face start to flush again. 'That's totally not the reason he's here later today. Maybe he is just running late. Emily said he's always late for everything!'

'What is daft?'

'Crazy, Massimo. Crazy, nuts . . .'

'Ah, I like this word. I will find many ways to use it each day in here with some of our daft customers. As for Giorgio,' he continued, 'he starts work at eight o'clock in the morning at his office. So, at seven-thirty in the morning it does not matter if he is a little late. But nine o'clock is different – this is definitely late, Nina, and there is no other explanation for it, other than you come here at nine o'clock in the morning this week and next week. This is the truth, Signora Nina!' He spoke with a flourish of his hand. 'Now, Nonna is asking if you will join us for dinner on Saturday night. What is your answer?'

'*Ah sì, Nonna, grazie*,' Niamh said, smiling at Nonna, who had still not let go of Giorgio. 'How do you say, "That's very kind" in Italian?' she asked Massimo. She didn't know what to make of Massimo's theory, but it made her feel good to think she might have had something to do with Giorgio showing up later than usual.

'*Molto gentile.*'

'*Molto gentile, Nonna*,' she repeated.

Nonna merely smiled and nodded her head. She motioned with her hand and mumbled that she would like a cappuccino. She hesitated for a moment, glanced at Niamh and then nodded towards Massimo. Even though she had just invited the new foreigner in town to join them for dinner on Saturday night, Nonna wasn't quite ready to trust her with her morning cappuccino. There was a correct order of things, and cappuccino was pretty high up on the list of the important elements of Nonna's life, along with food, wine and family. Massimo looked at Niamh and shrugged as if to say that there was no point in fighting that one.

'No problem, Massimo. There is a saying in English that goes, "All good things come to those who wait," and that definitely applies here. I'm nowhere near qualified to make Nonna's cappuccino just yet!'

Giorgio looked at her and shook his head, smiling. He peeled Nonna's arm from around his waist and turned to leave. 'My dear Nina, you still do not understand just how important coffee is to the Italians. You might have a very long wait before Nonna will order a cappuccino from an Irish girl!' He gave a wave to the small group gathered at the counter and was gone.

Niamh stood watching him leave, replaying his words *My dear Nina ... my dear Nina* over and over in her head. Don't overthink it. It's just an expression, she tried to convince herself, but she had plucked the three words from the air as soon as he had said them, just as a hummingbird might pluck sweet pollen from a bud.

# Chapter Twenty-One

By the end of the week, Niamh was brave enough to start making cappuccinos for some of the regular local clients. She had perfected the art of the cappuccino foam under Massimo's stewardship and was amazed at how much skill it took to get it just right.

Saturday morning came around and she was at her post behind Massimo's counter by nine o'clock as usual. She was deep in thought as she stared into the milk pitcher, steaming the milk for the two cappuccinos that had just been ordered, when she heard her name.

'Niamh? What on earth are you doing in here?'

She turned to see Jeffrey leaning across the counter, grinning at her.

'Jeffrey!' she exclaimed, her face immediately flushing with colour.

Thankfully the pitcher of steaming milk demanded her full attention, so she turned back, grateful to have a moment to gather her thoughts. Should she be mad or pissed off at having been stood up? Or should she try to appear nonchalant and dismiss it as unimportant?

'Of all the gin joints . . . ' He laughed. 'What the heck are you doing here?'

'I'm making coffee. What does it look like?' she replied, her gaze focused on the jug in her hand.

'Well, I can see that, but why here? I thought you were opening your own place?'

'I am, in a couple of weeks, but I've been coming here to learn the art of the barista.' She placed the two cappuccinos on the counter. 'What are you doing here?'

'I'm in town for the weekend with Franco. So, thanks for standing me up on the pier that day. It's been a long time since that's happened, I can tell you. I had forgotten how crappy it felt! I felt like a complete jerk.'

'Nice try, Jeffrey. Are you having a coffee?' she asked, trying hard to look busy.

'A cappuccino, please, and what do you mean by that? I stood there like an idiot for a half an hour before it dawned on me that I had been stood up.'

'Jeffrey ...' She sighed, and stopped, unsure which version of herself was going to respond. He would either get calm-and-collected Niamh, who would graciously dismiss his attempt at lying about his behaviour as meaningless and unworthy of anger, or he'd get demented Niamh, who had to admit that she felt a little humiliated at the thought of it.

'Jeffrey,' she continued. 'It's bad enough to stand a girl up, having invited her to lunch in the first place, but to lie on top of it and try to come over all smarmy and cocky like you were there the whole time is just pathetic. I was there. I was the idiot. And the fact that you stood me up and now are trying to fudge your way out of it, unable to admit that it was a shitty thing to do, makes me wonder why I even agreed to it in the first place.'

So it turned out that he got the demented version of Niamh in the end. She turned her back to him and focused her attentions instead to the milk pitcher. She was furious again and wondered if it was considered illegal to scald customers in Italy.

'I swear to God I was there. In fact, you can ask Franco. He'll be here shortly. Honest, Niamh, I was there. I was about fifteen minutes late because I had to drop Franco at the marine store to get what he needed to fix his boat's engine. It's about an hour away and on the way back there was some bad accident on the road so we were delayed. I swear that's the truth. I was there. Everyone typically runs late in Italy, so when you weren't there, I just figured you had stood me up. It never even dawned on me that you might have disappeared in less than fifteen minutes. Honest!'

She turned to look at him and he was standing with both hands held up in defence.

Bollocks, she thought, as she remembered how she had scarpered off just before quarter past the hour. He looks like he's telling the truth.

'Niamh, I'm so sorry you thought I had stood you up. I didn't have your number and neither did Franco. I went back to Genoa the next morning and I didn't know where you had moved to after you left the hotel that day, so I was kind of stuck. I honestly didn't think I'd see you again.'

She tucked her hair behind her ear and fiddled with a tub of spoons beneath the counter in an attempt to look busy. Where are all the customers now when I need them? she thought to herself.

'Well, you sure can make a decent cappuccino. Truce?' he asked with a smile.

'Truce,' she agreed.

'On one condition though – that you let me make it up to you for real. Let me take you out to dinner tonight.'

'Oh, that's nice, but I can't tonight. I have plans.'

'Of course you do. That's not surprising. OK then, how about tomorrow night? I don't have any assignments due on Monday so I'm staying in town this weekend. I can meet you any time that suits.'

'I thought you were done with school?'

'Almost. The exams are over but we had both been doing some tutoring for extra credit so we've got a bunch of reporting and paperwork due on that now and I've got one last assignment. Another week or so and we'll be free. So, what do you say?'

'Sure, why not?' Niamh said with a small smile.

'Be careful and don't be too enthusiastic about the prospect of dinner with me or I'll get a swelled head.'

'Call me cautiously optimistic. Just don't be late this time!'

'I won't now that I understand that I've got a fifteen-minute window before you go all Cinderella and her pumpkin carriage on me!'

'Well, if you're not late then you won't need to worry, will you?' she said, feeling more confident.

'Fair point,' he conceded. 'How about dinner at Da Paolo's?'

'Oh, that sounds lovely, actually. I was there once with Grace and loved it. We were told it's one of the best restaurants in town.'

'It is. I know the owner so he'll look after us. I'll see if we can get a table outside. OK, I've got to run. Thanks for the coffee,' he said with another wide grin. 'See you tomorrow night!'

The rest of the morning passed without incident, and she took off her apron and said goodbye to Massimo just after noon.

'*Brava, Nina. Oggi hai fatto bene!*' Massimo said, graciously telling her that she had done well today.

'*Grazie, Massimo.* I love coming here.'

'*Allora*, see you tonight, yes? Here is the address of Nonna's house.'

'OK, thanks. Is it here in town?'

'No, is up in the hills above the town. You can walk, but there are many, many steps. I forgot that you do not have a car.'

'That's fine. I can take a taxi.'

'Ah, yes, but they are not so reliable here. Sometimes they do not ... how do you say ... arrive? Why don't you meet me here at six o'clock and you can come with me?'

'OK, thanks. That's very kind of you. I'll see you here at six o'clock. *Ciao!*'

She made her way back to her little café on Via dei Limoni, grateful for some quiet after the busy morning at Massimo's. She surveyed the scene and took stock of what she needed to get done for the rest of the day. The place had been mostly cleared out and now looked a lot more spacious. The coffee machine had been serviced and was working perfectly, which was a relief given the inordinate price it would have cost to buy a new one. She had yet to try it for real herself and thought it might be safer to wait until she felt totally confident with Massimo's model before she started tinkering with her own.

Niamh paced up and down, counting out her steps and trying to decide how to configure the new tables and chairs for her café. For now, they were all stacked upstairs, still wrapped in their protective plastic. She had literally squealed in delight when she found them in an old furniture shop in Genoa. The place was a salvage yard of sorts, with all kinds of old doors, wrought-iron gates, fireplaces and an eclectic mix of furniture. She had wandered around the shop happily for about two hours and in the end had bargained for the little mismatched tables and chairs and an enormous chipped, art deco-style mirror. She had been quite proud of herself for pointing out all the flaws – which to her mind only added to their charm – but which had knocked several hundred euros off the price.

She had another few days of training to go at Massimo's and then she'd be ready to open up Café Limoni, as she had decided to call it. The new sign for out front was being delivered in the afternoon. It was a simple wooden sign with an etched-out coffee cup and the name of the café engraved on it. Massimo had introduced her to a local carpenter who was delighted to help her out. He gave her a reduced price for the sign as she was a friend of Massimo's, and said that he would hang it from the front of the building as soon as she was ready to announce the new café.

Now that she had the clutter cleared out it was easy to clean the small space. She spent the afternoon cleaning, scrubbing and polishing and the place practically sparkled by the time she was done. She admired the original tilework as she first dusted, then scrubbed them individually. Even the chips and dents from years of wear and tear suited them and gave them an aged patina. The back countertop had been covered in some sort of hideous plastic protective coating that was probably deemed practical twenty odd years ago. When she peeled it and the layers of glue off, she revealed a beautiful piece of solid oak wood underneath, which she polished to a high shine.

Her supplies would start arriving from Monday and she had allowed a few days to get everything sorted and organised before opening the following Saturday morning. She had found an old set of weighing scales buried under the counter, with individual steel weights that had obviously been used long ago to balance the scales, way back before the more modern versions existed. It too was chipped and rusted in places but she decided that even though she had nothing that needed weighing, it was too beautiful to discard, so she cleaned it up and it now stood proudly on a shelf inside the window.

Saturday was always a busy day in the town, even early in the season, as all the locals were out and about, so she decided that would be the best day to announce her arrival on Via dei Limoni. The thought of it alone made her anxious, and the closer the date got the more nervous she felt. She had forgotten all about tonight's dinner party as she got lost in her work, and only when the church bells struck five did she lock up and dart home to change.

# Chapter Twenty-Two

Niamh had no idea how formal or fancy an Italian dinner party would be, so she opted for a simple black dress that she had bought the day she went shopping with Grace in Santa Margherita. God, that seems like months ago but it was only a couple of weeks, she thought as she got dressed. She tugged at the dress to get it up over her hips. 'Yep, you're starting to wear all that pasta you've been eating Niamh,' she said, with an exasperated sigh. 'Please, God, just let it zip up.'

The zip eventually obliged and she pulled it up the last two inches.

'God Bless Coco Chanel for inventing the little black dress – every girl's most trusted wardrobe essential. Now, earrings – I need big, fabulous, dangly earrings to distract people from the fact that after all this time I still can't speak proper Italian.'

She reached Massimo's café just as he pulled up out front. They drove for ten or twelve minutes up into the hills behind Camogli, eventually turning off the main road and down a gravelled driveway to a space that could hold about six cars. Her heels crunched on the gravel as they made their way up the narrow path towards the three-storey villa. It was painted a deep, warm red, in keeping with the collective hues of red, orange and yellow in the town and on surrounding properties in the hills.

At the front of the house a long wooden table sat underneath a pergola loaded with bright purple bougainvillea. It was set for at least a dozen people and was adorned with chunky off-white candles. The view down over the hills towards the bay was magnificent. Niamh couldn't help but stand and stare, captivated by the sight of the town sitting in a semicircle, giving way to the sparkling bay beyond it.

There were some familiar faces from the café, as well as Massimo's family. Massimo took her around to meet those that she didn't already know by name. She cursed herself for not working harder at learning more Italian, as she was limited to basic pleasantries and introductions. Nonna was nowhere to be seen. Most likely in the kitchen, Massimo explained, as she always cooked when hosting people for dinner. He gave her directions to the kitchen when she asked, and she made her way through the elegant villa to find her host.

Nonna was in the kitchen with one of Massimo's children at her feet and the other rolling out pasta shapes at the table under her guidance.

'*Buona sera, Nonna,*' Niamh said, as she handed her the bouquet of flowers she had brought for her.

'*Ah, Nina, buona sera! Grazie!*' Nonna replied with a warm smile.

'I see they are learning the art of pasta-making from a young age,' said Niamh, gesturing to the little one with the rolling pin.

Nonna hesitated and then nodded her head. '*Ah sì, la pasta, sì.*'

'Can I do anything to help you?'

Nonna understood the question and nodded, handing her

an apron. She said something in Italian that Niamh didn't understand, pointing at the child covered in flour at the table.

'I'm sorry, I don't quite understand,' Niamh replied, frustrated that she wasn't better able to communicate.

'She said that the little one rolls the dough so slow, that we will be here all night and not eat until tomorrow.' Niamh turned to find Giorgio leaning on the doorframe. 'So, you know how to make pasta?' he asked, sounding surprised.

'No, not a clue, but she can tell me what to do. I'm a good listener,' Niamh said, smiling.

Nonna handed her a rolling pin and showed her just how far to stretch the pasta before cutting it into small squares.

'You have high ambitions, Nina. First coffee and now pasta. You are brave.'

'Or delusional. I'm not sure what I'm doing here, trying to make pasta at an Italian dinner party.'

Giorgio smiled again. 'Neither do I ... but is funny to watch!'

'Thanks for the vote of confidence, Giorgio. Cheers for that.'

'So, you are ready for everything? To open the café next week?'

'Yes, I think so. I hope so!'

'I think maybe you do not understand what you are thinking?'

He ran his right hand through his hair. She realised that he did that a lot. She couldn't even guess at his age, although to be honest she was never any good at putting an age on people. But if she were forced at gunpoint, she'd probably say late thirties. He had great hair, anyway, whatever age he was. Kind of like that Irish actor who played James Bond before anyone really knew him. Wasn't he from County

Meath or somewhere? I mean, who comes from County Meath? No one! And then, all of a sudden, Ireland has its own James Bond.

'Um, is that a question or a statement, Giorgio? I'm confused. What do you mean?' she asked with a frown.

He continued, in broken English, to explain the critical nature of the short season, the importance of tourists and the tourist season, and so on, but by now she was entirely distracted. How was it, she wondered, that salt-and-pepper hair looked so great on men, whereas women went to extraordinary lengths to camouflage any signs of ageing? She could definitely see some early flecks of grey in Giorgio's hair but she had to admit that it looked good. Women, on the other hand, didn't have the same advantage. Why was that?

'Nina!' he said, with an impatient, loud sigh.

'Oh, sorry,' she said, with a jolt. She wondered how long she had been staring at him and his hair. 'Sorry, I just lost my train of thought.'

'But you weren't saying anything. I was, Nina,' he replied, with another confused frown.

'Oh yeah. That's right. Sorry, what were you saying?'

Giorgio shook his head and repeated his earlier declaration, this time with more emphasis.

'I am asking,' he said, pausing again for effect, 'if you understand what you must do and how difficult it will be with this café.'

'Oh, that!'

'Yes, that,' he replied, his gaze meeting hers.

Niamh stifled a giggle. 'Yes, Giorgio. I think I do – I'm just a bit nervous about it, TBH.'

'What is "TBH"? What does this mean?' he asked, looking perplexed.

'Don't frown, Giorgio. My mother says that you'll get wrinkles if you frown. You know the little ones between your eyebrows? Some people have them so bad that they look like actual furrows between their eyes, like in a field. You know – furrows for growing vegetables.'

She put one finger in the space between her eyebrows and frowned repeatedly to see if she could feel the onset of any furrows.

'Nina, I don't know what you are talking about. I don't know what are these furrows, or the other thing you said before that.'

'What thing?'

'I don't know. You said something about TB . . . this terrible disease.'

'What? No, I didn't.'

Giorgio ran his hand through his hair again. 'Yes, yes you did. You were talking about the café. You said you were nervous about it, and then you say something about having TB.'

'What? Are we actually having the same conversation, Giorgio? What are you talking about?'

'Nina, I am not so sure any more,' he said, grinning at her.

Nonna lifted her head from her pasta-making and glanced from one to the other of them, understanding nothing of the words, but following their gestures and expressions.

Niamh's mind raced back through what she could recall of the conversation in her head.

'Oh! Wait! I said TBH!' she exclaimed, putting a hand over her mouth.

'Yes, this was it!'

'*Ha!*' She laughed out loud. 'That's not TB like the disease, Giorgio, it's T-B-H – as in "to be honest". It's short for "to be honest".'

Giorgio was now gesturing with both hands in spectacular Italian fashion. 'So if it means this, then why do you not say this? Why do you say just these letters?'

'I dunno, lots of people say it. I think it's a millennial thing. I think they made it up. It's like a pop culture thing now, you know, like LOL. None of them can type any more, either. I think that's where it comes from. You know, they shorten everything to fit into text messages and then suddenly they all wake up one day and none of them can spell! My uncle works in HR for Apple in Cork. He said it's totally a thing – that they can't spell properly.'

'No, I do not know what you are saying again, Nina,' Giorgio said, shaking his head. 'I think my English is OK, you know? And then you start talking fast like this and I have no idea what it is that you are saying. *Mamma mia*.'

His hands were enunciating every word as if the whole thing were orchestrated. Niamh bit her lower lip and turned her eyes to the ground as she watched the hand-gesture theatre unfold.

Don't laugh, don't laugh, she warned herself, as she tried to quiet the giggles rising in her throat. 'Sorry, yes,' she eventually said aloud.

'Why are you always sorry, Nina? Don't be sorry, just listen to what I say,' Giorgio said slowly, putting his phone on the table and pulling out a chair to sit on.

'You're right, sorry. I mean, yes,' she replied, her gaze still firmly directed towards the floor.

'*Allora*, Nina, is just that the season here is so short, for the tourists. All the Italian people will go back to Milano on the last weekend in August. And, in September you will find only some German tourists here. So you must make all of your money from this café in just a few months from now to the end of August, because after this, it is . . . how do you say this . . . there is no more.'

'It's over?'

'*Si! Esatto!* It is over!'

'I get it, Giorgio, and I appreciate the advice, but none of this made any sense from the start – not leaving my life in Ireland, not renting a café, not opening late in the season, nothing makes sense.'

'*Si, è vero!*' He agreed with a small nod of his head. 'So, you will change your mind?'

'What? No! Giorgio, nothing I've ever done in my whole life has ever felt so right or so challenging or so goddamn exciting!'

'Ah, so then you will not change your mind?' he asked with a confused look on his face.

'Hell, no!' Nina said with a wide grin.

'But, Nina, you know that you are a little bit crazy to do this, no?'

'*Si*, Giorgio,' she said with a happy laugh. '*Si!*'

He held her gaze across the table for a moment or two, until his concerned expression gave way to a genuine smile that crinkled up the corners of his eyes.

'You are funny, Nina, funny and courageous!'

She felt something contract in her belly. She watched as he gathered up his things. She watched him still as he pushed back his chair from the table. Her eyes followed him as he stood to leave and she wondered what he meant, or what he could have meant exactly. No one had ever before said that she was courageous, nor had they had any reason to, she pondered sadly. She found herself silently willing him not to leave just yet.

'Hey, so how come you know a word like courageous when

you can barely speak English at the best of times?' she said with a cheeky smile.

'Ah, I learn English from many movies!' he said, with an uproarious laugh. 'And all these movies about the war, they have the heroes who have the courage and they must go to war and be the courageous ones! And if they have the courage then they will win.' He looked quite pleased with himself.

Niamh tried to hide a smile at the idea of Giorgio watching some epic war movie and repeating the words and phrases to himself to learn more English.

'*Allora*, now I go. Nina, you have your advice about this place, so as your lawyer and your friend, I have done what is my job.' He stood, towering over her, and tucked his phone into his pocket.

'*Sei coraggiosa*,' he said with a wide smile as he tapped her nose with his finger before crossing the kitchen to say goodbye to Nonna.

She lifted her hand to her nose.

Did the fact that he had just touched her mean anything? she wondered. Did it have any significance? Was this how male and female friendships worked? Rick certainly had never been playful with her, or perhaps he had in the early days, but she couldn't remember it. Could people be playful with each other without it actually meaning anything more?

She repeated the word *coraggiosa* twice under her breath and decided that she liked both the rhythm and the round sound of it.

'*Coraggiosa*,' she repeated softly to herself. She wasn't sure that she was courageous at all, but she liked the fact that someone else harboured the thought that, for once, she might be.

'Now I will go so that you can concentrate,' he said, returning to her side. 'I will go back to the others on the terrace.

Come and join us when you have finished with the pasta. Nonna always leaves this type of pasta until last so that it is made just before the cooking, so I think this will be the last job to do tonight.' He turned and spoke to Nonna in Italian and she confirmed his theory.

'She says that she will keep you only for this job and then you will both join us on the terrace.'

'Will she need help serving? I don't mind helping. In fact I quite enjoy it. Makes me feel useful.'

'No, she always has people to do this part of the evening. How do you say ... she hires professional people for this? Is this the right way to say this?'

'Yes.'

'Good. *Allora*, she hires people to serve the meal and to clean up, but she insists on cooking and preparing everything herself.'

'Maybe she likes to feel useful, too.'

'Perhaps you are right,' he said with a shrug. 'I had not thought of it like that.'

He left the kitchen, but returned a minute later and handed her a tall glass of champagne. 'No cook should be without a drink in the kitchen. Is bad luck,' he said, and left.

She caught Nonna watching them and she heard her mumble something, but couldn't make it out.

'You won't have one, Nonna?' she asked.

'No! No!' she gestured towards the pasta, indicating that she would wait until this job at hand was complete.

They continued the pasta-making for another twenty minutes, with Nonna churning out at least three times the volume that Niamh contributed. When they had finished, Nonna patted her on the arm and thanked her, then ushered her out to join the other guests on the terrace. She made her way back out through the villa, wondering who she would have the best chance of having a decent conversation with, and hoping that some of the other guests that she didn't know so well spoke some English.

She was surprised to see Franco standing with a glass of wine on the terrace, and she scanned the small crowd to see if Jeffrey was there, too.

'Sorry, Nina, but it's just me tonight,' Franco said with a grin as he caught her glancing around the terrace.

'Hi, Franco,' she said, ignoring the quip. 'What are you doing here?'

'That's my mother over there,' he said, pointing to an older Italian lady. 'She and Massimo's wife are close friends and so we often get invited to Nonna's house.'

'Oh, right, of course. I don't know why I asked, sorry. Stupid question. I suppose everyone knows everyone else in this town.'

'Well, yes, that might be true, but it doesn't mean that everyone is friends, so it wasn't really a stupid question,' he said. 'I hear you were making some pasta in there?'

'Yes, it was great, although I hope you're lucky enough to get some of Nonna's version and not mine. Hers are perfect as you would imagine and mine look like they've had an epileptic fit and are all wobbly.'

'How's the café coming along? When are you opening?'

'Next weekend, hopefully.' Niamh sipped on her champagne.

'I'm only here in town for a couple of days so I'll miss your opening day, but good luck with it! Cheers!'

'Thanks, Franco, that's very kind of you. Oh yeah, Jeffrey said that he would be here in town this weekend. I should have guessed that you'd be with him too.'

'Yes, my partner in crime. He was very disappointed not to be invited to tonight's dinner party. He will be even more disappointed when I tell him that you were here,' he said with a mischievous grin. 'But I believe that you have plans for dinner tomorrow night, no?'

'Dinner tomorrow night? Where are we going?' Giorgio had stepped alongside them and put one arm around Franco just as he mentioned tomorrow night's dinner.

Shit, Niamh thought. Worst possible timing.

'Sorry, Giorgio, but we are not invited. Jeffrey is taking Nina out to dinner tomorrow.' He turned to Niamh and grinned. 'He already asked me what he should wear. I haven't seen him this excited about dinner in a long time.'

Giorgio looked from Franco to Niamh and then glanced down at his champagne glass. Niamh could feel her cheeks get redder by the second. She was glad it was getting dark and she hoped that neither of them would notice. She didn't know why exactly, but it felt wrong to be telling Giorgio all this, and there was no way to politely shut Franco up.

'Ah, I see. You met him at the party, no? At Sara's restaurant?'

'No!' Franco continued, laughing. 'They met one day in Portofino by chance, and then again at Sara's by chance, and then one final time by chance yesterday in Massimo's café! I think it is not just chance, but perhaps fate, no?' He was clearly enjoying this.

'Oh, I did not know,' Giorgio said quietly, glancing at Niamh.

'Franco, it was totally by chance and meeting at your sister's restaurant and Massimo's café was totally normal, as you always hang out there when you are in town.' Niamh tried desperately to tone down the implication that something greater was happening with Jeffrey. 'You're exaggerating, and it's only dinner. It's not a big deal.'

'Well, my dear, this is not how my friend Jeffrey is looking at this. He is very excited about tomorrow night's dinner date.'

Even though she was embarrassed at having this conversation in front of Giorgio, she had to admit to feeling a little bit pleased when Franco said how excited Jeffrey was about dinner. It had been a long time since she had had any excitement in her life when it came to a man. Life with Rick had become pedantic and predictable and he could never have been accused of ever getting excited about the prospect of having dinner with her. Her thoughts trailed off and she tried to remember if it had been different at the start. It must have been, there must have been a spark, but she was damned if she could recall it now.

Her attention was jolted back as they were called to the table to eat. With each glass of wine she got braver with her Italian and had several fragmented, confusing and downright funny conversations. She couldn't remember laughing this much in a long time. The group were warm and welcoming and they wished her luck with her new café, each of them promising to visit.

Two hours or so later she heard a car door close and footsteps coming up the gravel path. Sara arrived, looking as though she'd just stepped out of a couture advertisement, wearing a cream-coloured satin halter neck jumpsuit and carrying a wicker basket that contained several bottles of champagne.

'Jesus, she's like a model,' Niamh mumbled to Franco, who was sitting alongside her. She self-consciously tugged on her dress. It had gotten more and more snug with each course and at this point she was just hoping that the zipper wouldn't give way.

'Yes, I know she's my sister, but even I can see how beautiful she is,' Franco said. 'She used to be a model but got tired of it and went back to culinary school. I think half of her clients go to Sara's just to see her. The male ones, at least.' He laughed.

Giorgio got up to greet her and walked her to the table.

'They look good together, don't they?' she said to herself as much as to Franco.

'They do. A handsome couple, no?'

Niamh pretended to take a sip of wine in the hope of not having to comment further about Sara and Giorgio.

Franco raised his glass to hers. 'A toast to Café Limoni. I hope that this dream will make you happy,' he said with a kind smile.

'*Grazie*, Franco,' she replied, taking a long sip of the champagne. 'I hope so, too.'

# Chapter Twenty-Three

At exactly eight o'clock the next evening she reached the narrow little alleyway entrance to Da Paolo's. Jeffrey was already there waiting for her and greeted her with a hug and a large grin. The owner came and greeted Jeffrey and ushered them to their table in the courtyard outside.

'This is adorable. We didn't get to sit here last time,' she said, admiring the small space that held only eight tables.

'I pulled a few strings to get an outside table,' he said with a wink.

He held her chair as she sat at the table, noticing with a smile that a bottle of Franciacorta had been pre-ordered and was sitting in an ice bucket adjacent to them.

'Nice touch,' she said.

'Well, I felt lucky that you agreed to have lunch with me the first time, not to mention dinner tonight, so I wanted to show my appreciation at having been given a second shot,' he replied. 'May I?' He smiled as he tipped the bottle towards her glass.

'I rarely say no,' she said, returning his smile. She realised that it felt nice to have someone pay so much attention to her and she relaxed more into her chair.

Jeffrey did most of the ordering, as he spoke decent Italian.

The menu offered an array of fresh seafood and shellfish, but as Niamh had noticed when she had had lunch there previously, most of the tables ordered the same thing. Da Paolo's was renowned for their daily specials and in this case it was oven-roasted whole fish cooked in white wine, tomatoes and capers.

They chatted easily again over dinner, Niamh telling Jeffrey about her ideas for the café and he telling her about his attempts to secure a job back home.

'I must have applied to about thirty different law firms. The competition for the top firms is really intense – a lot of smart graduates looking for a small number of top jobs,' he said as he topped up their wine glasses.

'Are they all in Canada?'

'No, I've applied to a whole bunch in the US too. New York, Boston, Chicago and DC. Franco has applied to most of the same firms, so in a way we're even competing with each other. It will be tough if one of us gets our top choice and the other doesn't.'

'Stop being such a pessimist!' she admonished. 'When do you find out? I mean, when do these firms start contacting successful candidates?'

'Well, the first round of calls could be any day now. They know that candidates apply to multiple firms, so they are equally driven to lock in their ideal choice of candidate as soon as possible. My guess is that if we're successful in the first round we'll get a call next week. If not, it will be another couple of weeks after that, once they've gone through the first round. It's just a waiting game now.'

'That must be pretty frustrating.'

'It is a bit, because I actually don't know when I'll have to leave here. However, it does mean that until then I get to hang out in Liguria for the summer and that doesn't suck. To be honest it's probably the last time I'll have any real free time for the next few years.' He laughed. 'If you're lucky enough to get into one of the top firms then it means years of long hours.'

Several bottles of local, crisp white wine had followed the initial bottle of Franciacorta when eventually the waiter placed two espressos and a plate of biscotti in front of them. Niamh looked around and realised that they were the last two sitting out there. 'We should go and let these people go home.'

'Oh, you're right. I hadn't noticed that everyone else had left. How about a drink at La Terrazza? I'm staying at the hotel this weekend.'

'OK, that sounds nice, but only if I can buy the drinks – and thank you for dinner. I had a really nice time.'

'Me too, and I think I'm man enough to let a woman buy me drinks,' he joked.

They strolled to the outdoor terrace of La Terrazza and sat with an unobstructed view of the moon, fat and high in the sky, reflecting on the bay below. The waiter brought them two glasses of limoncello, followed by another two on the house, as Jeffrey told her about the various towns and villages she needed to explore locally.

'I better head home, it's getting late. I'll get the bill,' Niamh said, as she reached for her handbag. 'Where . . . ' she looked left and right on both sides of her chair.

'What's up?'

'Where's my bag?' She looked under the table, stood up and took her jacket off the back of the chair, but her bag was nowhere to be found. 'Oh fuck! I must have left it at the restaurant. It was on the ground next to my chair. Shit. Do you think we can call them?'

'Um, Nina it's one o'clock in the morning and we were the last people to leave. They are long since closed. Don't worry about it. I'll get the check.'

'No, it's not just that, it's my phone and my keys, too. Fuck!'

'The keys to your apartment? Oh shit. OK, let me call the restaurant just in case there's someone there late. I doubt it, though.' He pulled out his phone and looked up the number of the restaurant. 'There's no answer. Do you have a spare stuck outside or is there anyone else in the building who can let you in?'

'No, putting a spare outside would be the kind of thing a smart person would do. I don't qualify for that description. And no, I don't know any of the neighbours in the other apartments yet because I spend all my time at the café, so I haven't met anyone else in the building. I can't exactly go buzzing their doors in the middle of the night. Not the best way to endear yourself with the neighbours, wouldn't you agree?' She wasn't sure why she was being so sarcastic with Jeffrey, as he had nothing to do with it. She put her head into her hands and let out a loud sigh. 'I'm such a fucking eejit.'

'Look, just stay with me tonight. It's not a problem and I promise I won't bite.'

She sat bolt upright. 'No, wait, I could just get another room here for the night.'

'Nina, this is Italy, not America. They don't have twenty-four-hour staff. You'd be lucky to get some night manager who might manage to find a key if you had lost your room key, but check you into a room in the middle of the night? That's not happening. Just stay with me. I'll be good. Come on, I promise.'

'Shit. OK,' she said reluctantly, as she had no other choice, and followed him back to his hotel room.

'Death by minibar?' he asked as he opened the closet door and peered inside at the contents.

'Sure, why not? Why stop now?' she asked with a shrug. She couldn't remember having this much fun in a long time.

'So . . . we have a split of champagne, some dodgy-looking whisky, vodka and a half bottle of red or white wine. What's your fancy?'

'I think I'll stick to champagne, thanks.'

'OK, here you go, you have that. There are glasses in here somewhere,' he said, rooting through the small closet under the television.

'I can't believe I left my bag in the restaurant. I hope my phone won't be robbed.'

'Nah, the staff would have had to go out to clear up after we left so they'll have found it. Don't worry, it will be there in the morning.' He walked up to her and took her in his arms. 'Here, see if a hug will help.'

She was surprised at how bulky and strong he felt compared to Rick, his arms and across his back in particular. He felt good and it felt good to be held properly, even if it felt a little strange. She couldn't remember the last time Rick had held her in his arms like that, which made her feel sad. She lay her head down on his shoulder and sighed again. 'You smell good.'

'Thanks,' he laughed, releasing her from the hug. 'Stop worrying, will you?' he said quietly. He hesitated for a second and then leaned in and kissed her. She felt her shoulders soften. He pulled away from her and looked into her eyes. 'I'll sleep on that sofa thing over there if it will make you feel better. Honestly, I don't mind.'

'No, I don't want you to,' she said, standing on her tippy toes to kiss him.

'Are you sure?'

'Yes. Stop asking me.'

She wasn't sure if the drinks had given her fake courage or if it was the headiness of being kissed by someone new again, but this time she wanted him and didn't feign any moral objections. It was probably a combination of both. She didn't feel drunk, but then again that wasn't really a true indication of her level of sobriety, as most often it was the nights she 'felt fine' that ended in the worst catastrophes. Either way, she didn't care. Here was this tall, strong, good-looking Canadian who was utterly charming and sweet, and he liked her. She hadn't had this kind of attention in a long time.

Why the hell not, Niamh? she thought to herself, wrapping her arms around his neck.

The following morning, Niamh knew immediately upon waking that she was in a strange bed. She could tell by the sheets, which were silky smooth against her skin. They felt like fancy hotel sheets. The fact that she was naked rather than wearing a T-shirt or pyjamas was the second sign that something was amiss. She turned her head and could see that Jeffrey was still sleeping. A pang of embarrassment rushed through her, as she thought back to the night before. Straggly memories like pieces of a patchwork quilt coming together started to float through her mind. Suddenly, she had a mental image of her trying to imitate a pole dancer using the four-poster bed.

Jesus, did I pole dance for him? I'm mortified! she thought with a grimace. You don't do normal dancing well, Niamh, never mind pole dancing!'

She could feel the embarrassment work its way up her neck in a hot flush again. Mortified, she closed her eyes at the memory, struggling to put the remnants of recollections back together into a cohesive picture.

She turned to look at him again. He was sound asleep. Moving slowly and quietly, she gently eased out of the bed. She shook her head again in remorse as she picked up her various items of clothing that had so clearly been discarded in haste.

'Where the fuck is my bra?' she whispered to herself.

She lifted up his trousers and shirt from the floor, hoping to find it underneath.

'Where the fuck is my fucking bra?'

She checked his side of the bed, but there was no sign of it. She knew that if she was to get out of there unnoticed, she would have to be quick. She tiptoed into the bathroom and threw on her clothes. She didn't dare run the tap to splash water on her face for fear of waking him, but instead picked up her sunglasses, her shoes and crept out. She stepped silently into the hall and turned to close the door gently behind her. Her bra was hanging on the doorknob outside the room. In a flash she remembered deciding that they should do like they did in the old movies and hang a white cloth or towel outside the door, and had the bright idea of using her bra instead.

'Oh my God. I'm mortified. How many people have seen this?' she moaned quietly, as she pulled the door shut with a click. 'God forbid you'd just use the DO NOT DISTURB sign, like a normal human. No, you had to hang your bra on the doorknob, like some pornographic lunatic.' She stuffed the bra into her pocket, slipped on her shoes and made her way to the lobby bathroom.

She had black smudges of mascara and eyeliner under her eyes. She did her best to freshen up her face with water and paper towels in the bathroom mirror. 'Looking decidedly lovely today, Niamh. Look at the state of you. If you were on the street, sitting on a piece of cardboard with a blanket wrapped around you, people might throw a coin at you this morning.'

Her hair looked like a dead, matted cat on top of her head, most likely as a result of the half a can of hairspray she had used last night. Washing it was out of the question, though – she would rather die right there than have to massage her head, followed by the pain of blow-drying afterwards, and she didn't have the luxury of the type of hair that you could let dry naturally. She would have to pull out a baseball cap when she got home and hide underneath it for the day. She caught sight of herself in the mirror and decided that she looked like a failed drag queen. 'So much for the skincare routine,' she said, as she slipped back out of the lobby bathroom unnoticed.

She had no money and no way of getting home, so she went to the only place she could think of that was open at seven o'clock in the morning.

'Of course it had to be sunny,' she moaned, as she put on her sunglasses and walked quickly to Massimo's.

Massimo greeted her with his usual sunny smile. 'Ah, *buongiorno*, Nina! You need a coffee, no?' he asked with a grin. His voice sounded louder than normal.

'Yes, Massimo, but I've no money. I left my bag at Da Paolo's last night so I have to wait until they open to get it.'

'Nina, is no problem. They will open at eight o'clock to prepare for the lunch, so you have a half an hour to enjoy your coffee. Or maybe you need two today, no?'

'Yes, maybe indeed.'

She feigned normality as she ordered two cappuccinos. She sat outside in the hope of avoiding further conversation, put her sunglasses back on again and slunk down into the hard chair. She realised that she probably looked quite strange, sitting alone at the table with two cappuccinos, but she didn't care. The coffee was helping. She was massaging her temples when she saw the other chair at her table being pulled back and someone sitting down on it. She looked up to see Emily grinning at her.

'I can spot a hangover at ten paces,' she said, pulling in her chair. 'Good grief, you look wretched. I want to know everything. What did I miss?'

Niamh looked at her and groaned. 'You don't want to know.'

'Oh, I definitely do. Whose coffee is this?'

'Mine.'

'Ah, I understand. It's a two-coffee kind of morning. For future reference, it's best to order them one at a time so the second one doesn't sit there and get stagnant and cold while you try to stomach the first.'

'Agreed, but that would have required a second conversation.'

'Ah, I see. Well, this one looks cold already, so let me buy you a fresh one, then I'm coming back and I want details.' She clapped her hands together in glee at the prospect of some juicy stories. 'You don't look so good. Can I get you anything else?'

'I feel like absolute dog shit,' Niamh said in brutal honesty.

'Charming. All right then, I'll be back with some carbs.'

Niamh leaned forward and put her head on the table. She stayed that way, relishing the cold of the steel table top against her face, until Emily returned with fresh cappuccinos and warm croissants.

'You have a lovely pattern on one side of your face now,' she pointed out.

'Marvellous. Just add it to today's list of visual horrors. What are you doing here so early? You're not an early morning person.'

'I'm going to Milan this morning. Just stopping in for a coffee before the car arrives.'

'I kissed him.'

'What? Who?' Emily asked looking genuinely surprised. 'I was expecting a good story, given the state of you, but there was kissing? What have I missed?'

'What do you mean, "who?" Jeffrey.' Niamh groaned again and put her head in her hands.

'Good Lord, we haven't had this much excitement in town in ages. Go on!' Emily urged. 'How did this all happen and when?'

'Last night, at Da Paolo's. Well, not actually at Da Paolo's but afterwards, back at the hotel.'

'Go on! What on earth happened? This is very exciting!' Emily grinned.

'I don't know. One minute we were having a great time just chatting and laughing and the next we were kissing.'

'Were you drunk? Was he drunk?'

'I think we had three bottles of wine with dinner and I recall diving head first into his minibar, so yes, I think you can safely say we were drunk.'

'Wait … his minibar? You were back in his hotel room? How very *Dangerous Liaisons* of you!' Emily threw back her head and gave an uproarious laugh.

'OK, fine.' Niamh placed her forehead on the table and muttered, 'That's not the whole story.'

'It rarely is, my dear. Come on, out with it.'

Niamh lifted her head off the table and looked across at her friend. 'I slept with him,' she said. She sipped her second cappuccino, shaking her head. 'I mean, what got into me? A week ago I had sworn off of men, given recent disasters, and here I am kissing a practical stranger like a dog in heat.'

Emily waved her hand in the air. 'Don't be so hard on yourself. So you slept with him. He's very charming and clearly attracted to you. What's the problem? Stop overthinking it, you were due a bit of a blow-out night.'

'It was so stupid, though. I mean, he's leaving at the end of the summer so nothing can come of it, and now I've gone and slept with someone in a small town. Stupid of me to have complicated things.' She sighed.

'Look, A, he's not from here – he's Canadian and returning home in a matter of weeks, and B, he's not weird, he likes you and you like him. Niamh, you've been pining away over that dreary excuse of a man back in Dublin, even though he's the one who left you, and for some reason you think you belong in some self-imposed purgatory. Have some fun for a while. You're young and single, and so what if he's leaving at the end of the summer? Not every relationship or fling has to be for ever, you know. There's a lot of good in the temporary versions, also.'

Niamh squinted at her through her headache. 'I never thought about it that way, but I suppose I did put myself into some sort of sad-girl, self-imposed prison, didn't I? What a loser I am. Rick is the one who left and I sat around mourning him. God, I wouldn't recognise me if I saw myself like this a few months ago.'

'You know what they say about the best way to get over a man?'

'No, I don't. Grace said something about that a couple of weeks ago too before she left. Go on, then, what's the advice?'

Emily sat back and folded her arms across her chest. 'The best way to get over a man is to get under another.'

'Emily, that's a vile way of putting it. I'm no prude, but God, that's crude.' Niamh squinted across the table.

'Like it or not, it works. If you shag someone else then suddenly you don't have only Mr Misery Guts back in Dublin in your head. Someone else is swirling around in there, naked, too. It's called the Penis Distraction Theory. It creates the little bit of distance and distraction you need to gain some perspective and move on.'

'You totally made that up. That's an Emily Drake theory, isn't it?'

'What does it matter who made it up? It works and that's all that counts!'

'Sounds like you've done a thesis on this.'

'I've done substantial groundwork, yes,' Emily said with a grin. 'Now, I must go meet my driver.' She tossed back the remainder of her cappuccino and stood up. 'I'll call you when I get back.' And with a large wave she was gone.

# Chapter Twenty-Four

It felt almost ceremonial to turn the lock in the door and flip the sign around to read APERTO/OPEN to the outside world. Niamh gave a little clap with her hands and made her way back behind the counter, wondering who would be first to cross the threshold. She unwrapped the various dishes of salads that she had prepped earlier that morning and placed them in a series of large, hand-painted pottery bowls in the refrigerated display cabinet. The smell of torn fresh basil, ripe tomatoes and tangy cubes of marinated feta cheese rose up to greet her as she peeled back the layers of plastic.

Loaves of freshly baked ciabatta from the local baker stood ready to make the light, healthy sandwich options listed on her menu. She had purposely kept it short to start with, offering four types of salad and the same number of sandwiches, thinking it would be better to start slowly and get the basics right initially.

The door opened, triggering the bell that she had had affixed. An older Italian man shuffled in, stopped and looked around.

'*Buongiorno.*'

'*Buongiorno,*' she replied with the widest smile she could muster.

He fired off a stream of rapid Italian that she failed utterly to understand.

'Um ... *mi scusi, non ho capito*,' Niamh stuttered, trying to explain that she didn't understand.

'*Lei non è italiano, signora?*' he asked incredulously.

'*Io, no*,' she replied, trying to think how to say that she was Irish, not Italian. 'Um ... *io sono irlandese*,' she said, stumbling over the few words that she knew.

The little old man uttered a grunt that sounded like '*Meh!*' and with a dismissive wave of his hand he turned and shuffled back out of the door.

'Well, this is certainly a positive start,' she mumbled sarcastically as she wiped the countertop for the third time that hour. 'The first person to cross the threshold turns out to be a total racist and flees because I'm not Italian. Well, that's just rude!'

The little bell chimed again.

'*Buongiorno, signora*.'

She turned to see the postman stride across the floor.

'Oh, *buongiorno*,' she said, asking if she could get him anything.

'*No, grazie ... ecco*.' He handed her what looked like her first electricity bill.

'Charming – a rejection and an electricity bill. This has been a profitable first hour. Third time's a charm, perhaps?' she mused.

Her phone pinged with the sound of an incoming message.

*Hello, love. Just checking to see how it's going there?* her mother wrote. *If you're too busy to chat, I understand.*

'Chance would be a fine thing,' Niamh muttered under her breath as she replied with a whopping lie. *Yes, all good. A bit slow this morning but that's probably to be expected.*

*Of course it is, love. Just wait until word gets out and you'll be run off your feet!*

Niamh rolled her eyes and looked around the empty café. *Yep! Must run! Chat soon.*

She couldn't keep up a text exchange of blatant lies so she added two kisses and hit send. An hour later a text from Grace interrupted a game of solitaire on her phone.

*Hi! Can you talk or are you busy?*

*I can talk.*

Her phone rang immediately.

'Hey! I didn't want to interrupt you. How's it all going? I've been thinking of you all morning.'

'Fantastic,' Niamh replied sarcastically.

'Uh oh. What happened?'

'Nothing. Nothing is what happened. That's the problem. I've been sitting here since nine o'clock this morning and so far I've had a little old man who was lost and the postman dropping off my first bill. So far, it's a complete disaster.'

'Maybe it's just not an early town?' Grace offered.

'Grace, all the other cafés are packed every morning,' Niamh said despondently.

'Well, people probably don't know you're open yet.'

'The postman managed to find me,' she said sulkily.

'Well, he was actively looking for you. How did you announce the opening?'

'What do you mean?'

'I mean what kind of marketing did you do?'

'Well, I have the new sign outside and I put a notice up in a few places around town and I displayed a poster at Massimo's place, stuff like that.'

'But, Niamh, you're not on a main street – that location is

a bit off the beaten path! We stumbled upon it by accident, remember?'

'Are you saying this is a stupid idea?' Niamh said, her voice getting louder. 'Because it would have been great to have heard this before I ploughed so much money into this mad notion.'

'Stop being so defensive and don't get all pissy with me. I'm just saying that you might need to do some more marketing until people realise that you're there, that's all. For God's sake, don't make me regret calling you, Niamh. I'm just trying to help. Like, I don't know ... get a sandwich board and plonk it outside on the street, or put up some kind of notice or advert on the Camogli websites. They love promoting local places like that, don't they? Or, I don't know ... hire someone to walk up and down the pier with coupons or something.'

'Yeah, I suppose you're right,' Niamh agreed reluctantly. 'Maybe I could—'

Before she'd finished her sentence the bell rang and in walked two middle-aged men in shorts and bulging T-shirts.

'Gotta go!'

'OK, good luck!'

'*Buongiorno*,' she said cheerfully as they made their way to a table.

Definitely northern Europe somewhere, she mused, based on the way they were dressed and the massively overgrown moustaches. She gave them a minute to look over the menu.

'Can I get you something?'

'Ah, English?'

'Yes, well, Irish, actually, but I speak English,' she corrected in the way that Irish people the world over always felt the need to do.

One of them looked at her directly, clearly expressing that he didn't give a toss either way.

'We take a beer.'

'Ah ... well, I don't actually have any beer, I'm afraid.'

He looked at her again, this time blankly.

She sighed quietly. 'I'm afraid I don't have any beer,' she repeated slowly, enunciating her words.

He looked towards his moustached friend and back to her again. 'No beer?'

'No, sorry. I don't have a beer licence yet.'

He muttered something in German to the other moustache and they both stood abruptly, nodding to her as they left the café.

'Philistines,' she spat under her breath. 'What? You can't have a bloody sandwich without beer? I mean, I like a boozy lunch like the next girl, but it's a bloody sandwich. Have a cup of tea!'

It was almost another hour before the bell rang again. Niamh leaped up from behind the counter. 'Whatever it is you want you can have it for free, just please for the love of God don't go.' She hadn't intended to say it aloud, it just kind of came out.

She turned to see Giorgio standing just inside the door, a bemused look on his face.

'Of course, it's you,' she said, realising just how happy she was to see him at that moment, but trying desperately not to show it.

'So, this is your strategy to make money with this business? I am not so sure this will be a big success for you. But thank you, Nina, I will have an espresso, for free, no?' he said, his face breaking into a wide smile.

'You're actually going to allow me to make an espresso for you?' she asked, feigning shock.

She bent, pretending to root around for an imaginary something under the counter. Please don't notice that I'm blushing, goddamnit, she thought, as she tried to distract herself with a box of sugar sachets.

'Well, today, I am feeling brave – *coraggioso*, no? And you said it is free, no?'

'Yes. I'm just happy to have something to do, Giorgio,' she replied as she turned to face the coffee machine.

'Why? Not so many customers today?'

'Zero, actually, Giorgio. Zilch. Nada. Niente. Fuck all.'

'Ah, I understand. So you are frustrated about this, no?'

'You could say that, yes.'

'Don't worry, it will take time. You must be patient, Nina.'

'Not my greatest virtue.'

'What is this . . . virtue?'

'Um, it's a strength or positive characteristic.'

'Ah! OK, good. So what does this mean?'

'It means that I'm not the most patient person.'

'Ah, *sì*, yes, now I understand – and this does not surprise me,' he said with a grin, as he tipped back the tiny espresso cup.

He was always immaculately groomed and today was no exception. He wore a single-breasted navy suit, with another crisp white shirt unbuttoned at the neck.

I bet he's the kind of man who gets better looking with age, she thought, staring at him. He had a strong jaw and had the faintest hint of dark stubble. She only realised she was staring at him when she felt a strong urge to tuck a stray strand of hair back behind his ear.

'Exactly how many white shirts do you own, Giorgio?'

'I don't know,' he shrugged. 'I have never counted. A lot, I think!'

'You look good.'

He glanced up at her.

Fuck. Inside thoughts, Niamh, inside thoughts, she told herself in alarm.

'In white shirts I mean. It's a nice shirt ... on you ...'

'Ah, *grazie. È da Napoli.* I buy all of my shirts in Napoli. They are the best quality.'

'I think I'm missing the sartorial gene.'

'What does this mean? I don't understand ... sartor ...? What is it?'

'Sartorial. It means good sense of style, a good inkling for fashion.'

'Inkling?'

'Oh, um ... a good idea.'

'Ah I see. OK. *Bene.* Inkling,' he repeated.

His phone rang. This was the first time the two of them had been alone together in a while, and as she watched him pull out his phone she realised that she had missed his company.

'*Pronto.*'

She loved the way Italians answered the phone. Not by saying hello, but by saying '*pronto*' meaning 'I'm ready.' It was one of the delightful quirks of the language that she had picked up on since moving there. She had even tried saying '*pronto*' herself when her phone rang. She thought it made her sound sophisticated and helped her fit in more, but it had pissed her mother off no end and she had hung up twice, mistakenly thinking she had dialled the wrong number.

'But why do you say that when you answer the phone, Nina?'

'That's how all the Italians answer the phone, Mam.'

'But you're not Italian.'

'I know, but I'm living here now so I'm just trying to fit in as best I can. It's just a habit now.'

'But don't you see that it's me calling? Doesn't my number show up on your screen when I call you?'

Sweet Jesus, this could go on all day, Niamh thought. 'Yes, it does. You're right. Don't worry – I'll say hello in future.'

'Thank God. It's costing me a fortune with all these phone calls and having to hang up every time thinking I've dialled the wrong number.'

Niamh rolled her eyes. 'Yes, OK. I'll only answer in English from now on when you call.'

Giorgio stood and covered the phone with his hand. 'I must go back to the office. The coffee was not so bad. I think you will be OK, Nina,' he said with a wink as he left.

'What a gorgeous specimen of a man,' she said under her breath with a sigh. 'But don't wink at me if you don't mean it.'

She sat and debated whether she should just give up and close up shop for the first day, tempted just to crawl home and get under the covers. 'That's ridiculous. It's your first day, Niamh. Cop on,' she berated herself.

A hesitant knock on the door got her attention. Two short, white-haired old ladies stood outside, peering in through the glass.

'Just please don't be looking for an actual Italian person, for the love of God. Please want something ... anything ... that can be served in English. Please!' Niamh muttered as she opened the front door.

'*Buongiorno*,' she said with a smile.

The two ladies looked at each other and back to her.

'Do you speak English, dear?' one lady asked in a soft British accent.

'Yes, I do.' She held the door open for them.

'Oh, marvellous.'

They made their way to a corner table and ordered some tea.

'Are you here on holidays?' Niamh asked, as she placed two menus on their table.

'Yes, we come every year.'

'Oh, lucky you. Can I get you anything?'

'This caprese sandwich sounds lovely, but is it very big, dear? We don't eat that much for lunch at our age, you know.'

'I can divide it in half for you if you would like to share it,' she offered.

'Oh, that is so kind of you. Would you like that, Louise?'

The other lady had yet to utter a word.

'Yes, lovely,' she replied in a quiet voice.

They sat there for two hours, ordering several pots of tea and enthusiastically proclaiming her caprese sandwich to be one of the best they had ever had. Two other couples wandered in for coffee and sandwiches, an Italian lady for an espresso and a young couple asking if she had Wi-Fi. Too embarrassed to leave when she said no, they opted for a cappuccino and a slice of pie.

The two British ladies introduced themselves as Millie and Louise from London, and said that their friend had told them about the café.

'You heard about it?' Niamh asked, surprised to hear that they hadn't just stumbled upon it. 'But I only opened today.'

'We arrived yesterday from London. Our friend told us about this place last night on the terrace of the hotel. You must know her – Emily Drake?'

'I do,' Niamh replied with a smile. 'That was sweet of her.'

'She told us not to miss it and she was right. Well, good luck to you, dear,' Millie said as they shuffled out. 'See you tomorrow.'

And with that she had her first regular customers.

The next few weeks went by in a blur. Jeffrey had been

surprisingly sweet and had called a couple of times. He had even suggested another dinner date on her next free weekend. Niamh wasn't sure if it was her reluctance to get involved with anyone else again so soon, or the fact that she was totally wiped out every night and relished the thoughts of sleep over anything else these days, but either way she had put him off. She saw little of her new friends outside of the café as everything was new territory to her and when she wasn't opening, serving or closing she was getting ready to do one of those tasks. Word spread around town and some of the younger locals ventured in to try her salads and light lunch options. Unsurprisingly, she didn't do a big trade in coffee apart from the tourists, but the doorbell kept jingling as people wandered in and out. The most significant request that she was unable to fulfil was wine and it quickly became clear to Niamh that if she was to compete with the other lunch options in town she would have to figure out how to get a wine licence. Given that she herself believed that wine with lunch on holiday was more of an assumption than a luxury, she couldn't really blame those who opted to slink back out when they discovered that Café Limoni was, to all intents and purposes, a dry lunch option.

With that aside, she had built up a decent trade and, while she wasn't about to get rich based on the current numbers, she could, for the first time, see the potential of building it to a sustainable future. The older locals were curious and peered through the window, but they were never going to be her customers and after a couple of weeks she learned to make peace with that, and focus instead on those she could attract.

# Chapter Twenty-Five

After a particularly long and busy week, Niamh finally turned the key in the door of Café Limoni and headed home, grateful that tomorrow was Sunday and she had the day off. It had been her busiest Saturday yet, and she walked home feeling happy about how the week had gone, and particularly proud about the day she'd had today. This was the kind of satisfaction you could never get from working for someone else and she relished the feeling after all the weeks of uncertainty. She tried to call Emily on her walk home but her phone battery was dead. She had forgotten to charge it all day due to the relentless stream of customers.

Probably for the best, she thought, as she ambled along, or Emily would be inviting me to one thing or another. Instead, I have a date with my fancy new Italian sheets and my blackout blinds.

The following morning, Niamh woke to check the time, and remembered that her phone had died the previous evening. She had obviously fallen dead asleep before she had thought to plug it in. She was standing under the steady beat of the water in the shower when she heard the noises that went on and on. Unable to make out the sound, she turned off the water to listen but it had stopped. She wrapped a towel around her and stepped into the bedroom. Her phone was lit up. There were seventeen missed calls from Grace, four from her dad and dozens of text messages. Her breath tightened and her hand started to shake instinctively from the sudden surge of adrenaline rushing through her body. She sat on the edge of the bed, with the phone cable extended to its fullest, and dialled Grace's number.

'Jesus Christ, I thought you were dead. Where the fuck were you, Niamh?'

'I'm sorry I—'

'I've been trying to reach you since ten o'clock last night.'

Niamh quickly calculated that that would have been eleven o'clock Italian time and she was already asleep.

'I'm sorry. My phone died and I forgot to charge it. What's wrong?'

'Mam is in hospital. It's bad. You have to come home.'

'What? What happened?'

'I don't know, we don't know yet. We're waiting to see the doctors this morning. She collapsed at home.'

'Jesus. Is she OK?'

'They have her wired up to all kinds of monitors at the moment. I was there last night. I haven't been in yet this morning. Robert is away so I have to drop the kids off to a friend in an hour and I'll go in then.'

'But what are they saying?'

'I don't know. I mean, they don't know. They haven't said anything yet. They're doing all kinds of tests. She was in a bad way last night, Niamh.'

'Oh shit. OK, umm, I'll check flights. I don't know when the next flight is but if you think I should go then I'll go.'

'They aren't my words, Niamh. The doctor asked about family and I said you were in Italy. He said to tell you to come home.'

She could hear Grace crying quietly on the other end of the phone. She felt the water drip from her hair down her back and onto her shoulders.

'Where's Dad?'

'He's with Mam. He stayed with her last night.'

'OK. I'll check flights and I'll call you back.'

Her hands shook as she pulled out her laptop. 'Come on, Wi-Fi, just fucking work today, OK?' she yelled at the screen.

There was one flight that afternoon but she had no idea what the train schedule to Milan was like on a Sunday.

'What's the goddamn train company name?' she muttered as she typed into her Google search bar. The timetable showed several trains departing Camogli, but all of them had multiple stops and none of them got to Milan in time for her to make the flight. She picked up her phone and texted Emily.

*Please call me if you get this. It's urgent. I need your help.*

Four minutes later her phone rang.

'What's the matter?' Emily asked.

She started to sob as she explained the situation and relayed the phone call from her sister. 'There's a flight at two o'clock but none of the trains will get me there on time.'

'Stop crying and get yourself together. You don't have all the facts so don't waste your energy on tears just now. Pack a bag and wait. I will take care of this for you. I'll call you back shortly.'

She hung up abruptly and Niamh did as directed. 'What do you pack for something like this?' she wondered as she dried her eyes and stuffed clothes into an overnight bag. Her phone rang six minutes later.

'Giorgio will be outside your door in thirty minutes. He will take you directly to the airport.'

'Giorgio?'

'Yes. I couldn't reach my driver by phone so I called Giorgio. He was at home when I called. He said he would be there in thirty minutes. Now, get your passport and put it into your bag right now. You're upset, Niamh, and likely to forget it. Then go online and buy a ticket for that flight while you wait. Don't leave it until you get to the airport, as that's a disastrous situation to deal with in Italy. And bring a pair of large sunglasses. I'm not joking about that. If you are upset then you're better off hiding behind them rather than deal with nosy individuals gaping at you. Wear them on the flight too if you need to.'

Niamh was nodding as she spoke, grateful to be told what to do. Her mind was swirling with thoughts and worries. She thought about her mother and what condition she was in, she thought about her dad, sitting by her side all night. She thought about her sister frantically dropping the boys off with a friend so she could get to the hospital quickly.

She was waiting downstairs when Giorgio pulled up.

'Nina, I'm so sorry,' Giorgio said as he got out of the car. He wrapped her in a hug.

'Thanks. I'm so sorry to ruin your Sunday,' she said, wiping her eyes dry.

'No, I am happy that I was here to help.' He took her bag and flung it on the back seat. 'Your flight is at two o'clock, yes?'

'Yes,' she said, nodding.

'OK, we will get there in plenty of time. Don't worry.'

'OK. Thank you, Giorgio. I . . . '

'There is no need to say anything. Family is everything, no?'

Her eyes welled up with tears and she clenched both fists and blinked furiously to hold them at bay. She took Emily's advice and hid behind her oversized sunglasses.

He drove like a maniac and made it to the airport in

two hours. The journey was mostly in silence, with only the Italian radio for distraction, most of which she didn't understand anyway.

He parked the car and got out, whipping her bag from the back seat.

'Thanks, Giorgio. I'll . . .'

'Come,' he said, taking her hand. 'I'm coming with you. Do you have a boarding pass yet?'

'No, I just bought the ticket online at home.'

'OK, I will take care of this for you. Don't worry.'

She felt like a little girl as he held her hand, took charge and strode ahead. She hadn't even thought about boarding passes or anything like that. The security liquids rule flashed into her head and she couldn't remember if she had even packed cosmetics or not. Giorgio presented her passport and luggage at the check-in counter. She could just about make out the conversation with him arguing with the attendant that she was not going to check her bag in. He picked it up, shook it, twirled it around, all the while gesturing with his other hand and reeling off rapid, stern Italian.

She didn't know what he said exactly, but the attendant conceded and she took her bag and boarding pass with her.

'You must be at the gate in forty minutes. The entrance to security is there,' he said pointing to a series of empty turnstiles.

'There's no one there,' she muttered confused.

Giorgio smiled at her. 'Nina, it is Sunday. Sunday is for family. No one travels on a plane in Italy on a Sunday unless it is absolutely necessary. So, this means that you will be at the gate in ten minutes from here, from this place. Do you understand?'

'Yes.'

'OK. Now, vodka or whisky?'

'Sorry?' She realised that he had escorted her from the security check point entrance to a little bar just ten yards away as they were talking.

'Vodka or whisky? It is a simple question, no? You have had a shock and a drink will help. Just one, not ten, you understand? Ten will not help, Nina.'

'Vodka, please.'

He sat her down on a chair and disappeared to the bar, coming back with a double vodka, an espresso and some sort of a baguette sandwich sticking out from a paper bag.

'I have to have an espresso too?'

'No, the espresso is for me as I will drive back to Camogli again now,' he said with a small smile and a shrug.

'Oh right, of course. Sorry, I'm not making any sense.'

He sat with her as she drank her vodka. He reached over and stuck the baguette into her bag. 'I am certain that you have not eaten today, and the food on the aeroplanes is . . . how do you say . . . food for dogs?'

'Dog food,' she said with a smile. She couldn't imagine Giorgio ever eating anything from a plastic airline tray.

'Ah, easy! Yes, dog food. Promise me that you will eat this before you get to Dublin.'

'I promise.' She realised for the first time today that she was hungry. It was almost one o'clock and she hadn't eaten all day.

'Do you need me to do anything for you?'

'No thank you,' she said, staring down into her drink. 'Oh, wait. Can I give you the keys of the café? I had planned to go in there today. Would you mind checking to make sure that everything is OK? There's food and stuff in there and I'm not sure when I'll be back.'

'Yes, give me the keys. I will take care of it. I will take care of everything. Don't worry . . . *va bene?*' he said, taking her hand.

She nodded her response, not trusting herself to speak, and squeezed his hand back in return.

He walked her back towards the security entrance, put her bag on the ground and held her in a strong, tight hug. She closed her eyes wanting to melt into him right there and pretend that none of this was happening. He pulled back from her slowly, put his hands on her shoulders and looked at her intently. Her heart started to pound in her chest.

'*Non preoccuparti*. Don't worry. Everything will be OK,' he said gently, as he leaned forward and kissed her on both cheeks. He put her bag on her shoulder and nudged her gently in the direction of the waiting security attendant. '*Vai*, Nina,' he said, encouraging her to go.

'Thank you,' was all she dared to say for fear that the emotions racing through her would cause her knees to give way or her eyes to flood with tears. She handed her boarding pass to the attendant, who gave it a cursory review and nodded that she could go. She turned and looked back over her shoulder. Giorgio was standing where she had left him, his hands in the pockets of his jeans, watching her. He nodded, indicating in his own way that she should continue on forward and that everything was going to be OK. The fact that he had brought her here, that he had helped her and had taken charge was utterly generous and kind. The fact that he had stayed here until she had left was enough to make her fall apart. He could easily have turned and walked away, but that one small gesture of waiting there and watching her go was the sweetest, most selfless thing anyone had done for her in a while, if ever. She gave a small wave and turned away as she wiped the tears from her face, making her way slowly and with a heavy heart to her gate.

She sat down and pulled out her phone to text her sister and saw that she had several messages. The noise of the airport must have obscured the message alerts coming in. Grace was at the hospital and their mother was stable. Emily sent her best wishes, saying to text her if she needed anything. Giorgio had sent another note simply saying not to worry and he would see her again as soon as her mother was well.

How sweet. What lovely people I've met here, Niamh thought as she stood up unsteadily, ready to board her flight home, uncertain of what awaited her when she got there.

# Chapter Twenty-Six

Niamh went straight to the hospital on arrival. Her mother was weak but conscious and happy to see her. She took her hand as Niamh stood alongside the bed.

'I'm sorry to worry you, love, and have you fly all this way home.'

'Stop, Mam, it's fine. How are you feeling?'

'I don't know, to tell you the truth, with all this medicine they have me on.'

She was beyond pale. She was more a grey colour and she looked old and vulnerable lying there in the hospital bed. Grace had warned her before she entered her room, but it was still a shock to see her like that.

'You never think of your own mother as an old woman, but she looks like an old woman in there tonight. Just be prepared for that,' Grace had said as they entered the room together.

She was wired to a drip and all sorts of monitors that Niamh didn't understand. The doctors had said that they needed to run more extensive tests in the morning so that they could determine what had caused the problem. The two girls spent the evening there with Paddy, talking to doctors and nurses and sitting by their mother's bedside.

Later that night Grace said goodbye and went to collect

the boys. 'I'll be in again in the morning, Mam. Have a good rest tonight.' She bent over and kissed her on the cheek. 'Love you.'

'I love you, too. Now go get those gorgeous boys and get them to bed,' Una said with a small smile.

When Grace had closed the door behind her, Una turned to her daughter and motioned for her to sit down. 'I had a visitor earlier, when you were on your flight home. Rick came to see me.'

'Who?' Niamh asked, her mind refusing to function.

'Rick. Your Rick.'

'What? He's not my Rick. Not any more, Mam. How did he know you were in here in the first place?'

'Well, actually he called to the house looking for you and the woman next door was in her garden. She had been there when the ambulance came for me last night so she told him. It was nice of him to come and visit me, wasn't it?'

'Why was he looking for me?' Niamh asked, frowning.

'Well, he said he wants to make amends. That he made a mistake and he called to the house to see you.'

'What did you tell him?' she asked suspiciously. Niamh was afraid that her mother had always secretly harboured a hope that she'd live happily ever after with Rick. 'Boobra must have dumped him. Serves him right.'

'Who in God's name is Boobra?'

'Oh, nothing, forget it. So, what did you tell him? Did you tell him that I've moved to Italy and I'm loving my new life and I'm skinny now? Not that I am, but he doesn't know that so I hope you told him.'

'No,' her mother said slowly. 'I said you were in Italy all right, and he seemed surprised at that.'

'I bet he was. I bet he was very surprised that I was actually living a life somewhere fabulous without him. You know what? I bet he expected me to be at home watching television, depressed, sobbing and eating my way through tubs of ice cream. Ha! Little does he know. Prick.'

'Nina, it's hard enough to talk. Will you stop that rambling and listen to me, for God's sake?'

'Sorry. Go on.'

'I know he hurt you but he told me that he made a mistake and he wants you back. People can change or fix their mistakes. What's the point of all those self-help books and life coaches if people aren't able to change their ways and become better versions of themselves? If you can forgive him for hurting you and if you love him entirely then you have a chance at a good future together, but there can be no room in your heart for any doubt – or anyone else.'

What exactly has Grace told her? Niamh wondered, horrified that her mother might know any details of her romantic life, scant as it was.

'Reluctance and hesitation creates space,' her mother continued, 'and space creates opportunity for problems. Why are you so adamant you don't want him back? Do you really mean it?'

'He cast me aside so easily, Mam, and I heard nothing from him for months.' She could feel herself getting frustrated already with the conversation and she was irrationally angry at the idea that Rick had seen her mother before she had.

'Well, his own family are certainly no role models for great couples. His parents hardly talk to each other and both of his brothers are divorced, but he does love you, that I'm certain of.' Una paused and took a long breath. 'But you must love him back, Nina. You have to be certain. And if you want to build a future with him then you'll have to forget about these notions of Italy. I'm just saying this because you never even spoke to the man after you broke up. You went on holiday and didn't come back. It was all very reactionary and you need to be sure that you made, and are making, the right decision. The fact is he'll never be happy anywhere else. He's too Irish. It's only a certain kind of person can uproot and start over somewhere else. It speaks to strength of character and a quiet confidence in oneself.'

Niamh sat in silence, twiddling with her fingers, unsure of what to say.

Una shifted her position in the bed. 'Will you prop up my pillow a bit for me? You know, Nina, I see how your face lights up when you talk about this village in Italy – what do you call it again?'

'Camogli, Mother.' Niamh rolled her eyes. Her mother was never going to remember how to say it, no matter how long she tried. It was English or nothing.

'Right, yes, that place. Well, I see how you are when you talk about it. You like it there.'

It was said as a statement more than a question, but Niamh answered it anyway, as if to confirm the fact. 'Yes, I do.'

There was silence for a few moments and she could see that her mother was thinking of what to say next.

'Well, that's a good thing, I'm glad you're happy there. People start new lives in new places all the time. Sometimes for no reason except they just ended up there, but other times it's a choice. When it's the right choice it can be good for your soul. Only the lucky few get to live somewhere that feels good in their soul. Most people just survive and live somewhere because that's where they live and they are too reluctant or afraid to change. Young people today have much greater opportunities to change their life and start over, but you need to decide because you can't have both, Nina. If you think there is any chance of you two getting back together then you'll have to come back home to Ireland.'

'But he threw it all away, Mam, so how can I trust him? I heard nothing from him in all this time so how can I know for sure? I mean, how do I know if he was actually the one and he just screwed up and we're really meant to be together and I should stay?'

She could hear the level of hysteria rising in her voice, try as she might to control it, but she hadn't been prepared to talk about Rick and hadn't thought about him in a while. Now, the fact that he was back and saying that he had made a mistake – it was all very confusing.

'Nina, there's no such thing as "the one", that's just a concept made up by movie companies and the people who sell books full of those romantic stories. Surely you know that much? You're a smart girl.'

'Publishers, Mam, the people who sell books are called publishers,' she sighed.

'Well, whoever they are, Nina, they just made that up to drive us all mad searching for that one true love. Then, women all over the country are depressed when they see the movie or read the book and realise that they haven't found true love but they're running out of time, so they marry the next decent fella that they meet. It's all nonsense.'

'Mam, it's not nonsense. I'm not going to just marry anyone.'

'Who said you have to get married? For God's sake, Nina, you just broke up a few months ago. Sit down and take a minute before you go rushing into marrying him, will you? All I'm saying is you should listen to him. Surely everyone deserves a second chance, or at least the chance to be heard? Isn't that what you're always saying? You ran off with this hare-brained notion of living in Italy, and somehow it has worked out and you like it there, but your reaction to all this was just as bad as his. You can't just run from your problems. You have to face them. And I think you owe it to yourself to find out if there is still a chance for you two before you write him off, that's all.'

'I don't know. This is all very confusing. He left and I heard nothing this whole time. Not a word! And now suddenly he shows up and wants to talk and wants me back? Rick and I were great together at one point but even that had kind of faded into mediocrity. And everything else was kind of average, at least for me it was. I mean, he's the one who had the great job. Mine was only OK. He had a great apartment. I was still stuck living at home because I couldn't afford my own place. No offence.'

'Yes, Rick and you were good together – until you weren't, but neither of you handled the situation very well.' Her mother shifted again in the bed. 'Will you hand me that cup of water, please? My throat is getting dry from the length of this lecture.'

'Mam, I . . . '

'Will you stop it, Nina, and just listen to me for a minute. All I'm saying is that loving someone isn't enough. There has to be more than that. Look at all the relationships that the average person has before they settle down with someone – many, correct?'

'Yes,' Niamh answered reluctantly, wondering where this might be going.

'Well, don't tell me that all those people weren't in love at some level or another or at one point in time. Of course, there was love or at least real happiness, otherwise what's the point of being in a relationship? But there has to be more.'

'What do you mean?' Niamh asked, now more confused than ever. 'You're starting to contradict yourself, Mam.'

'Nina, you have to love yourself. That's what I'm trying to tell you. That's the most important relationship you'll ever have. You have to be happy within yourself so that you can be happy in the relationship with your partner. You have to like who you are as a person and you have to like who you are in the relationship, because people change a little bit when they are in a relationship, they have to . . . they have to compromise to make it work. And you have to like the version of you that you become with the new person.'

Una handed her back the cup to place on the bedside locker. 'Relationships burn out or end because they didn't have all the ingredients – there was love, maybe, but it's not enough. Attraction to the other person isn't enough in itself, Nina. When you meet the right partner you'll feel good about them but also about yourself and how you act or feel around them.'

'Jesus, this is like something you'd hear on *Oprah* or one of those American talk shows. Where is all this coming from?'

'Don't be ridiculous! It's nothing like those shows on television where they beat up their relatives. It's pure common sense, if you think about it.'

The nurse stuck her head around the door and nodded in Niamh's direction. 'Ms Kelly, I'll have to ask you to leave now, please. The doctor is on his way.'

'Oh, OK, no problem.'

'Don't worry too much about making the right decision,' her mother continued. 'There's no rush. When everything lines up the way it's supposed to the universe has a way of letting you know. Just give your subconscious a job to figure it out and sleep on it for a while. When you can see no clear reason not to do the thing because it all makes sense to you, then you have to just go for it. Just be true to yourself, Nina. It's OK to go after what you want, and don't settle for good enough just because you should, but weigh up all the options and have all the conversations. If you don't, you're selling yourself short and you'll always wonder what might have been.'

She patted her daughter's hand and smiled, leaning back against the pillows. 'Now, run off home with you and get some rest. I'll see you tomorrow after my tests. They are pretty straightforward so they said I should be back in the ward by about eleven o'clock.'

'OK,' Niamh replied, giving Una a kiss on the cheek.

'Oh, and bring me some black grapes and some Rich Tea biscuits. The biscuits here are terribly boring altogether.'

'Right so,' Niamh said, giving her another kiss. 'I love you.'

'I love you, too. Go home to your father and make sure he has some dinner, will you? And don't forget my biscuits tomorrow.'

# Chapter Twenty-Seven

In her dream Niamh was being shoved and pushed back and forth on a boat. The boat was rocking and she with it. She didn't hear her bedroom door open. She had been home almost a week and her life had become a rotation between hospital visits twice a day and cooking dinner in the evening for her father and Grace and the boys.

The tests had shown that their mother had suffered a mild heart attack. There was a blockage in her arteries that would require surgery. It was a fairly routine procedure, but it still posed risks and would require a long rehabilitation period. Una was going to have to remain in hospital for a number of weeks, a reality she was not at all happy about.

Niamh had refused to see Rick, insisting that all her energies needed to be focused on her mother and the rest of her family right now. She knew that in truth she was partly using this as an excuse to delay having to see him, but it sounded entirely legitimate and appropriate, so he could hardly argue. She knew she'd have to see him eventually, if only to gain some closure, but for now her days were on repeat: hospital, lunch, hospital, dinner.

The surgery was finally scheduled for early the following day, which was a cause for both relief and anxiety for all of them. Niamh and Grace left the ward earlier than usual that night so that their mother could get a proper night's sleep before she was taken down to the theatre first thing in the morning. Paddy had arranged to be there early in the morning and the girls would follow a bit later. The doctor estimated that she should be out of recovery by noon.

She and Grace had stayed up late with their dad, chatting by the fire, each of them trying to defer the idea of going to bed only to lie there restless.

She was aware of being shoved, back and forth, back and forth as her brain caught up with her physical self. She heard her name called but it sounded like it came from far away. She woke slowly, opening her eyes to find Grace standing over her, her face wet with tears.

'Mam's dead,' she sobbed.

Niamh's head was fuzzy and dull from lack of sleep. Her eyes were refusing to open properly. She squinted, trying to focus on her sister. She couldn't catch the words that Grace had just spoken. She heard them, but couldn't process their meaning. She sat up with a slow fear creeping through her body.

'What?'

'Mam's dead, Niamh,' she repeated, sobbing loudly now.

The fear swelled inside her with a surge. It started in her stomach and welled up, expanding into her chest until it hurt. Her heart was pounding wildly.

'What are you talking about? I saw her last night. She was fine, Grace.' She sat up on the edge of the bed, her heart pounding loudly in her chest and her ears.

'She died, Niamh. She's dead.'

Grace sat on the bed and wailed, rocking back and forth.

'What the fuck, Grace? Tell me what's going on,' she

shouted in a panicked voice, as an unsummoned rage took hold of her. Her head was pounding.

Grace's voice had a staccato rhythm to it now as it fought with heaves and sobs for a sound. 'This . . . morning . . . '

'Yes, what? WHAT?' Niamh shook her shoulder frantically. 'WHAT, Grace? Tell me!'

'It was the anaesthetic,' she sobbed. 'It happened all of a sudden . . . she had a reaction to it. She went into . . . her blood pressure dropped, and she went into anaphylactic shock . . . and they couldn't revive her.'

Niamh sat and stared at her, suddenly weakened as the surge of fear she had felt rushed down through her body to her toes. She felt silent tears roll down her face, struggling to understand what Grace had just told her.

It must be true, she thought as she watched her sister fall to pieces alongside her. 'Grace, what? What actually happened? What do you mean?'

'She had a reaction to the anaesthetic . . . she was allergic to it. It's rare, but it does happen. They didn't know in advance.' Grace sobbed uncontrollably. 'They couldn't reverse it in time. Her heart just gave out.' She was wailing now, as if the words were puncturing her soul as she spoke them.

'What time is it?' Niamh asked, grabbing her phone. It was half-past eight. Her mother's surgery had been scheduled for seven o'clock. She hadn't even woken up to send her a text message before she went down.

'I wasn't even awake,' she said quietly. 'I was asleep when it happened. I was asleep when she went down to the operating theatre. I was asleep, Grace. I was asleep while she was dying.'

Grace looked at her, wiping her eyes with a soggy tissue. 'What?'

'I was asleep while Mam was dying. I wasn't there. I didn't even send her a note this morning.'

The adrenaline in her body was making her nauseous.

'Was she alone, Grace?' she asked, tears coursing strongly down her face now.

'No, Dad was there,' she sobbed. 'He was there early.'

'Oh my God.'

'He just called. Just now before I woke you. He said to go down there right away,' she sobbed. 'To say goodbye while she is still in the room . . . ' She sobbed uncontrollably again.

'But . . . how is she dead, Grace? Why did she die? I mean . . . she's in the hospital. It was a standard operation. You're not supposed to die in the hospital?' She sat on the bed, staring at her sister, beseeching her for answers.

'I couldn't really make out what he was saying . . . just that it's a rare condition, but some people have a reaction to the anaesthetic and Mam did . . . and that they couldn't bring her back.'

'Jesus.'

'I don't know anything else. He wasn't making much sense. We should get dressed,' Grace said, standing.

Niamh remained motionless on the bed. The tears that fell were silent. She hadn't started to sob yet. That would come later. Part of her felt as if she were living in someone else's bad dream. She shook her head hard and put her hands to her eyes. None of this made sense to her. It must be real, yet it couldn't be. She couldn't understand it. 'How is this happening?' she asked herself out loud.

Looking back on it, she had no recollection of getting dressed. She had no memory of her nephews' chatter when she went downstairs, or what she might have said to them. She had no memory of the car journey except for sitting stoically in the passenger seat of Grace's car, her hands clasped together in her lap, staring straight ahead into the grey, rainy day. She had no memory of dropping the boys off at crèche. She wasn't even sure if it was she or Grace who had walked them in. The only memory she had was of standing, frozen at the top of a sterile white corridor. It looked bleak, empty and soulless. The walls were hazy, blurry. It looked as if you could walk down the length of the corridor for miles and not reach the end. She remembered how her feet wouldn't move. She was rooted to the spot, her brain trying to process what was happening, what was about to happen. If she stayed there in that spot, then perhaps it might not be true. Perhaps she could stay there for ever on the precipice of both the corridor and of utter heartbreak.

Grace nudged her forward and her feet obeyed. She didn't know where they were going, only that she didn't want to go there. She wanted to slow down the walk, to not reach whatever door it was they were moving towards. Her heart was pounding again now in her chest. Grace reached the door before her.

How does she know which door it is? Niamh thought, forgetting that they had been there just the night before.

The door was numbered two hundred and twelve.

'Are there two hundred and twelve sick people in here?' she wondered. She couldn't be sure if she had said it out loud or in her head.

Grace hesitated at the door and turned to look at her sister. Niamh just turned to face her and returned the look. There was nothing to say.

Grace pushed through the heavy white door. The room was silent. Their father sat on a grey plastic chair next to the bed. He was holding his wife's hand. He looked up when the door opened and stared at them, his eyes wide with sorrow and loss. He stood and hugged them both. It was then that Niamh turned her gaze towards her mother. She lay there, silent. She looked peaceful, as if she were just sleeping, except for the colour of her face. It wasn't white. It wasn't grey. It was something in between. She didn't know if there was a colour name for it, but it wasn't a normal colour. She wondered if this was the colour that people turned when their life slipped out of their bodies and went elsewhere, or nowhere.

Grace was sobbing quietly, her head bent and her shoulders shaking as she held her mother's hand. Niamh could feel tears course down her face as she stared at her mother, but she couldn't hear any sound. She hugged her dad and felt herself sob into his chest as he did the same.

Grace stood back to allow Niamh the chance to step in beside their mother. She held her hand and leaned in to kiss her cheek.

'I'm sorry I was asleep, Mam. I'm so sorry.' The sobs were hurting her chest now as she gazed down at her mother's face.

That was all she could manage to say as her voice gave out. She surrendered to the tears and the pain that took over and bent her head down into her hands.

The door opened and a nurse bustled in. She spoke but the sound didn't seem to come from her. It seemed to come from far away and reverberate around the room. Niamh had no idea what the woman had just said. Her dad was sitting on the plastic chair, holding his wife's hand again, staring quietly at her face. Grace was sobbing inconsolably. Niamh decided then that she would have to try to be strong. Her mother would have wanted that.

The nurse was twiddling dials on the monitors alongside the bed. They were no longer connected to their patient, so

Niamh figured that she must be shutting them down, readying them to help the next patient. She wondered how much time they had, here in this little room with their mother. She stopped the nurse at the door as she went to leave the room.

'What time ... um ... how long ... ?' She couldn't find the right words to ask the question.

The nurse smiled a kind smile and placed a hand on her arm. 'Take your time, love. There's no hurry.'

Those simple, kind words summoned more silent tears. Niamh nodded her gratitude. She looked back into the room and felt a searing pain in her chest as she watched her father look at her mother. She wondered if this pain was what people meant when they talked about real heartbreak. She had never really thought it was an actual thing, an actual pain, but this pain was real and she had never felt it before. Breaking up with Rick had hurt, but she hadn't felt this or anything like it. She put her hand to her chest at the point of the pain but she couldn't reach it. She couldn't touch it. It was deep inside, some sort of primal pain reserved only for the most truly devastating moments in life.

Her father sat motionless, holding her mother's hand and gazing at her face. He looked as if sadness had wrapped itself around him and he sat there smothered by it. She knew then that she could not watch him say goodbye to the woman he had loved for over forty years. Not here, not in this grim, soulless hospital room.

She had no idea how long they had been in there. The nurse came in for a second time. She never told them that they needed to leave, but Niamh sensed that their allotted time might be running out. She stepped forward and motioned to her sister. Grace nodded and leaned forward giving her mother another kiss goodbye. She was unable to speak.

Niamh leaned down and did the same, squeezing her cold hand. 'I'm sorry I wasn't here, Mam.'

She put her hand on her dad's shoulder as if to coax him from the far away, sad place he was currently languishing in. He looked up into her face and just stared at her, his eyes empty. She didn't think she had ever seen such sadness on anyone's face before. Not just sadness, but heartache. She hadn't known that a face could register heartache. She learned that it could that day. She learned that heartache was a real pain, and that your eyes would hold and show it as an emotion for as long as you felt it.

'We'll be right outside, Dad, OK?'

'OK, love,' he said as he started to get slowly, unsteadily to his feet.

She turned then and walked away. She didn't look back as she didn't want the moment that he said goodbye to his wife, to her mother, etched in her memory for ever.

The rest of the day bled into the following and into the one after that. All she recalled was the constant stream of visitors calling to the house, the low hum of quiet conversations, the steady stream of tea, vodka, sandwiches and cake as visitors both brought food to help the family and stayed to eat and drink with them in consolation.

Her mother hadn't wanted to be waked at home. She had always thought that it was a rather gruesome notion to have the coffin in the middle of the living room.

'You lying there dead and all those people just gawping at you while they have tea, and in your own living room, too. I'll be having none of that.'

Instead there was a rosary and then another prayer service the evening before the funeral. The day of the funeral was grey and wet. Niamh stood alongside her father and her sister under a black umbrella. By the time they had buried her mother and she had reached the car, she was soaking wet, but had no recollection as to why. Had she dropped the umbrella? Had she been holding it wrong? Had the rain been blowing sideways? She didn't know. All she could recall was the sight of the coffin being lowered slowly into the ground as she stood there and tried to reconcile that her mother, larger than life, was now lying lifeless inside that wooden box. She failed. Her brain failed to compute the reality of the situation as she watched it reach the bottom. She had never felt so empty in her entire life.

# Chapter Twenty-Eight

For over a week after the funeral Niamh had been actively avoiding any contact with Rick. He had sent several text messages of condolence and had left two voice messages on her phone, but she was not ready to see him, not ready to talk to him. She was living in a haze of pure sorrow and lack of sleep. She hadn't had a proper night's sleep since before leaving Italy weeks before. Finally out of desperation to get out of the house as much as anything, she agreed to meet him at a wine bar in the local village.

'We were really good together. I blew it. I'm sorry,' Rick said quietly as he reached his hand out and took hers. 'I've missed you. I wasn't ready to make a commitment back then but I am now – I know what I lost, Niamh.' He squeezed her hand and looked her straight in the eye.

She sat silently staring down at her hand in his. It felt different.

'We can even talk about moving in together if that's what you want, Niamh.'

She sat opposite him at a tall round table in a quiet corner. A couple of drinks and months of ill feeling sat between them.

'This is all my fault and I take full responsibility. I was wrong. I should never have let you go. I heard that you had gone to Italy with your sister, but then I heard that you hadn't come back. I couldn't believe it. I was kind of shocked, to tell you the truth. It didn't seem like the kind of thing you would do. I felt bad about it, actually, because I had caused it or something.'

She resented the fact that he thought he had so much power over her, enough power to cause her to turn her life upside down and stay in Italy instead of coming home at the end of the week like every other normal person. She sat twirling the stem of her wine glass in her fingers, watching the legs appear on the inside of the glass.

Did he have that much power over me? she wondered. Is that really why I refused to come back home? Was I really just running away from something, from him?

She looked up at him, realising that she had stopped listening to him. 'I'm sorry, what?'

He sighed. 'I'm trying to talk to you here, Niamh, and you're making it very difficult. Can you listen to what I'm trying to say?'

'Yes. Did you know that wine has legs?'

'What?'

'Did you know that wine has legs?'

He looked at her as if she had suddenly sprouted a second head. 'Wine?'

'Yes, wine,' she repeated.

'Yes, I knew that wine has legs. I think anyone who knows anything about wine knows that wine has legs. Why?'

'No reason. I didn't know that, so I guess not everyone on the planet knows that wine has legs, but I know it now. I learned that in Italy.'

'That's great, Niamh. Can we get back to our conversation now, please? I'm really trying here.'

This was suddenly starting to feel like a lot of effort.

'Yes, you were telling me how much you missed me and how much you wanted me back.'

'What's gotten into you? Have I said something to piss you off?' He pinched the brow of his nose between his two fingers and shook his head.

'You mean tonight or back a few months? A few months ago you dumped me with some lame spiritual phrase like "we're going nowhere" or "it's not working" or something along those lines. You sounded like something out of a really bad American sitcom that got canned after the first season 'cause it was so corny. I mean, who says that to a person, Rick? Who actually says something like that?'

It was a tirade now and there was nothing she could do to stop it. It was probably a combination of exhaustion, grief and two glasses of wine. The words just came pouring out as if each of them had their own intention and determination to be heard.

'Did someone tell you to say that? I don't remember you ever being such a massive moron before that night. Did you talk to people about it? Did you get counsel on how to dump your girlfriend in such a way as to avoid mass casualties? What ... I mean, what the actual fuck was all that about?' She drew a breath, and took a large slug of wine, knowing already that she'd regret this in the morning.

'I'm sorry I didn't handle it better. I said all the wrong things, Niamh, I know. I just panicked. I thought we were going too fast and I just felt an urgent need to pull the plug. It was an asshole move, I know, and I'm sorry.'

He stared down at the table and had the decency to appear legitimately remorseful.

'What about the skinny blonde who was all but mounting you in that skanky club?'

'What club? What are you talking about?'

'Town. It's called Town, Rick. That club. I saw a photo of you with Boobra draped all over you.'

'The one at the office who works in Sales? Are you serious? She's just a player, Niamh. She'd throw herself at any man who has money and will look at her. She's desperate to land a man and it shows. She has "Rescue Me" written across her forehead. Do you have any idea how unattractive that kind of shit is to a man?'

'So why was she sitting on your lap, balancing on your balls?'

'Oh for God's sake. She sat on my lap and had someone take a photo of us. It was twenty seconds.'

'So you're telling me you didn't enjoy it?' She realised that she was at risk of sounding like a wounded victim if she kept this up, but the thought of him with the walking cleavage from Sales made her furious all over again.

'She posted that picture, not me. She took the photo and she posted the photo. It was twenty seconds and I haven't seen her since that night except in passing at work. I swear to you, there was nothing more to it than that.'

'I have to be true to myself,' she said, recalling her mother's words and sitting up taller on her bar stool.

Rick rolled his eyes. 'For fuck's sake, Niamh. What does that mean?'

'It's what Mam said to me one night before she died,' she replied quietly, blinking away the tears that threatened.

'Well, I don't go in for that kind of enlightened, self-preservation rubbish. How can you be true to yourself when you don't even know who you are or what you want?' He was frustrated now and signalled the barman for another round. 'You fucked off to Italy for a grand adventure when things

282

weren't going your way. You started a business that you knew nothing about, blew your savings most likely and as usual you didn't know a thing about what it was you were supposed to be doing. You've never even worked in a café, Niamh, let alone run one. That's not the most responsible way to behave.' He sighed loudly, shook his head and ran his hand over the stubble on his chin. She used to like to do that. She had always liked it when he didn't shave on the weekend, and would look like a relaxed version of himself for a day and a half. 'What about your future, your career?' he continued. 'Did you ever stop for a minute to think about that? Christ, Niamh, it's not like there's a Hollywood version of your life where you get to run off to Italy and just start a new life for yourself and live happily ever after. Real life doesn't work like that and you need to think about your goals, your plans and your future. You're a dreamer, Niamh! A dreamer! Hell, I bet you haven't even closed up that café or thought about it, have you? You just left it to run home and now you're sitting here feeling sorry for yourself. You ran away from problems and made a rash decision, and now you've gone and left that one, too. Hardly big-picture thinking, wouldn't you agree?'

She could feel her posture slipping and her shoulders rounding down. Her gaze dropped to her fingers and she started to pick at the piece of loose skin by her thumbnail. Maybe he was right. Maybe it had all been a huge mistake. She did just run away from it all and never stopped to think about how anyone else felt or what it might mean for her future. The barman put two more drinks in front of them. Rick paused to take a sip of his gin and tonic.

'Look, I'm sorry that your mother died, but she'd tell you the same thing if she were here. She'd say that you're just being childish and selfish and you need to cop on and pull yourself together. Maybe you just need to hear this. You've had a mad adventure arsing around Italy for the past few weeks or however long you were there, doing whatever you felt like doing. You've had weeks and weeks out of real life, eating pasta every day and drinking barrels of wine. That's more than most normal people have their whole lives. It's time for a reality check, Niamh. It's time to quit the fantasy, grow up, come home and get back to your real life.' He paused, shook his head and stared at her.

She could feel herself getting teary and she desperately didn't want to cry in front of him. She had way too much eye makeup on, for one, and it would be sliding down her face in a slow, black rivulet if she shed a single tear. This wasn't going to plan at all. She noticed the barman frown slightly as he watched her try to hide her face in her glass, sipping slowly. She had to pull herself together.

Maybe Rick was right. Maybe it was all just a stupid fantasy, running away from her real life like that. It would certainly be easier here. Her family was here and she had friends here. She could even get her old job back if she wanted it. She didn't think she wanted it, though. It was tainted now. She used to be good at that job so there was no reason she couldn't find another one like it. It hadn't been very inspiring, but the pay was decent. Maybe she could apply for a more senior position at a different firm and make a bit more money? She could live at home until she found a place to live, or maybe there was a chance after all for her and Rick. Maybe they could start over. Maybe this time he would be really open to moving in together as he suggested because he wanted her back so much. They could get a place in town like she'd always imagined and she'd buy one of those fancy white sofas with loads of white and beige throw cushions. He'd want a massive television, of course, but they liked to watch movies together, so that would be nice. She'd get a new set of matching serving dishes and dinner set, the fancy kind that her friends would admire when they'd come over for dinner. Maybe they could get a dog? Rick loved dogs, big dogs especially. Maybe if they got a dog they'd spend more time together on the weekends. Maybe instead of going to the gym for hours at a time he'd want to take the dog on long walks in the park with her . . .

His voice cut into her reverie, scattering the mental image of her perfect new living room in their shiny new apartment along the canal, with their Labrador puppy. 'You quit in an email. After everything we've been through. Not in real life, in an email, Niamh! I'll tell you, that made me look like a right wanker at work. I got all kinds of grief over that, especially from the women, saying that I had mistreated you and you were now an emotional basket case. There's nothing wrong with you, Niamh. I hate it when women play the female card, all tragic and vulnerable. It's such bullshit. You made me look like a right prick.'

There it was. It was so obvious that it was shocking. She could feel her jaw drop slightly as her eyes settled on him. The barman raised his eyes from the other side of the bar.

'What are you looking at me like that for? What?' Rick asked, now clearly frustrated.

Another time she'd just have got mad. She'd have been furious and argued back, thrown some mean comments at him and threatened to walk out. He'd sulk, they might not talk on the way home, but eventually they'd apologise the next day and have make-up sex, and while still wrapped in each other's arms would say that they shouldn't argue with each other like that, that they were too good together, and everything would resume as normal and be fine again for a few weeks.

'I made *you* look like a prick?' she asked almost inaudibly.

'What?' he asked, exasperated.

'I said, I made *you* look like a prick? You dumped me. Dropped me without a second thought after four years. And I made *you* look like a prick?'

She started to laugh. The couple further down the bar turned to look at her. She could hear that she sounded a bit hysterical, but she couldn't help it. She wasn't being facetious or trying to annoy him – it actually sounded funny when she repeated it in her head. She slowed her laugh enough to speak.

'It's just funny that you think I'm somehow at fault here for making you look bad at work. And I just realised something. You always have to be right. You always have to be in charge, all put together and in control. You dumping me, that was OK because that was you in control and in charge, but I was supposed to just suck it up and deal with it and return to work like a good girl. Or quit! But I didn't. Instead I ... how did you describe it? I believe you said that I had "fucked off to Italy for a grand adventure" and in your head that made *you* look bad!'

He stared at her as if she had lost her mind.

'Over the course of the last two drinks I was beginning to think that maybe you were right. It was all a big mistake. I was wrong and you were right. You knew better, as usual. And I just realised, Rick, that this is what you do – you make me feel like a smaller version of myself, like a little girl who doesn't know better. You probably don't intend to do it, and probably don't even know you're doing it, but you do. This has never been a relationship of equals but I never realised it until now 'cause I never really heard it from you so bluntly.'

'Look, Niamh, I don't know what—'

'No, let me finish,' she continued. 'You're a nice guy, Rick, and you're a decent man for the most part. You're successful and good-looking, but I just don't like who I become around you. I somehow let you take charge of everything, including me, and I become a smaller version of myself, and I don't like it. I'm loud and I'm messy and I say the wrong things and I'm not very diplomatic and I'm a little overweight and my feet smell when I wear runners and my eyebrows are too thin. I can live with all that, but I don't want to live a smaller kind of life any more.'

She scrunched her hands into tight fists on her lap and stared down at them, remembering the words her mother had said to her before she died. She looked up into his face with a sad smile, tried unsuccessfully to blink back some tears and said: 'Loving someone isn't enough. There has to be more than that.'

She slipped down off her bar stool and picked up her jacket. 'You were right to end it, Rick. We were good together for a while but we're just not the right people for each other. We're not the "happy ever after" kind.'

He shrugged his shoulders. 'How can you be so sure that there is a "happy ever after" kind?'

She wiped away what were almost certainly black tears by now. 'I can't. But I'd rather try to find it and fail than settle for good enough. Like you said, it's the dreamer in me. Goodbye, Rick.'

It was the most in charge she had ever felt around him.

# Chapter Twenty-Nine

The next two weeks went by in a quiet, sad kind of ritual. There was a tangible air of true sadness in the house, dispersed temporarily only when well-meaning visitors dropped in. The number of visitors had been diminishing as people got back to the business of their real lives and left Niamh, Grace and their dad to resume theirs. The house was markedly quieter than before, the only sounds being those made by Niamh clattering about in the kitchen as she pulled together some semblance of lunch and, later, dinner.

She slept late most mornings and awoke groggy and with a headache, having had too much wine the night before, but it was the only thing that gave her solace. If she drank enough then she would fall into an unsettled sleep, but at least it was sleep and a respite from the thoughts in her head. Grace dropped in every evening with the boys and they provided a welcome distraction from those thoughts in her head and the silence that hung in the air. They also brought a smile to her dad's face, the only time she would see it all day, and when they left, it would slip away and he would settle back into a quiet sadness. He was lost without his Una, and there was nothing that Niamh could do to change that.

'That's the hardest part,' she said to Grace one evening

at the kitchen table, after their father had gone out into the garden to tend to his plants. 'Watching Dad trying to deal with being alone, without Mam. They were always together and had their little routines, you know?'

'I know,' Grace said, as she stood and looked out of the window at the back garden. She watched him lift Ben out of his carefully tended flowerbed. 'I don't know what he's going to do, but there's not much we can do to help. He'll just have to get used to it. Old age sucks. Oh God, I hope they haven't stomped on any of his flowers.'

'She wasn't even that old, Grace. She wasn't supposed to die – she was in hospital. Why couldn't they save her? I just don't understand it.'

'Yeah, I know. Poor Dad.' Grace watched him pull up some stray weeds while the boys played chasing with the dog. 'Do you want another glass of wine?'

'Yes please. I'll open a bottle. We finished that last one. Are you staying here tonight?'

'Yeah, Robert is away tomorrow at some match so I thought I'd stay over tonight and keep the boys around for Dad. I better get some kind of dinner started for the boys. What do you fancy?'

'I don't care. Whatever is in the fridge is fine.'

'Well my two terrorists aren't quite that lenient when it comes to food. How about some shepherd's pie?'

'That sounds good. Dad will eat that, too.'

Grace pulled a couple of pots from the kitchen cupboards as Niamh opened a bottle of red wine. 'What are you going to do?' she asked her pointedly.

Niamh sighed and leaned back against the sink. 'I've no idea. I've been kind of playing ostrich and not thinking about it, to be honest.'

'You mean you're in complete denial?'

'Yep.'

'Well, you can't go on like this, you know. Neither can I. Eventually we both have to return to our real lives, altered for ever as they are. I need to go back to work next week and I can't keep coming over here every evening, and you need to decide what you are going to do. As it is, you're living between two worlds. What's happening with the café while you're here?'

'That's the problem. Nothing is happening with it right now. I had no choice but to close it up and get on a plane. That was weeks ago. I put most of my savings into getting set up in Italy. I had to rent an apartment before I realised I might have been able to live upstairs. So, I had committed to it for a month initially and then I got distracted and it was easier to just extend that rather than buy furniture for the place upstairs. Then I had to buy all kinds of stuff for the café, so basically my savings are more or less obliterated. It was slow at the start, obviously, but then I started to get some regular customers, mostly tourists who wanted something other than pasta. I don't think the Italians really get it, but I had some decent tourist trade. But now it is literally just sitting there costing me money,' Niamh said with a defeated sigh.

'How come?'

'Because I still have to pay rent and bills for the place,' she sighed.

'Oh right, of course. Sorry, that was a stupid question. But look, you can go back and start it up again. You said that you had started to get good feedback from people and that the tourists liked it, so just go back and get stuck in again.'

'Well, that's the problem. Summer is almost over now and everyone has told me that once the first week of September arrives and schools reopen, all the tourists are gone. My only customers were tourists. It's all a bit of a mess and I don't actually know what to do, Grace!'

'Wait a minute. What does that actually mean – the bit about all the tourists leaving?'

'It means that there is no business, no customers from September until next April or May. Apparently it's a really short tourist season.'

'But that's ridiculous. Surely that's an exaggeration?' She rapped loudly on the window. 'Ben! Will you for Christ's sake get off that dog?' she roared through the glass. Her father turned around from his rose bushes and said something in the direction of Ben. He stood up and the dog bolted for the shed, with Ben in hot pursuit. Their father shook his head and stared after Ben, smiling for a moment before going back to his pruning.

'It's not. I asked Emily and she agreed. She said the place is pretty deserted in winter, which is charming – unless you are dependent on a stream of tourists to make some money. Why didn't I know this before I signed the bloody lease? I suppose it was a rash decision in the first place. Shit! I've gone and made things even more complicated. What a first-class gobshite I am. What am I going to do, Grace? I don't want to just give up. I don't want to be a failure and have all this hard work come to nothing. I'm demented trying to think of a solution but I can't invent tourists if they're not there.'

'Well, look,' Grace said, stirring onions in a wide pan. 'There's no point beating yourself up over this. You tried something and it didn't work the way you had thought it would. So what? It was worth a shot. It was always going to be a risk, and you knew that, but at least you tried it, at least you took a risk. I've never taken a risk like that in my life. I've always held down the safe, sensible job. This took balls, Niamh, and you should feel good about having tried it at all.'

'I suppose,' Niamh said reluctantly.

'Do we have potatoes?'

'Yeah, I'll get them,' Niamh replied, staring out of the window. 'I just don't know what to do now.'

'Well, you have to go back, don't you? I mean, you still have stuff there, you can't just disappear.'

'No, I know. I have stuff in the apartment and I have to find out what I need to do about the café lease. God, what a mess.'

'Look, it's not going to get any easier and you're wasting money paying for an apartment that you're not in, so just make the decision to go back and close it all up and come back home.'

'It feels like I'm giving up, though. I hate to think that I have to give up after I've come so far!'

'Well, what is the alternative? You said you're practically out of money and nothing happens there for the winter, so what are you going to do?'

'I don't know. It feels like total defeat if I give up and move back home. I really felt like I was starting to get somewhere, you know – starting over, building a new life, and I love it there. But I don't have any more money to throw at it and I can't afford to keep paying the rent and cover living expenses until next May. It's all very frustrating.' Niamh put her head in her hands.

'You can get a new job, Niamh. You can live here and take your time to figure things out. Anyway, it will be good for Dad to have you around.' She opened the back door and roared out. 'BEN! Get off your brother! He's not a horse. You're squashing him. Dad, can you keep an eye on them before they kill each other, please?'

'Ah, they're grand. They're only playing,' he said without even turning around.

292

'Look,' Grace continued, 'you had a shitty situation to deal with and you got a bit carried away and ran away from your life for a while. No one is going to blame you for that. But you can't fuck up your whole life by continuing to live in denial. It was a good run while it lasted and you got to take a few months out of real life and live some foreign fantasy for a while. That's more than most people ever get to do in their lives, me included. At some point you have to put on your big-girl pants and buckle down to some real work.'

Niamh stopped peeling potatoes and stared at her sister. 'Hang on a second, Grace. I appreciate the life advice but it's not as if I was living out some full-blown fantasy for the past couple of months. I was working my arse off. I fixed that place up and spent weeks on my hands and knees scrubbing. I was in there every morning at six o'clock to get it set up. I had to do everything myself.'

Grace rolled her eyes in frustration. 'I never said that, Niamh. Stop putting words in my mouth. All I'm saying is that you're here lolling about, unable or unwilling to make a decision and you're at risk of fucking up the rest of your life through blatant indecision. If you can figure out a way to make money in Italy for the winter and you're happy there, then by all means go back, but if you can't then you have to accept the fact that it didn't work out for whatever shitty reason, and decide what to do next. That's all I'm saying. And if you don't want to hear it then fine, I'll shut up, but someone had to say it.' She turned back to the stove, taking her frustration out on the pot in front of her.

'Oh Jesus, did I pick a bad time to come back in? Is it safe in here at all?' Paddy joked as he stepped into the kitchen. 'Just so you know, Grace, Ben ate a worm and got dirt all over him before I noticed it, so he's filthy but it's only dirt.'

'He ate a worm? Ah, for Christ's sake, Dad, why did you let him eat a worm? That's disgusting.'

'I handed it to him. I picked it up from the dirt I was digging in and handed it to him and said, "Here, Ben, eat this. It's good for you, lots of protein."'

Grace looked at her father as if he had completely lost his mind.

'For God's sake, Grace, lighten up. It was a joke. Of course I didn't give the child a worm. I turned around and he was already chewing on it with one half of the thing hanging out of his mouth. He found and ate it all by himself and swallowed it before I could stop him. Many children before him have eaten a worm and lived to tell the tale. What's for dinner?' he asked with a small chuckle as he washed his hands in the sink.

Niamh caught Grace's eye and made a 'knife across your throat' gesture indicating that they should drop the subject of Italy now that Paddy was back in the house.

'We're making shepherd's pie, Dad,' Grace replied cheerily.

'It smells good so far, fair play to you girls. You learned from the best – your mother always made a great shepherd's pie.'

The two girls stopped still and looked at him.

'For the love of God, will the two of you stop it? You can't bring her back, you know, and I'm not going to stop talking about her. If she were here now she'd give out yards to the both of you for being so soft. Your mother made a great shepherd's pie and that's all there is to it. We can't pretend that the woman never existed.'

'No, I know, Dad, it's just that, well . . . we thought it might be upsetting to talk about her, that's all,' Grace said slowly.

'Well, that's just daft, Grace. What are we going to do? Never talk about your mother again? That makes no sense at all. We all miss her and we wish she was still here, but she's gone and you can't pretend otherwise.'

It was the most direct and no-nonsense speech the girls had heard him give in weeks and it gave them both pause to take a sigh of relief. Maybe they didn't have to walk around on eggshells after all. Maybe their father was actually coping better with their mother's untimely death than they were.

'Now, just make sure you do a decent job with that shepherd's pie and don't cock up her recipe,' he said, eyeing the two of them over his glasses. He picked up his newspaper and headed for his armchair. 'Oh, and you better bring those two in out of the rain or they'll be like little mud babies out there.'

'Christ!' Grace said, bolting for the back door. 'I didn't know it was raining.'

The two were covered in earth and mud and would need to be deposited directly into the bathtub. 'Can you do dinner, Niamh? I have to power hose the garden off of these two.'

'Yep,' Niamh said, grateful for the change in conversation and the distraction. She turned down the heat under the pot of boiling potatoes and pulled open a drawer. She took out an old black apron and shook it out of its wrinkled coil. She made as if to place the strap around her neck but hesitated. She could see her mother standing there in the kitchen. She held the apron to her face and could smell her mother's perfume from the last time she'd worn it. She closed her eyes and inhaled deeply. She could feel tears sting the backs of her eyes and blinked them away furiously. For all the casual comments her dad had made, she knew instinctively that seeing her get upset was more than he'd be able to handle right now. She folded it and placed it gently back into the drawer. It was just too soon, she decided, as she closed the drawer and turned her attention back to dinner without the apron. 'Some things just take more time than others.'

# Chapter Thirty

Niamh loved it when Grace stayed over with the boys as it gave her a purpose and provided a genuine distraction from her thoughts. She could tell, though, that Grace was anxious to get back to her regular life and routine, but that she was making herself available to give Paddy time to readjust to the new order of things.

Both of them were surprised at how well he seemed to be coping. They had expected a lot of sadness, which there was, of course, but they had also expected him to be listless and helpless, and neither condition was apparent in any shape or form. He got up each day and busied himself with his little jobs around the house, he took a stroll into town each day to get the paper, do a bit of grocery shopping or just drop into the local café, and he tended to his plants and garden religiously each afternoon. He was doing a decent job of keeping himself occupied.

Niamh was beginning to think that of the three of them, she was the one having the hardest time moving on and accepting things as they now were. She suspected that being in limbo between her old world here in Dublin and her new world in Italy wasn't helping and that the sooner she made a decision either way, the better off she would be. Although she was reluctant to admit defeat and relinquish her new life in Italy, she was beginning to see how easy it would be to slip back into a regular life again in Dublin.

She had no intention of going back to her old job – that was one thing she knew for sure – but she had to admit that it would be so much easier to find something else here in Dublin, rather than try to reinvent herself in Italy. While she hadn't been in love with her previous job, she had been good at it and she knew now, with the benefit of hindsight and the perspective that her escape to Italy had given her, that she could apply those skills again in another company. She had good experience at a growing startup, and that whole industry in Ireland was booming. From her experience at PlatesPlease she knew that there was a ton of funding being invested in new and exciting companies, and most of them were going through major hiring spurts. She knew a little about raising money, recruiting employees and running the administrative side of things, so that experience was bound to have some value.

Niamh also had no intention of going back to Rick. That notion had now been firmly ruled out in her mind, and if she were to remain in Dublin she would rather do so on her own terms and start over. In fact, being more independent for a while might not be the worst thing she could do. She would dust off whatever friendships she could still claim post-breakup, and get out there and make new ones to replace those that she lost to Rick.

She had a place to live here at home until she decided what she wanted to do in the future. Her dad was easy to live with and wouldn't bother her, and he made for pleasant, easy company in the evenings. She suspected that it would be good for him to have her around, too, rather than being left all alone in the house. All in all, the signs seemed to be pointing towards returning home and starting over, but to do so meant that she had to deal with all of her responsibilities in Italy and close everything down. There was no way to avoid it. She would have to go back and deal with it all in person.

Now that the peak summer period was over there were plenty of cheap flights to Milan. She could just take the train from there to Camogli, spend a few days packing stuff up, deal with any necessary paperwork and finances, ship a few things back to Ireland and fly back. She figured that she could get everything done in a week. She could ask Grace to stay over for a few nights while she was away so that Dad wouldn't be on his own. I'll ask her the next time I see her, she thought.

She opened a bottle of wine and poured herself a glass as she started to get dinner ready for the two of them.

'Is it just the two of us tonight?' Paddy asked, as he walked into the kitchen.

'Yep. Just us.'

The house was decidedly quieter without Grace and the boys. Niamh put on one of her mother's aprons, one that hadn't been worn since it had last been laundered and so it wouldn't torture her with the scent of her mother's perfume. Before sitting at the table her father poured himself a glass of milk.

'Have you thought about when you'll go back to Italy? I was only thinking today that you must be home about a month at this stage. Am I right?'

'Yes, just a couple of days short of a month, actually,' she said as she placed their plates on the table. 'I don't know. To be honest I was beginning to think that maybe it was all just a mad idea in the first place and that I'd be better off here at home, especially with everything that's happened.'

'What do you mean "with everything that's happened"? Surely everything that's happened is even more reason to get back to your new life out there? I thought you were loving it?'

'Well, I was, but then when I had to come home I had to close the café and now it's heading into winter and it's a bit of a ghost town from what I hear.' She hesitated, wondering how much she should tell him.

'Go on . . .'

'Well, I've used up most of my savings in getting the place ready, and paying rent and all that, and I had only just opened the café when I had to come back, so it's all kind of screwed up now, and I don't really have the means to survive through the winter, 'cause I can't get any other job.'

'So you're just going to give up?'

'No, it's not that I'm giving up. It just didn't work out in my favour. The timing was wrong. It took me too long to get the place open so I missed most of the summer, and everyone tells me that there's no one around for the winter. Some things are just not meant to be, Dad. I tried and it just didn't work out. Anyway, it will be easier to get a job here.'

'So you *are* just going to give up, then. I'm surprised at you, Niamh. You were never a quitter.'

'That's a bit unfair, Dad.' Niamh waggled her fork in the air. She took a sip of wine and stared down into her plate.

'Niamh, life is unfair. Shitty things happen to good people every day. No one said that any of it was going to be easy or fair, but you haven't given this thing in Italy a fair shot.'

She looked up at him, wondering where this was going.

'It was unfortunate that you had to come home, but that's just how it played out. Your mother was sick, you came home and then she died, and you've been moping around here ever since. Do you think that's what she'd want for you? Do you think she'd want to see you around the house like a lunatic with the hoover, cleaning the place as if your life depended on it, instead of going out and making your mark on the world?'

'Well . . . '

'Of course she wouldn't,' he continued. 'She'd want you to go back there if it would make you happy, and that is what I want too. You've no business living at home with your father at this hour of your life, looking for another job that will just pay the bills.' His voice trailed off and he sat quietly for a moment, staring into the distance. 'You only get a few chances in life, Niamh, and I think that this move to Italy, mad as it was, might be one of them. It made no sense whatsoever when you announced that you weren't coming home, but that meant that you were following some kind of dream or something in your heart.'

Her mother had always been the one to give them lectures on life and share her many nuggets of wisdom, but her father rarely did so. Her mother's ramblings must have rubbed off on him.

'Most people don't get to live like that, Niamh. They grow up, get a job, get married and have children or not, and that's them for the rest of their lives. Most people don't get to just up sticks and start over somewhere else, because they have too much tying them down at home. You don't, so for the love of God will you do something with that privilege?'

'But won't you be lonely here at home in this house, all by yourself?'

'I'm actually thinking of going over to my brother in London for a while.'

'Oh,' she said, unable to mask the surprise in her voice. Her father hadn't been out of the country in years.

'Sometimes life is unkind to us Niamh. Your mother is

gone too soon and there's nothing we can do about that. But if this teaches us anything it's that life is too short, and that we should take advantage of every day we've got. So, I'm going to see my brother for a while and you should get your head out of the clouds and think about what you actually want to do, not what you think you should do. And, for God's sake, don't go choosing the easy way out, it rarely ends in happiness.'

She couldn't think of a single thing to say, so she just nodded.

'They were grand lamb chops, weren't they? You did a fine job of those, I must say.' He put his knife and fork on the plate. 'My show is about to start now. I'll put on the kettle. Will you have a cup of tea?'

'I will, thanks,' she said slowly.

She sat at the kitchen table as her dad made two cups of tea and slowly realised that she had just been given the permission she hadn't known she needed to follow her heart and choose the unknown over the practical, to leave her life in Dublin, to do it properly this time, and try again. She knew then, sitting at the kitchen table in her mother's second apron, that she had to go.

# Chapter Thirty-One

While it had been hard saying goodbye to Dad and Grace, Niamh felt a sense of relief that she had made the decision to return to Camogli. She had booked a one-way ticket to Milan, but the flight landed too late to connect with the last train to Camogli, so she would have to spend the night in the city. She had texted Emily for a recommendation as she herself knew nothing about the city and had spent no time there. The last time she had arrived in Milan had been with Grace, whose company had paid for a car service to meet them at the airport and take them to Liguria.

'Not so this time, Niamh,' she said to herself as she sat down to text Emily. 'This time you're on your own. No fancy car service for you. You'll be putting your broke arse on the train or the bus!'

To her surprise, Emily came right back to her. She was not normally one to live on her phone. In fact its usual state was to be on silent, stuck in the bottom of a handbag or in a drawer.

*Oh, perfect! I'm going to be in Milan then, too. I am badly overdue for a haircut, and I'm staying for the weekend. Oh, this will be fun! I know exactly where you must stay. Let me check to see if they have availability. I'll be right back!*

*You travel to Milan to get your hair done? It's a two-and-a-half-hour drive each way,* Niamh texted back, unsurprised at the fact, but still amused by it.

As soon as she sent the message, her phone rang. It was Emily.

'Good Lord, it takes far too much energy to type like that. When did people stop actually talking on the phone?'

'Well, you're just slower than most because you insist on using proper English and correctly spelled words all the time. Most normal people use abbreviations, so it's faster.'

'You know, if we're not careful we'll all become a nation of savages, unable to form complete sentences any more. As for my hair appointment – we live in a fishing village. A fishing village, where real people actually fish and then others actually cook that fish for a living. Not a whole lot of experienced hairstylists milling about the place.' Niamh could just imagine Emily shaking her head at the other end of the phone at the thought of even contemplating a hair appointment anywhere but at a top salon. 'Now, I just spoke with a good friend of mine who happens to be the hotel manager at the most divine property and I reserved a room for you for Saturday night. It's my treat. I'll just be so relieved to get you back to Italy that it can be cause for a little celebration. What time does your flight land and where?'

'I land just after six o'clock at Linate airport, and you don't have to pay for my hotel room. Thank you but—'

'Perfect, you'll be at the hotel within twenty minutes, darling, and the hotel room is already taken care of. You can change and we'll meet for drinks. I'll book dinner for about eight-thirty. Oh, how fun! This will be fabulous. I thought I'd be wandering the halls of the hotel all by myself. This is so much better!'

Niamh doubted that Emily would have been wandering the halls of any hotel on her own as she always seemed to be surrounded by keen suitors or elegant friends. 'Is the hotel really fancy?' Her question was met with silence. 'OK, sorry,' she continued. 'Stupid question! Don't worry, I'll pack accordingly. Do I need a cocktail dress, or exactly how fancy are we talking here?'

'You won't need a cocktail dress, no, but the hotel is very elegant and the restaurant we'll go to is exquisite.'

'Got it,' Niamh said, rolling her eyes. She shook her head, realising that the majority of her new cute outfits were still in Camogli. It wasn't as if she had needed to pack any for the trip back to Ireland. 'I'll have time to shop for something tomorrow before I leave Dublin.'

'Marvellous. I'll send you the hotel details. Send me your flight information so that I can track your flight. See you tomorrow night, darling!'

Niamh smiled as she ended the call. She wouldn't have considered Emily the type to track a flight. In fact she would have gone so far as to suggest that she wouldn't know how. She certainly wasn't the most technically adept individual, but in a short period of time Emily had become a good friend. She was the one person who had checked in with her regularly over the past month in Dublin. She had even offered to come to the funeral, but Niamh had dissuaded her.

Her plane landed a few minutes early. She stepped off the plane and onto the steps leading down to the tarmac. They had been directed to a gate in the older section of the airport, as yet unrenovated, and so most of the flights disgorged their passengers onto the tarmac. She stood at the top of the steps and took a deep breath of air. It smelled foreign yet familiar. She made her way through to baggage reclaim, grabbed her overweight suitcase from the luggage carousel, heaved it up onto a luggage trolley and proceeded to customs.

Before leaving Dublin she had made several trips to Penney's – Ireland's preferred, inexpensive shopping solution to any impending night out or holiday. The average piece of clothing ranged from eight euros to thirty euros, yet she had somehow managed to spend almost three hundred euros in each of two Penney's locations. All the new autumn and winter lines were in and she figured that though they were radically inexpensive, no one in Italy would have them, or know just how inexpensive they were in reality.

As she exited through customs, she was greeted by a man wearing the typical uniform of black suit and tie, with a black cap. He was holding a sign with her name on it. She giggled to herself as she said hello. So that's why she wanted my flight information, she thought. The driver took her luggage trolley and she stood a little taller, swinging her handbag over her shoulder. She just wished it were summertime right now so she could fish out an enormous pair of sunglasses and act like she was fabulous or wealthy.

Chauffeur-driven cars had priority parking so they were in the car within minutes, and before she knew it she was whizzing through the city. She stared out of the window as the city morphed from functional business districts to increasingly elegant streets and buildings. The car slowed to a crawl in less than twenty minutes, and the driver turned onto Via Manzoni and pulled up in front of an imposing limestone building.

The five-storey hotel stood proudly on a corner, with double doors leading to a plush, elegant lobby. A highly polished brass plaque on the wall read LEADING HOTELS OF THE WORLD. She knew she had seen that plaque somewhere before and she gasped as she realised that this was the same group that the hotel in Santa Margherita had been a part of. If that experience was anything to go by, then she was in for a treat.

She checked in and was graciously welcomed as a friend of Signora Emilia, and escorted to her room on the fourth floor. A note from Emily and a bottle of Franciacorta was on ice awaiting her arrival.

'Welcome back! Open this and imbibe as you get changed. I'll meet you in the lobby bar on the ground floor at seven o'clock!'

'Don't mind if I do,' Niamh said with a grin, as she popped the cork on the champagne.

Unsurprisingly, Emily was holding court at the bar when Niamh arrived downstairs. As she made her way through the lounge she was relieved to see that she hadn't overdressed, but in fact could maybe, at a stretch of the imagination, pass for being as glamorous as the other ladies in the room tonight. She had picked up a capped-sleeved black sequinned dress that fell to just above her knees. It shimmied as she walked and, given its shift pattern, it was very forgiving. She wore a pair of new nude heels and walked slowly towards the bar to ensure her feet wouldn't slip out of them. Maybe that's why celebrities always walk slowly and purposefully, she thought. Maybe they're just trying not to fall out of their shoes.

Emily turned and saw her. She jumped down from her bar stool and hugged her tightly. 'Welcome back, darling! So good to see you!'

'You too! This was a great idea!' Niamh turned to greet the two men in suits and stopped short. 'Giorgio!' she said in utter surprise, and with just a little too much enthusiasm. Her breath caught in her throat. God, he looks good, she thought to herself, hoping she wouldn't blush.

He looked equally as surprised to see her. 'Nina! *Buona*

*sera*. What are you doing here?' He stood up and kissed her on both cheeks.

'I'm on my way back to Camogli. What are you doing here?' She glanced at Emily, who shrugged and raised her eyebrows as if to say this was all perfectly normal.

'I am also on my way back to Camogli. I arrived from America this morning. I have been to visit my brother in Chicago.' He hesitated for a second, glanced at the other gentleman and then said quietly, 'Nina, I am so sorry for your loss.'

'Thank you,' she said with a small smile, as she looked down at the floor. 'If it's OK, I'd rather not talk about it. I can't yet. I don't mean to be rude.'

'No, no, of course not. I am sorry. I understand.'

She saw him glance at Emily awkwardly. Emily knew better than to bring up the subject of her mother at this time, so instead she introduced her to the other gentleman at the bar. 'Niamh, this is my dear friend Antonio. He is the general manager of this wonderful property, a firm favourite of mine.'

'It is my pleasure,' Antonio said, taking her hand. 'Emilia is too kind, but she has been a very good friend for many, many years now and one of our best clients.'

'Less of all that talk of many, many years, darling, if you please? It never does a lady good to highlight the years.' Emily smiled as she sipped a Martini. 'Niamh, darling, what will you have to drink?'

'Oh, umm, a Martini sounds great, actually.'

'My pleasure, *signora*,' Antonio said as he motioned for the barman. 'We are delighted to have you stay here with us. If you need anything at all during your stay, please do not hesitate to contact me.' He handed her his card. 'Emilia's friends are always welcome here, and now you are a friend too.' His

English was flawless and he was impeccably dressed. 'Now, I will leave you all to catch up. I will see you later this evening, no?' he asked with a nod and a smile towards Emily. She tipped her glass in his direction and smiled back at him.

'Cheers, darlings!' she said raising her glass to Niamh and Giorgio.

'Cheers,' they replied in unison.

'You look wonderful, my dear,' Emily said as she leaned over and patted her friend on the knee.

'Yep, amazing what dropping five pounds will do for those second and third chins,' Niamh said with a grin. 'Can't say I'd recommend it, though, the grief diet that is, pretty miserable actually.' She bit her lip and stared down at the floor, regretting the fact that she had brought it up at all.

'Well, you look marvellous, that's all, and it's great to have you back. Isn't it, Giorgio?'

'Yes, she does. You do,' he said, staring at her. 'I almost did not recognise you when you walked in.'

'That's just because you've never seen me in sequins and mascara,' Niamh joked, grateful for the abrupt change in conversation. 'You usually see me buried under layers of dirt and dust.' She had meant it flippantly, but the word 'buried' slipped out before she knew it. *Fuck, this is hard*, she thought. *How do you carry on as if everything is normal and behave appropriately when every other thought drifts back to your mother's funeral just weeks ago?* She could feel tears threaten, but she refused to let them win right now. That could wait until later when she was back in the privacy of her own room. She pretended to drop her handbag and moved to get it, only to bump into Giorgio's head, who appeared equally keen to jump to attention in order to change the direction of the conversation.

'Ouch, shit,' she mumbled, rubbing her forehead.

'*Dio, io*,' he uttered, doing the same.

'Are you all right?' Emily asked, feigning concern. It was clear that she was trying not to laugh outright. 'Not to worry, drink up, it will numb the pain.'

Niamh sat back on her stool, rubbing her forehead.

'I'm so sorry, are you OK?' Giorgio asked, touching her forehead.

'Yes, I'm fine,' she said with a smile. It felt good to be out in a nice social setting with these good people. She hadn't realised how much she had missed it. 'This hotel is stunning, Emily.'

'Yes, I stay here all the time. When I heard that Giorgio was arriving back this morning I insisted that he join us. I just hope you aren't too jet-lagged, darling?'

'No,' he said firmly. 'I don't believe in jet lag. I don't accept it.'

'Spoken like a true lawyer,' she joked. 'So, how was your trip?' She turned to Niamh and placed a hand on her knee. 'Giorgio just walked in about four minutes before you did, so I've heard nothing of his trip yet. Speak, darling, speak!' She raised her Martini glass to her lips.

His face broke into a wide grin. 'I am going to be an uncle!' he said, with an effusive hand gesture.

'What? Really, but, how?' Emily asked, her tone of voice causing Niamh to cast her a second glance.

'My brother, he has met someone in Chicago. They have been together for almost a year and now she is pregnant.'

'That's terrific. I didn't even know he had a girlfriend out there. Did you know?'

'No, I knew nothing. He didn't want to say anything until he was certain that this was, you know, real, that it would work – especially after Lena.' A look of sadness crossed his face momentarily. His brother's loss probably reminded him of his own subsequent loss too, Niamh thought.

'Yes, of course, that's understandable, darling. How wonderful.'

Giorgio's grin reappeared almost immediately. 'And now she is to have a baby, and I am to be an uncle! It makes me so happy!' He raised his glass to no one in particular.

'I didn't know you liked children so much,' Emily commented, narrowing her eyes slightly. 'Is this new?'

'No, I always wanted children, and if I can't have them of my own then this will have to be good enough.'

'If you're not careful, darling, that grin might become permanent and people might accuse you of actually being happy.'

'It is wonderful news, no?'

'Indeed.' Emily seemed genuinely surprised at his reaction to this news.

'That's fabulous, Giorgio. When is she due?' Niamh asked.

'Ah . . . in the spring. She is two months pregnant. I will be a spring uncle!'

'I know what it's like to have little nephews. You're going to be a great uncle.'

'*Salute!*' he said, raising his glass again. His happiness was almost infectious.

'All right my loves, we should make a move soon,' Emily said, changing the subject. 'We can talk more about this over dinner. Our car should be out front by now. Finish up your drinks and I'll meet you both out front in five minutes. I need to grab my wrap from my room.'

She moved through the elegant crowd with ease.

'She has a way of walking that makes it look like she's gliding or something, doesn't she?' Niamh said quietly as she watched her leave the room.

'Yes, she is a very elegant woman.'

They were both staring after her now.

'I was surprised to see you here,' Giorgio said, turning back to face her. 'I was not sure that you would return to Italy.'

'I wasn't either, to be honest. I only decided for real a couple of days ago. It was hard, you know? Part of me wanted to stay at home for my dad's sake, and the other part of me wanted to come back here, so it was hard to decide in the end.'

'So what made you decide to return?'

She realised that she had probably never had as long or as real a conversation with him before this. She certainly hadn't had his attention for this long before, and she found his presence intoxicating. She wanted to admit right then that he was part of the reason she had wanted to return. She had tried to deny her feelings for a long time, but realised on her return to Ireland that it wasn't only the country of Italy she had missed. She had missed Giorgio, too. She wanted to say that she hadn't expected to fall for someone else so soon, but she had. She wanted to tell him that, foolishly or not, when she visualised herself in Italy, he was always part of that picture. But she knew that she couldn't or, at least, shouldn't. He was with Sara and she had to accept that, reluctant as she was to do so.

'Well, it was something my dad said. He said, "Your mother would want you to go out and live your life, not sit around here moping", or something like that.' She looked down at her hands and fiddled with her fingers, willing herself not to get teary.

'Your father sounds like a kind and sensible man,' Giorgio said kindly. He reached over and placed his hand over hers. 'You are lucky for this reason, no?'

Her eyes welled up with tears despite her best effort. 'Sorry,

I thought I'd do a better job of holding it together. I didn't mean to get all teary and emotional,' she said, wiping a tear from the corner of one eye. 'I'll pull myself together, I promise.' She took a deep breath and sat up straight.

'Don't apologise for being sad. You have every right to sadness, just as you do happiness. Now is a time for some sadness. The time for happiness will return again soon.'

Sensing that she needed a shift in tone, he stood up from his bar stool. 'In the meantime, how about we choose happiness, just for now, over dinner? I will tell you about my plans for being an uncle. It would be a shame to cry onto our plates, no?'

She laughed despite herself, and got up from her stool. 'Yes, that would be a shame. Your English is getting better, Giorgio!'

'I have been learning a little,' he replied, and held out his left elbow for her to take.

She glanced up at him and all she could see was a kind smile on a handsome face. She hesitated for just a second, and then she accepted the genuine gesture and linked her arm through his. Emily was waiting for them at the door. Niamh saw her eyes drop for a split second down to her arm linking through Giorgio's and could have sworn she saw the faintest hint of a smile. She couldn't be certain, though, because a second later Emily waved at them wildly and swept out through the door into the waiting car.

# Chapter Thirty-Two

Niamh had forgotten to close the blackout blinds fully before collapsing into bed at one o'clock in the morning. Slatted bands of light crept slowly across her bed, inching their way towards her pillow. She had fallen into a deep sleep as soon as her head hit the pillow, and had barely moved in the night. The hotel room was cast in the soft white glow of early morning light and she lay there quietly admiring her elegant, monochrome surroundings. Even though she was exhausted, she felt relieved to be back in Italy.

She sat on the edge of the bed, willing herself to stand up. The past few weeks had been an emotional minefield and today somehow felt like a new beginning, a fresh start. She was back and, although she felt a pang of nervousness about what lay ahead, she was cautiously optimistic. She had to figure this out. Shaking her head to dislodge the last of her sleepiness, she felt as if today were symbolic in a way. She padded barefoot to the bathroom.

'I've got to figure out how to work these bloody Italian radiators,' she muttered as she put a hand on the ice-cold old cast-iron radiator. It had an old dial that only went on or off, meaning that you either remained cold or you had screaming hot steam hissing and screeching from the pipes. The noise had been too much for her as she'd got into bed in the wee hours earlier this morning, so she had twisted it to off.

The hot water rattled in the pipes now as she ran the shower. It coughed, spat and splattered its way out, as if resenting the fact that it had to do anything at all. At first it was too hot to step into and then gradually it got cooler until it turned cold. She had read somewhere once that Jennifer Aniston only took three-minute showers, so she felt that three minutes should be enough for her, too.

'You look like you slept in a ditch, Niamh,' she said to her reflection in the bathroom mirror. 'If today is symbolic of a fresh start back in Italy then you need to look the part,' she mumbled quietly as she stood under the pulsating showerhead.

Thirty minutes later she spotted Emily at a window table in the ground-floor restaurant, sipping on a cup of steaming hot tea – a British tradition that she had refused to relinquish on moving to Italy.

'Did we order more champagne when we got back here last night, darling?' Emily asked with a smile.

'Yes, we did,' Niamh said. 'It was a great idea at the time! I'm exhausted.'

'Good Lord, where is your spirit this morning? You're in Milan, darling! So much opulence, so much elegance, so much fun!'

'Where's Giorgio?' Niamh asked, sipping on a freshly squeezed orange juice.

'He was up and out early. He was meeting some friends for breakfast. Now, the plan for the day is as follows. The car is picking us up here at four o'clock. I have my hair appointment this morning followed by a spot of shopping. Let's meet for lunch, shall we?'

'OK, that sounds good.'

'Just get out and take a walk. There is shopping to be done and you're in the right neighbourhood! Every shop you could wish for is right here.'

Niamh had a feeling that Emily's idea of shopping and hers were two very different creatures. She decided she had been right later that morning as she strolled past the high-end labels and couture shops. Not an H&M in sight. Even Zara wouldn't get a look-in here, she thought, as she wandered the narrow, elegant streets of the Montenapoleone neighbourhood. She happily passed the time wandering the neighbourhood until lunch, when she followed the directions from the concierge to reach the restaurant that Emily had reserved for them.

Niamh smiled as she reached the entrance. It was inordinately elegant – not that she had expected anything less. A narrow, wrought-iron door led from the street down an arched alleyway that opened up into a small wine bar. The wall opposite had two sets of double French windows that opened out onto a charming courtyard. Ivy and wild roses grew up white trellises and three-foot urns held ancient olive trees. It was the epitome of understated Italian elegance.

Emily had already been seated at a corner table in the courtyard, her back to the fragrant roses on the wall behind her, facing the elegant crowd of diners. She wore a beige cashmere coat and oversized sunglasses, her hair piled atop her head in an elegant chignon.

'I had to start with a glass of something chilled. Won't you join me?' Emily said as Niamh took a seat across from her.

'Yes, that sounds lovely. This place is beautiful, Emily,' Niamh said, taking in the scene around her in the courtyard.

'Yes, it's one of my favourites here in the city. The menu is short and simple, the food is all local and they only serve what is in season.' She turned to the waiter, who was seating

Niamh at the table. 'Can you please bring another glass of this?' she asked, raising her glass and drumming her perfectly manicured fingernails on it.

'*Certo, Signora Emilia, subito.*'

'I wasn't sure what your preference might be, so I hadn't ordered a bottle yet. Now, take a look at the menu and let's order. I'm famished.'

All the items on the menu were small plates. The menu was designed with tasting and sharing in mind, with dishes that could be sampled and shared amongst friends.

'For such a fancy place, this menu is surprisingly simple,' Niamh commented.

'It is. The chef is very talented and the focus is on the produce as opposed to overtly fancy dishes. I think it's only a matter of time before she gets a Michelin star for this place. I love their wine list, too. They have the most amazing selection of wines by the glass here, which is quite a treat.'

They ordered a selection of dishes, including late summer tomatoes and burrata, fusilli pasta with wild mushrooms, garlic and thyme, and grilled baby quail. Each item listed on the menu came with a suggested wine pairing, which they elected to have.

'So I'm guessing that we're not in any hurry and that this is going to be a long lunch, then?'

'Yes, darling, the best always are. Cheers!' Emily said with a smile as they clinked glasses.

Overhead outdoor heaters kept the chill from the September air. The high surrounding walls fashioned a kind of natural amphitheatre, cocooning the sounds of chatter, laughing and the clinking of glasses and crockery, creating a warm, buzzy atmosphere. Emily was always easy company and Niamh could feel herself relax more with every sip of wine. Knowing that she didn't have to worry about making her way around a still as yet strange city, or deal with public transportation to get back to Camogli made it all the easier to sink into a sense of relaxed comfort and enjoy every moment of the lunch. The idea of slipping into the back of a chauffeur-driven car and having someone else take care of everything was very appealing right now.

Each of the courses were delectable, but even more interesting were the wines they were paired with, some of which Niamh had never heard of before.

'I love this wine list, so many local choices ... I've always been into wine – I think I told you that – but most of these bottles you just can't get outside of the country. Some of them I've never even heard of and I thought I knew a lot about wine.'

'Very perceptive of you, Niamh. This place is actually renowned for its wine list. A lot of these wines come from small producers and are never mass marketed or exported, so the only way you'll find them is to drink them at the source. That's rather the beauty of it.'

'I'm really impressed. I know the usual suspects like the big-name, famous wines from Tuscany and Piemonte, but I didn't realise there were so many little local producers and local wines.'

'Most people don't until they come to Italy. The big winemakers are like merchants in any business. They've got marketing dollars and savvy and they take a few good bottles and mass-promote them to large markets. It's merely "Marketing 101" in its simplest form. So what you see outside of the country are wines from big producers with big influence. The small, local producers just don't have the marketing dollars to compete but they are still excellent wines.'

'It's a pity there's nothing like this in Camogli, isn't it?

Although I suppose places like this are usually only in big cities.'

'Well, I suppose that's part of the attraction of the best cities – a wide variety of great restaurants, cafés, wine bars. I mean, shopping you can get anywhere, but some cities do food and wine better than others. It's why I come to Milan as often as I do. It's elegant, refined, cultured but yet it's relaxed, and it's nothing like as frenetic as other major metropolitan cities. I like the pace of life here.'

'I can understand why,' Niamh said, sitting back in her chair and looking around at the contented faces of the other diners. 'It's just lovely here. I mean, I love Italy in general, and have definitely fallen in love with Camogli, but I had no idea that Milan was such an elegant city. Everyone talks about Rome being so beautiful, but you don't hear as much about Milan.'

'No, it's rather misunderstood, actually, but that's part of its charm because as a result it's not as overrun with tourists. It's much more of a local city and feels very Italian. Once you get under the skin of Milan it's actually rather like an onion that keeps revealing layers and layers. It's most definitely my favourite Italian city and you're beginning to see why.' Emily smiled as she turned her attention back to the menu.

Niamh sipped on her wine and let her mind wander. They sat in silence for a few minutes, each of them lost in their own thoughts.

The quail course arrived and, just like the other dishes before it, was beautifully presented. Another waiter arrived at the table and poured each of them a glass of Barbaresco. Niamh swirled her bulbous glass around and around on the white tablecloth and inhaled deeply. She watched the orange-brown hues of the wine circle the glass and, holding the glass to her nose, closed her eyes and inhaled the earthy scent. Taking a sip, she looked across the table towards Emily.

'Delish,' she said, precisely. 'I've never met a bottle of Barbaresco that I didn't love, but to be honest it's not that easy to get in Dublin – only in the fancier restaurants. I went a few times with Rick for special occasions, but he wasn't that into wine so I never really got to experiment as much as I'd have liked,' she said, thinking how long ago that all seemed now.

'My sentiments exactly, my dear. Barbaresco doesn't get enough credit in my mind. It's always overshadowed by its more popular neighbour Barolo, but there is an earthiness to Barbaresco that I just adore.'

'That's exactly the word I was thinking when I tasted it. It's like you can actually taste the earth, or maybe you can smell it, I'm not sure, but either way it's there. Do you know what I mean?'

'I do, and I agree. Divine,' Emily said, taking a long sip of the luscious red wine.

'Camogli needs a place like this. I know it's only a little village, but wouldn't it be lovely to have a place like this to hang out in, with great wines? You know, a local spot that wasn't a restaurant, just a wine bar – and Liguria has such great local wines. I'd never heard of most of them either until I got there.'

'That's true,' Emily replied, swirling her glass on the table. 'To get a glass of wine anywhere you have to beat off the tourists at the restaurants. And even the restaurants with tables outside on terraces are more likely to seat people who want to have dinner, not just drink wine.'

'Unless it's you, of course,' Niamh laughed. 'I can't imagine anyone refusing to seat you ever – Camogli or elsewhere!'

Emily laughed. 'I should hope not! Thank God for La Terrazza where we go for Aperol spritz at sunset. That's about the easiest place in town just to get a drink.' She picked up her wine glass and looked across at Niamh. 'What?' she asked. Niamh was staring at her in the oddest way. 'You have a very peculiar look on your face, darling. What is it?'

'No,' Niamh began slowly. 'It's just that I think you're right. There is nothing even close to this in Camogli apart from La Terrazza and that's part of the hotel. Other than that the only place you can go to have a glass of wine is a restaurant. In fact, I think that the best selection of wines by the glass is at your apartment, Emily.'

Emily laughed. 'You're probably right.'

'But seriously,' Niamh continued, leaning in across the table. 'What if the café wasn't a café? What if it was a wine bar instead? I mean, change it up and set it up as a proper wine bar?'

'Do you know?' Emily leaned back into her chair. 'I think you might be on to something. This wine bar idea has appeal for both locals and tourists alike, so you wouldn't have the same problem of relying merely on summer traffic. And Lord knows, as you correctly stated, there isn't a decent place to go and get a drink without them wanting to force-feed you pasta or fish. And that, my dear, is an opportunity. Plus I love the idea of being able to go somewhere fabulous, that's not my apartment, and drink great wines!'

'Why didn't I think of this the first day?'

Emily shrugged. 'Sometimes the best ideas take time.'

'Do you really think I could pull this off?'

'Niamh Kelly, where is the enthusiasm and excitement of mere minutes ago? Don't let the old, hesitant you creep back in!' Emily admonished. 'Of course you can pull this off!'

'You're right, you're right. Sorry,' Niamh said in agreement. She sat up straight and folded her arms in front of her on the table. 'OK, where do we start? I have to change the place enough that it doesn't look like a wannabe wine bar. It has to look legit, and I'm on a budget, so I have to do it all on a shoestring. Last time around I went all in but now I'll have to prioritise, so I'll have to be really smart this time. What do you think?'

'I think it's probably quite simple, actually. You just need to reconfigure the inside so that it looks less like a cheerful café and more like a soulful wine bar, you know, colour scheme and soft furnishings, things like that. Then, get rid of the existing menu and food displays and offer something simple, something more suitable to a wine bar, like this.' She pointed to the small snack menu that stood on the table. 'And stock up on great wines!'

'And if I offer a fabulous selection of wines by the glass that locals can't get anywhere else in town, then I have something new and shiny to offer.'

'Exactly! Ooh, how very exciting!'

'But isn't it impossible to get a licence to sell wine? I tried when I opened the café but I couldn't get one.'

'Nothing is impossible, darling. It will just take a bit of time and will require that we approach the right people.'

'What do you mean?'

'Italy is about as corrupt a first-world country as any and there are still officials not opposed to greasing the tracks a little for you, in return for an incentive. Also, there are the normal channels to go through for all the oceans of paper-work, and then there are other channels that one can use, to ensure a faster, smoother result. It's simple. You just didn't know the right channels to go through. You were an outsider who filled out an application form. Nobody cared. It was a standard rejection and that was that.'

'I have no idea what you are talking about, but it sounds like you know how to make this actually happen?'

'Everyone does. You just have to ask the right people the right questions. Most European countries are bureaucratic to the point of exhaustion. You just have to know the right people and the right channels.'

'So you're fairly sure I could get a wine licence?'

'I know you can,' Emily said with a wink. 'This isn't my first time dealing with Italian bureaucracy so I've already learned what not to do, and who to recruit to help smooth the way.'

'Unreal. I never really stood a chance with the café, did I? I had no idea about anything, least of all how local politics worked.'

'Don't beat yourself up. It's the same the world over. There are easy ways to do things and hard ways to do things. You just chose the latter because you didn't know any better, that's all.'

Emily had a knack of making everything sound less complicated that it was. She seemed to go through life effortlessly, but whenever they talked about anything tough or challenging, Emily would always refer to 'hard lessons learned', as if she had personal experience of them. Niamh didn't know if she was just a great orator of other people's struggles and victories or if in fact she had lived through so many challenges, and learned so many lessons, that everything now was truly effortless.

'Now, the first thing you are going to need is advice on how to approach the legal application with the local council. Know of any good lawyer that we could seek advice from?' she said, a slow smile spreading across her face.

'Giorgio?' Niamh asked, wide-eyed.

'Precisely. He's not corrupt but he knows his way around

the system, he knows everyone in the council and he has some friends in high places. That should be our first conversation.'

'You're actually serious, aren't you? You really do think that I can turn the café into a wine bar and pull this off,' Niamh said, a wave of emotion rising inside of her.

'It was your idea, darling. I believe in jumping all over an opportunity when it presents itself and this sounds like a great opportunity to me. Plus, I don't really see any other options if you want to remain in this country, and I'm quite certain that you do – am I right?'

'Yes,' Niamh replied emphatically. 'More than anything.'

'Well then, that's settled. We have some work to do, don't we?' With that Emily waved for the bill and fished her sunglasses out of her bag. She picked up her phone and tapped at it for a few seconds. 'The driver is waiting outside.'

'Was he just sitting waiting for you the whole time?' Niamh asked, amazed that Emily had so many people at her beck and call.

'I pay him to do that. You can solve many problems by throwing money at them, darling. It makes life so much easier,' Emily replied, grinning as she stood up from the table. 'Excellent lunch, and we're leaving here with a Plan B for Niamh Kelly. Not bad for an afternoon's work, wouldn't you say?' She picked up multiple shopping bags and swept through the restaurant gracefully, leaving a trail of turned heads in her wake.

Niamh walked quickly to catch up with her, wondering if she would ever possess the grace and charm that Emily had in spades. As she tripped over the handle of a woman's handbag on the ground and bumped into an adjacent chair, she rolled her eyes and thought, most likely not.

# Chapter Thirty-Three

Niamh turned the key in the door of Café Limoni as the sun started to come up. The little streetlamps cast orange shadows in random patches across the cobbled street. The door creaked open, the sound reverberating in the early-morning silence. She stood, taking in the scene around her. It was exactly as she had left it. Thoughts of the last time she'd stood here in the café came flooding back. The rush the next day, the desperation to get out of there and get to the airport, the crush of worry she had felt in her chest. They were now replaced by thoughts of the hospital visit, the funeral and the weeks that followed. Everything flashed through her mind like a movie projector at high speed. She didn't even realise that she was crying.

She switched on the overhead light, the sharp jolt of the bulb stinging her eyes. There was a fine layer of dust on each of the tables. She ran one finger across the table closest to her as she walked by it, watching her finger leave its trace as she went. She stood behind the counter, running her hand across the tiles. The place had the musty smell of an old property that had been closed up for too long. She knew she should fling open the windows and let in the autumn breeze, but instead she sat on the stool behind the counter and put her head into her hand, suddenly feeling overwhelmed. She pressed the backs of her wrists hard into her eyes until she saw circular rings pulsating in the darkness behind her eyelids. The last conversation she'd had with her mother ran over and over in her head and she wished she could just pick up the phone and call her. But she couldn't, and with the pang of loss she felt the physical ache again in her heart.

'Cop on to yourself now, Niamh,' her mother would have said to her in her no-nonsense voice. 'You have work to do and it won't get done with you sitting there feeling sorry for yourself.'

She smiled, despite herself, at the memory of her mother's way of wrapping up words of encouragement in words of minor admonishment, wiped her eyes with the backs of her hands and started cleaning. Small clouds of dust rose from each table as she made her way around the little café.

The door burst open. 'I brought baguettes and coffee from Massimo's!'

Niamh jumped up with a start to see Emily standing just inside the doorway, her nose scrunched up in disgust.

'Good Lord, Niamh, open some windows. It smells like old men's shoes in here!'

'What are you doing here? It's eight o'clock in the morning.'

'I couldn't sleep.'

If Emily noticed Niamh's tear-stained face, she didn't show it. She placed the paper-wrapped warm baguettes on the countertop.

'Seriously, Emily, what are you doing here? You're not a morning person. You don't do early mornings.'

'Well, it's quite simple, darling. The sooner you transform this place into a wine bar, the sooner I'll have somewhere lovely to drink great wines that is not my own apartment. I was too excited about this whole wine bar notion to stay in bed, and I figured you might need coffee.'

'Fair enough.'

Emily stood, hands on her hips, and took in her surroundings, as if looking at it with fresh eyes for the first time.

'It won't take much at all to convert this place into a wine bar. To be honest I think all it really needs is a drastic shift in ambience. Kill the overhead lights, bring in an overabundance of lamps and candles, paint the walls a moody colour and get some top-quality wine glasses.'

'What's wrong with the colour of the walls?' Niamh asked, aghast at the thought of having to paint them. 'I thought accent pieces might be enough to change the look of the place, no?'

'Well, darling, first of all, white is too clinical for a wine bar. It is perfectly fine for a café, early morning, lunch, bright, sunny and shiny and all that, but people won't frequent a wine bar until evening, and you need to create the right mood. I think a nice cool grey colour would work very well in here, and it's trending in all the great interiors magazines. Cool grey, that is. And secondly, you didn't have to paint the place last time around. You just dusted it off and touched it up. So, I'm sure it's desperately needed at this point. This is not the time to be cheap, darling. It will show.'

By now Emily was pacing the room downstairs, pointing out things that had to go and things that had to change. Apart from the idea of having to repaint the walls, Niamh was actually relieved to have someone with strong opinions to suggest what she needed to do.

'We'll have to have some kind of spectacular, over-the-top wine display for dozens and dozens of bottles. We don't want to have confusion or uncertainty about what this place is. I think the only answer is to get one custom made.'

'What?' Niamh cried. 'We need a custom-made wine cabinet? Are you mad? That would cost a fortune.'

'Not at all, my dear. I know someone locally who can make it out of regular wood and we'll have it painted and scuffed – kind of shabby chic. What do you think?'

'As long as you know what you're doing, that's fine by me. I wouldn't know where to start.'

'Now, one other thing. Why don't you move in upstairs until you get back on your feet financially? Get rid of the Airbnb and stick in a bed upstairs. I think it's ideal given that there is already a bathroom and it would save you a small fortune. What do you think?'

'No, you're right. I had thought about doing that and getting the place all cleared out and then, well, you know ...' Her voice trailed off.

'Yes. Quite. You got distracted.' Emily stood up and closed her laptop. 'Well, Niamh, you're just going to have to grab hold of this one by the arse. Own it! Things were different before and you didn't have to try to think at this level, but now you do. You need to conserve what finances you have left to get this place up and running. Just terminate your Airbnb rental, which you are fully entitled to do with sufficient notice, and move in upstairs. I really don't see any other way around it. I can talk to them if you like.'

'You can?' Niamh asked, her mouth agape. 'Would you? I don't even really know them. I'd be so grateful.'

'Yes, of course. They are good people. I'll have a chat with them and explain the situation. It won't be a problem.'

'If you can that would be marvellous. It would be great to be able to live upstairs. Thanks, Emily, I really appreciate it.'

'Not at all.' Emily gave a casual wave of her hand. 'Now, what are we going to call the place?'

'What about just calling it "The Wine Bar"? You know, so when people ask, "Where are you going?" the answer would be "to The Wine Bar".'

'I love that idea! We'll need to get a sign made for outside, and a logo. We need to decide on an opening night and then promote the hell of it around town. Anything else that I'm not thinking of?' Emily asked, tapping her fingers against her bottom lip.

'I don't think so, except for the obvious.'

'What's that?'

'The wine?'

'Oh right, yes, of course. I'll come up with a plan for the wine to get us through opening night, at least, and I'll see if we can get some time with Giorgio today or tomorrow. We'll need his help with the licence and probably getting a sign made and hung if we're to open in a couple of weeks. Remember, it doesn't have to be perfect for the launch, just fabulous. There is a difference, you understand!'

'Yes, I'm learning that.' Niamh smiled, pulling on a pair of rubber gloves.

'Now, I'm in desperate need of another coffee, so I'll dash. Come to my place for lunch. I'll have lunch ordered in for us and we can get online and order all your lamps and candles and other supplies. I think the place needs some cool artwork, too. We can do all that over lunch. Say one o'clock at my place? I'll have a plan figured out for the wine by then. In the meantime, you get stuck in here and get rid of any glaring signs that this was ever a café. Stick everything in a corner for now in case Giorgio wants to keep some of the marginally valuable stuff that was here before you, but otherwise, it all goes. *Va bene?*' Emily had a wide grin on her face. It was clear that she was enjoying this.

'*Va bene*, OK,' Niamh agreed with a nod.

'God, I hadn't realised how bored I was until I started thinking about this project. This will be fun, darling! See you at noon.'

Apart from ducking out for a cappuccino around ten o'clock, Niamh got stuck in and didn't stop dumping, moving and cleaning until almost one o'clock. It felt good to be busy again, and she had to admit that she was excited about the wine bar idea, especially as she had support from Emily. She wasn't sure she'd have managed to pull it off on her own. She freshened up in the little bathroom downstairs and dashed to Emily's place with a few minutes to spare.

The two of them spent the afternoon mapping out plans for the wine bar. They decided that Niamh could start with the painting and they could recruit help as needed for the parts she couldn't reach. They decided on a soft, pale grey colour from magazine images and Emily told her where to go and buy paint in town. They'd deliver it by the next day so she could get started right away. They scrolled through websites that offered Italian-designed products and delivered locally, both of them agreeing that the place should have an Italian feel to it if they were to attract the locals. By comparison, more modern designs in restaurants and bars both in Camogli and other towns locally had never been popular with the locals and had therefore proven unsustainable.

They found a company just outside Milan that created spectacular old-school candelabras and scrolled through pages of designs. They ordered several tall floor-standing versions as well as elaborate twelve-candle countertop designs.

Miniature single candleholders in the same design would be perfect for each individual table.

'Lamps would definitely be easier and less messy, but this is going to be stunning and more unique,' Emily announced with a proud smile as they hit the order button on the website.

'I think the servers, myself included, should wear all black, but it should be stylish, not some lame shirt and pants,' Niamh suggested

'Excellent idea! Why don't we pick something from a high street store that carries that kind of thing all year round so, as your people change, you can just order more. I don't like those restaurant-industry options, they're too stiff for what we're trying to create here and they're terribly expensive. They don't all have to be identical but they do need to be functional and elegant. You need to get this up and running on a shoestring.'

'And the wine glasses should be those really fancy thin-stemmed ones that they have in the good places in Milan and Portofino. I know they're more expensive and they break easily, but they kind of say something about the place, don't you think?'

'Agreed, and I know the brand you are referring to. I'll pull up their website.' Emily leaned back in over the laptop again.

'I wonder if Massimo might be able to get me a trade discount on the glasses, you know, because he has a café?' Niamh wondered aloud.

'It's worth asking, darling. Every euro counts now, and the further you can spread it, the better the place will look and feel. OK, so it looks like everything will be delivered within the next seven days,' Emily continued, scrolling down her laptop screen. 'So I think it's safe to say you'll be ready to open in ... what? Two weeks?'

'That sounds doable. All of the really hard work is done from the first renovation of the café, apart from repainting the place. The only question is how long it will take to make the wine-display cabinet. How long do you think?' Niamh asked, slashing items off their to-do list.

'Let me worry about the wine-display unit. We can always throw money at the problem to get it done in time.'

The one thing they compromised on was artwork. They didn't have a budget for original art and they didn't have the time to scour local artists, so they ordered a number of oversized prints from an online outlet, including artists like Rothko and Picasso.

'We don't want a sunflower or French lily pond vibe, we want something more striking and less ... I don't know ... melancholy or moody.'

'Right, not a Monet in sight. Got it!' Niamh said, giving Emily a mock military-style salute.

By the end of the day they had everything ordered, planned and plotted out on paper. They settled on an opening date in a little under three weeks' time. It had to be a Saturday night to try to maximise the local crowd. Niamh gathered her things and stuffed the lengthy to-do list and a whole lot of notepad pages into her bag.

Emily's phone buzzed. 'Oh good, it's Giorgio. He says he's on his way. I asked him to drop by after work.'

'Does he know what for?'

'No, he has no idea, but I didn't want to get into it over the phone, best to ask these delicate questions in person, I find. Do me a favour and pull a bottle of white wine from the wine fridge and fill the ice bucket.'

'Sure. Does Giorgio even drink white wine? I don't think I've ever seen him drink anything but Italian reds.'

'Of course he does, especially the good stuff. But, more importantly, I do, and we're in my apartment,' Emily said with a grin.

Niamh went to the small room just off the kitchen and pulled a chilled bottle from the impressive collection. It had originally been intended to be a larder or storage room of some sort but Emily had had it converted into a wine cellar that now held several hundred bottles. As she put the bottle in an ice bucket, the door buzzed.

'Niamh, can you get that?' Emily shouted from the living room. 'I'm on the phone with one of the vineyards.'

Niamh opened the door to Giorgio.

'Oh, *ciao*, Nina,' he said, smiling. 'I didn't expect to see you just now. I thought it was just Emilia.'

'We've been here all afternoon working on stuff. Come on in.' She tried to sound casual but there was something about his presence that always made her feel . . . she couldn't even describe it . . . unsettled. She didn't know what it was, exactly, but she had never felt it before with any other man. He was handsome, certainly, and impeccably dressed always, but there was something about his demeanour, the way he held himself, his confidence and his quietness that she felt drawn to. He had a warm side that wasn't immediately apparent. Niamh felt that it was most likely due to the nature of his work and the need to maintain a professional persona with clients. 'I'm opening a bottle of wine in the kitchen. Emily is on the phone. Would you like a glass?'

'Yes, thank you.'

He followed her to the kitchen. She pulled the bottle from the ice bucket.

'Carricante. Nice choice,' he said appreciatively.

'It's a nice collection!' she said with a big smile. 'I'm trying to beef up my knowledge of local wine and taste some of the ones that I wouldn't have had access to in Ireland. So this Sicilian Carricante white wine is today's market research.'

'Beef? Why do you say beef?' he asked, tilting his head as he did when asking a question.

'Beef? What?' Niamh responded, confused.

'Just now . . . you said you beef . . .'

'*Oh!* Beef up!' she replied, laughing. 'I said I was trying to beef up my wine knowledge. It means improve, like . . . improve my wine knowledge.'

'Ah, another new expression! See? The more time I spend with you, the more English I learn. This means you are good for me, Nina, no?' he said with a grin.

She felt her stomach flip upside down.

Jesus, Giorgio, you really can't say things like that to a girl. Not when you're that hot. She could feel her cheeks start to flush as she fumbled with the corkscrew.

'You look happy today, Nina. It is nice to see,' he said, stepping towards her. 'Please . . .' He took the corkscrew from her hand. Subconsciously, she touched the place where his hand had touched hers.

She leaned against the kitchen island and watched as Giorgio proceeded to open the bottle with a couple of deft movements. She couldn't help but think that if that had happened with Rick she'd have gone all bat-shit crazy feminist, ranting about how she was perfectly able to open a bottle of wine and how presumptuous and controlling he was. But with Giorgio it always felt like more of an invitation than an order. She always felt like part of the conversation or the event with Giorgio, as opposed to having to argue for her place in it.

They sat on high stools waiting for Emily to get off the phone, and Niamh rattled on, telling Giorgio about the plans for the wine bar. She avoided the subject of the licence as she thought Emily would be better equipped to handle that conversation. And, anyway, she herself didn't know exactly what was involved, only that they needed it fast.

'When you get everything ready and you are finished with all of this extra work, on your first Sunday off I will take you sailing,' he announced with a smile.

Her heart gave a little skip. He had never invited her anywhere before.

'Most Sundays I take the boat out with Sara, Massimo and some friends. You must come with us!'

Niamh cringed inwardly on hearing him say Sara's name. She couldn't understand their relationship. Yes, Sara was easily one of the most beautiful women that Niamh had ever met, but she had been cold to her from the very first time they had met, and no matter how pleasant or polite Niamh had been towards her, nothing had changed. Giorgio wasn't the type to be struck by looks alone, surely, so what was she missing? She realised that she envied Sara her relationship with Giorgio, which was irrational and futile, but she couldn't help it. She had to try hard to make an effort to be nice to her around Giorgio, as her instinct was to be jealous, which her mother would have pointed out was a nasty character trait that should be stomped on.

'That sounds great, thanks,' she said. She was saved from having to feign delight at the invitation to join him and Sara on his boat by Emily's arrival in the kitchen.

She wasted no time in explaining what they needed and

she asked him directly if he could help them. In true Italian fashion, he shrugged his shoulders in response and picked up a grape from the bowl.

'*Sì, certo*,' he said in response. Yes, of course.

Niamh marvelled at how it all worked here, but didn't dare to interrupt. They were making real progress and she had just got one giant step closer to opening The Wine Bar and to her rescuing her dream of a fresh start and a new life in Italy.

# Chapter Thirty-Four

The following weeks went by in a rush and Niamh's days were full of tasks like painting, fixing, ordering, stocking and planning. They had multiple wine deliveries from small producers several times a day, so Niamh based herself in the little café, leaving only to run a necessary errand or grab a coffee at Massimo's. The painting of the walls took her four days and she was particularly proud that she had managed to do it entirely on her own. The place changed every day and she was beside herself with excitement as she watched its progress.

She had erected the candelabras and placed a miniature version on each table. She had been lighting the ivory-coloured candles for a few hours every day, just as Emily had advised, to avoid having the place look shiny new. Instead it would have a patina of age on it with the candle wax dripping and frozen in time. Niamh smiled as she examined them every morning and saw how they were already creating wax shapes like those ice structures you see in caves – either stalagmites or stalactites, depending on whether the ice rose upwards from the ground or hung down from above, but she was damned if she could remember which was which. 'Either way you already look very pretty,' she said to the candelabras as she walked by them, touching their new wax sculptures gently.

With only a few days to go before opening night, she really didn't have any spare time, but when Giorgio had called on Saturday evening, he had been insistent that she meet him at Massimo's early the next morning.

She dressed in jeans, boots and a sweater, grabbed her coat and an oversized scarf and picked up her bag. She opened the door onto the narrow, cobbled street and stepped out into the cool air. Late October had brought with it a distinctive chill both early morning and late at night.

She walked the ten-minute walk to Massimo's café, the chilly sea breeze helping to wake her up.

'And on a Sunday, too,' she mumbled into her scarf.

She walked along the series of narrow streets, her head down against the wind, mentally running through her check-list for the day.

She stepped into the warmth of Massimo's café and peeled off her scarf.

'Ah, Signora Nina! *Buongiorno!*' Massimo said warmly. 'You are ready for the big party, no? Everything is prepared? I know that you are very busy with all this work. You need a coffee, no?'

'*Sì, Massimo, certo oggi,*' she replied with a smile. Yes, definitely today.

Giorgio sat at a table at the back of the café. That's unusual, Niamh thought. He usually stood at the counter for an espresso or cappuccino, or on occasion he would sit at a table right in front, and she had never seen him sit at the back of the café. Maybe he doesn't want to be spotted by clients on a Sunday morning and he's hiding out, she thought, as she made her way towards him.

'*Ciao, buongiorno,*' she said with a smile.

'*Buongiorno*, Nina. How are you today?' he replied, but he didn't smile.

'Umm ... tired, busy, stressed. I think that about sums it up,' she joked.

Massimo arrived with two cappuccinos and a plate of biscotti. '*Ecco signori!*' he said, placing the cups on the table.

'*Grazie, Massimo,*' Giorgio replied, looking up at him. He turned his attention back to his cup as he stirred a sachet of sugar into his cappuccino.

Niamh realised that she hadn't seen him smile yet this morning.

'So what's up?' she asked with a small frown. Although she loved nothing more than to be in his company, she was woefully behind schedule and Giorgio didn't seem to be in the best of moods.

'I'm afraid that I have some bad news, Nina,' he responded, not lifting his eyes from his cup.

Her heart sank in one plunging dive to the pit of her stomach.

'What do you mean? What kind of bad news?' She sipped her coffee nervously. 'Oh my God. Have they denied my application?'

'What application, Nina?' Giorgio asked, looking confused.

'My wine licence? Have they denied it?'

'No,' Giorgio replied, his eyes cast down towards his feet. 'I'm afraid there is an offer on the building.'

'What do you mean, an offer?'

'There is an offer for the building ... to buy the building. I didn't know how to tell you this news. I just found out last night,' he said without looking at her. 'But I think that there is no good time to tell you this.'

'My building?' she asked incredulously.

'Yes. Well, it is not your building, it is my brother's building, but yes, that building.'

'But I don't understand. How could there be an offer on it. Is it sold?'

'No, the offer was just made yesterday, but my brother says that he is happy with the offer and that it is perhaps a good thing for him, so I must tell you that he will accept it.'

'What?' she asked, incredulous.

'I know. I am sorry, Nina.' He shook his head slowly, staring at his untouched cappuccino.

'But how, Giorgio? I mean, how could this happen? The building was empty for two years ... two whole, entire fucking years. Nothing. Then I fixed it up, opened the café, am getting ready to reopen it as a wine bar and now it's being sold?' Her voice was rising with every word. 'And my lease expires after the initial six months. Oh my God. What a rookie mistake that was. I didn't think I needed to lawyer-up for my little café in Camogli. I feel pretty fucking naïve right now. No one even rented the godforsaken hole until I fixed it up, and now some fucker buys it from under me? How is this happening?'

'Yes, I am sorry, Nina. I think my brother is a fool to sell the building. It is only going to increase in value with all the investment that is being made in Camogli. I told him this, but he did not listen to me.'

'I couldn't give a shit about your brother's investment, Giorgio. What about my investment? What about me?' Her voice was rising and she could see the couple at another table look in her direction.

'*Lo so, lo so. Mi dispiace, mi dispiace* ... I am sorry,' he said, running a hand through his hair.

He looked remorseful, but Niamh didn't care. She had bet

everything on coming back and starting over again, and now she was in danger of losing it all. She wasn't sure which of them she was more furious with right now. Giorgio's brother, certainly, even though she had never met him, and whoever put an offer on the building, and even Giorgio himself just for being the messenger.

She felt an irrational sense of rage but was simultaneously welling up with tears.

'Sorry? Fuck, sorry, Giorgio. I put everything into that place. All my savings – you know that! How could you do this?'

'Nina, calm down. I—'

'Calm down? Calm down? I just got back from burying my mother and thought I was coming back to pick up my life again and get back to work. But no, I can't do that 'cause the building is about to be sold. How the fuck was the building sold? I didn't even know it was for sale.'

'I know. I am sorry. It is complicated because I don't have all the information. And no, it was not for sale.'

'OK, you are making zero sense now. Zero! How could the building be sold if it wasn't for sale? Is the goddamn building sold or not?'

'Please don't get so mad, Nina. Yes, yes, the building is being sold, but it was not for sale. I mean that my brother had not put it . . . how do you say . . . for the market?'

'Don't get mad? It's too late for that. I've just been royally screwed! And it's *on* the market, Giorgio. *O.N.*'

'OK, on the market. So, it was not on the market. But yesterday my brother called me from Chicago to tell me that he had agreed to sell the building to someone.'

'Agreed to sell it? To who?'

'I don't know. He just told me that he had an offer on the building and that he will sell it.'

340

'So, it's not sold yet?'

'Yes, he has agreed that he will sell it.'

'But have they signed anything? I mean is it actually sold?'

'I don't know. I don't think so but I only know what he told me when he telephoned me yesterday.'

'I don't believe this! You have find out, Giorgio! I need to know if it's too late or if I can do anything about it.'

'I can call him first thing in the morning, in his morning time, I mean. Now, it is still night-time in Chicago.'

'OK, OK.' Niamh sighed as she put her head down onto her folded arms. 'I really don't believe this is happening now, after everything I've been through. Who put an offer on the goddamn building?' She wiped one silent tear from her eye and turned her face away from him.

'I am sorry, Nina. It is not mine. The building is not mine. There is nothing I could do. He just called and told me that this had happened and I was the one who had to tell you.' He reached out and put a hand on her arm. She sat back, pulling her arm away and stared out towards the front of the café.

'Can you please call him later today and let me know what he says?' she asked, standing up and pushing her chair from the little table. It made a scraping sound on the tiles.

'Yes, of course. I will call you as soon as I speak with him. Nina . . . ' He stood up and stepped towards her, but she swept up her bag and strode towards the door.

She left the café and made a left turn, walking back along the promenade. It was quieter now that the tourists had left. Some locals walked along the seafront, older couples wrapped in coats and scarves against the cold sea breeze. She folded her arms and hid behind her sunglasses, head down as she walked into the breeze, back in the direction she had come only twenty minutes earlier. Tears fell silently down her cheeks. She didn't even attempt to wipe them away. It didn't matter. She didn't care.

She had thought that this time it would be different. She had really believed that she'd get her second chance and things would turn out better. She had put so much into turning the café around, trying to prove as much to herself as to anyone else that she could do it. All the feedback she had received over the past few weeks was hugely positive. Even the locals seemed curious about the idea of having a wine bar in Camogli. But everything was now in question, and once again she didn't know where she stood. She didn't know if she would even have the place by the weekend, or if she was basically running it for someone else now that it had been sold. It was all a disaster – again.

She turned to go up the steps to the upper level, making her way back to the apartment. She locked the front door behind her and did the same with the door that led to the upstairs. She twisted the dial on the heater until it hissed out steam, took off her jeans and curled into bed. She leaned one elbow against the pillow and switched her phone to silent, realising as she did so that the building was also the place that she now lived. 'Homeless too. That's a thrilling prospect,' she muttered into her pillow, before falling into a restless sleep.

# Chapter Thirty-Five

She awoke just after four o'clock in the afternoon and turned to sit up, feeling normal for just a moment. Then the conversation with Giorgio came racing back into her mind and she sank back into the pillows. She pulled out her phone and texted Emily.

*Can you meet me for a drink? I need to talk to you.*

Her phone lit up almost immediately with a response.

*Of course. Where and when?*

*Now and I don't give two fucks.*

*Ah. OK. How about the little place at the end of the pier?*

*OK. Heading there now.*

*OK. See you in 20 mins.*

Niamh was already sitting on the terrace of the restaurant all the way at the end of the pier when Emily arrived. She was facing the sea but wrapped up in a jacket and scarf as it had started to get colder in the evenings now. It looked very different to how it was in the summer. The light was thinner, not as big and golden, but it was still beautiful.

She had replayed the earlier conversation with Giorgio over and over in her mind, trying to find a solution, but it was hopeless. She knew that if she lost the building and the wine bar failed then she didn't have an alternative, as this was all she could do here without any proper Italian skills. She didn't speak enough Italian to get a regular job, there were no English schools in the area so teaching English wasn't an option and the tourist season was already over for the year. She had put everything into the café and, with Emily's help, had mustered the energy and resources to do it all again with the wine bar idea, but she was at the end of the road and she knew it. The wine bar had been Plan B and she didn't have a Plan C.

Emily pulled out a seat at the table and motioned for the barman. She was wrapped in an oversized camel-coloured cashmere wrap and wore her signature Chanel sunglasses. Her nails were perfectly manicured, as always, Niamh noticed.

'Thanks for coming,' she said quietly.

'Of course, darling. It sounded rather urgent but in truth you know I rarely turn down the opportunity to drink outdoors.'

She ordered a bottle of local red wine.

'Now, what seems to be the problem?'

'Giorgio asked me to meet him this morning at Massimo's café. The building is being sold.'

'I know.'

'What do you mean, "you know"?'

'I know. He told me yesterday. He called me to ask me how he should tell you. I must say he was distraught at the idea of being the one to tell you the bad news.'

'Why didn't you tell me?'

'Because Giorgio was adamant that he should be the one to do it as you had agreed the whole deal, contract and all, with him.'

'And now it's all shot to shit.' Niamh sat forward and put her head in her hands. 'I can't believe this is happening. Can't the universe just give me a break and throw me a goddamn bone?' She sighed dramatically.

'Look, all is not lost,' Emily replied, pulling her wrap tighter around her shoulders against the chill of the sea breeze. 'You know the little man who sells pizza by the slice?'

'The one at the other end of the pier?'

'Is there another one?' Emily asked, raising one eyebrow.

Niamh wasn't in the mood for jokes. 'I don't know, Emily. Yes, I know that guy. What about him?'

'Well, he had an internet café here in town some years ago. He spent an absolute fortune kitting the place out with computers, modems and cables – whatever one needs for an internet café . . . I don't know. Anyway, my point is that he ran an internet café, which made perfect sense when he opened it, but then a year into it laptops and smartphones became mainstream and suddenly he had no business.'

'*Ecco, signore,*' the waiter said, smiling as he deposited two glasses and a bottle of wine in front of them.

'Anyway, as I was saying, the man suddenly had zero business and so he totally reinvented himself. He borrowed money from somewhere, recruited some locals to help and turned the place into a very basic pizzeria offering pizza by the slice. Of course, the town was appalled at first, as they'd never even considered pizza by the slice, but the tourists loved it and so grew his business. He had the courage to stay in it and figure it out. He found a solution to his problem and moved forward.'

She sat back with a wide smile, looking very pleased with herself. Niamh was certain that there was a lesson in this somewhere – something about the need to reinvent herself, but she couldn't determine what exactly it was.

'Great story, Emily, but there's one minute detail that differs from his story and my Greek tragedy of a life.'

'What's that?' Emily asked, still beaming.

'That guy had a building. He just traded a bunch of computers for a pizza oven and some dough and off he went with his new business. Small problem – I don't have a building. I *used* to have access to a building until some wanker went and put an offer on the building and my greedy landlord jumped at it.'

'Well, if that's how you feel about me?'

'What?' Niamh squinted up at her with a pained expression on her face. She was tired, emotional, and stressed and this conversation wasn't making much sense. This was clearly one of Emily's 'Let's have a deep and confusing conversation about nothing' kind of days, but Niamh just couldn't cope with it right now.

'I'm your wanker.'

Niamh looked up from her wine glass and stared her right in the eyes. 'What?' she asked again, shaking her head. This was becoming maddening.

'You said, "some wanker went and put an offer on the building" – you said that just now.'

'Yes. So?'

'So, I'm your wanker, darling. Although I'm not terribly fond of the term. In general it's perfectly fine, and in fact I know many wankers personally, but not to describe me. I understand where it was coming from, of course. Perhaps we could find another word for me, though. Something a little more flattering?'

She sat back against her chair, took a sip of wine and watched the realisation work its way across Niamh's face.

'You?'

'Me.' Emily nodded.

'You bought the building?'

'No, I put an offer on the building.'

'But ...'

'But what?'

Niamh could see that Emily was enjoying this now. She sat up straighter. 'But, I mean, why did you ... do you want to buy the building? Why would you do that to me?'

'Not *to* you, darling, *for* you. I want to do this with you. Don't you understand?'

'No actually, I don't.'

'Look, Niamh, it's really quite simple,' Emily said, leaning into the table to face her. 'You were gone for almost a month and I realised that you are the only non-Italian person here that I really like. The rest of the expats are either pretentious snobs or entitled pricks and they think that the fact that we all speak the same language somehow binds us together in unity or solidarity as expats and they've forgotten the fundamental principle of forging friendships – that you have to actually like someone before you allow them into your life. And I don't, for the most part, *like* most of the expats here. Anyway, then along comes you, not really giving a toss what anyone thinks of you and just getting on with it, and you open this café that sells lovely salads that no one except tourists wants to eat because the Italians haven't quite grasped the Californian ideals of "clean food" and heart-healthy alternatives. To top that off, you offered average coffee that no Italian will ever spend money on, and you opened smack in the middle of summer. The odds were stacked against you from the start, my dear.'

'But you're buying the building ...' Niamh said slowly.

'Precisely,' Emily said firmly, with a nod. 'This really is awfully good wine. It has great body for a four-year-old wine, don't you think?' She swirled her glass and took a long sip.

'Yes, I suppose. Anyway, you were saying ...' Niamh

offered, trying to rein in the conversation and nudge Emily back in the direction it had been going.

'Look, darling, it's all quite simple really. While you were gone the town council finally granted permission to build that new luxury hotel on the periphery of the town. That's going to increase the spotlight on Camogli and the town is only going to get busier. More hotel inventory means more tourists, which is a good thing for locals who will benefit from increased tourist traffic. However, it will also have implications for real estate and so people are already speculating that property prices – especially those in the centre of town – are going to rise. So, you come along, dust off the grime from the old café and then announce that you're turning it into a wine bar. Lo and behold, some simpleton with absolutely no imagination of their own decides they should buy it now that it's all shiny and new again. They couldn't see the value of it when it was ramshackle, but the moment it shows promise as an investable entity, they dig into their grotty little pockets, call Marco in Chicago and make him an offer.'

Niamh couldn't believe what she was hearing. She just sat and stared at Emily, trying to process what she was saying.

'But how did you know that someone had made an offer?'

'Giorgio called me yesterday and asked my advice on how to tell you. He was devastated at the thought of disappointing you.'

'But if someone else made the offer, how are you going to buy the building?'

'Well, I merely intervened. There is one caveat, though.' Emily sipped her wine and turned the bottle towards her so she could read the label. 'Hmm, this is surprisingly good. I haven't seen it on the menu before. It must be new. You see – this is why we need the wine bar, so we don't have to sit outdoors on freezing cold terraces in autumn!'

Niamh thought she might lose her mind soon. 'Go on,' she urged.

'Oh yes, so I called Marco earlier today and said I would pay one euro more than the offer he had currently on it and that I was his dear friend and I reminded him that he owes me a favour. So he laughed and said OK. He doesn't care about the ins and outs of the deal, he just wants to take some money out now that he's going to start a family.'

Niamh's head was beginning to spin. Her mind was racing. 'He just laughed?'

'Yes, like I told you, he really wants nothing to do with all this negotiation and paperwork, he just wants to take the cash and get back to his life in America.'

'So, what's the caveat?' Niamh asked, nervous at what she might say next.

'Well, a lot of my capital is tied up in other investments and it will obviously take me some time to access it . . . ' Emily's voice drifted off as she did some mental calculations.

'Obviously,' Niamh repeated, having zero concept of how long it might take.

'I'm probably going to need sixty to ninety days, and the issue is that the other buyer is a cash buyer.'

'So what does that mean?'

'It means that we need Marco to be agreeable to the idea of turning down the initial offer and having to wait a few months for my money to come through.'

'OK, but even if he did agree to those terms, how would it work? The financial part, I mean?'

'Simple. I'll front the capital required to buy it initially and we'll work out a revenue-share arrangement so that you can contribute to the payments of the building and ultimately be co-owner. Are you following?'

'Yes, I think so,' Niamh replied slowly, finally taking a breath and reaching for her glass of wine. 'So you'd buy it and I'd buy my share of it over time?'

'Exactly. I'm not loaning you the money, Niamh. I want to be your business partner. I'll buy the building, you'll run the business and commit to a payment plan over time.'

'But why? I mean, you could have bought a building any time before this but you didn't, so it can't just be for the real estate opportunity.'

'Well, primarily, darling, because I'm bored, and secondarily, I like the idea of having a place I can go to drink great wine and feel like I own the place. Can't get barred from your own wine bar, after all!'

'So what do we do now?' Niamh asked, determined to keep the conversation moving forward.

'Well, I don't want to get into a bidding war, so we need Giorgio to keep the other buyer at bay temporarily until we sign the deal with Marco. If the other buyer gets wind of a counter offer then he/she might well counter again, and I can't afford to let this escalate in price.'

'Does Giorgio know about all this?'

'I don't think Giorgio even knows that I've made a counter offer yet. But Niamh, you have to act as if nothing has changed and open the wine bar on schedule as planned. Understand? We need to act as if we know nothing about this offer, and continue with life as normal, because whoever made that offer is most likely here.'

'*Here?*' Niamh said loudly. 'Do you think it's someone we know? Like, someone who knows us? Oh my God! Traitors!'

'Yes, treacherous, darling, but such is life. That is precisely why you have to proceed with opening night without as much as a hint of anything being awry. If they made an offer once, they could well do it again,' Emily replied matter-of-factly as she pulled out her phone and dialled Giorgio's number. 'Might as well bring him into the plan if he hasn't already heard.'

The conversation with Giorgio was short, with Emily saying a lot of 'yes' and 'that's correct' before hanging up less than two minutes later. 'Turns out he had heard. Marco called him as soon as he hung up from me to tell him to stall the deal with the first offer. Giorgio just needed to verify what was discussed.'

'So he understands what's happening? I mean, about us needing time to get all this straight?'

'He does. He said to leave it with him, that he was well used to having to play politics with property deals and that he would delay getting back to the original bidder as much as possible.'

'Do you have any idea who it might be?'

'The original bidder? No, and I hope that I don't find out because if it's anyone I know and I find out that they have undermined me and tried to buy the building that houses my new business – sorry, our new business – out from under me ... well, you know what they say. Hell hath no fury like a woman scorned.'

For the next four days, Niamh continued with life as normal to all intents and purposes. The reality was that on the inside she was a mess. She felt completely powerless, as she herself could do nothing to resolve the situation. She continued to run about town, preparing for opening night on Saturday, but the precariousness of her situation was never far from her thoughts. The uncertainty was overwhelming.

Emily had tried to lift her spirits by saying that there was a chance that the other buyer, if successful in his or her bid, might want to keep the wine bar open, in which case Niamh could most likely remain on. But in Niamh's mind, the fact that she would then be working the bar for someone else, made her just a barmaid, an entirely different situation. It was untenable and she knew it.

'How much is the building?' Grace asked, when she called Niamh that afternoon.

'The offer was eight hundred thousand euros, so Emily offered eight hundred and one thousand euros to counter.'

'She's nuts! Imagine having that kind of money.'

'Well, that's the problem, she doesn't have all that, at least not liquid, anyway, that's what she said,' Niamh explained as she sat at one of the small tables in the wine bar. 'So she needs to liquidate some other investments in order to buy the place before the other buyer can make a counter offer.'

'Right, so she'll just liquidate a few investments and hope that the other buyer doesn't get wind of it. Well, that should be easy enough,' her sister said sarcastically. 'And in the meantime, are you losing your mind?'

'Yes. Totally. I can't do anything. It's all down to Emily, and I just have to carry on as if nothing is happening. She's talking to some people back in London and Giorgio is trying to keep the other buyer at bay until she has some idea of how quickly she can access the cash.'

'But what's the hurry? Why the urgency, all of a sudden?'

'Well, now that the brother has had an offer on it, he's decided to go ahead and sell it. They're having a baby in the spring, and apparently he's applying for his green card, so it's not like he's coming back here any time soon, so I guess the money sounds attractive. Can't say I blame him. I'd cash out too if I suddenly found out that some random building I owned was worth almost a million euros and someone wanted to buy it in an all-cash deal.'

'That's true. What are you going to do? If it doesn't work out, I mean. Sorry to be Negative Nelly, but I don't want you to be blindsided if it all goes pear shaped. Have you thought about it?'

'Thought about it? That's all I do! I haven't slept properly since this all started. My head is melted from it all,' Niamh said, exasperated.

'I can imagine – but do you have a Plan B? What if it all goes pear shaped?'

'No, Grace, *this* was Plan B. I had this mad idea and forged ahead with it, never in my dreams or nightmares thinking that some fucker would turn the whole thing upside down behind my back.'

'And you've no idea who it is?'

'None. The brother hasn't said, which makes me think that I know the person.'

'Well, not necessarily, maybe that's just a professional courtesy or something. You know, don't name the bidder until the deal is done or something?'

'I don't know, but it's a weird feeling thinking that someone around here just did that to me and I don't know who.'

'Well, you don't know that it was someone who's actually there. They could have been passing through and spotted it. Don't go getting all Sherlock Holmes, thinking your neighbours are out to get you. That will just drive you mad.'

'Yes, you're right. OK, I better get back to work. I've some wine deliveries arriving this afternoon. I'll see you Friday!'

'OK, I'll text you from the airport before I fly. Good luck with the last-minute stuff.'

'OK, thanks. Bye!'

# Chapter Thirty-Six

'I still can't believe that you flew over here for this,' Niamh shouted to Grace through the bathroom door a few days later.

'Well, I've never been one to miss a good launch party!'

Grace had arrived earlier that afternoon and the two sisters had caught up over a quick lunch along the promenade before returning to Niamh's apartment.

'Anyway, it's not every day your little sister has the balls to do something like open a wine bar! The fact that it's in a gorgeous part of Italy is just icing on the cake,' she shouted back.

Grace came out of the bathroom in a mist of perfume.

'You look amazing, Grace. Did you lose weight?'

'Maybe,' Grace said with a shrug.

She wore a simple, Bardot-style black dress with off-the-shoulder detail.

'So did Robert lose his mind at the thought of having the boys for the weekend?'

'They're his kids too, Niamh,' Grace snapped.

'Jesus, sorry. Sensitive much? Who peed in your Cheerios?'

'No, it's just that it's frustrating that's all. Why is it that I'm expected to look after them twenty-four-seven, but if Robert has them for one weekend then it's "How is poor Robert going to cope?"'

'Didn't mean to trample on a nerve there, Grace,' Niamh retorted, rolling her eyes.

How was it that after only a couple of hours together they always ended up sniping at each other over something stupid? Niamh wondered.

'Honestly, you'd swear a man wasn't to be trusted to keep his own kids alive for one lousy weekend,' Grace continued, undeterred. She rummaged about in her suitcase, pulled a necklace from a small suede pouch and clasped it around her neck.

'That's fab!' Niamh exclaimed, happy to have found an opportunity to change the subject. 'Is it new?'

'Yep.'

'Nice gift!'

'As a matter of fact, it was a gift to myself.'

Niamh raised her eyebrows. 'Oh?' She fingered the amber pendant at the end of the gold chain.

'Well, when your husband is away on business for your birthday and comes home only to have forgotten all about it entirely, what do you do but go shopping for a consolation prize on his credit card?'

'You did not!' Niamh laughed.

Grace looked at her without so much as a smile. 'Give them an inch and they'll take a mile, Niamh. Perhaps the shock of seeing the line item for twelve hundred euros on his credit card bill will be enough to ensure he doesn't forget as easily in the future.'

'You spent twelve hundred euros on a necklace?' Niamh shouted incredulously.

'Yes, I did. Isn't it divine?' Grace said coolly as she eyed her reflection.

'That's nuts, Grace. That's rent money! Who spends that kind of money on jewellery?'

'Well, not sane people, I'll give you that, and normally I wouldn't either, but I just got pissed off and that was the one piece that caught my eye. Trust me, this was on the lower end of the scale based on what I saw on display in Brown Thomas. Normally I'd be lucky to get something from Zara from him, but he completely forgot and it pissed me off so I thought "fuck it" and went shopping.'

'Did he freak out?'

'He lost the plot initially, but when I suggested that he just not forget about his wife's birthday in future he shut up. He was fuming, but how could he object when he had been such a knob? I mean, who forgets their wife's birthday? Now, come on,' she said, swiftly changing the subject. 'What are you wearing to the grand opening? And what time do you need to be downstairs and ready? Didn't the invitation say six o'clock?'

'Yes, but I need to be ready before that. I need to start opening the place up in about half an hour,' she said, pulling a hanger from her wardrobe.

Grace looked from the green midi dress to Niamh and back to the dress. 'That?'

'There's no need for that tone of voice, Grace,' Niamh said defensively. 'What's wrong with it? It's *new*!'

Grace sighed. 'It's fine, but it's just not . . . I don't know. It's fine for a regular summer's day. It's cute, but I don't know – it's fine if you want to blend in and don't want to make a statement.'

'If I just want to blend in?' Niamh repeated, as she stood defiantly with her hands on her hips. 'Yeah, I go out all the time with the intention of wanting to blend in and be wall-paper, Grace.'

She turned around and rammed the hanger back into

the closet. 'One day I put on a really cute dress by mistake but I saw myself in the mirror and immediately said, "Take that off right now, Niamh! That one looks cute – you don't want to impress anyone, remember? Your goal is to be wallpaper!"'

'Oh, for crying out loud, calm down. The dress is fine ordinarily, but tonight is a big deal – you're opening your own wine bar, Niamh! Who gets to do that? Tonight you need to look like a million dollars! You need to be your A-game, most glamorous, sophisticated version of yourself. Now stop arguing with me, take that pissed-off expression off your face and pull out your sassiest numbers.'

'Sassy?' Niamh said reluctantly, staring at the options in front of her. 'You forget that I shop in H&M and Zara, Grace. I don't think I can afford sassy. I can afford cute, like normal people.'

'OK, stop with the defensive attitude. Let me in there. You're bound to have something suitable,' Grace said confidently, as she flicked through hangers. 'It's not about how much you spend. It's about fabric, the cut – you just need to have an eye for detail and know what looks good on you, that's all.' She pulled a black chiffon dress from Niamh's wardrobe. 'What about this? It still has a tag on it.'

'Yeah, it's new. I just wasn't sure it would work for tonight. Is it too formal?'

'Nonsense. This is perfect,' Grace replied, as she snapped off the price tag.

Within twenty minutes, Niamh was dressed in the new dress that fell just below her knee and had accessorised it with oversized gold hoop earrings and black wedge sandals. She twisted her chestnut brown hair into a messy bun and secured it with a couple of hair clips.

'There!' Grace said with a satisfied smile. 'Now you look like someone to be reckoned with.'

'Hmm, OK, thanks.' Niamh nodded with a small smile as she checked her reflection in the mirror. She looked at her watch and her stomach gave an anxious flip.

'Go! Don't even think about getting nervous. I'll see you in a half hour,' Grace said, as she shoved her sister towards the door.

Opening night had been planned meticulously. Niamh had sent a formal written invitation to everyone she knew locally and Emily had done the same in both Camogli and across the neighbouring towns. Giorgio had invited all his clients and Massimo had put up a promotional poster and had told anyone who would listen at the café. Franco had promised to show up with a bunch of his local friends and even some from as far away as Genoa. Niamh and Emily had decided to offer a red wine, a white wine and Franciacorta on the house, but the other, more expensive bottles would have to be charged for if requested. It was a business, after all.

Niamh had been counselled by Emily in earnest the week prior. She advised her not to make the mistake of being too busy serving that she couldn't meet and talk to her guests. Emily explained that in any business it was critical to have a relationship with your best clients, and that these Camogli locals would ultimately be her best clients, so it was a big opportunity to meet them and have them get to know her.

'You need to put your personality on this place. You need to become known as the owner. People like to be recognised and welcomed when they return somewhere, so it's important that you get to know your customers. Wear something fabulous on opening night and put an apron over it, that way, you can show that you're serious about it and not afraid to work, but when you remove your apron you will appear as the owner, not the server. I've watched Sara work this strategy to her advantage for years, so you'd be wise to do the same. At the end of the day, people do business with people they like, it's as simple as that.'

Niamh grimaced at the mention of Sara's name and she wasn't sure she liked being compared to her in any manner. Still, though, she couldn't help but admit that Sara's business was a raging success, so she let the comparison slide and took the advice as being well intentioned.

She stood alone now in the centre of the wine bar, turning full circle to look around.

What have I forgotten? I'm bound to have forgotten something, she mused, drumming her fingertips to her lips. She whipped out her phone and checked her To-Do app again.

Nope, this is weird. This feels weird. Actually having everything ready is a bit weird, she thought, still in the centre of the room. She walked behind the counter and checked all the wine coolers. Everything was fully stocked. She pulled open the door of the fridge to make sure all the hors d'oeuvres were ready. Platters of food were filled with bite-sized pieces of food, specially prepared to ensure they would be easy to eat with one hand while the other was holding a wine glass.

Rows of long-stemmed wine glasses stood ready for deployment, alongside still more rows of old-fashioned champagne coupes. Niamh had decided to inject a little old-world opulence into the interiors and opted for the coupe over the regular champagne flutes. She had mirrored those choices in the mismatched porcelain plates she had bought for the small plates on the menu.

She tested the surround sound system one last time and then checked her watch. It was ten minutes to six. Her stomach gave a nervous flip as she selected 'Fly Me to the Moon' on the stereo. It had been her mother's favourite song. She thought of her then, for a moment, as she adjusted the volume and decided that Una Kelly would have been proud of her in that moment. She crossed her fingers and said a silent prayer that it would all work out. She was afraid to hope, but couldn't allow herself to dwell on that now. She had guests to greet and a role to play, and she intended to do it justice.

'Oh my God, the place looks amazing!' Grace gushed as she burst through the door from upstairs. 'I'm so bloody proud of you, Niamh!'

'Thanks. Yeah, it does look nice.'

'Nice? Are you mad? It's fabulous!'

'Sorry, you're right. It is.'

'Don't you go apologising for nothing again now, Niamh Kelly. I haven't seen sight of that old version of you for some time now and I'm not allowing her back! Look at what you've accomplished! This is amazing!' her sister said, engulfing her in a hug.

Moments later, the first of the guests started to file through the door. Niamh had hired two local guys to help serve drinks so that she could divide her time between serving drinks and playing hostess. There had been a steady stream of guests for the first hour and the room was filled with the buzz of happy chatter.

As the crowd started to build in the cosy front room of the wine bar, Niamh was becoming increasingly frustrated as she struggled with bottles of wine in the little galley kitchen.

'What's up with these bottles of red wine?' she said with a loud frustrated sigh.

'*Che c'è?* What is wrong?' Giorgio asked, sticking his head inside the door.

'These bloody corks keep breaking. It's not like I haven't opened a million of them in my life, but these are getting the better of me.' She tucked another bottle between her knees and tugged on the corkscrew.

'And this is how you do it?' he asked, nodding towards the bottle jammed between her knees.

'I'm doing it the same way I've always done it, but they keep breaking, dammit!' she said as the corkscrew flew up with half the cork attached.

'*Dammelo*,' he instructed, reaching out his hand for the corkscrew. 'Give it to me.'

She sat down on a tall bar stool with a huff.

'I think we have had this conversation, Nina, no? You have to be more patient. *Pazienza, Nina.*'

She watched him deftly manoeuvre the corkscrew into the mangled cork and gently coax it out.

'*Allora*,' he said as the cork gave way. 'You just need to do it slowly. Some of these older bottles of red wine, the corks they are tighter, so you must be gentle. *Pazienza, Nina.* If you rush, then you will have this problem.' He nodded his head towards the three aborted wine bottles on the counter.

'Thanks. I'll just add this to the list of things Italians do better than me,' said Niamh with a sigh.

'Maybe, yes,' Giorgio said, turning back to face the counter. '*Allora*, you go and pour some drinks for your guests and I will rescue these other bottles for you.'

He had seemed tense when he arrived and still wasn't his usual calm, easy-going self, but she was grateful to him for rescuing the bottle situation.

'You're very quiet tonight.'

'Ah, just many things on my mind today.'

'Well, come and have a drink when you've rescued those

other bottles and forget about it. Pull your happy face out of your pocket, will you? This is supposed to be a party, after all!' She gave him a playful shove.

He responded with what was definitely a forced smile. 'Yes, yes, I will come.'

She looked at him for a moment but, he wasn't giving anything away.

She stepped back into the main room, which by now was packed and she couldn't stop a grin from spreading across her face. Grace was holding court with two Italian men in suits and caught her eye across the room. As far away as she was, Niamh could tell that she was in good spirits and loving the attention. She looked like a peacock with her feathers out on display, she decided. Squinting over at the two men in Grace's clutches, Niamh realised she didn't even know who they were, which she took to be a good sign, and her frustration from the kitchen started to dissipate.

Real strangers means that word has spread! How cool is that! she thought with a chill of excitement.

Niamh felt a tap on her shoulder and turned to see Sara standing in front of her. 'Congratulations, Niamh, this place looks wonderful,' she said with a smile.

Niamh wasn't sure if she was more surprised to see her standing there or to see her smile. She was quite sure that Sara had ever smiled at her directly before and she couldn't mask her surprise.

'Oh, umm, thanks. I didn't think you would come.' Niamh had uttered the words before she could stop them. 'I mean, I didn't think you'd be able to make it, you know . . . with the restaurant and all that.' She wondered what the hell Sara was even doing there.

'No, I understand, but I wanted to come,' Sara said quietly, casting her eyes to the ground. 'I owe you an apology.'

'Me? What for?' Niamh asked, genuinely confused.

'It's kind of you to act as though you don't know what for, but I know that I have not been very kind to you since you arrived.'

'Oh, that.'

'Yes, that. I know that tonight is not the right time, as you are so very busy, but I wanted to come and say congratulations and to offer my support – and to apologise.'

'But I don't understand. I mean, did I do something to upset you? Because if I did then you should have just told me. All I heard from everyone the whole time was how wonderful you were and how friendly and how sweet and blah, blah, blah. But you were kind of a bitch towards me so I just never saw it.'

'I know. I'm so sorry, I . . .'

The fact that Sara had chosen this night and this moment to have a meaningful conversation about their lack of relationship irked Niamh. She had enough to deal with on opening night, not to mention the issue of the building being under offer. She didn't have time for this right now, but neither could she afford to be seen as the witch in this scenario. Sara was extending an olive branch, so Niamh could hardly beat her over the head with it.

'Look, Sara, I'm sorry, but I really don't have time right now. I don't want to be rude but I have a room full of guests to attend to so maybe we could . . .'

'I understand, of course. There is no excuse for my behaviour and I know that it was wrong of me. It's just that I was jealous of you, that's all. It has always been a terrible character trait of mine, that I try to keep in check, but this time it got the better of me.'

Niamh stood rooted to the spot. 'Jealous? *You* are jealous of *me*?' she asked incredulously.

'Was. I *was* jealous of you. I'm not any longer. You did nothing wrong and I know that now and I'm sorry that I misjudged you.'

'But . . . how? I mean, what possible reason could you have for being jealous of me?' Niamh asked, unaware that her jaw had dropped in absolute incomprehension.

'But you must know, surely? Niamh, from the very first night I met you at the cocktail reception in Santa Margherita I have spent so much time wishing you had never dropped into my life. I realise now what a mistake that was, and that I should have been grateful to have you here, but I was wrong.'

'Santa Margherita?' Niamh squealed, now utterly confused. 'What?'

Sara gave a little laugh. 'You really don't know, do you?'

'Know what?' Niamh asked suspiciously.

'That since the very first night that I saw you with Giorgio, I knew we wouldn't last much longer and I blamed you for that. You see, Giorgio and I had been friends for a very long time, and soon after his fiancée left him we became a couple. I was the one who initiated it. I had been in love with him for a long time and I knew he didn't feel the same way about me, but when she left he was heartbroken and so we sort of fell together.' Sara clasped her hands together, avoiding eye contact with Niamh. 'I think I hoped that his feelings would change over time and that he might love me the same way I loved him. I was just grateful for what I had . . . for what it was, and it was wonderful for a long time. But when I met you that night and saw you with him I knew without any doubt that he would never look at me the way I saw him look at you. It was as if perhaps he realised that then, too, and so everything between us changed.' Sara glanced up at Niamh's face. 'I thought it was your fault. I blamed you.'

Niamh stood silent as the small crowd of people swirled around her.

'When there is an attraction, a chemistry between two people, it cannot be denied and it was obvious to me from the very beginning, even if it was not so obvious to you,' Sara continued. 'It took me some time to realise that, of course, it was not your fault. I behaved badly towards you and for that I am truly sorry,' Sara said, this time meeting Niamh's gaze properly.

Was this actually happening for real? Could Sara actually have been jealous of her? wondered Niamh. Where was Giorgio, anyway? She hadn't seen him since the wine bottle incident in the kitchen. She searched the crowd but couldn't see him.

Then Grace was at her side, having seen the conversation between Sara and her sister from across the room and coming in case Niamh needed to be rescued.

'Niamh, I think it's hard for people to reach the bar, there are so many people here,' Grace said, pointing in the direction of the narrow bar counter.

'Oh, right, I hadn't noticed,' Niamh admitted, grateful for the distraction. 'Are the two guys not passing enough drinks around?'

'No, no, that's not the problem. All the food is on the bar counter and people can't get to it. I think you should pass it around the room.'

'You're right,' Niamh replied. She turned to speak to Sara, but Sara shook her head. She put a hand on Niamh's shoulder. 'Please. I have distracted you enough. We can talk later. Tonight you have important work to do. I brought two of my new staff members here tonight to see your wine bar. Don't worry, I will ask them to help. If you want my help, that is?'

Niamh hesitated for a moment, still reeling from Sara's confession. She didn't quite know what to say, but she had to agree that she had other priorities right now and that she could use a little extra help.

'That would be great, Sara,' she said appreciatively. 'I thought two people would be plenty but they are stuck serving drinks. I didn't think we'd get this big a crowd, to be honest.'

Sara smiled at her as she gestured to the two girls. 'Niamh, this is a good problem to have. It means that you have underestimated the crowd and tonight will be a big success. Don't worry, the girls will be happy to help.'

The two girls, figuring they had the night off, had already had a couple of drinks, but they donned black aprons in the kitchen and loaded mini bites of food onto round trays. As they headed towards the door, Niamh thought she saw one of the girls stumble in her heels.

'Are you OK?'

'Ah, *sì*! New shoes,' the girl replied, kicking up her heel to explain the stumble.

Niamh decided that she really needed the help, so she probably didn't have a choice and, anyway, the girl worked for Sara so she was definitely properly trained.

It didn't take more than a couple of seconds for her to hear the commotion on the other side of the packed bar. Emily, stationed on a high stool at the counter, had seen the initial pieces of prosciutto-laden crostini become airborne as the girl, deep in conversation with two Italian guys her own age, took another wobble. The girl hadn't even noticed a couple of appetisers roll off the side of her tray and down the sleeve of an expensive Italian suit. Emily scanned the crowd and caught Niamh's eye across the room, drawing one hand across her throat in a 'cut her off' motion. Before anyone could intervene, a fit of giggles caused the offending tray to wobble again, and this time several pieces of tomato bruschetta landed on the lap of a very elegantly dressed woman. Niamh watched in horror, making her way through the crowd. She had been introduced to the same woman earlier that evening and knew that she was a highly respected writer from *Food & Wine* magazine in Milan.

'No! Not her!'

Before Niamh could even reach the scene, Sara had stepped in and plucked the tray from the unwitting girl who was still, at this point, deep in conversation. With an ice-cold look that could freeze molten tar, Sara snapped her fingers loudly. '*Vai!*' she said in a voice that indicated she was not to be argued with, and motioned towards the door.

Niamh stood mortified as Sara spoke in a rapid stream of Italian, apologising to the lady and assuring her that she would take care of it. The lady stood and turned to Niamh, whose face was now bright red.

'Don't worry about it. It's my own fault,' she said graciously in flawless English. 'Who wears white to the opening of a wine bar? Please don't even give it a second thought. The dress will be fine.' She gestured towards the pale red stain. 'And I'm here as a friend of Massimo's so, officially, I'm not on duty.'

It was such a kind gesture and Niamh, already on edge and anxious, was almost brought to tears.

'I am so embarrassed,' Sara whispered in her ear, clearly fuming over the incident. 'I didn't know she had been drinking. I am so sorry. I need another apron.'

She turned to the second girl and fired off a couple of sentences in stern Italian. Niamh didn't catch what was said but the threatening tone was clear.

'No, no,' the second girl insisted, seeming to reassure Sara somewhat as she continued about the room with her tray.

She turned back to Niamh. 'You have another apron?'

'Yes, in the kitchen, on the back of the door. But who . . . ?'

'Tonight, I work for you,' Sara said with a nod as she disappeared in the direction of the kitchen.

Stunned, Niamh turned to watch her go.

'What excitement!' Emily declared with a sparkling laugh, as she came to stand alongside Niamh and Grace. 'Sara had been speaking to some people in that corner and she saw the whole thing happen. I watched her lurch across the room like an animal stalking its prey,' she continued with an amused smile. 'I'd hate to be that poor girl tomorrow!'

'Well, it's not her fault, poor thing. She didn't know she'd end up working tonight,' Niamh offered in the girl's defence.

'Niamh, darling, you don't go out with your boss and get hammered. My word though, did you witness the snap of her fingers?'

'Yes, impressive!' Grace said in reluctant admiration.

'I kind of want to learn to do that, and to be more like her actually. She was fierce!' Niamh said, her head reeling. 'Although if I acted like that I'd probably be sued for harassment.'

'Now,' Emily said, leaning in conspiratorially towards Niamh. 'Not meaning to change the subject or anything – but I'm going to. There's a man in that corner I simply have to meet. Do you know him?'

'Who?' Niamh asked, craning her neck in the direction Emily was pointing.

'That gorgeous creature in the pale blue shirt. Just look at those arms. He's positively bursting at the seams, and so am I. I think I feel flush!' Emily said with a salacious grin.

'No, I've no idea who he is. How did these people find out about this? And how are there so many hot men here? Is this actually happening?'

'Word of a party travels fast in a small town. Now, hand me two glasses of your finest champagne, please, dear girl!'

'You're just going to rock up there and talk to him?'

'Good grief, no. With a bit of luck I'll rock up there and seduce him!' Emily grinned before making a beeline for the corner.

The crowd had started to whittle down after eleven o'clock, with only a couple of stragglers left in the bar.

'God, this certainly isn't an Irish party,' Grace said, gripping her champagne glass tightly. 'I don't think an Irish party can officially end until all the alcohol has been consumed. Emily! Are you leaving? You can't leave!'

Emily was making her way to the door on the arm of her prey.

'We're going to La Terrazza to meet some of ... what's your name again, darling?' she asked the man, who was easily fifteen years her junior.

'Alessandro,' he said, leaving her side to introduce himself to Niamh and Grace. '*Piacere*,' he said politely. 'We are going to meet some work colleagues of mine. You are welcome to join us.'

'Ooh, sounds like fun,' Grace said, with champagne-fuelled enthusiasm. 'Niamh?'

'Sure, why not? I think I've earned a drink tonight,' Niamh said. 'Go ahead. I'll follow you in a few minutes. I just have to lock up here and grab my coat from upstairs. I'll leave this mess until tomorrow.'

# Chapter Thirty-Seven

Niamh flipped the little sign on the door to read CLOSED. Giorgio was outside, pacing up and down, talking on his phone. Niamh's stomach flipped as she stood watching him through the blinds. She wondered if he was coming back to join the party or if he was coming with an update on the deal. She could feel her heart pound harder in her chest and felt irrationally nervous. He was coming in with some sort of news. That much was obvious. What she didn't know was whether it was good or bad.

He kept pacing, and had all the shoulder shrugging and gesticulating of an Italian in intense conversation.

Niamh texted Emily:

*Have you heard anything from Giorgio about the deal?*

Moments later a response flashed up on her screen. *No, nothing. Why?*

*Because he's pacing up and down outside the wine bar like a deranged caged animal.*

There was silence for a moment and the three dots to indicate that someone was actively typing had disappeared.

*Why have you gone silent? What are you not saying?* Niamh asked.

*He does that when he's stressed or angry. I've seen it before.*

*Shit. Do you think it's bad news?*

*I don't know.*

Giorgio pushed open the door. The little bell tinkled overhead.

'*Buona sera*,' he said, as he dropped his briefcase on the banquette along the left wall. 'Are you busy? Can I speak with you?'

'For the love of God, Giorgio, yes, spit it out. I've been watching you pace for the last ten minutes,' Niamh said, her arms flung out at her sides.

He frowned and looked confused. 'I don't understand, but I have some news about the deal.'

He sat on the banquette and she took a seat alongside him.

She groaned and bent over at the waist, putting her head in her hands. 'It's not going to work out, is it? I can tell by your face. You're all serious. I knew it was impossible. Goddamnit it, anyway.' She lifted her face and shook her head with a wry smile. 'I was so close.'

'Nina, will you listen to me?'

'Sorry, go on,' she said in a quiet voice. Her mind had already left the conversation as he talked about different numbers, percentages and valuations. She wondered how long she had before she would have to return home. She wondered exactly how much money she had left in her bank account. She thought about the invoices to suppliers that had yet to be paid. She would have to cover those, for sure. She couldn't just walk away from those and not pay them just because she'd screwed up her own finances.

'Nina, are you listening to me? I don't think you are listening to me,' he said, sounding exasperated.

Niamh turned to see Giorgio gesturing with both hands.

'Sorry, no, I wasn't. I am now. Sorry.'

'So my brother will own half.'

'Sorry, what? I wasn't listening. Sorry.'

Giorgio sighed and shook his head and spoke slowly. 'I explain to you, Nina, that Signora Emilia will own fifty per cent of the building and my brother Marco will own the other fifty per cent.'

'But how come? I don't follow.'

'*Dio io.* You were not listening to one word I have said.' Giorgio got up and stood in front of her. 'I tell you now again. OK. I have spoken with my brother on the phone in Chicago three times yesterday and two times again today. I have told him that he is crazy to sell the building. The building will only increase in value. Each time I tell him this he tells me that he will soon have a baby and a wife to think about and so he now wants to sell the building. So I ask him how many dollars exactly do you think you need to buy ... *Dio io,* what do you call these things? Nappies! Yes, and milk for the baby? Do you think you need eight hundred thousand dollars' worth of these things?' Giorgio was gesticulating wildly again and running his hands through his hair. 'So finally today he hears me for the first time. I say is it not better to have an investment for the future if he is to have a child? I say is it not better to save for university in America as this costs so much money? I tell him that right now he does not need the money, he just wants the money – there is a difference, no?' He continued uninterrupted while Niamh stayed rooted to the seat, clinging to his every word.

'So finally I suggest that if he wants money now that he sell half of the building to Emilia and retain the other half ownership. That way he gets money for baby milk and he keeps a share of the building for the future. And Emilia does not need to worry about liquidating her other investments. After two days of these conversations he tells me that this is a very good idea.'

He looked exhausted.

'So, you mean he's going to sell half of the building to Emily? Like fifty per cent? And he's happy to hold on to the other fifty per cent?' She realised that she was speaking as a nine-year-old might, in trying to understand the situation, but she was terrified that she had somehow misunderstood.

'*Sì.*'

'And is Emily OK with this?'

'I have not spoken with her yet. That was my brother just now on the phone. But I think she will agree that it is a better deal for her as she can retain her other investments. She would have had many, many tax implications if she had had to liquidate her investments before they had matured.'

It still amazed Niamh how articulate Giorgio could be when he talked about business or finance, and yet at times couldn't utter a simple sentence in English, but she decided that this was not the time to mention it.

'And, he's not selling to the other bidder?'

'No.'

'So, we keep the wine bar?'

'*Sì,* you keep the wine bar,' he said, looking at her with a smile.

'*Oh my God!*' was all she could say. She put both her hands to her mouth. They were shaking.

'Nina, why are you so surprised? I know a good deal when I see it. I just had to explain it to my brother that he is being a fool to sell. So now, this way, everyone wins.'

'Thank you, Giorgio! Thank you! Thank you!' She leaped up, threw herself against his chest and kissed him. She hadn't meant to. At least, she didn't think so. She certainly hadn't thought about doing it – it just happened. She was over-whelmed with relief and excitement that all this was finally over and she could get on with her new life here. She pulled back, put her hand to her mouth and looked at him. 'I'm sorry. I didn't mean to. I was just ... I don't know ... sorry,' she mumbled from behind her hand, her head reeling once again. She sat back down on the banquette and could feel the tears welling up behind her eyes.

'Are you? Sorry?' he asked, looking down at her.

'No, that was a lie,' she said with a small laugh, wiping away one errant tear.

He took her hand and slowly pulled her up from her seat.

'Why are you crying?' he asked softly, tilting his head to one side again, a gesture she had come to love.

She didn't trust herself to speak for fear she might give in to all the emotions welling up inside her. Relief that the building would not be sold from under her, excitement that opening night had gone so well, pride that she had pulled it all off and was on the way to rebuilding her life, this time the way she wanted, and emotion that she was afraid to name or afraid to hope for, given the conversation with Sara. Instead, she just shook her head and blinked away the next round of threatening tears.

She took a deep breath. 'Sorry,' she shrugged. 'It's just a lot right now, that's all.'

'There you go apologising again,' he said, putting his hand under her chin. 'But this is OK. It is a lot and you have done so much. I hope you are proud of yourself tonight, Nina. I know that I am.'

He put his hands on her shoulders and looked at her for just a moment before pulling her back into his arms and enveloping her in a hug. He tilted her chin up towards him and this time the kiss had intention. She could feel her body soften and relax against him as her heart beat faster in her chest. He put one hand behind her head and, with the other on the small of her back, he pulled her gently in towards him. She wrapped both her arms around his back, her hands on the curve of his shoulders and breathed into him. She wanted to stay there for ever, not moving, not changing anything.

He pulled back from her and smiled, his eyes crinkling at the sides. He slowly brushed her hair back and put both his hands on the sides of her face. 'I have wanted to do that for a very long time. In fact since the first day that I met you, the crazy Irish girl with the funny name and the big laugh, I have wanted to do that. Most of the women I have known in my life are the same. They want the same things, they do the same things, and they behave the same way. You are different.'

'But what about Sara? I spoke to her earlier, but . . . '

Giorgio shook his head. 'Sara is a dear friend, we were together for a while but it was never . . . *come si dice*, how do you say . . . a forever kind of love. I helped her with some problems in the past, and she was there for me over the past year. I think we both knew it was not this forever love, but . . . but then I met you.' He brushed her hair back again and smiled at her as though allowed to for the first time. 'I love that you are different. You do things your way and you are not afraid of anyone or anything.'

'That's funny, because I think I'm terrified of most things actually, but I like the version of me that you see.' She stopped dead in her tracks and put her hand to her mouth with a gasp.

'What's wrong?' he asked, seeing the change in her expression.

She felt tears well up and threaten behind her eyes and she blinked them away furiously. 'Sorry, it's just something that my mam said to me before she died. She said that you have to like the version of you that you become with someone new, you know, like in a new relationship, and that's kind of what you said just now. It made me think of her.'

'That is a good thing, no? Your mother was right. I wish I could have met her.' He smiled and bent down to kiss her softly again. 'I was afraid to hope for this for a long time, Nina.' He put one arm around her shoulder and pulled her into his chest.

The bell jingled over the door. A young couple holding hands stepped just inside the doorway, but hesitated on seeing the CLOSED sign on the front door.

'Excuse me ... oh, I'm sorry,' the young man said, seeing that he was interrupting something. He looked back at the sign and back again towards Niamh and Giorgio.

'Umm, the sign says this place is open until midnight and it's not midnight yet,' he said, checking his watch. 'Umm, we were just wondering ... '

'Are you open?' the young woman asked with a hopeful grin as she stuck her head around the door.

Niamh looked up at Giorgio, raised her eyebrows and gave a little shrug of both her shoulders as she had seen him do so many times. She looked back to the couple at the door. 'Yes,' she replied with a wide grin as she squeezed his hand. 'Yes, we are!'

# Acknowledgements

I'd like to get one thing straight – I would not be here today without Hannah. Some people are great at their job, others are, without a doubt, superbly talented. Hannah Weatherill, my remarkable agent, is the latter. Hannah took a chance on me and championed *The Italian Escape* from the beginning. If I haven't said it enough, I'm putting it in writing – thank you!

Thanks also to Diane, founder extraordinaire, and the entire team at Northbank Talent for the unwavering support.

To Viola, for believing in the story, for giving me a shot, and for tea. Her help and feedback made this an infinitely better book (and it was such fun in the process!) Thanks also to the entire team at Sphere/Little, Brown who have been so welcoming and enthusiastic. They have made this process entirely seamless and, frankly, such a pleasure. Special thanks to Lucy and Thalia for carrying the torch and bringing me into the fold.

Massive thanks to my sister, Martina, for taking my one-hour, transatlantic calls on a daily basis as I questioned everything, for offering suggestions, for pointing out when I had (literally) lost the plot, and for being the first reader of this book in its entirety. #grateful

Thank you also to my youngest sister, Angela, for providing

a constant stream of inspiration through hilarious running commentary and storytelling from the desert.

Thanks to Nancy, for her (true to nature) selfless and generous offer to help with my contracts. I owe you countless dinners in NYC!

Can't help but note all the fabulous, strong women in my life . . . just as it should be!

Thanks to Mom, who taught us that we can be whoever we want to be (except the Queen of England, whom I apparently aspired to be at the age of four). And to Dad, who always accepted stumbles and failures with a shrug of his shoulders and his favourite refrain: 'back to the drawing board'.

*Grazie* to Fulvio and Mario, for showing me 'their' Camogli and inviting me in to experience such a magical place, away from the madding crowds.

And finally, thank you to Tom, The American, for so much, including, but not limited to (see Nancy, I pay attention!) holding down the day job while I wrote for months, offering reassurance when I needed to be reassured, laughing when I wrote something funny, and for believing that this book, and this journey, was destined to be.

*Escape to Italy this summer and fall in love with*
*the perfect holiday romance . . .*

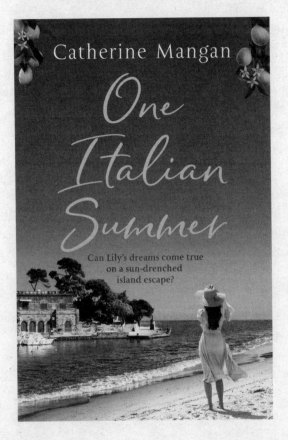

When Lily's long-term relationship ends, she flees her life
in New York to travel to her best friend's wedding on the
sun-drenched Italian island of Ischia – but could there be
more to the secluded island than she ever imagined?

# Chapter One

Lily Ryan weaved her way through the glamorous, post-work crowd, waving excitedly when she spotted her best friend Dee already seated on a high stool at the bar.

'You really need to work on your entry, you know. That wave was far too energetic,' Dee said with a sarcastic eye roll.

'I know, sorry. I'm just glad it's Friday,' Lily said, wrapping her friend in a big hug. 'My boss caught me on the phone to my sister in Dublin at lunchtime and was totally passive-aggressive with me all afternoon, *and* she said I'm short one vacation day for the Italian trip so she's docking my wages. I swear to God if she ever had a kind thought it would die of loneliness in her head. She's such a miserable cow.'

Lily sat heavily on the stool alongside Dee, hanging her bag on a hook directly underneath the bar. They had arranged to meet at the Monkey Bar, a retro-chic cocktail bar and restaurant in the high-profile East 54th Street neighbourhood of Manhattan. The Monkey Bar had long been a favourite of publishing and entertainment executives, but a feature in the hugely successful *Sex and the City* sitcom brought it to the attention of the younger, up-and-coming executive crowd.

'You're looking very glam,' Dee said, raising her glass of wine to her lips. 'What's that all about?'

'Are you joking? I have to make an effort when you pick a place like this, and unlike you I'm not dressed in a power suit with sharp edges and fancy jewellery all day. God, it's so swanky, isn't it? Look at these people,' Lily said, turning to scan the well-heeled crowd.

'Yep, you can smell the money. All these powerful midtown types. Honestly, these chicks spend more on their outfits than I do on my monthly mortgage payment,' Dee said, glancing around the crowded, dimly lit bar. 'It's not really my thing,' she shrugged, 'but it's close to the office, so it takes less time to get to my first post-work drink.'

'I think it's fabulous! I can pretend to be glamorous and sophisticated for a couple of hours, before I head home, put on my PJs and order Thai food online.' Lily grinned. 'But not tonight – I'm meeting Peter for dinner after this at Marea.'

Dee raised an eyebrow in mock disdain. 'Swankier still!'

The bartender placed a monogrammed coaster on the bar in front of Lily.

'What will it be, ma'am?' he asked, with a friendly smile.

'I'll have a vodka Martini, please.'

'How would you like it?'

'Sorry? Oh right, yeah. Um … dry, please, and um … with a twist. Thanks,' she replied, feeling her cheeks flush.

'Coming right up.'

Jesus, Lily … Vodka Martini, dry with a twist. How hard is it to say that all in one go? she said to herself with a loud sigh.

'Since when do you drink Martinis?'

'I've been practising.'

'How do you practise drinking a Martini? I mean, what is there to practise?'

'I had to get out of my pink drink phase,' Lily said, nudging her stool closer to the bar. 'It just reeks of girly drinks. Peter drinks Martinis, so I thought I'd see if I could like them.'

She cringed inwardly as she heard the words come out of her mouth. The look of disapproval from Dee was instant and unmistakable.

'Eh . . . since when do you drink what Peter drinks?' Dee asked, frowning slightly.

'I don't!' Lily said defensively. 'I just like the glasses. Don't go all "women's rights" on me. I just needed a more grown-up drink to go with my new life as a successful copywriter. Cheers!'

'Ah, that's right. Cheers to that. New job, new man, new drink of choice. Got it. So, are you still madly in love?' Dee asked, referring to Lily's boyfriend of six months, Peter.

'Yes, but it's costing me a fortune in lingerie. I had to dump my entire underwear drawer. Nothing matched any more. So now I think I'm contributing significantly to Victoria Secret's EBITDA this quarter.'

'Okay, first of all, you do know you can wash and re-wear your knickers, right? You don't have to don new undies every time you see the man. Second, since when do you know or care about EBITDA?'

'Oh, I had to learn all this new financial language at work. I'm attending the senior team meetings now and I felt like a total dope when they started talking about finances.

So, I paid one of the junior finance guys to teach me what I'd need to know in order to survive the senior team meetings. I paid for drinks a couple of nights a week for three weeks and now I sound smart!' she said, proudly. 'Man, this Martini is good!'

'You're sounding more American by the day,' Dee laughed.

'So, did you get your tux?' Lily asked, her eyes not leaving her Martini glass as she raised it slowly to her lips.

Dee rolled her eyes. 'No, they screwed up the order. I really don't want to talk about it, I'll just get into a rage in my head again. Anyway, they're a bunch of imbeciles. I should have known better than go to a department store in the first place,' she said, shaking her head.

'*What?*' Lily screeched. 'So, what are you going to do now? You're getting married in a few weeks.'

'Yeah, don't remind me. Why did I ever let Morgan talk me into a fancy wedding in Italy? We should have just gone to City Hall and buggered off afterwards to Bora Bora, or something like that … Hang on a second,' she said, placing her right hand on Lily's arm. 'Excuse me!' she said, signalling the waiter. 'Can I have another one of these, please?'

'Coming right up, ma'am,' he said with a nod.

'So, what are you going to do now?'

'Oh, Morgan has stepped in.'

'Uh-oh. Is she displeased with you?' Lily asked, with a grin.

Morgan, Dee's soon-to-be wife, had a notoriously short fuse and a wicked temper. She was used to the finer things in life and would stand for nothing short of exceptional service. Morgan was sophisticated, successful and loyal to a point, but incompetence and sloppiness were easy triggers for her rage.

'No, she has just sworn off said department store for life. She took the matter in hand and went directly to her stylist at Tom Ford.'

'Tom FORD?' Lily shrieked. 'Tom Ford is like, a thousand dollars for a pair of pants!'

'It could be more actually, and yes, the tuxedo is costing four thousand dollars. But apparently that is okay because a) it is my wedding, and b) it's a bargain because it's off the rack.'

'Sweet Jesus, that's two months' rent.'

'Trust me, it's easier to spend the money than listen to Morgan.'

'I suppose so,' Lily said, her eyebrows raised in disbelief. 'Right, so what other details do we need to finalise? I haven't had to do anything as your maid of honour yet.'

'This is why people go to the registry office.' Dee grimaced. 'All this wedding crap. I never wanted any of it.'

'Yeah, well we both know you don't have a say in the matter.' Lily laughed. 'Should I get a second one of these, or would that be bad?'

'Eh, sorry, excuse me? Since when do you question having a second drink? I hope this man isn't changing you too much, Lily Ryan!' Dee said in her thick Dublin accent. Turning to catch the barman's eye, she motioned to the two glasses. 'We'll take another round when you have a chance, please.'

The barman gave a wink in their direction. 'Sure thing, ladies. Settling in for the night?'

'Could be.' Dee nodded. 'Do you have any nuts or anything?'

'I've got popcorn. I'll get some right over to you.'

'Awesome, thanks.'

'And you say that I'm the one sounding more American?'

'Listen, I've been here twenty years. That's one year longer than I lived in Dublin, so I'm allowed say "awesome".' Dee laughed. 'Christ, do we have to talk about this wedding? It's all we talk about at home.'

'Well, if you want me to help, then yes, we do.'

'Okay, so I have to finalise the ceremony details. Morgan wants nothing to do with that part. She's taking care of the resort, music, food, all that stuff. I'm doing the wine – there's no way I was letting her choose the wine. We'd be flying in some reserve bottles from France if she had her way.'

'God, yes, she'd lose her mind altogether with that,' Lily said, as the barman placed another round of drinks and a bowl of warm popcorn in front of them.

'No, we're going Italian and we're going local. I put my foot down.'

'Wow, how did that feel?' Lily asked with a frown, as she carefully lifted her second Martini glass.

'Terrifying,' Dee said, throwing her had back with her signature raucous laugh. 'Anyway, I have to do the ceremony and I don't actually know what's involved. I googled foreign weddings but all I get is all this soppy crap and hymns. I'm looking for the basic requirements here to actually get out the other side of this.'

'Um, I'm not sure if I'm allowed ask this question, but why is this the first time I'm hearing about this? Have you done *anything* for the ceremony yet?'

'Don't start. We just had a disastrous quarter and I had to claw back forty million dollars from our budget, so I'm really unpopular at work and given the state of the economy, fintech in general is screwed right now. My life's a mess.' She shook her head. 'I really don't have the head space for any of this ceremony shit so yes, I need your help.'

Dee was chief financial officer for Paratee Financial, a publicly traded financial technology platform, and so was ultimately responsible for the finances of the 200 million-dollar company.

'Funny, I always think of shark costumes when I hear "fintech",' Lily said, grinning.

'Not helping, Lily!'

'No, I know, sorry. Okay, so what can I do? I could find some not-too-soppy readings or verses, or whatever they're called. Ooh, what about music? I could google some songs for the violinist to play. You booked a violinist, didn't you?'

'No, she has since been replaced with a string quartet, and that's Morgan's remit so I'm not messing with that. Can you just find some readings that are not too vomit-inducing? I don't want any of that perfect love stuff. Just some normal love stuff.'

'Normal love stuff. Got it.' Lily nodded in support.

'Right. I've got to head. I'm meeting Morgan at Nobu.'

'Okay, me too. I'm meeting Peter in twenty minutes,' Lily said, her face brightening into a wide smile.

Peter was older than her by twelve years and divorced with two sons whom he rarely saw. He ran his own head-hunting company, which was massively successful, and was very well connected in the New York social scene, as connections were imperative for his business. While Lily wasn't easily impressed by money, she had to admit that the past few months had been a fun rollercoaster ride of great restaurants, fine wines and some lovely pieces of jewellery.

'So, are you wearing new underwear for your date?'

'Yep! Teal green. He says it brings out my eyes.'

'But you don't have green eyes.' Dee frowned.

'Yeah, I know, I think he might be colour-blind, but I don't want to ask. I like the compliments, even if they're for eyes of a different colour. I don't want to put him off!' Lily giggled.

'That's not weird at all . . . Okay, so do you want to meet for brunch tomorrow or are you fleeing to the Hamptons?' Dee asked, signalling for the bill.

'Can't, I have that goddamn baby shower tomorrow.'

'Christ, do people still have those? I thought they went out with the nineties?'

'I wish. Nothing worse than sitting in a room full of new mothers all congratulating each other on how clever their babies are, and my favourite part is when they give me a sympathetic smile and tell me that my time will come too,' Lily said, rolling her eyes. 'I think I've caught your eye-roll habit.'

'Condescending bitches. Just because they've got a sprog stuck to their hip they assume that every other woman on the planet wants the same thing.'

'So, you don't fancy coming with me then?' Lily joked.

'I'd rather shove chopsticks under my nails.'

'So, that's a "no"?'

They both laughed.

'I've got this,' Lily said, pushing Dee back and handing her card to the barman. 'I think I've been a crap maid of honour so far, so at least let me pay for the drinks.'

'Okay, just make sure you find some half-decent poems

or whatever,' Dee said, picking up her purse and making way for the four well-heeled women hustling to land on her bar stool first. 'Try not to drop any babies tomorrow. Doesn't look good on a résumé.'

'I told you, I have my perfect job now!' Lily said with a proud smile.

'Oh, that's right. I keep forgetting that you are no longer my normal, scatty friend, but you are now successful, in love and on the path to true happiness. What's that like?' she said, grinning, as they reached the door of the Monkey Bar.

'I'm living my best life!' Lily joked, waving over her shoulder at her friend. She turned the corner and made her way down Madison Avenue.

# Chapter Two

Lily arrived at the front door of Marea, an elegant seafood restaurant on West 59th Street, just before seven o'clock. Summer in New York brought searing waves of humidity that sat like a heavy cloud between the tall skyscrapers flanking both sides of every street. It only took a few blocks to go from being perfectly made up to looking like a hot, sweaty mess. Pushing through the double doors, Lily made her way through the vast lobby, keeping to the right so she wouldn't be seen from the bar – a firm favourite of the glamorous midtown set. Elegantly dressed women air-kissed each other as friends and colleagues met for pre-dinner drinks.

'How come none of them have moisturiser rolling down their faces?' Lily muttered as she pushed open the solid oak door of the bathroom.

'You're a shiny mess, Lily,' she proclaimed, as she patted her face with a tissue, grimacing at her reflection in the mirror.

It was the kind of establishment that considered paper towels too commonplace and instead displayed baskets of neatly rolled, miniature cloth towels. Lily soaked one under the cold tap and, reaching under her dress, dabbed under her arms, and under her bra, letting out a sigh as the cold towel touched her skin. A click behind her alerted her to the fact that an older lady in a pinstripe skirt suit had stepped out from a cubicle. In horror, Lily realised that she was flashing her underwear in the mirror as she dabbed sweat from her underwired bra.

'Oh God, sorry! So hot out, isn't it?' she said, faking a smile.

The lady dropped her gaze to the floor and raised an eyebrow as she quickly rinsed her hands and breezed past Lily without uttering a word.

'Please don't be sitting at the table next to me at dinner,' Lily whispered, this time under her breath, as she flipped open her purse and pulled out several pieces of rescue make-up. 'I can't sit next to someone who has seen my knickers in public.'

She never used to carry so much make-up, or even wear it, but then she didn't frequent such upscale restaurants, with such a stylish crowd. Leaning in towards the gilded mirror, she reapplied some foundation and finished with some Charlotte Tilbury magic powder.

'Much better,' she said, with a smile, as she snapped the gold compact shut.

Trying not to limp too obviously, she walked across the foyer in the direction of the main restaurant. Her new shoes were pinching her heels. Shouldn't have worn leather in this heat, she thought, shaking her head. Fixing her posture – chin up, shoulders back – she reminded herself to slow her pace, just as she had observed other New York women do when they walked in high heels.

'It looks like they've been in training to walk like that,' she had observed one evening to Dee.

'They are in training. Haven't you heard? There are twice as many single women as there are single men in this city. That's a tough landscape to navigate for those in pursuit of a husband.'

'No, I mean to walk that precisely, like models on a catwalk.'

'Well they are some pretty lethal heels. I think it's a case of either slow down or fall down. You can't charge across a marble floor in four-inch heels. It won't end well,' Dee had said as she sucked the end of her mojito through her straw.

Lily smiled at the memory as she paused momentarily outside the door of the restaurant, adjusting her skirt before rounding the door in the direction of the hostess stand.

'Welcome to Marea. How may I help you this evening?' the hostess asked with a wide smile that displayed perfect white teeth.

'Good evening. I'm meeting someone here. Mr Peter Allen,' Lily replied, standing up a little taller as she looked up at the elegantly dressed woman.

'Of course. Mr Allen is already here. Please follow me,' she replied, with the same automatic wide smile.

The hostess turned and made her way slowly towards the back of the restaurant. Lily caught the unmistakable flash of red from the soles of the hostess's shoes.

Louboutins! She's wearing six-hundred-dollar shoes! she thought to herself with a pang of envy. I have got to up my shoe game.

Peter was seated at the table, speaking quietly into his

phone. He winked at Lily and smiled as the hostess pulled out the chair for her to sit.

'Enjoy your evening,' she said, smiling her perfect smile and nodding to both of them before turning to return to her post.

'Sorry, this will just take a second,' Peter whispered in his soft London accent, covering his phone with his hand. 'Get yourself a drink!' he added, before returning to his phone call.

God! You look hot, Lily thought as she watched him gesture towards his phone.

He was immaculately dressed as always, this time in a lightweight, dark navy suit and a pale blue shirt. The tie had already been discarded and the top button opened. Lily had come to learn that this was his way of transitioning from the workday to dinner, unless of course the restaurant called for a jacket and tie, in which case he would loosen the tie just a smidge.

'Sorry!' he mouthed across the table.

'No, no problem!' Lily said, waving her hand in dismissal.

'Can I get you something to drink perhaps ma'am?' a waiter asked, having appeared to her right.

She recognised him but couldn't remember his name. John ... James ... something like that, she thought, running through a list of names in her head.

Peter knew everyone's name as this was one of his favourite restaurants.

'Um ... yes. Do you have a Prosecco by the glass?'

'No ma'am, but we have several champagnes by the glass. Would you like to see the drinks list?'

'Oh, sure, thanks,' she said, feeling a flush of

embarrassment rise up her cheeks. Of course they don't have Prosecco, Lily, she admonished herself silently. This isn't your friendly local. They don't do Prosecco. They do *real* champagne.

The waiter returned and handed her a heavy, leather-bound drinks list, which he held open at the page listing champagne by the glass.

Sweet Jesus, the price of them! she thought in quiet horror. Normally, Peter did all the ordering as he was particular about what wines he did or didn't want to drink, and as a result, Lily was blithely unaware of the prices.

The cheapest glass of champagne was twenty-seven dollars, the most expensive an alarming two hundred dollars.

'Um . . . I'll have a glass of this please,' she said, pointing to the least offensive option.

'Right away,' he replied with a smile, as he snapped the leatherbound book closed.

She sat back into her chair, admiring the soft décor of the room. It was exceedingly elegant, but welcoming, and was already filled with well-dressed people, engaged in quiet conversations. Lily shifted in her chair and flicked her long, dark brown hair back over her shoulder. She glanced down at the buttons of her dress to make sure they were still firmly in place. The second button down had threatened to pop out before she left her apartment, so she had secured it with a safety pin. She tugged self-consciously at the fabric now, as she sat casually surveying her surroundings.